THE
Indiscretion

Resounding praise for
Judith Ivory

"Ivory's writing is absolute magic."
Kathleen Eagle, author of *The Last Good Man*

"One of the most talented fiction writers working in historical romance. . . . Ivory is one of those writers who not only delights readers but also inspires awe and envy in fellow writers."
Albany Times Union

"Splendid, elegant . . . lush, artistic romance."
Romantic Times

"Ivory's writing is exceptional, often exquisitely precise, and she is a master at portraying emotional intensity."
Minneapolis Star Tribune

"Memorable . . . endearing . . . well-done protagonists . . . shimmering sexual tension and page-singeing love scenes."
Library Journal

"Ivory enchants her readers."
Publishers Weekly

Other Books by
Judith Ivory

BEAST
THE PROPOSITION
SLEEPING BEAUTY

Judith Ivory

The Indiscretion

AVON BOOKS
An Imprint of HarperCollinsPublishers

This is a work of fiction. Names, characters, places, and incidents are products of the author's imagination or are used fictitiously and are not to be construed as real. Any resemblance to actual events, locales, organizations, or persons, living or dead, is entirely coincidental.

AVON BOOKS
An Imprint of HarperCollins*Publishers*
10 East 53rd Street
New York, New York 10022-5299

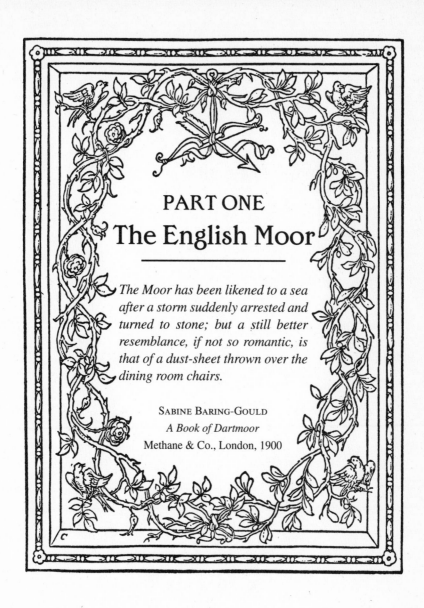

PART ONE
The English Moor

The Moor has been likened to a sea after a storm suddenly arrested and turned to stone; but a still better resemblance, if not so romantic, is that of a dust-sheet thrown over the dining room chairs.

SABINE BARING-GOULD
A Book of Dartmoor
Methane & Co., London, 1900

1

Any woman who can make you happy has all the information she needs to make you miserable if she wants to.

SAMUEL JEREMIAH CODY
A Texan in Massachusetts
Lataille, Brace, & Co., Boston, 1884

DEVONSHIRE, ENGLAND, 1899

Sam Cody wasn't usually a hard-drinking man, but today was an exception. His ribs were sore. His mouth was cut. His eye was swollen. The woman he loved wasn't speaking to him. Her family, if they got hold of him, was fit to hang him, and his own friends and relatives were so riled they'd probably hie the horse out from under him to help. So here he was, in a godforsaken coach station in the middle of nowhere—whatever it took to avoid the pack of angry friends and family—while he sulked, as irritated with himself as they were: But there was no way to avoid himself.

Or almost no way. He tipped back his flask, gingerly putting its lip to his, and knocked back another sour mouthful of what passed for whiskey in England. He drew in air over the liquor as it ran down his throat—a little trick he'd learned today, since he had to breathe through his mouth, because breathing through his nose made it burn so badly his eyes watered. The whiskey settled hotly in his belly. Oh, he was working up a dandy drunk. Once he was on the coach, if the doggone thing ever came, he intended to drink himself unconscious.

The only company in the little wooden room was an oversized trunk someone had deposited here before he'd arrived. It sat in a halo of dust motes, blocking most of the light from the only window, a big box container that looked nonetheless clean and freshly packed, so he thought maybe he'd be having company on the ride to Exeter—though whoever it was must know something he didn't, because the other passenger was as late as the coach. Sam could only guess as to which way to walk, up the road or down, if the coach didn't come. He was a stranger here—and pretty much felt like the proverbial fish, its gills sucking air.

He was new to England by two weeks, and so far he didn't have much use for the country or anyone in it. Today especially. Today he hated every goshdamn Brit right up to their prissy, raised eyebrows. He hated every one of their little pasty-faced children. He hated their yappy dogs, their fat cats, their tiny carriages, their windowless walls and narrow alleys. He hated the way they didn't say what they thought—if one more slick-eared, stall-fed Brit answered him one more time with the word *indeed*, he'd rip the fellow's tongue out—

Oh, what did it matter? He was headed home.

In that spirit, he ambled over to the only furniture in the room, a wood bench, and sat on it, drawing one long leg up to hook his boot heel on the edge. He lay his arm over his knee, his metal flask dangling in his fingers.

You idiot, Gwyn. His now former fiancée. Oh, he hated her. He loved her. He missed her. How dare she be so mean to him? He had another quick mental argument with her. He'd been arguing with her all afternoon even though she was present only in his imagination. Once more, he explained carefully and convincingly exactly what had hap-

pened today. It made perfect sense. Over and over, his explanations made everything all right again.

A shame the real woman wouldn't be hearing his fancy
speeches.

He raised his flask again—light, hollow, near-empty—
and polished off the last of the whiskey. He was just wondering what the limit was before the rest of his body
interpreted English whiskey the way his taste buds did—as
poison—when his vision jumped. It was a new variation to
the swimming of his head. He leaned back on one arm to
make the movement stop, which it didn't. He closed his
eyes. Oh, how his body hurt. Closed, his swollen eye felt the
size of a peach; the lid didn't unfold right.

Sam bent his elbow, shifting around to lower himself
backward onto the bench. Hard as the surface was, meeting
it seemed a relief, almost comfortable. He let his shoulders,
then head, drop the last inch, a *clonk* onto wood. Fully horizontal, he knew a dicey moment as to whether he could stay
in this position or whether he'd have to heave his sorry self
up so as not to choke on all the liquor and coffee keeping
his breakfast eggs company, all of it considering a return
trip.

Exhaustion won. He sank past queasiness . . . falling, a
plummet, into sleep . . . like a U.S. silver dollar dropped,
blinking then disappearing, down, down, out of sight, into
the deepest part of a choppy Channel sea.

"Penis," suggested Lydia Bedford-Browne. She and her
lady's maid sat side by side on a one-horse farm cart as it
pulled to a stop. "Ask him to tell you about his *penis.* That's
what anatomy books call it."

Rose, round-cheeked, round-bosomed, and a head shorter
than her mistress, tied the reins as she giggled nervously.
"Oh, I couldn't possibly say that," she answered and set the
brake.

Married this afternoon, Rose had just stammeringly admitted that she hadn't the foggiest notion about "that part"

of a man. Not a clue what it looked like, what it did exactly when it came to a woman, or even what to call it so as to open a discussion about it with her new groom.

Alas, back in Yorkshire, Lydia's father's library at Castle Wiles contained numerous representations. She even knew where her brother kept his forbidden copy of the Beardsley drawings to *Lysistrata* with their amazing exaggerations of the fanciful item under discussion.

Of course, she could have found Rose pictures of fairies and werewolves, too. They were roughly as real to Lydia. And as relevant to the life of the Viscount Wendt's daughter.

She laughed. "Beyond recommending anatomy books, I can't help. I'm sorry."

Rose nodded. "I just thought you might know a good word. You always know words."

"Well, I've already given you the best word I know." She lifted a handful of skirts and stood up, thinking to abandon Rose, the conversation, and the cart. "You mustn't fret," she counseled over her shoulder. "Thomas will help. It doesn't matter how you say it. Just ask what you need to ask, however it comes out."

She studied the ground below, gauging the distance, then felt Rose's hand at her elbow.

"Wait," the girl said. "I'll come around to help."

Lydia shook her head. "I can manage—"

She took aim on a spot several feet below, where she intended to land. Indeed, in London, someone would have been there, arms outstretched. In London, a dozen people would have helped her down. Her father or brother, a servant, half a dozen willing gentlemen, or even her mother. Everyone was always helping her, as if she were an invalid.

Not here, though. With a sense of freedom, she leaped from the cart seat, her arms out. Her skirts billowed. She was momentarily airborne, thrilled. When she landed on hard, uneven ground, though, one foot and knee slipped out from under her. She went down onto her back, colliding with the earth so forcefully it knocked the wind out of her. She lay there flat out, stunned, staring up into a sky streaked with fluffed clouds. Then she rolled to her hands and knees, a little shaky, and pushed herself up.

As she dusted grit from her palms, her maid came rushing around the cart. "Did you break anything? Are you all right?"

The girl set about brushing the back of Lydia's plain brown dress until Lydia sidestepped her reach. Even then Rose's plump little hands followed, darting upward, trying to right an askew hat.

"Stop." Lydia laughed as she straightened the hat herself. "No, I didn't break anything. Yes, I'm fine." She let out another light burst of laughter at the antics of a short young woman who, for a few steps, half-chased while trying to adjust the edge of her jacket. "It was a little fall, Rose. Nothing more."

The lady's maid made another pass at her, a swipe of her hand that tried to brush the back of her shoulder.

Lydia captured the girl's hands and drew them down to her sides. "Will you stop," she said. "You've gone completely dotty. I'm fine. Honestly."

The girl shook her head, biting her lip. "Well, between the two of you, I'm in a state. You, going off alone—"

Ah. "I won't be alone. I'll call on Meredith in Bleycott—"

"And Thomas—" Rose all but choked, her face filled with dread and angst. "Thomas can't talk of it either. We've tried. We're both simply mortified to speak of it." They were back on the uncomfortable subject of Thomas's John-Thomas. "He is as innocent as I am. A fine honeymoon it will be, both of us as ignorant as rocks."

"No, no," Lydia reassured her, "Boddington"—her near-fiancé—"once likened the process to cricket. Something about bats and wickets and team play." She hadn't explored it further, since both Boddington and cricket bored her to tears. "Nothing to worry about."

"Cricket? Cricket matches are endless!" Rose protested. "Surely it is nothing like cricket."

"One can hope." Lydia laughed. "You must find out and tell me. I entrust the matter to your research. I want a full report."

She looked around them, taking in the surroundings as she carefully hid a hurt ankle. She'd twisted it in the fall, but better not to mention it. Rose had enough to fret about. While Lydia herself felt so hopeful and happy that, by contrast, she was almost ashamed of herself.

In her twenty-four years of living, she had never been on her own for more than an afternoon. Now she had three whole days to herself, and they stretched before her like paradise. She drew in a breath. The air was clear and bracing, the afternoon bright. A pinch in her ankle meant nothing in the context of so much freedom and choice. She would do fine. So would Rose.

In spite of her good mood, though, when she turned and faced fully for the first time the coach station to which she and Rose had brought themselves, Lydia felt a little let down. Here was where her independent adventure would start? She stared at a small wooden shack as bare and raw as the land that spread out behind it.

The Dartmoor. Its open tableland lay beyond the tiny building, dwarfing it in a vastness of granite and sparse grass. As far as the eye could see the moor looked . . . hard, unyielding. It brought to mind the stories associated with it: giant black dogs that ran at night, devouring lost souls; the ghost of a murdered noblewoman rattling through the dark in a driverless coach; a devil with burning eyes who appeared out of nowhere, riding a black stallion, who with his horse could leap into the air and gallop on the wind.

Romantic rubbish, Lydia scoffed. Yet seeing the moorlands stretch out, unimpeded by civilization, made her aware of how such nonsense got started. Without the village of Swansdown to jolly up the landscape—and its warm, joyous wedding celebration now left behind—the terrain was at once majestic and bleak. And the ramshackle ticketing office for the bimonthly coach across it was of a piece: a stark little structure that looked about to collapse, about to give its slats and beams back to nature, barely deserving the word *building*, let alone the dignity of *station*.

Rose continued in her dour vein. "I don't like it," she said as she walked around the back of the cart. "The coach isn't even here." Indeed, there wasn't a horse, vehicle, or human in sight.

"Your mother said it always ran late, or I wouldn't have stayed for the last round of toasts to the bride and groom. I trust that it will be along shortly."

At the rear of the cart, Rose reached for Lydia's long satchel, frowning over her own arm at her mistress. "Why not take the train? You could hire your own compartment. You'd be hidden. No one would see that you were traveling alone."

"Until I got off at a busy station without you. No, thank you. I can't risk running into someone who knows me or, worse, knows my parents—and disapproves as much as they do of my going anywhere unchaperoned. Besides, a private compartment would be expensive." Rose scooted the satchel to the edge of the cart, and Lydia took hold of it, too. They had a little tug-of-war as she continued. "No, no one will pay a speck of—" She frowned. "Let go, Rose, I have it," then continued, "a speck of attention to me on an out-of-the-way public coach. If, indeed, I even see another soul."

Rose relinquished the satchel enough that it dropped between them; they each had hold of a handle. It was an awkward bag, longer than the maid was tall, not heavy so much as cumbrous for its tightly packed length. "We'll do it together." They began in tandem. "I packed your extra handkerchiefs."

"Thank you."

"Do you have your tonic?"

"In my purse."

"I put your wool wrap on top here, in case you get chilly."

Lydia nodded, not mentioning that she planned to put the satchel in the coach's boot. It was too unwieldy to keep with her.

"Oh, and I packed sandwiches at the side, one cucumber, one chutney and cheese—"

"It's only a three-hour ride, Rose—"

"You should make yourself eat them. And your hot water bottle is under the sandwiches for when you get to Bleycott."

Lydia let out a soft snort. "You sound like my mother."

"Your mum would kill me if she knew I was letting you go alone." Rose glared over the bag as they trudged with it, then yanked it suddenly. "Let go. I have it." As if carrying the bag alone might ward off the wrath of the Viscountess Wendt— wrath that, in point of fact, was almost impossible to prevent in any predictable way, though God knew people tried.

Rather than fight further, Lydia obliged. She could not have done what Rose did: With a grunt, the shorter, stockier woman hefted the long satchel into her arms and took off at a good pace—a woman carting an enormous, leather-and-damask baguette, the circumference of which her arms didn't quite encompass.

As they climbed the front steps of the station, Lydia said, "Put it down there. I'll get the driver to load it for me."

Rose answered by clutching the bag to her, a gesture that suggested Lydia's lack of robustness—which certainly translated into less muscle and stamina than her maid—and general susceptibility to chills and rashes and sneezing were life-threatening. Which, generally speaking, they weren't.

Rose talked over the diagonal end of the satchel. "If you won't take the train, why not hire a private coach?"

Lydia laughed outright. "Now that *would* be expensive, wouldn't it? I can't." She mugged a face, making fun of herself. "Too budget-minded." She sighed. "Rose, it's good for me to go out on my own. I don't get to often enough. It feels wonderful." Gently, she told her again, "Put the bag down, please."

Rose relinquished it slowly, putting one end down, then letting the other slide down her body. As the whole dropped onto her toes, she opened her mouth.

Lydia held up her hand. "No more. We're meeting in Bley-cott in three days' time, then taking the train back to London as planned, like the very proper lady and lady's maid that we are. No one shall ever know I struck out on my own to attend your wedding." She made a face of mock horror, then rolled her eyes. "Oh, forbidden pleasure that it was."

When Rose only bit her lip, Lydia let off teasing. "I wouldn't have missed it," she said. "Thank you for abetting me." Her parents had expressly forbidden her to go "out among the moorspeople to a wedding between servants," while she herself could think of nothing better than watching a miracle happen: seeing her very sweet lady's maid marry their footman, Thomas Simms.

Rose—Lydia's friend, companion, and generally co-conspirator for nine years now—pressed her little bow mouth into a solemn expression. "Thank you for coming," she said, her eyes round with sincerity. "Thomas and I were so proud to have you here."

The bride was speaking her ostensible reason for leaving her groom and wedding celebration in order to drive Lydia the mile down the road to the coach station: to "have a private moment to thank my dear mistress, the Honorable Miss Bedford-Browne, for coming."

Lydia looked down, nodding. Imagine, she thought. Rose, married. She was overwhelmed by a sudden, confusing rush of feeling: sadness, joy, jealousy, affection.

Rose, too, bent her head, mirroring Lydia's movement. The two women stood there, nodding in some sort of mysterious agreement. A moment later, they raised their heads simultaneously, looked at each other, and grew still in the same instant. And there they were—inappropriately across class lines, yet somehow inexplicably—connected.

Finally, the only way to break the tension was to do what was natural. "Oh," Lydia cried out and threw her arms around the young woman with whom she had grown into adulthood. "Oh," she said again, hugging Rose to her. "You are dear to me. And I am so happy for you." She pushed her away. "Now, off with you. Go have your honeymoon with your handsome new husband."

Rose sniffed. Her eyes grew teary.

"No." Lydia pushed at her. "Go on now."

"You'll be all right?"

"Guaranteed."

"I'll walk you into the building, stay till the coach—"

"No, no," Lydia protested. Apparently a secondary reason for the bride wanting to take her mistress to the station was to carp endlessly about the choice of transportation. To distract, she teased, "Besides, you have that research question to report on. You must find out what Thomas calls himself there and what exactly all the fuss is about." The anatomy books, Lydia thought, made it all sound like pistons and packing rings.

"I've waited twenty-seven years. I can wait half an hour more."

Lydia sighed. "All right. But once the coach arrives, you run off. No need to wait till it leaves."

Rose nodded, an accord at last. At which point she made a move toward her mistress, hesitated, then gave in: She boldly linked her arm through Lydia's, opened the door, and the two women walked through it together into the small, wood-plank structure that was the local coach house to the only coach line that ran, village by village, across the Dartmoor.

2

Love, any devil but you!

JOHN DONNE

The two women walked through the door to be immediately confronted by Lydia's large black trunk. It stood on end not five feet from the doorway, smack in the middle of the one-room station. Rose's brother had delivered it earlier that morning.

"Now why would Artemis put it there?" Rose asked. "Couldn't he have put it to the side so we could move about?" She shook her head as they rounded the corner of the trunk. "Why are men such fools—"

They both stopped, confronted with the fact that there was a . . . a fool in here with them.

A man lay stretched out on a bench against the back wall, his arm over his eyes at one end of the wood plank, his legs dropped off the other, his feet planted on the floor. He didn't respond to their noise, presumably deeply asleep. His spraddled feet caught Lydia's attention. On them he wore strange, eye-catching boots, while between his feet lay a black hat, high-crowned and banded by a piece of thin black leather on which were threaded, spaced, and knotted half a dozen silver beads. The two together—hat and boots—were foreign yet familiar.

She remembered: They were American, the attire of Wild West cowboys, the likes of which had whooped and shot their way through Buffalo Bill Cody's Wild West Exhibition when it was on tour in London two years ago; her brother had dragged her to it. She had at first been resentful of having to sit there with him, then excited by the strangeness— there were dramas, for instance, "re-enactments," of savages chopping the hair off people with axes—then faintly appalled by her own excitement. She would not have thought she could respond to such a display of horror—horror done badly for sensational effect—and didn't know what to make of the thrill she felt.

She and Rose walked between the trunk and the man to get a better look at him, his shoes, and his hat. She stared down, full of curiosity, taking him in from one end to the other, and felt a whiff of that same odd excitement. He was big, built on a grand scale, like the idea of the Wild West itself. Then, as she drew closer, she caught a whiff of something more tangible: liquor. Ah, he wasn't sound asleep so much as passed out, perhaps.

For whatever reason, the man's body was a study of sprawl and balance: positioned not to fall off the narrow bench yet relaxed enough to be truly asleep. Given the width of the bench and the size of him, sleeping on it seemed a small athletic feat.

"Do you think he's all right?" she asked.

He didn't look all right. His very un-English clothes were a mess. Perfect really, just exactly what she'd expect of someone who'd been chasing Indians all day: His slate-gray coat was dusty and torn at the shoulder. He had a cut at the corner of his mouth—his arm was flung over his face, so the lower portion was all that showed. His complexion was browned by the sun, so tan that his lips looked pale by comparison, though this didn't keep his dark, clean-shaven jaw from exhibiting a darker-still bruise. The hair of his head, a shiny tousle above his arm, was on the long side, unruly, uncombed; it looked black in the low light of the room.

"He's breathing," Rose said. "I think he's healthy enough: just foxed."

Lydia angled her head to get a better look at his boots. With his knees bent, the cuffs of his trousers pulled up. A long stretch of boot showed—leather the color of black cherries with a lot of stitching that made embossed wings along the sides. Fancy boots, though they were creased and scuffed. The heels were worn down. Still, they looked soft, creased in a way that said they moved exactly with the man's foot and ankle. His slate-colored trousers, besides looking as if they'd been wadded into a ball before he'd put them on, showed scraped skin through a tear at the knee. From the tear something else peeked out, the edge of something red. It was his underclothes. They were red! Lydia wanted to giggle.

"He's in terrible shape, isn't he?" she said.

Rose tittered, making Lydia glance over at her.

Aah. Before Thomas there had been a string of male callers, every one of them good-looking. Rose had an eye for the handsome ones.

Lydia frowned back at the inert man, feeling disgruntled somehow. His body extended off the bench in both directions. He was too long for it, his shoulders too wide, which of course to Rose would translate to *tall* and *broad-shouldered*. All right, Rose was correct. He was nicely proportioned in a long, loose-limbed way. His arm lay gracefully over his eyes, his hand relaxed, its palm a pale hollow against its otherwise darkly tanned skin. Aside from the rumpled mess of his clothes, he looked . . . healthy, strong. Healthy, that is, for a beat-up foreigner who smelled of whiskey. Rose was also right in that he was deep in his cups—Lydia recognized the smell from her father. Scotch whiskey, his favorite beverage, bar none.

Lydia made a face, about to criticize further. Then thought better of it. Here was almost surely her companion

for a coach ride. No sense in adding to Rose's chagrin. She
shrugged. "He looks harmless enough." She tried to believe
it herself.

At that moment, outside in the far distance, the sound of
a coach—the whir of wheels, the rapid clatter of hooves—
rose faintly out of the silence.

The man on the bench stirred. He lifted one boot and
crossed it to his knee, groaning at the effort.

The sound of horses and wheels grew louder, distinct.

She reminded Rose, "You promised: time for you to go.
I'm as good as in Bleycott. I'll see you there Tuesday
evening."

Reluctantly, the girl kissed her, hugged her again,
thanked her for the hundredth time for coming, then offered
to cancel her honeymoon and travel home with her.

"No, no," Lydia said, laughing. "You must answer the penis question, remember? You must report when I next see
you on all that is decent to tell."

"O-o-h," Rose groaned and bent her head to Lydia's.
"There must be other words. . . ." She lowered her voice,
whispering, and they were suddenly in conversation about
honeymoons again.

The penis question. The phrase drifted through Sam's mind,
though he couldn't gather its sum and substance. He was
dreaming.

The dream seemed to spring from a noise, a sound akin to
the movement of high wind in tall grass. Skirts rustling. Yes,
that was it. Silk against silk.

Voices intruded, women's voices. They were soft and
nearby. Ha, they were talking together, confiding about men
and sexual relations. Oh, yes. His sleeping mind strained toward these voices. He could make out bits. *Honeymoon . . .
decent . . . indecent.* That was all he could catch, though a
few moments later—or a few hours, it being hard to tell,
since he kept coming back from the netherworld without
knowing how long he'd been there—he knew the smell of a
woman's hair. As if she bent close through the darkness. The

smell of soap, ginger-lemon floral, the scent warmed by her scalp, her skull, her neck. Hair. His dreaming mind imagined coils of it, cascades of feminine hair. Oh, he loved soft hair and silky skirts.

Gwyn, he thought. She had nice skirts, beautiful dresses, though her hair wasn't her best feature. He liked her hands, her long fingers. He could feel them suddenly in the dark. The last time he'd seen her alone on peaceable terms, she'd surprised him. She'd slid those fingers down his shirt, over his belt, and along his fly, till through his trousers she found the outline of him. He'd been kissing her and was already pretty darn firm. The pressure of her fingers through his clothes, though, made him rigid. She laughed coquettishly at what she'd done, at his response, then said, *Your manhood.* Which struck him as a silly word for his fully erect penis, though he sure couldn't complain about the context. He pressed her palm down onto him with complete approval, whatever she wanted to call him.

Voices again. The sound of a carriage. It entered the dream raucously, horses snorting wet breath, shrieking, stomping. A man yelled at these unhappy animals, but Sam couldn't make out the words, as if vowels had been moved around just enough to turn the meaning into garble. Then the door to the coach opened like a maw. Perhaps Gwyn was inside. Where had she gone?

The pleasure of a moment ago became a vague awareness of pain. His nose hurt. His face stung. Slowly, rib by rib, he realized his chest ached. His shoulder blades had a pinch in them where he was lying on something hard, the whole effect painfully reminiscent of the after-hours following the brawls of his youth. He didn't do that anymore, he assured his sleeping self. No brawling. But, God bless, he hurt like he'd been ridden hard and put up wet.

Sam stepped into the waiting dream coach, into its dark interior, hurting now, wanting someone to soothe him. There was no one, though, nothing in the coach, only cold, then suddenly he was falling, swallowed up into blackness. He tumbled until, in the far distance, appeared what became a rocky piece of grassland, opening up wider and wider, coming at him. He was hurtling toward it. The land came faster, expanding in all directions. He knew terror for an instant as he realized he was going to smash into it—

"The coach is here," someone said.

Abruptly, Sam jerked, his breath came out in a gulp. The back of his head hit on something, wood. And he was suddenly awake, his heart pounding.

Disoriented, he blinked up. He lay on a board bench that cut into his shoulder blades, staring up at—of all things—a woman's upside-down face, behind her head a raw rafter ceiling.

Her face hung over his, a wince fixed on her features—not what he was used to seeing in a women's face at this close range. Which said a lot for how his eye was looking.

"Is it blue?" he croaked. His speech, normally deep and drawling, sounded downright raspy: rusted, whiskey-voiced.

"What?"

"My eye."

Her face—heart-shaped with a little, pointy chin—frowned, looked disconcerted, then answered, "They both are."

He let out a snort, a dry laugh. "Blueing up. Black and blue."

She nodded. "A bit. Mostly just jolly well swollen. How did you do it? It's horrid."

"I got myself into a little fight where I was sort of outnumbered."

"You lost."

"No, I didn't," he said quickly. He'd won, damn it.

She blinked, then asked, "What were you fighting over?"

"Whether a man, then him and four of his friends from a back alley, could rob a woman on the street." Sam tried to sit up, but he moved too quickly. He groaned and lay himself gently back onto the bench. Lying there, he told her with some satisfaction, "You can't, it turns out." He grimaced when he might like to have smiled smugly. "Two of them were hospitalized."

"You put them there?"

"I did."

"And you're proud of that?"

He lifted his chin, tilting his head backward enough to frown at her upside down. "Under the circumstances, yes. Listen, Gwyn—" he began. Then what he'd said brought him up short.

He tried to sit up again, this time moving slowly, stiffly forward till he had rolled up onto his backside and lowered his legs over the edge of the bench. "*Achhh*," he groaned, laying his head into his hands. Success. Of sorts. He hurt so many places he couldn't separate out all the aches and spasms. He was too old for this, he thought.

"Indeed," the woman said as she backed out of his way— and possibly his reach: She looked wary.

Indeed. He lifted his head enough to throw her a scowl over his spread fingertips.

She was thin, hardly more than a hundred pounds soaking wet, while being maybe five-six—which was nine or so inches shorter than he, making her taller than average and downright skinny. He couldn't resist telling the scrawny thing, "Putting two of them in the hospital was fair return, if nothing else. And the other three were messed up about as badly as me. The woman got away with her purse without a scratch. First-rate results, though of course, it cost me some—" At which point, he remembered all it cost him and that humbled him into silence.

Arguing with a stranger after calling her Gwyn. How crazy was this?

"Indeed," she said again.

He twisted his mouth at her as far as it would go without killing him with pain. "In-goddamn-deed."

She'd turned partly away and moved toward the door— the trunk that had been in the middle of the room was missing. She looked at him now over her shoulder, her neck making a long, willowy arch. A pretty stretch of spine.

He assessed her where she stood in part shadow, part lit up the front—the door was swung open, the low sun shining into the room: fair complexion, brown hair mounded up onto her head, a perfectly worthless little straw hat perched on top. Her clothes were plain but . . . stylish somehow. Simple. No jewelry. She put herself together in a way that made her prettier, he thought, than nature intended. She was decent looking. For a thin-boned woman. Of the serving class, he'd guess, since she was traveling cheaply and alone. A lady's maid. No, something about her was fancier than that. A governess. Or shopkeeper maybe. A frugal milliner. Oh, hell, he didn't know what she was other than she didn't appear to be a society tulip. No, nothing like Gwyn, nothing at all.

Outside he heard horses. The coach. It must have arrived. The woman sauntered into the open doorway, watching presumably the final loading and readying of their vehicle.

Sam put his head, his temples, back into his hands, sitting there light-headed and queasy, waiting for the courage to stand up. He'd have to any minute.

"You shouldn't drink so awfully much," said the soft-sweet voice by the doorway in its high-horse accent.

"I hurt."

"And now you hurt worse because of the drinking."

"Thank you for your kind advice," he said, lifting his head enough to look at her again. Stupid creature. "I'm all right," he told her.

"No, you're—"

He cut her off. "How much I drink is none of your business."

"Well," she said, "I didn't mean it as a slight against your manhood."

"My what?" He straightened slightly.

"Your manhood. Your masculine pride."

He nodded. Of course. Right. He knew that.

Looking out into the coach yard, she asked, "So, how long is it?"

"Excuse me?"

"How long is it, do you think?"

"How long is what?" Sam felt a tingle of panic. What the hell kind of conversation was this?

The woman swayed her pretty neck toward him and fixed him with narrow look. "The ride," she said.

It took him a moment. Then with a sense of relief, he said, "Ah, the coach ride."

"What else?"

"Nothing." He repeated the word, delighted to say it: "Nothing." He shook his head at himself. It was an accident that she had used Gwyn's silly name for a fine part of his body. Entertaining, in fact. He smiled till the movement of his mouth pulled at the corner where his lip was split. He caught the side of his mouth with his fingers, holding it still, only able to smile with half of it. "I don't know how far it is. Twenty or thirty miles across the moor. Depends on which town you want, I guess."

He picked up his Stetson from the floor, laying it into his lap.

Her eyes followed it. "Not that long then," she said.

She stared at his hat. Sam blinked, frowned, looked down. *Quite long. Manly and long.* Then he let out a short laugh of release. Lordy. He leaned back till his shoulder blades found the wall and relaxed against it. What a cross-eyed conversation.

"Is something wrong?" she asked.

He shook his head, letting the half of his mouth that didn't hurt too much crack a smile again. He was feeling better. Not wonderful by any means, but not sick at his stomach and finally, fully awake. "Nothing's wrong."

He laughed outright then and eased himself up, standing cautiously as he dusted his hat against his leg.

A short, bushy-bearded man stuck his head in. "E'ery-one rea'y?" Even his thick regional accent didn't hide the man's slurred words. Well, here's hoping the horses know the way, Sam thought, because their driver was drunker than he was.

Setting his hat far back on his crown, he followed the young woman out into the afternoon sun. The driver was actually carrying a bottle of gin. He had trouble holding on to it as he tried to climb into the driver's box. Sam thought about confiscating the liquor, but that was way too hypocritical in the end, so he just shoved the man up the foot treads and into the box instead. Then Sam offered his hand to the woman to help her up into the coach.

After a curious moment of hesitation, she accepted his assistance. She lay her thin fingers in his. They were surprisingly soft, delicate, the ball of her thumb warm and plump like the breast of a little bird. He pressed his thumb over the backs of her knuckles and balanced her up the two wood steps, letting go as she took hold of the door frame. Before she bent fully under it, though, she stepped awkwardly on the threshold, as if her ankle twisted.

"*Oof,*" she said and fell backward.

Instinctively, Sam put his hands up, and her buttocks landed into them.

If he'd been more sober, he might have found a more gentlemanly way to help. Right or wrong, though, he cupped her backside in his hands. Her bottom, another surprise, was round and firm, even generous; it fit just right into his palms. He pushed her back up into balance by her bottom and liked doing it, a pretty rewarding piece of misbehavior. It made him laugh to do it.

She grabbed hold of the door frame, stabilizing herself in the coach doorway, then turned before she made her way in. He was right behind her, and there they were, nose to nose. For a minute she looked for all the world like she was going to whack him, if only she could have found a place on his face that didn't look like it had already been whacked enough.

Sam doffed his hat by way of apology. Her expression changed. She looked confused, though her cheeks remained two clear blotches of indignation. "Sorry," he said, half-meaning it, then annoyed. Why was he apologizing for keeping her from falling? She should be thanking him for it.

She frowned, opened her mouth, then closed it—too noble to express appreciation she didn't feel.

"It was entirely my pleasure," he said.

She blinked, and that did it. To his surprise, she shoved him in the chest with both her hands, moving him with unsuspected strength for such a delicate-looking woman. Of course his balance wasn't all that good, given the whiskey in his system. He had to catch himself with a backward step onto the ground.

She told him, "You, sir, are not only drunk, you are unspeakably rude. Rude, crude, uncouth, barbaric—"

"For something unspeakable, you sure have a lot to say about it—"

"—uncivilized, reprehensible—"

"I have the gist: A polite man would have let you fall down the steps."

"An English gentleman would have caught me by my elbows."

This took him aback for a split second. Right. She was probably right. He should apologize earnestly. But what came out his mouth was, "Your bottom was a lot easier to find than your elbows."

She glared at him. Then articulated in her soft, round British syllables, "Do you know, sir, you have a wide streak of immaturity?"

For some reason, this made him grin—with only half his mouth, but he was getting good at lopsided smiling. "I sure do," he agreed. He winked just to get her goat further. "It's one of my charming qualities." He tipped the brim of his hat again, then gestured toward the interior of the coach. "After you, ma'am," he said. When she hesitated, he added, "We're late enough. Can we get started?"

She swirled herself and all her skirts around, then ducked through the coach doorway, successfully this time, without saying another word.

He said to her back, "You're welcome," then vaulted in after her, into the shaded, musty enclosure of a big, old coach that rocked. Its antiquated, creaky springs declared noisily that he and she were going to feel every bump the road had to offer. He dropped himself into a threadbare seat, him facing backward, Miss Prissy Brit facing forward.

Belatedly, with her staring pointedly out the window, she muttered, "Thank you."

"No problem," he said. "I live to save ungrateful women."

He folded his arms over his chest, slid down into his seat, stretching his long legs out till they were comfortable, then tipped his hat brim low over his eyes. He figured he'd sleep, since he'd done enough—argued with his only companion, called her Gwyn, handled her backside, then enjoyed tormenting her till he'd alienated her beyond conversation. Nope, he was pretty much finished here.

The driver *hee-yah*ed the horses. The coach wheels slid in the gravel for an instant, and with a lurch the vehicle sprang forward. Off they went, heading east on a route that would stop at every podunk on the stony prairie the English called the Dartmoor. With Sam playing possum just to keep things civil.

It was going to be a long thirty miles.

3

*A cowboy is inured from boyhood to the excitements
and hardships of his life.*

From the program of Buffalo Bill Cody's
Wild West Exhibition, London, 1896

Lydia watched out the window as they rolled and bumped along. Happily, the perverse man across from her had fallen asleep, so the ride settled into a peaceable rhythm. If one could call going for all a rickety old coach was worth peaceable.

Once they left the station, they departed civilization itself, all but for the ribbon of poorly paved road on which they traveled. Not a town or farm or person in sight. Just gray terrain broken by patches of grass and the occasional shrub. Coarse-grained rock climbed and descended along their route; it rolled along under them. She had never entered a place that was so barren, open, and wild. It lay in strong contrast to the gentle country scenery she was used to in the summer, the patchwork lowlands of Yorkshire. The familiar farmlands and moors of her home shire were divided up, partitioned by winding roads and hedgerow boundaries peopled with villages and farmhouses, even castles.

Today, the bare horizon was broken only once by anything that looked related to a human being, a tall silhouette, as if a man walked the moor on foot. A priest, perhaps, in a cassock, his arms folded into his sleeves. As they drew closer, though, he turned out to be a stack of flat-looking rocks, its precarious balance defying the millennia of its existence. A tor. The moor was covered with them. Most just looked like haphazard piles of rocks on a hilltop, rubble. But some formed a kind of natural statuary, like the fantastical display on the horizon they jostled past. People used to think druids had built them, that they were altars. Science, though, said otherwise, that they were only the remains of the moor's ancient mountain range, weathered and worn to hillocks crested with heaps and towers.

Whatever the origins, Lydia enjoyed the sights out her open window, even as her view pitched and shook. If the driver careened them too fast for the vehicle's age and suspension, still God knew they were making good time. At least his recklessness, she told herself, didn't have to share the road with other traffic of any sort—they passed nary a soul. Half an hour ago Lydia had slipped her wrist into the hand strap, where she could get a good grip, and now held on for dear life while looking forward to a shorter trip, if a more topsy-turvy one.

Out the corner of her eye, she occasionally glimpsed the American. Long angles of sunlight and deep shadows cut across him, an irritatingly dramatic result of the sun lowering for the most part behind them. Less remarkable, his arms lay folded across his chest, his boots braced across the floor to the far seat base, his head down, his body rocking to the rhythm of the coach. Apparently, he could prop himself into stability, then fall asleep anywhere.

She stared at his black hat tipped down over most of his face. If ever he should play in a Wild West show, he'd be a stagecoach robber, she decided. Or a gunfighter with a "quick temper and a quicker trigger finger," which was a line out of one of her brother Clive's Buffalo Bill novels. She entertained this fantasy for a few minutes, smiling over it. Yes, something about him, a leanness, "a build as hard and de-pendable as a good rifle" (she, in fact, had pilfered one of Clive's contraband American novels just to see what they were about), not to mention something in his brooding atti-tude, spoke of a possibly harsh, very physical existence.

Her imagination put him in a big, tooled-leather saddle on a horse caparisoned in silver stars down its breast. Along with his black hat with silver beads, she added silver guns in holsters at his hips and American spurs that jingled as he walked. She remember what such spurs looked like and, more memorable, what they sounded like: a lot of metal to them, a silver band low on each heel, silver chains under-neath, with jagged, spinning wheels at the back. Nothing like an English riding spur with its single, neat point affixed to a gentleman's boot.

As with the Wild West show, Lydia found the jangling, clomping difference shamefully thrilling. It brought to mind Indian battles, buffalo hunts, coach robberies, life and death. Lurid, provocative, yet safe of course, like all fantasies, since here she sat. She should be in Bleycott by late evening. He wasn't wearing spurs or guns or anything dangerous. She laughed. He was probably a traveling salesman.

Something about his posture, his attentiveness, made her call over the road noise, "Are you awake?"

After a second, with a finger he pushed his hat brim up enough that his eyes were visible, if shadowed. "Yes, ma'am."

He had a nice voice when polite, like a bow groaning slowly over the deepest strings of a bass. He took his time saying things, slow-talking his way over sliding consonants and drawn-out vowels. His speech was full of *ma'ams* and *you're welcomes*. A politeness that turned itself inside out when he used it to say surly things.

"Who's Gwyn?" she asked.

He tipped his hat back further, till his face—its frown— was in full light. "You have a good memory."

"Who is she?"

Sam sat there slouched, hearing a lady he'd been sure

wouldn't utter another word to him ask about his love life. He chewed the inside of his cheek, then thought, Why not tell her?

"The woman I was supposed to marry this morning." He sighed, feeling blue again for simply saying it. Hell, what sort of fellow left the woman he'd courted for almost two years at the altar in front of all their friends and family? He expected a huffy admonishment from Miss Prissy Brit now—

"I'm so sorry," she said.

The coach turned sharply, and they both leaned to counter the force of the motion, with him stretching his leg out to brace himself with the toe of his boot and her swinging from the hand grip.

Over the noise of their travel, she asked, "What happened?"

Sam frowned. Now where had this little lady been five hours ago? Because that was the one question he had been dying for someone to ask all day, though not a soul till now had thought to. Her concern, and his needy longing for it from someone, anyone, shot a sense of gratitude through him so strong he could have reached out and kissed her.

He said, "I was on the way to the church, when, out the window of my hackney, I saw the robbery I told you about. The fellow stopped the woman on a Plymouth street and grabbed her purse. She fought him. He was puny but wiry and willing to wrestle her for it. It made me crazy when he dumped her over. I figured, with me being a foot taller and sixty or so pounds heavier, I could hop out, pin the hoodlum to the ground, then be on my way with very little trouble. I wasn't prepared for his four friends." Sam sighed. "I spent the morning at the doctor's when I was supposed to be standing at the altar."

"But your bride—"

"My bride won't talk to me long enough to hear my explanation."

Their eyes met and held. Hers were sympathetic. And light brown. A kind of gold. Pretty. Warm. He watched her shoulders jostle, to and fro, as she said, "Well, when she saw you like this, she must have—"

"She didn't see me. She only called me names through her front door. No one would let me in."

"How unreasonable."

"Exactly." What a relief to hear the word.

"You could send her a note to explain—"

"She returned it, unopened."

"You could talk to someone, get a friend to tell her—"

"No one will speak to me. I had to bribe the stable boy to get me to the coach station."

Her pretty eyes widened. "But people have to understand—"

Exactly what he wanted to hear, the very words he'd been telling himself all day. And now that he heard them, he realized how stupid they were. "Apparently not. 'Cause not a person I know does."

Bless her, her mouth tightened into a sweet, put-out line. "Well, how unreasonable," she said again. Oh, God bless her.

"Yes." But no. He looked down. "It is unreasonable. Until you realize that I left Gwyn at the altar once before, eight months ago."

She straightened herself slightly in her seat, readjusting her wrist in the hand strap. Aha! her look said. Then she came back loyally to his side. "You were beaten this time." She paused, frowning. "What happened eight months ago?"

"Nothing." He sighed. "I slept in."

"Didn't you have a best man to help you? Grooms get nervous. Grooms need help."

"I wasn't where anyone knew how to get to me." He was with the caterer's sister, the cook, who also missed the wedding. But, shoot, he wasn't married yet. It hadn't seemed that wrong. Though, no excuses, missing the wedding was completely wrong. Twice he'd been wrong now. He admitted it. Someone should let him admit it, then forgive him.

He watched the dignified young Englishwoman sit back, as if she could physically remove herself from riffraff who spoke to strangers about his embarrassing life.

Might as well get it all out. "And once before, with another woman, I missed that wedding, too."

Sam sat up, taking his hat off a minute to examine it, then scratched his head as he looked out the window. A damn sorry case he was.

Today was his typical sort of mess—and the reason most of his friends and family considered him a hero on one hand and a cad on the other. When he wasn't standing women up at the altar, he was forgetting to come get them for picnics or dinners or leaving them hanging while he tried a new horse or simply slept past his rendezvous with them. For one reason or another, he went through women the way ranch hands went through eggs in the morning. It was purely disheartening, and he figured he'd die alone because of it.

He fully expected the woman rocking across from him to end their conversation now that he'd told her. He'd been playing on her sympathy. Sympathy he didn't deserve. Now she'd hate him not just for what he'd done to Gwyn but for playing up to her as well. He sure could be an idiot without half trying.

"Well," she said from her side of the coach, "you have made some terrible mistakes, haven't you?"

He nodded. "I sure have."

"And you are paying through the nose for them."

He looked at her. "I am." His nose literally ached from his heroics today.

"I hate it when that happens."

"Me, too," he muttered. He wondered what it was she wanted for being so nice to him.

She seemed to ponder his sad tale, as if turning it over in her mind. Then she said, "Well. Any bride who won't listen to that story perhaps isn't worth marrying."

"Oh, no," he contradicted. "Gwyn is worth marrying. As soon as she cools down, I'll send her something nice to get her attention. I'll court her again." Gwyn was worth it. He'd beat out four or five fellows to have her. She was prime company, the best. "And you?" he asked.

She looked at him, startled. "Me?"

"Yeah. Why are *you* on this coach?" He smiled, vaguely curious, as he stretched his arm out along the seat. "It's the saddest vehicle I can conjure up. Me, I'm trying to keep out of the way of all the family and friends who'd like to finish off the job the bandits started. They'll all be on trains. But you? What have you done?"

"Nothing," she said quickly, sitting back.

He'd been kidding her, making fun of himself. But, interestingly here, Miss Prissy Brit looked alarmed, then blushed. Even in the late afternoon shadows where she sat, he could see the faint, pretty, rosy-porcelain pink. Her eyes shifted to his hand on the seat back, to where his thumb found a wear in the fabric. "All right," he asked, "so why are you on it?"

She blinked then shrugged. "I just like it."

He laughed, watching her. "So what do you like best? The dust? The bad springs? The wild joyride of the pace? Or is it the company?"

Her eyes met his again, while her expression ran a gamut: confusion at being confronted, anger, which turned into, surprisingly, a small, rueful smile. She tried to hold it back, couldn't, then shook her head, looking down. She would admit nothing. But her posture—the way she bent to hide the smile as she hung there rocking in the hand strap—suggested that the proper little governess here, or whoever she was, was exploring the edge of what was and wasn't very proper.

It was an endearing silence. Sam leaned forward, extending his hand. "Samuel J. Cody," he said. "Pleased to meet you."

She stared at his hand, licked her lips. It took him a second to realize: She was inventing a name to tell him. He wanted to laugh outright.

Once she found it, she smiled boldly across at him, bless her. She had a fine smile, wide-mouthed, full of nice teeth. "Lydia Brown," she said as she reached forward.

They both leaned, her coming into the direct sunlight from the window to offer her hand. She had large eyes, her salient feature. Big, round, long-lashed eyes the color of honey. They were more than pretty, Sam decided as he took her thin hand again in his; they were beautiful. He and she remained connected like that across the space of the coach, wobbling together to the rhythm of the road. He held her fingers longer than was cordial, enjoying again how delicate they were. Soft, cool, smooth—this woman did no physical labor. He enjoyed for a second longer how he, literally, held her off balance, then let go, leaning back. "What do you do?"

She sat back deeper this time, into the corner of the seat. "Do?"

"Yes, you sound cultured—is that rude to mention? And you're traveling—"

"A lady's maid," she said quickly.

"Really?" He asked with wonder and delight.

He wouldn't say she was a bad liar. She wasn't. Anyone else might have given her straightforward answers some credit. Just not a man who'd ridden an hour and a half so as to get to a remote coach station so he could ride in an extremely late, uncomfortable vehicle all the way across an English plain that was as devoid of beauty as the inside of a rock.

"Yes, really," she told him, then looked out the window, chewing her lip.

The vehicle jerked slightly. The carriage was picking up speed, if that was possible. The horses complained, whinnying in excitement. They were being driven too hard by someone who didn't have a good hand on them—something that would take care of itself, Sam reasoned. The driver would have to slow down, since the animals themselves couldn't keep this up.

He had to call to ask, "Who is in Bleycott?" He remembered the name of the town from somewhere. It was her destination.

She pretended not to hear him, so he repeated the question.

She frowned for a second, then called back what she must have thought would shut him up: "My husband."

She wasn't wearing a ring.

He puffed his lip, pulling his boot up to cross his knee, and tapped his fingers on the leather. He looked at her, wondering what her real story was and feeling a little bamboozled, since he'd told her his, lock, stock, and shameful barrel.

He could think of no more inroads. They were at an impasse. While the coach was becoming a giant pain in the backside, bouncing them around in ways that promised bruises tonight. He watched her round shoulders bump against the upholstery to the rhythm of the pounding horses' hooves. Her hand at the strap held on so tightly her knuckles were white.

She lost her hold of it completely in the next instant, though, as they were both thrown sideways—the carriage veered. Before they could brace themselves, the wheels went off the road's shoulder and into a ditch. Sam caught himself; Mrs. Brown did likewise, screeching at the top of her lungs. They rattled along, racing at a catawampus angle before, miraculously, the vehicle recovered itself, finding the road again. Lord, though, what a scare, what a ride.

"That gosh-dang driver," he said. "The fellow up there in the driver's box has more gin in him than good sense."

They didn't slow one bit.

Sam grabbed the top of the window frame then straightened his body through the window, up and out, bellowing at their driver as he did. "Slow down, you idiot!"

There was no answer, so he craned himself further out, hanging on for dear life as he yelled louder. "You hell-bent, peanut-sized, lizard-brained—"

His hair stood on end as, hanging outside the coach, he watched it, with them in it, weave across the road then back—for all the world as if no one drove them at all.

"Jesus," he breathed, then grabbed hold of the window casement. He used his arms to leverage himself out the window to his hips.

"Hey!" he bellowed. "Hey!"

The driver was drunk, he told himself. Just drunk. Or deaf. Maybe the fellow couldn't hear him for all the noise of the coach and road and horses. Whatever the explanation, the vehicle veered again, all but throwing Sam out the window.

Gosh-dammit. He hated what he was going to have to do. Bringing his leg up, he hooked his heel into the window opening and heaved himself all the way through it, twisting to hold on to the side of the coach. Outside, the noise was blaring, all clatter and clamor and rasping, bouncing springs. It was hard as the dickens to hold on as he climbed sideways along the vehicle. He heart thudded as he inched his way toward the driver's box, each bump in the road jarring him so hard he had to keep his teeth clenched to keep his jaw from rattling or his teeth from biting his tongue. If he ever got a bead on that driver, he'd shake him by the—

There was no driver.

Over the coach rooftop, Sam could see the whole of the bare seat. There was no one to yell at.

Nothing else for it. Hanging off the coach, Sam continued his way sideways like a crab toward the rail of the driver's box. The damn vehicle leaned precariously, veering in the direction of his unbalanced weight. As they headed for the ditch on the other side this time, he muttered curses and tried to get a footing, his boots seeming to slip no matter what small leverage he found. For a moment, both feet went and he hung by his hands, dangling like a side of beef, swaying to and fro. Then a bump in the road swung him wildly *fro,* away from the box, then enough *to* in the other direction that he got his leg up and over, a kneehold on the rail of the driver's box.

He climbed over and sat down into the rocking seat. God only knew how long it had been unoccupied.

At which point, the coach hit the far ditch, the one they'd missed last time. The frightened horses swerved, taking the whole dang-blasted carriage sideways with them. For an instant, as it turned sharply, the vehicle only had contact with the road at two wheels. From inside, Mrs. Brown shrieked, while Sam, if he hadn't had a good grip on the side rail, would have been tossed from the helter-skelter vehicle as it descended straight down into the ditch then all but overturned before it pitched its way back up and out.

Meanwhile, the reins, he realized, were dragging on the ground in among twenty-four galloping hooves. Ah, hell, here was something he didn't want to attempt. Yet even as he dreaded it, he'd already begun. He climbed down into the harnesses, while, driverless and at the mercy of the stony moor and six frenzied horses, the coach headed out onto open land, across the Dartmoor itself.

Sam had just managed to wrap a rein around his hand as, one foot on the shaft, he clung backward to a harness saddle and the mane of a horse—*awkward* wasn't the word—when with a sudden whoosh and a rooster tail of water the carriage suddenly came to a complete and surprising halt. Sam was thrown over the top of the horses to land with a cold, wet splash into water. Of sorts.

He was dazed for a moment. Very quickly, though, he was aware that he was up to his knees in bog scum. And sinking. For a few seconds there was only the eerie sound of befuddled horses. They, too, struggled in mire. The whole of the carriage and horses were caught in a kind of swamp. Into this neighing, whinnying, and relative quiet, Mrs. Brown's voice called, tentative, frightened. "Mr. Cody? Are you there? I can't get the door open."

The coach sat at a strange angle in the water. He realized not only was he sinking in mud, but the carriage was inching down, taking Mrs. Brown and the horses with it.

After few moments' struggle, he pulled himself up by the neck of an uncooperative horse—the damn beast was so upset it tried to bite him. The mud was silty and sucking, hard to fight. It took an age, it seemed, to lift himself back and up through harnesses, poles, and over the break lever, then to climb up onto the roof.

From there, he reached down and fought the bog for the door. Though only a few inches of the door was underwater as yet, the muddy pressure was too much.

"You'll have to use the window as I did," he told her.

"I can't get my foot up," she whimpered from inside.

"Give me your arms."

After a moment, two long, slender arms extended upward

through the window, while behind a horse screeched, then bellowed.

Sam leaned down, wrapping her arms around his neck. "Take hold and let your feet climb through the window as I pull you."

He lifted, getting a grip around her back and waist as soon as he could, and Mrs. Brown appeared through the window, disheveled but none the worse for wear. She was wet and shaken—apparently the water had splashed generously to the inside of the vehicle. She was probably bruised as well. But, in fact, they would have both been fine, if only the carriage hadn't been sinking beneath them.

He pulled her all the way up onto the coach roof.

Once she was safely deposited, he left her for a moment—with her protesting—to climb forward, back down over the carriage toward the horses. There, he took out his pocketknife and sawed till the small blade had cut through the traces. Lighter now without the carriage taking them down, the whole team struggled forward. The two lead horses seemed to be on firmer ground. He hoped they could pull the rest out.

He turned his attention back to Lydia Brown, who sat folded onto her knees and shaking on their unstable rooftop.

As he joined her again, he looked around. The bog was large and covered in a thick layer of bright green moss. It lay like a blanket, broken only around the area where the horses and carriage had sailed into it.

From the luggage rack of the rooftop, he unstrapped a long, satchel-like case—it was more awkward than heavy, as if it had a fold-up ironing board packed at the bottom. He lifted it over his head and heaved it out across the marshy water.

"That's mine!" she yowled as it arced through the air.

To Sam's amazement, the bag hit with a slosh, bounced downward, then bobbed back up. It remained where it landed, nestled in a cushion, a mat of floating vegetation.

"The moss is thick," he decided, "and porous enough to be buoyant. It's going to hold us." He hoped he was right.

Turning to Mrs. Brown, he said, "You're next."

"Ai-ai-ai—" she complained as he took hold of her and glided her backward off the wet rooftop, dropping her, fanny first, onto the thick, green quilt.

The moss promptly dipped at the edge where it had been cut through by the coach. She slid down it partway into the water, her skirts soaked, before she rolled, reaching, shrieking—and clinging by fistfuls of moss for all she was worth.

Nothing like a little taste of mud and bog water to make a body scurry. She managed to turn over and skittle forward, getting up onto her hands and knees. Then a miracle: The lovely green pillow, quaking and shuddering under her movement, became a buoyant surface for her crawl upon. There was a path of it all the way across the mire to where he could see land, dirt, blessed rocks. His idea worked. He almost couldn't believe it. Who would've thought?

"Toward that rocky area," he called. "Where the bright green dulls and looks drier. About twenty yards off, that's were it ends."

A good, practical woman, if terrified, the good Mrs. Brown grabbed up her skirts, hitching them into her bloomers (which were a lot fancier than her outer clothes, a lot of lace and thin silk and ribbons; he was mesmerized for a second), and began to crawl. Sam watched her silk bottom— two ivory-pink moons with wet silk clinging to them—make its way out onto the bright, velvety green float of vegetation. Under the circumstances, he thought maybe he shouldn't have found her bottom pretty, but in fact it was downright breathtaking. She had a dimple in over each buttock where it met the small of her back. A neat, perfect matched set.

The skinny lady with the fine backside made her way, her hands up to her wrists in water, her knees in puddles with each step, but she stayed afloat and made progress. Sam could see her legs trembling.

"You're doing real well, darlin'," he called, then corrected, "Mrs. Brown."

Behind him, he heard the horses make land in a frightened frenzy, the sound of hooves on something harder than gosh-damn mud and slime. Thank God. Though, somewhat dishearteningly, he heard the ungrateful nags take off in panic once their feet found traction. They galloped off.

No matter, he told himself. The horses'd settle down. He and the lady could chase them once they got themselves sorted out.

Only then did he notice his knees were getting wet. The lowest corner of the roof was going under.

Quickly, he set to relieving the coach of everything he could till the last moment. The trunk in the boot was a lost cause, but he managed to lift two strongboxes, a small and a large, from under the driver's box. He had just tossed the larger, heavier one onto the bright green floating surface and watched its corner tip—whatever was in it was unevenly balanced—cut into the moss, and the whole thing drop into the dark underneath, when the entire carriage gave a gurgle. He felt it drop suddenly under him.

As fast as he could he lowered the small strongbox onto a piece of likely vegetation, then slid himself into the water too, grabbing the largest intact piece for himself. He had just gotten up onto a piece of moss that more or less supported him, when behind him—with a loud, vortex-like rush—water sucked. And the coach went down suddenly as if something underneath it had hold and pulled. In seconds, all that remained was the vehicle's far corner—and a lot of glugging bubbles as its interior below the surface took on water and sludge.

Then silence. All but for the faint whimpering of the woman up ahead.

Sam lay on his piece of bog moss—it was thick and spongy—drenched, muddy, and breathing like a man who had . . . well, who had just spent the last twenty minutes try-ing to survive to this moment. Now that he had, the moment itself didn't look too promising. God knew where the horses had gone. He realized it was late in the day. The sun was low. Soon they would be without light in this desolate hole of a place.

The good news was that, if he kept himself mostly flat

and his weight dispersed, he could scoot on his wet belly along the floating, green blanket. Up ahead, he saw Mrs. Brown's beautiful backside crawl up onto what looked to be real land. Hallelujah. A few minutes later, he was dragging himself up onto the same plot beside her.

She sat, clutching her knees to herself and crying. "I'm not very brave," she said.

He laughed. "You were a crackerjack. I don't think I've ever seen a woman so hellbent on staying alive. You did fine, real fine." He added to distract her, "And I liked the way you tucked up your skirt. You have about the prettiest bottom I've ever seen crawl across pond scum."

Through her tears, she made a face, a glare, at him. Though she stopped crying. She wiped her eyes.

Good for her, he thought. She'd be back to her old uppity self in no time.

When he stood and surveyed the situation, though, three hundred sixty degrees, there wasn't much to survey. He turned this way and that with nothing but rocks, tufts of grass, or bog in any direction: not a single sign of civilization. He couldn't even be sure which way the road was, though it had to be close.

Across the mire, he saw what looked to be deep wheel marks where the vehicle had entered the water, but there was no telling if the road was in the direction the tracks indicated. In fact, he was fairly certain it wasn't. The last part of the ride had been so wild, he could only guess how many times they'd veered off one course then another. Two or three times at least—

It surprised him when he heard, "Thank you."

He frowned down at the woman sitting with her arms around her legs.

She said again, "Thank you. Thank you for getting me out of that thing before it sank." Then with perfect illogic, she swung her fisted forearm back and knocked him across the shin.

"Hey," he said. "You're welcome. I think. What was that for?"

She looked up and around, over her shoulder, to frown her wide, watery eyes at him. "Hey nothing. You threw my bag—"

"To see if it would float." He snorted. "Is gratitude a difficult concept for you?"

"Throw your own bags."

"Mine are on their way to Dover, to enjoy a honeymoon I won't be having."

Relentless, her lip trembling, she said, "Y-you threw *me* on that—that—that *scum*, when you didn't even know if it would hold me."

"The coach was sinking. Did it matter?"

"*You* didn't try it first."

No, he hadn't. Why not? "You were lighter. It might have held you but not me." Good. That sounded good.

It was, apparently. She scowled a second longer, her look going from ornery to uncertain, then her mouth formed a word: *Oh.* She nodded.

She turned around, wrapping her arms around her knees again, then asked, quieter, "So you wanted to save me, if possible, before you drowned, if you were going to? Is that it?"

"Sort of." No, what he wanted was to smack her. But he said instead, "So you wanted my help, but you're not very grateful because you don't approve of the form it took? Is that it?"

After a pause, she said, "Sort of."

He thought he saw a smile, just a crack of one, before she threw him a look, a raise on one eyebrow, then made a face, *ew.* Demonstratively, she lifted a pinch of wet dress, her pinky held out delicately, the hem heavy with mud. In her prissy English accent, she said, "Your day to save women."

"Yeah, I'm the king of it."

"As an act, it's a trifle rough around the edges."

"It beats the bottom of a bog, you have to admit."

She admitted nothing. They both sighed.

"Here," she said. With a crooked finger, she invited him to bend down.

He squatted, an arm balanced over his knee, to see what she wanted, half expecting her to tweak his nose or slap his face.

He jerked when, with the edge of her wet dress, she reached up and dabbed at the corner of his mouth. "The cut here opened again," she said and pressed.

With her thumb and finger, she took hold of his chin, bracing it against the pressure as she held her skirt against the side of his lips to stop the bleeding. For a full minute, she had a little routine: She pressed, stopped, contemplated the corner of his mouth, frowned, wiped gently, then pressed again, the whole time her brow knit with concern.

Sam was discomfited, then slowly wooed by the process. She had a temper, but it didn't last. And her fingers again— he couldn't shake the awareness of how soft they were. Unusually soft, smooth; now cool and dewy from their crawl across a floating quilt of green. The wet hem of her skirt had a sweet odor, an organic scent that reminded him of lily pads, water lilies—white, long-necked flowers with pale pink centers, their stalks swollen with water. Mrs. Brown here and the English bog were a surprising combination, the smell oddly, powerfully redolent of Texas, where water— where life—was clear and he didn't feel lost.

"There," she said.

As she let go, he flinched. Yessir, his mouth stung again. Freshly opened up.

Mrs. Brown's expression pinched with empathy for the fact, her lips compressed. She lifted her little wad of wet skirt. It hovered in the air, offering to dab at his mouth again, her eyes so full of generous sympathy—so surprising and sweet—he didn't know where to look.

He shook his head. "It's all right." He let himself drop backward onto his rump to sit beside her, resting his forearms onto his knees.

She said, "What an awful day."

"The worst," he agreed.

"Yours especially. I'm sorry about your wedding and honeymoon."

"That's not even all of it. I came over here for a job, one of the requirements being I was married, a stable family man." He laughed dismally. "I'm pretty sure I'm fired now." He looked over at her there beside him. "Your day hasn't shaped up much better."

"Mine started out well." She shrugged, then took a deep breath. "But at least now we're over the worst. All we have to do is find the horses and get back on the road."

Yeah, that was all they had to do. Piece of cake.

Looking around, she queried, "What became of the driver?"

"He fell off, I imagine. He's probably lying in the road somewhere, fuddled and wondering what happened."

"Do you think we should look for him?"

"Where?" he asked. More importantly, "How?"

"He might be hurt."

"I hope he is," Sam said with feeling. "We'd be dead, if it was up to him. Wherever he is, he's on his own so far as I'm concerned." He thought to add, "Will your husband be worried?"

She stared at him blankly for a second, then nodded vigorously. "Yes. I'm sure."

"Good. Then he'll send someone out after us when we don't arrive on the coach in a few hours."

Again she nodded, though the way her eyes lifted to stare solemnly out across the bog said no one was coming with help.

After a moment, he broke into her solitude by asking, "Is it still bleeding?"

She looked over at him, her gaze dropping to his mouth where his tongue tasted blood.

"A little."

She leaned toward him, studying the cut. Pieces of her hair had come down, shaken loose. A long bronzy-gold piece lay in the curve between her shoulder and neck. The strand bent with a little curl at the end. It looked soft, floppy, and shiny as a satin ribbon.

He found himself watching her kind expression at close

range, the way she bit her lip and mulled over whether she needed to dab his mouth again. He played on her tenderheartedness, touching his fingers to the place as he opened his mouth gingerly, wincing to demonstrate how much it hurt.

Her own mouth was wide, her bottom lip full, while her top one was so thin it was almost not there. Yet he couldn't help but think, Mrs. Brown of the dimpled backside sure had an elegant pair of lips.

She was a pretty woman, he realized. The contour of her face came from bone and hollow. On the thin side. But with genuinely pretty features. High cheekbones, a delicate jaw, a narrow, straight nose. And that wide, well-made mouth.

Enough. He took his hand away, twisting the lower part of his face sideways—askance, amused—letting her know he could move it, that he was pulling her leg. Then countered any offense she might take with his most boyishly charming smile—or half of it, anyway.

His antics startled a laugh out of her. A triumph. She had a fine laugh. Then, bless her heart, she looked down, blushing like no married woman he knew. Yep, a sweet little liar.

Sam ended up laughing with her, downright entertained.

Brave, resourceful. Soft-hearted to the point of being soft-headed. Double-dealing somewhere. And, given the way that skirt came up into those bloomers, no slave to propriety.

By God, he liked Mrs. Brown or whatever her name was, faults and all, prissy or not.

After a moment, she asked, "Why are we laughing?" though the question only made her laugh harder. From deep in her belly the sound burbled with little sharp skips, like a rippling brook that could flash now and then, almost blinding in appeal.

"Nerves," he answered. He took off his boot, dumping out water and mud.

"Nerves," she repeated.

"Plus I'm flirting with you, and you like it—while both of us are wet, muddy, and out in the middle of a moor, where it's probably downright dangerous to be stranded. You have to admit, that's pretty funny."

She quieted and looked at him. "Are we stranded, do you think?"

"No," he lied. "Of course not." He laughed again, a snort this time, then said, "So," turning to look into her dishonest gold eyes, "here's what I think: First we go through the satchel and strongbox and see what's worth hauling with us. If we hurry, that should leave us with maybe as much as an hour of daylight. Then we either chase after the horses, hoping to catch them and ride them. Or walk in the most likely direction of the road, then hope someone comes along. What'll it be? It's your call."

4

The light that lies, In woman's eyes.

THOMAS MOORE
"The Time I've Lost in Wooing"
Irish Melodies, c. 1807

The strongbox contained two bottles of gin wrapped in a clean shirt and pair of socks. The odd-shaped satchel with something hard at the bottom—Sam thought of it as the ironing-board bag—belonged to the good Mrs. Brown, who didn't want him to go through it: only carry it.

"It holds a lot of private things," she said.

They argued. She won. The satchel wasn't heavy enough for him to put the energy into the debate that she was willing to. He picked the odd thing up by its handles.

"You carry the gin," he told her, handing her the bottles, one wrapped in the shirt, one in the socks. "It could be our dinner."

They decided to go after the horses, mostly because, though the animals had galloped off a ways, they were visible around a rocky rise near the horizon. Two had broken loose from the others, the remaining four presumably behind the dark outcrop of granite. It was Sam's intention that they walk up to the animals—a fifteen-minute trek, he estimated, if they could approach the horses without spooking them or having to give chase. Once close enough, he and Mrs. Brown here would decide on the two horses most willing to be ridden, improvise riding bridles from the coaching tack, then take to the road bareback: a good, solid plan, even if the riding part was a little tricky for a "lady's maid," but he could always take her up on his horse if she couldn't ride without a saddle.

Thus, with Sam carrying the elongated satchel and Mrs. Brown carrying a wrapped bottle of gin under each arm, they took off on foot, heading toward the distant silhouettes of the two horses that looked fairly calm—in fact, the animals appeared to be happily grazing on low bushes.

The land itself proved less accommodating. It was uneven and hard to cover at a steady rate, spongy in places, stone-hard in others. There were no trees to speak of, only the occasional cluster of scrubby vegetation. And rock, everywhere dark gray rock. It lay in random bits, in buried chunks or loose under a person's feet. It topped the smallest hills in stacks that stood in the clutter of their own deterioration.

The generally flat vista was broken regularly by stony ridges that erupted from the ground like the prows of ships emerging from a rolling ocean of land. Grim landscape. Gray and still. Walking across such terrain, it didn't take Sam long to realize that the only lively, colorful thing in it, Mrs. Brown, had something wrong with her foot.

"You havin' trouble walkin'?" he asked.

"No," she said immediately. Then, "Well, yes. I twisted my ankle earlier today. It hurts a little. I can walk on it, though."

He smiled—her first impulse had been to lie—but contained himself as he held out his free arm.

After a second's hesitation she took it, transferring that gin bottle to the crook of her other arm, carrying the bottles against her chest.

As they tromped along, she let herself lean on him ever so slightly every right-footed step. The feel of her weight reminded him of half an hour ago, her arms around his neck as he'd pulled her out of the coach. He could've worn her like a bandanna; she was as light as sunlight. Where she linked her arm in his, where she held on, her fingers gripped like a vice, yet their hold was feminine, soft and warm through his sleeve; he was surprised again by the contact, the contradiction.

They walked along beside each other, neither speaking, while Sam in surreptitious glances studied the young woman so reluctant to take help, yet so much better off for it.

What a funny girl she was. Pretty, yet fragile somehow. The hand that gripped his arm was lily-white, small with a faint pattern of blue veins. Though well kept and, God knew, soft to the touch, it looked bloodless. Her complexion was pale. From angles, she seemed frail, as if she were built of delicately laid match sticks—he could have put his fingers around her wrist with a knuckle to spare. She didn't have a lot of bosom, though what there was sure was round: small but plump—unexpectedly ample for a girl as slim as a bedslat.

In contrast, he couldn't help remembering that backside of hers, seeing it again somehow in the movement of her hips. A healthier-looking female backside did not exist. And those breasts, now that he noticed, bobbled as she kept pace—probably average-sized breasts, though on her long, thin rib cage they looked . . . almost voluptuous. A skinny woman with a swinging backside and breasts as round as peaches.

After a few minutes he said, "You're keeping up just fine, hurt ankle or not." Nice hair, too, he thought, though some of her curls were down. Her hat was askew—he decided not to tell her, because he liked it that way.

"Yes, I am," the woman on his arm said cheerfully. "Though my family would be full of cautions if they knew." She looked down, watching her feet as she added, "My tonic went down with my drawstring in the coach."

"Your tonic?"

"My medicine. It stimulates my circulation, the doctor

says." She laughed again, though a thread of worry ran through her laughter before she rallied her good humor. "I suppose I must circulate on my own now, hmm?"

Sam stared at her a minute, wondering how much to believe. He asked, "So you live with your family, but you're a lady's maid?"

"Um—yes." She blinked at him, hesitated, then lied; it was so obvious. "My parents are in service, too. At the same house."

He smiled, nicely he hoped. "The cook and gardener," he proposed. Might as well make it easy on her.

Her eyes fixed on his, a troubled look, but then she nodded, a single abrupt agreement. Either she didn't like lying or didn't like help with it; she wasn't enjoying herself.

"So the cook and gardener give you a hard time about your health?" he asked.

She made another quick nod.

"Really? Your family really worries?" Should he, he wondered? How ill was she? And with what?

She nodded again, this time almost sadly. Resignation.

Sam felt his own smile falter. "You're worrying me."

Her light brown eyes widened as she looked up, turning them fully on him. "Oh, no! There's no point. I'm sorry. I shouldn't have said." She cleared her throat and looked straight ahead then, standing away from him a little, marching off steps. Then he did worry, because, he could see, she was trying to manufacture confidence in her next words: "I'll be fine," she said. As if by convincing him she could believe it herself. She was scared to death.

"So what's wrong with you exactly?"

She shrugged. "I don't know. Nothing so far as anyone can tell. My parents just think I shouldn't strain myself."

"What's wrong with your parents then?"

She laughed, taken aback—and delighted—with the notion, then said, "Oh, they just fret. When I was little, I was sickly. To this day, half the time, food doesn't agree with me. The air makes me sneeze. I'm careful not to take too much exercise; the doctor says it's bad for me, and he's probably right—I don't have the stamina for it. My family is, oh, rather watchful over my health." She laughed. "While I try not to be. I think they make more fuss than is good, but it's hard to fight them." She bowed her head. "One of the reasons I came to Devon was to get away from that. To feel . . . free, self-reliant for a few days. Though I have to say—" She frowned, laughed, her giddy mixed feelings again as she rotated her head to take in their austere surroundings. "This is a tad more self-reliant than I had intended." She laughed again, this time at herself. Very charmingly, he thought.

It was about then—they had been walking perhaps ten minutes—when the two damned horses ahead of them lifted their heads, looked right at them, then swung around and trotted off, one of them disappearing behind the stand of rocks completely. The lone horse stopped at a new position, again as far away as they had already come, and stared back at the two people following him, as if an envoy sent to tell them, *We horses want no part of the creatures who brought us to these circumstances.*

Sam and Mrs. Brown slowed. They approached more leisurely, less obviously. But five minutes later, the one visible horse did the same thing again, putting more distance between himself and his approaching, would-be masters.

"Shoot, will ya look at that," Sam said, halting. "We're no closer to riding out of this trouble than we were when we crawled out of that swamp." He looked at the woman beside him. "Maybe you should wait here. I'll go get 'em and—"

"No, it's going to get dark. I don't want"—she hesitated—"I don't want us to become separated." She lowered her voice; it quavered. "I'm afraid," she said, as skittish as the horses.

He let out a breath, nodding, frowning under the brim of his hat, then started to walk again. He could see her point. By her careful movement, he was pretty sure her ankle hurt more than she wanted to let on; she was trying to be brave. What to do with her and the horses, though?

When, ten minutes later, the last horse in sight bolted again
to just this side of the stand of rocks, Sam let out a long,
windy sigh. "Sit down," he said. "You have to wait here."

"No—"

"You have to." The sun lay on the horizon behind thick
clouds, making the sky glow, while it gave every rise and
bump of the moor the faint, long, fantastical shadows of
early twilight. "I'm leaving you here. I'm running that
way"—he pointed west—"at an angle away from them, then
I'm circling back around behind that outcrop of rock—"

She turned to face him. "You can't leave me here
alone—"

"I can, and you have a part to play, so listen to me. It's
getting dark, and I don't have time to argue."

"I'm coming with you—"

He put his fingers over her mouth, which made her mad.
She shoved them away. Before she could say anything,
though, he told her, "Stop complaining. Listen."

"You stop. Stop acting as if you have everything taken
care of. As if I had no say."

He snorted. "All right, what's your plan?"

Silence. She pressed her pretty mouth tight, scowling up
at him. After a moment, she admitted, "I don't have one."

"Then, till you do, can we try mine out?"

More glaring, more lip pressing. "Oh, jolly good," she
said. She meant the opposite. "Certainly. Whatever you say.
You're a one-man Wild West show. I'll just stand here and
watch."

"Listen, Liddy"—it just came out. Lydia, Liddy; close
enough. It sure as blazes beat calling her *Mrs. Brown,* when
she was no more a missus than a fly and Brown probably
wasn't her name anyway. "I'd feel insulted if I wasn't so
busy feeling bad for you. You're worried, scared witless, and
it's addling your brain."

She blinked, frowned, and drew her head back, still mad,
then surprised him. "Fine," she said grudgingly, "what do
you want me to do?"

Well. All right then. "I'll go round that rise and send the

horses around this way. I'll run them toward you. When you see me come out from behind them, stand up and wave your arms. Make a lot of noise. Turn them back toward me. We'll get them between us, and I'll latch onto one, one way or the other."

Her bottom lip pushed out, she nodded. Her chest, those fine, wobbly breasts, rose and fell like she was running a race. Poor thing. She was. Against him. Against herself. Against her own bucking fright—she didn't think for a second she could take care of herself, and she didn't have much more faith in him.

Before he could think about her more and reconsider, he left her there.

Without looking back, Sam sprinted toward the sun. He paced himself, taking long, even strides, watching the ground as best he could in the fading light, trying to keep himself on the even tract as he ran parallel to the rise of granite.

The big shock came as he rounded on the high rocky rise. He slowed, then moved around it till he could see the horses: In the dim light he spotted not six but at least a dozen, a small herd. They weren't the coach horses at all. They were ponies. Wild ponies. And they scattered, every last one of them, in all directions, the moment they caught the drift of his scent and movement.

Sam stood there stunned, watching small, bushy-tailed ponies flee him at a gallop. Stupid. Oh, so stupid, Sam. You've known horses all your life, yet you mistake *these* for horses twice their size? Up close, they weren't anything like the coach's horses, except maybe in color; a couple of them were shiny brown with long black tails and manes. How could you be so dumb as to see a coach team in a couple of short, shaggy animals? Idiot . . . pea-green fool . . . what a waste of time and energy . . . all for the wrong horses . . . a long walk for nothing. . . .

He was berating himself pretty fiercely, feeling lower than low as he trudged up to Lydia. She was sitting on a big rock there in the twilight, her head bowed, waiting for him.

Oh, she would really light into him now, he thought. And he'd just let her. He had it coming. She was more than half right. He really was a Wild West cowboy sometimes—full of show and jingle, wanting not just to fix things, but to fix them spectacularly, while being so damn stupid sometimes he wanted to shoot himself. He didn't feel like he was worth spit—

"Dartmoor ponies," she said as he came up. "Two came close enough for me to see them better."

He began his litany. "I'm sorry. I should've known they weren't the right ones. I should've—"

She interrupted. "You should have what? They were far away. How could anyone tell from a mile off?"

"Their proportions were wrong. They—"

"We wanted them to be the horses, and the light was poor. We weren't expecting any other horses but ours—"

Her excuses made him mad. "Listen, you don't have to be nice to me—"

"Yes, I do. I have to be nice to myself—I mistook them too. It was an understandable mistake."

"It wasn't. I should've realized—"

"How? Magic? Or are you just God? You know everything?"

Yeah, he liked to think he did. About horses anyway. He glowered, trying to see her expression in a face so shadowed by evening he could barely make out her features. When it got dark in this neck of the woods, he was guessing, it would get real dark. He doubted they'd be able to see their hands in front of their faces in a few minutes.

Sam exhaled a long sigh and pushed his hat back on his head. "So it's okay with you that we walked for God knows how far, away from the road, in the wrong direction?"

"No, I wish we hadn't. But what can we do?"

"Nothin'."

"I wonder where *our* horses are."

He frowned, looking along the dim horizon as if he might see them. "Long gone," he said. It was information that should have depressed him more, but he sighed again and realized,

no: The heavy blue feeling that had walked with him all the
way back, like an old familiar companion, had stepped away
from him, fading.

After a second she asked, "Would you be hungry?"

"Starved," he said, surprised to realize it. Though he
couldn't think what the hell he'd feed them.

Immediately Sam started to think: He could build a fire,
see if he could find rabbit trails in the bushes. That shouldn't
be impossible, even in the dark; there weren't that many
bushes. He could set snares or traps on the most likely paths.
Why, by morning, they might have—

"I have two sandwiches," she said and laughed. Like a little joke, she continued in her meticulously articulated syllables, "One cucumber, one chutney and cheese. I don't know
why precisely, but I do believe you will hate them both." She
laughed again, that delightful, burbly sound, so feminine, so
merry.

He couldn't figure her out. She could be mean, argumentative, skittish, but she was . . . kind: possessed of a genuine
kindness, a sensitivity mixed with good intentions that felt
just plain good to stand next to, to be around. It was at her
core.

"Cucumbers?" he asked. "You make sandwiches out of
cucumbers?" It didn't sound terrible so much as it sounded
like nothing to eat. Like sandwiches made out of water or
air. "You eat the sandwiches," he told her. "I'll set up some
traps, see if we can't snag something bigger for breakfast.
Then I'll build a fire, make us comfortable."

"No, no. We'll share."

She bent over, a wonderful bottom-up shadow in the
growing dark as she unlatched a corner of the mysterious
long satchel at her feet and dug her hand down inside. He
twisted his mouth, thinking he should go through that thing,
whether she liked it or not, to see what else it might hold for
them.

And to see better what Liddy Brown was all about.

She brought out a package wrapped in butcher paper. It
crinkled loudly in the stillness as she unfolded it, the pale

paper flashing in the dimness. Open, she held the packet out.

He bent his head over the edges, sniffed—something smelled odd, like bay rum—then grunted, *ugh*.

Which made her burst into light, little peals of laughter, openly relishing his displeasure. "Do you want the cucumber or the chutney and cheese?" she asked.

He was stymied for an instant by the choice. Or lack of it.

"We'll split them both," she announced.

He frowned down at the dainty bread she handed him, its crusts cut off. He offered it back. "No, you have it. You could use it."

"Certainly not. You need to eat, too."

"I don't need to as much as you do." He was being gentlemanly.

She huffed. "You think I'm too skinny?"

"No," he told her honestly, "I think you're as pretty as— as a pie supper." Given how hungry he was, it was a high compliment.

Her head raised to look toward him. It tilted; she was trying to assess him through the dark. After a suspicious moment she said, "You mean that nicely, don't you?"

"Yeah." He laughed.

She nodded, seeming to debate herself whether or not to be flattered.

He explained, "A pie supper. Can't you imagine how pretty that'd be? Nothing but pie to eat?" Then he asked, "You hungry? 'Cause if you really don't care, I'll take half those sandwiches, now that I think of it." He teased her. "You're too fat anyway."

"I'm not."

He laughed harder. There was no predicting what she would or would not quarrel over, this woman. She'd argue over nothing.

Or hand him sweet grace on a platter, right when he was ready to chew himself up alive.

The expression *Night fell* was never more appropriate. When the last inch of sun sank out of sight, the moor became so lightless, it was eerie. The cloud cover was thick. Not the faintest star twinkled overhead. There was not the first light of civilization in any direction. Only a murky, fuzzy sliver of moon, dimly haloed, peeped now and then from the occasional passing hole in the clouds.

Lydia could see Mr. Cody's movement—that was about all—as she helped him gather sticks from bushes and shrubs around the perimeter of where they were setting up for the night. They'd decided to camp against the granite outcrop that had hidden the ponies, since one wall of haven seemed better than none. They piled their few things near it—her satchel, the gin and clothes—then set off for the far bushes in search of the makings for a fire.

Though she eventually carried a skirtful of twigs, Lydia didn't think she was worth much as a partner in fire-starting. Mostly, she just trailed after Mr. Cody, afraid to let him get too far away.

"It's so dark," she murmured.

"Dark as a pocket."

"You make it sound cozy. It's not—*yike!*" Her skirt caught on something that grabbed at her, not allowing her to follow for an instant, so that her words came out more alarmed than she'd meant. She tried to laugh away her unease. "I've not been in such pitch black since my brother locked me in my mother's wardrobe as a joke, then threw the key out the window."

Mr. Cody's shadow stooped and helped with her dress. "Nice brother."

"He is, mostly. And I was the one who got in trouble. I screamed and beat on the door so hard I literally broke my way out—my mother was not happy that I destroyed her wardrobe."

"Well, we have what we need to break out of this dark." He reached and caught her hand, his dry palm pressing to hers as his fingers wrapped around the backs of her fingers. "Come on. It won't be so hard as that. We'll start a fire."

His hand and words calmed her. She let him lead her back.

Just out from their roofless, one-walled shelter, Lydia dumped her skirtful of branches and twigs, then, squatting, watched Mr. Cody's vague shadow stoop over the wood. He began to arrange it, though she couldn't see well enough to say how. It didn't matter. A fire. Oh, glory. Lydia was impressed that he was going to be able to start one—she'd heard the American Indians could do it by rubbing sticks together.

She watched his obscure movements intently, trying to determine what he was doing, her hands in the squatting lap of her skirts. Finally, frustrated, she couldn't resist asking, "How are you going to light it? What do you do?"

A little pass of clouds revealed his silhouette in slightly better definition, a man with one knee on the ground, his other foot under him, his chest pressed against his thigh as he bent over their sticks. This shadow turned its head toward her. "You reach in your pocket," he said as he shifted his weight, "and pull out some matches." He let out a snort of humor as he struck a tiny flame into existence.

"You had matches," she said flatly, disappointed. And annoyed.

His face, over the tiny match, came alive for a moment: golden, shadowed, lit faintly—devilishly—from beneath. But familiar and a relief to see, even if he made fun. He threw her his teasing half-smile as he cupped his hand around the flame, then disappeared back into shadow as he held it low, applying it to the twigs beneath the heavier wood.

Some kindling lit. She watched the brighter light dance up into his visage as he bent over their small fire. Under the brim of his hat, his face drew sharp-planed, the injured side hidden by angle and darkness. She was taken aback to realize how handsome he was. Had she known this? That, without the distraction of bruises, cuts, and swelling, his features assembled in mature, masculine good looks. It was in the flare of his nostrils, the width and muscle of his jaw, the ridge and cut of his cheek.

She would guess he was in his mid-thirties, though his face seemed older—from too much sun and perhaps, she thought somehow, too much sorrow. It wasn't a youthful face. Even by firelight, lines fanned out at the sides of his eyes, crinkles—they weren't from smiling. His were the lines of a furrowed brow, of squinting and frowning into the sun. It came to her: He never smiled from happiness, only from glee when he teased, when he tormented with his quirky humor. His smile was ironic, sarcastic, faintly sadistic in a tame way. As if the closest thing he knew to joy was a sort of mirthless confirmation that, yes, life was as absurdly bleak as he'd always thought, so much so as to be ridiculous, funny.

Speaking over the small fire, he said, "Besides matches, I also have half a dozen cheroots in my pocket, mostly broken, but two, I think, still whole. You'll pardon if I have one."

She was uncomfortable having to say, "I'd rather you wouldn't."

He glanced at her with a derisive lift of one brow. "I wasn't really asking permission."

"A lot of smoke gives me asthma."

"Then this fire'll kill you." He didn't hide his belligerence.

"Do you always do this? Get angry over everything?"

He turned to look at her fully, as if pondering the question, then said, "Yes. Pretty much."

"Well, we have to have the fire for light and warmth, but I don't have to have the cheroot smoke, so I'd appreciate it if you didn't make any. Or, if you do, that you make it far from me, so I can breathe easier."

He said nothing, returning his attention theoretically to the job of lighting more sticks, spreading the ones that had caught to places where they would best catch the rest. Until he said quietly, "All right." He nodded, then added, "And I'm sorry. That was a jackass thing to say—to make you into a priss for not wanting the extra smoke, whether you have asthma or not." He glanced at her and offered his faint sideways smile. "You *are* a priss, but not because of the cigars. I don't have to smoke 'em."

"Thank you."

"Yes, ma'am." He nodded. "You're welcome."

He got the fire going to a nice, crackling blaze, and their little campsite opened up with warm light that cast their shadows onto the rock wall. They sat against it, him whittling on more sticks. Once sharp, he'd set them down.

"What are they for?" she asked.

"Rabbit traps."

"I haven't seen any rabbits." She knew there were some. She just hated the idea of his leaving her, wandering off into the dark to set up sticks that probably wouldn't catch rabbits anyway—in Yorkshire, they shot them with guns.

"Oh, no, there're rabbits here. Or foxes or gophers." He let out a single syllable of humor. "Maybe a prairie dog. It doesn't matter. Whatever we catch is our breakfast tomorrow." Gathering up his pile of sharp sticks, he sprang to his feet.

"It's a waste of time—"

"You got some other way to spend the evening?"

She frowned, but took his point. "Wilderness man," she muttered.

"Pardon?"

"Nothing."

Something in him actually *liked* being out here on his own, she realized, and she couldn't help but resent his liking what terrorized her. She tried to be more generous, more rational. So he enjoyed being part of the rugged outdoors, enjoyed being without any convenience but what he could invent. It was probably nothing for a man like him to live outside. If she had to be stranded out in the middle of nowhere, wasn't Wild West Wilderness Man the perfect partner for it?

His shadow loped away from her, toward the far scraggly scrubs again, disappearing into the dark all but for faint movement. Lydia stood, watching diligently, worried suddenly that he would vanish entirely. What if something happened? What if he never came back?

She hobbled after the flickering, firelit glimpses she got of his silhouette—her ankle was swelling a little. Swelling or not, though, she caught up and tagged along through the low bushes where he dug small holes, then planted the sticks, points up. The digging proved arduous in the rocky earth. In the end he gave it up for snares, using lace ripped from her petticoats as the nooses.

He set half a dozen traps that took forever. She wished he'd give up. It seemed pointless, but he wouldn't listen. Eventually, she shut up and just let him do it.

As he stood up from what she hoped was the final one, he said, "You go back to the fire. I'll be right there."

Lydia grabbed his coat sleeve as he turned. "Where are you going?"

"I'll be back."

"No! Where are you going?"

"I have to, um, you know—"

"What?"

His shadow shrugged noncommitally. "You know—"

"Oh."

He moved away, leaving her standing at the edge of dark brambles, hesitant to go back without him, hesitant to follow. As he disappeared completely, Lydia felt panic rise, as tangible as if a seed of it had stuck in her throat. Before it could grow, blossom, she crashed her way through the bushes toward a sound—that of a strong stream hitting the ground.

She'd do something about that herself. Yes, that was it. Her bladder felt as if it would burst. She came up on his silhouette. His back was to her, the sound of his relief hitting the ground strongly.

He jumped. "What the—"

"I'm sorry. I can't be alone. Don't watch. I'm not looking. Not that I could see anything in this blackness." About three feet away, to the side and back of him, she lifted her skirt, scooted her drawers down, then, holding them out of the way, squatted.

Oh, once she started, goodness, she was sure she would be here for half an hour.

"Well, this is cozy," Mr. Cody said, his silhouette glancing over his shoulder. "I sort of thought I'd do this alone."

"Well, you can't. I'm too scared."

He laughed. The faint bit of moon came out behind him, making his broad back, his spread-leg posture loom like a giant as he stood doing his very ungodlike task. There they were, him standing, his back to her, her crouching to do the same, the two of them within a yard of each other on a slope of ground that kept the physics right, their feet dry. After a moment, Lydia let out a giddy laugh. Their sounds set her off. Her stream was different from his, quieter for the shorter distance and less of it. When his activity slowed, becoming fits and bursts, Lydia felt silly, giddy again, to have this information. Above her, his silhouette's back and shoulders lifted, a man fixing the front of his trousers.

Then he turned around and hunkered down right there in front of her, his face close enough to dimly recognize features. "You're giggling again."

"I am," she said. "I'm sorry. It just comes over me, and I don't know what to do about it." She shook her head. Almost finished herself with her little personal task, she realized there was nothing with which to dry herself. A question came to her all of a sudden. "So what do *you* do?" she asked.

"Do?"

"Yes. Isn't your—well—you know, um, wet when you're finished? What do you do?"

"My 'you know'?"

She huffed. "Your penis." There. The word was out. More giddiness. And, now that the subject was broached, she had a few questions. Since they seemed to be on such intimate terms and since, as soon as they rescued themselves and were on their way, she would never see him again.

In the dark, his shadow let out a disbelieving snort. "We're talking about my penis again?"

"What do you mean, *again*?"

There was a pause. "Nothing. What do I do?" he repeated. More pondering silence, then he said, "I shake the wetness off. Anything else you want to know?" He laughed. Nervously, she thought. Though, she'd say, she had his attention.

As a matter of fact, there was. "My friend Rose is very

upset about the whole honeymoon idea. Were you looking forward to yours?"

Another, longer pause. "Yes, I was." Then he asked, "What about yours? Did you like it?" Then, "Why haven't you talked to your husband about these things?"

Ah. A small box-up. The fictitious husband. And, more unsettling, the way he asked, something in his tone, gave Lydia the oddest feeling, as if he knew she was lying. She couldn't think for a minute, then answered with the first explanation that came to mind. "He's deaf."

Mr. Cody burst into laughter and stood up. "Oh, that's good," he said.

"Well, he is." She defended her ploy irritably. This wasn't what she wanted to talk about.

"I don't doubt it. Deaf. Blind. Dumb—"

"There's no need to make fun—"

Good-naturedly he told her, "No, no, never think I'm making fun. I understand perfectly."

Again she felt uneasy, as if he truly did understand perfectly, which wasn't exactly the degree to which she wanted to be understood.

He started to retreat.

"Don't leave!" she said quickly. "Turn around, yes, but please stay. Please wait."

He did. He halted, his shape outlined largely again by the eerily starless sky, near-black against black.

She bounced a little, trying to "shake" off. It didn't work exactly, but it was the best she could do. She stood, pulling her drawers up with her, feeling derailed, stupid. How on God's green earth did a woman find out anything about men without having to marry one? It seemed like an unfair extreme just to satisfy curiosity.

When she stood—perhaps it was the shift of the direction of the meek light—she suddenly couldn't find Mr. Cody's outline. She was rational one moment, then the next coping with a kind of terror that spiraled up from nowhere so quickly that, when she called out his name, it sounded shrill. "Mr. Cody? Sam? Sam? Where are you?"

She jumped, giving a little shriek, when a warm hand took hold of her arm from behind. Then relief. He turned her, pulling her to him. Her forehead found his shoulder, and she let her head drop there. "Oh, my God," she muttered into his chest, "I'm such a mess. I'm terrified of the dark, and that's all there is here. I feel so helpless."

"You aren't. You take real good care of yourself, Liddy."

She shook her head. "I'm frightened and weak and sickish—"

"There's nothin' wrong with you," he said. He petted her head, which she liked so startlingly much she could barely move: for fear he'd stop. His hand was warm as it sculpted itself to the back of her skull, over her messy hair, pressing it against her nape. "Other than normal stuff," he continued. "A hurt ankle. A rightful fear of bein' out in the dark, lost on foot."

She said nothing, didn't move. Lydia remained as still as a puppy miraculously scratched at a place she hadn't known itched, at just the right spot.

They stood silently, neither moving, neither uttering a word for several long seconds. Then he said, "There," and set her away from him. He stepped back.

Lydia swayed a degree on her feet. He caught her again, his hand around her upper arm to steady her. And again it felt so good, she was all but ashamed; she blushed. "I'm a disaster," she said.

"You're a little strange," he admitted. He added quickly, "But nice. Liddy—" he said, then stopped. His head turned slightly, lowering, as if he were trying to see his own hand where it remained casually on her.

"What?"

He hesitated, looked toward her. "You're skittish." Another lengthy pause, as if he weren't sure he should pursue the subject. "You're like a stall-bound filly: undernourished, unexercised, under—" He halted, his silhouette shifting, a change of stance. He'd been going to say something else, but said instead, "You should gallop a little, let the wind blow your mane"—he laughed self-consciously, let his hand drop, and stepped back—"if you get my drift."

"Under-what? What were you about to say?"

He clicked his tongue, resistant, then said, "*Underpleasured*, but it felt wrong to tell you that with the two of us waltzing here together in the dark—even though I believe it's true: You are." He drew in a breath, then let it out in a long gust. "And now that I've told you what I shouldn't have, I think I'll just shut my mouth. Let's go back."

"Underpleasured?" She laughed.

"Okay, it was a stupid word. It's just that you need to figure out—" A pause. "To figure out what's your heart's desire, then try for it. You need to lap up the cream of life, find your own particular variety of it, you know?"

She didn't. But he turned, and she followed him toward to the campfire, half amused by his speech, half contemplative. Her heart's desire? A galloping filly who lapped up cream? Well. Topics for thought.

They hadn't walked a dozen feet, though, before he offered one further piece of advice, in a mutter as if he wanted to tell her but he didn't want her to hear it. He said, "You got a spirit in you, Liddy Brown, that is strong enough to carry you through anything. You don't need to be so afraid." These words truly surprised her.

Then they didn't. Strong. Lydia sensed it for a moment, like something in her blood she hadn't been aware of. Real strength. As if it had always been there, but she'd been afraid to see it, afraid to allow it: to turn it loose.

Well. I'm strong, she thought. She was. How enlightening. Strong. Just thinking the word was like seeing for the first time some previously unknown part of herself. I'm the reason. This tenacity, this force of nature that keeps me going is . . . is me. I'm looking at me.

Hello.

Once back at their campsite, Sam had little to say—he'd made himself tongue-tied. He wasn't sure he'd be able to say another word to a woman who made him say things like *underpleasured*. What kind of a word was that? And what would Gwyn say? What would she think of his telling some other woman, in the dark with the two of them all alone, that she needed more pleasure in her life? While he stroked her back?

Oh, yeah, he'd forgotten. Nothing. Gwyn would theoretically say nothing. They weren't together anymore. She'd lost her say.

For the first time today, this information, instead of depressing him, gave a lift to his spirits.

5

Around their fire, everything settled into a surprisingly peaceful evening. There was warmth and light. The night promised to be chilly, but if one had to be stranded on the moor, Lydia thought, July was the month to do it. Chilly shouldn't kill them. She relaxed as she pulled her legs up under her skirt. Her feet had actually become too toasty stretched out near the fire. Her back was cold, but overall she was comfortable. And oddly content. Her stomach growled from time to time, hungry—the sandwiches weren't enough—but she felt . . . safe.

Behind her stood their rocky windbreak. Facing the fire off to her left sat a laconic man who, head down, spent most of his time poking in the rocky soil between his legs. He and she didn't talk for a while, which also seemed all right. Strange, this, that she should know contentment out in the middle of a moor without enough food in her stomach, with-

out a single convenience or familiar friend, sitting in com-
panionable silence with a man she barely knew.

The fire cast dancing shadows over Mr. Cody as he dug in
the dirt—he put the rocks he found into what was becoming
a good-sized pile. At first, she thought he was ridding his
area of stones, making the place where he'd eventually bed
down more comfortable.

But then he picked up a rock and flung it, saying,
"There's something out there. I can see the glow of eyes."
He picked up and pegged a second stone hard out into the
dark.

He pitched rocks at some far off, invisible animal he
wished dead, offering no more conversation. Lydia watched,
entertained by his purposefulness at such a pointless task.
Purposefulness and . . . there was a kind of poetry to his syn-
chronized movement in the firelight.

He would cock his arm. From her angle, she could see his
coat pull across his shoulders as it opened in front, then his
tendinous wrist came from his sleeve for an instant. (While
behind them on their rock wall, his shadow-self, three times
larger than the man himself, drew back as if to hurl missiles
from Mount Olympus.) When he let go, his arm followed
through, quick, straight, and easy, as if its energy were nothing, a flick, a toss. Yet each stone flew over the fire—the little zipping whistle of it having long died off by the time the
crack of contact with the earth finally echoed back across
the darkness.

Then he'd pick up another stone, cock his arm, his coat
would open . . .

The hunter. Wilderness Man, she thought again and
bowed her chin to her knees, smiling. He wasn't happy
enough merely to set traps. Now he must sling rocks at the
glow of distant eyes, so sure he was that he could slay something to eat.

He unbuttoned his vest for better mobility, a good-looking
vest, she realized. In fact, his entire suit fit well and, she suspected, wasn't cheap. The cut was too straight and plain for
English fashion, but it was a nice enough suit of clothes. The

vest was blue, quite a lovely color, if she remembered correctly, though it looked a murky, charcoal-purple now by firelight. Even a cowboy apparently found himself nice clothes for his wedding.

In a pause between rocks, she couldn't help asking him, "You were going to wear that hat down the aisle?"

He halted as he picked up his next stone to look over at her. The fire snapped loudly, a sputter of green wood, then he said, "Nope. They had a top hat waiting for me, theoretically at least." He faced her, his lopsided grin pulling up in the faint light. Shadows jumped along the swelling at his right cheek and eye, lumpy and painful to look at. "Though I intended to wear my own boots." He knocked the sole of one with the rock in his hand. He sat cross-legged (Indian style, Buffalo Bill called it). "They're first-rate and comfortable. Moroccan kid and calfskin. Good enough to wear anywhere, to my mind."

He drew his arm back and let fly the rock he held—out, out it went—then removed his hat. He turned it over once— *clack* went the stone in the distance, punctuating his movement as he dusted the crown of his hat. He leaned nearer the fire as if to better inspect it, then straightened the silver beads on its leather hatband. After which he surprised her by leaning sideways toward her, offering her the hat across the few feet that separated them. He said, "This hat would've been up to a wedding, if the bride hadn't pitched a fit over it. It's a Stetson, handmade in Philadelphia by Mr. Stetson himself." Rather proudly, he announced, "Out of beaver felt. They don't make any finer." He offered the hat upside down, inside toward her. It was lined with satin.

Lydia took Mr. Cody's Stetson. It was quite light, weighing much less than she'd have thought, its texture soft, while the structure of brim and crown was stiffly resistant. Reaching her hand into her hair, she found her own straw hat, seriously askew, she realized, and pulled it from her head. She tried his hat on. As it passed over her face, she caught a whiff . . . pure Sam Cody. His warmth mixed into a smell . . . like oiled leather or fresh-cut wood.

Meanwhile, Mr. Cody went back to the manly role of rock hunter in the dark. She almost said, You'll never hit anything. But no, why discourage him when she so liked watching him try? She liked best the instant when he turned loose the stone, the way his arm conveyed a momentum into the little inanimate object, the way the stone flew from his fingers. He sent each one straight, no arc, just a zinging trajectory over the campfire, traveling like a bullet that might never land.

A bullet. Bullets and cowboy hats. Her own private little Wild West show on an English moor. She touched the brim of his hat, still on her head—her hair wouldn't allow it to settle properly. Queen of the Amazons hair, Rose called it. Nets and curling irons tamed Lydia's hair into something acceptable for society. Now, though, it had to be frightful; wild, unruly. Removing Mr. Cody's hat self-consciously, Lydia patted her hair down—it felt tangled and springy, like a pile of long, spiraling wood shavings. She remembered she had a brush and a tin of pins in her bag.

She retrieved them, then sat back down. As she handed his hat back to him, she asked, "Are you really from the wild American West?" She pulled pins from her hair and dropped them into the open tin.

"Born and raised in Texas, though I've lived lots of places."

"But Texas is the real West."

He glanced at her. "We Texans like to think so."

"What's it like?" She took a handful of hair, pulling and brushing at it.

"Texas?"

"Living there."

He shrugged. "Like living on a ranch."

"A ranch?"

He threw her a frown, at so many questions perhaps, but then seemed to take stock and contemplate a forthright answer. He hurled a stone and said, "It's a good life. But a hard one. A big ranch is sort of like one of your manors here. There's the main house and offices, then the rest where the help lives, like a village almost. A big ol' mess house, a yappy poultry yard, a bunkhouse, a dairy, the usual—barns, corals, stables: lots of people and animals all joining together to make the place work."

"But not as elegant as a manor house," she found herself saying as she pulled and brushed at the tangle of hair.

He glanced at her, making a pull of his mouth. "No, ma'am, I guess not."

She looked down a moment. "So are you a real cowboy then?"

"There's hardly any 'real' cowboys left"—he snorted—"not since drought then blizzard made raising cattle a pretty small operation. The open ranges are all fenced in now. But I was raised in the era when cattle was king, on a"—he made that dry laugh, the sort he didn't mean, in his throat—"an inelegant ranch. My father was a real cowboy."

Lydia let the hank of hair fall. "I was just making the point that, as a matter of elegance and civilized life—"

He threw her a wry look. "You were just making the point that you look down your nose at where I come from."

"No, I wasn't." Was she?

The life he spoke of *wasn't* a very refined existence. She thought of wild savages running around half naked, while one's fortunes hung upon whether a lot of cows got fat enough to herd over long, difficult distances—distances more than many multiples the length of Great Britain herself—all so that the surviving cows could be slaughtered.

"It just seems there are"—she almost said *smarter*, then chose instead, "easier ways to earn a living."

"If one *must* earn a living," he said and snorted. "I've been here two weeks, and I already know what the English think is the best way to get money: to be born to it. That's who you respect. Those clever fellows who have the good sense to be bred by rich parents." As if he'd heard the word choice she'd rejected, he added, "Now, there's something that takes a lot of brains. Wish I'd been smart enough to do that."

She'd offended him. Again. It was easy enough to do. But

this time she felt more uncomfortable about doing it. Perhaps she did feel superior, when she shouldn't, and it showed. Though she didn't really feel superior, she told herself. Not *really*. She liked him. She tried to dig herself out. "So, whether you're called a cowboy or not, you work with cows, yes? What do you do with them?"

He let out another short laugh. "By cows, I take it, you mean Texas Longhorn steers?"

"All right, yes. I think so," she allowed.

Another sidelong look. He was annoyed, though in the faint light it was also possible he was smiling, too. "You are the damnedest woman," he said. He shook his head. "Yes. I've worked with cows, as you call them. I drove cattle from Texas to Kansas for a while. It's hard work and deserves respect."

She nodded. "So why don't you like being called a cowboy?"

This won her a mean glance. "I don't mind: It's sorta true."

"You don't like it."

He turned fully, frowning at her; a direct, narrow scrutiny by firelight. "All right, I don't."

"Then why wear that"—she had to remember the word—"Stetson and those boots?"

Not very nicely, he said, "Because they're comfortable and practical and what I grew up with and like."

Bewildered, she asked, "Why are you angry now?"

Sam scowled at the question. Angry? Was he angry? He had to think a moment. What the hell was this irritable feeling? Yes, anger. She'd made him angry again. Why? He turned to her. "My life is worth something to me, even if it isn't the finest there is by your standards."

"I wasn't questioning your worth. Are you always this irritable?"

He thought about it. "No. But a lot of the time."

Most of the time. Truth be known, he woke up angry most mornings, spent most days angry, and went to bed angry most nights. Life itself pretty much infuriated him. It was stupid, but a fact.

"Well, you're being ridiculous," she told him.

"Witch."

She blinked. The name-calling took her aback, but she rallied. "Beast."

"She-coyote."

"Clod," she said.

He snorted. "Drip-nose bear bait."

She frowned, bowed her head. He'd won, he thought; she had no retort—until she took his breath away: She lifted her head, looked right at him, wrinkling her nose, and stuck her tongue out. The full, pink curve of it extended down her chin at him.

Sam startled, opened his mouth to say something, then couldn't: He burst into laughter. He laughed till his cheek hurt. He couldn't stop, and he didn't want to. So much for Miss Lydia's dignity. Or consistency, so far as he could penetrate it. He'd never known a person who could be so serious, then turn on a dime and be downright silly. When his laughter finally quieted, he was left beaming at her, glowing.

He told her, "Watch out. That tongue of yours is pretty cute. You better keep it in your mouth or I'm gonna want it."

Game point. She jerked her gaze away and shifted on her rump, rocking and rustling her skirts. She made a big show of ignoring him and his indecent comment, while she re-arranged herself on her rocky patch of ground, theoretically making herself more comfortable. As if now she could.

He picked up another rock and plugged the dark with it, thinking he might say something more to her, something nicer . . . something about how pretty she looked sort of tousled in firelight. Though, come to think of it, if he did, she'd probably only argue with him about it. In any event, he didn't get the chance: This time, his rock immediately struck something different. Instead of the long wait till the expected *clack,* there quickly echoed back a soft, dull thud.

They both straightened, turning their attention toward the noise, alert.

Sam squinted toward the far, all-but-invisible bushes. "I hit something," he said, amazed. Then he rolled forward, getting his legs under him till he was on the balls of his feet, and sprung up.

He bounded toward the bushes as the realization struck them both. His rock had stopped an animal, something small. A rabbit or a fox. Dinner. Food.

It was a hare. A fat hare that Mr. Cody brought back with a hatful of berries he'd noticed in the bushes, "as if God was suggesting the sauce." The animal had been apparently hiding in a whortleberry bush—the berries being a summer delicacy from Devon, usually served with cream for breakfast. Lydia and Mr. Cody snacked on them—a delight!—while he dressed the animal, devised a spit, then proceeded to steal the tin from her hairpins, dumping the pins onto the ground.

"Hey!" she complained. "You have to talk to me before you throw me or my things wherever you happen to want them!"

She didn't protest very vigorously, though, when he explained he wanted the tin to catch the juices and set it on a rock under their roasting dinner. He seemed to know what he was doing, and once the rabbit was cooking, Lydia forgave him completely. It smelled divine. She thought she would expire from anticipation. She couldn't remember being so hungry and eager to eat.

Mr. Cody turned the spit by hand, proving he could not only find them dinner but cook it as well. It seemed a small miracle that he could, since she couldn't have: He knew how to prepare food.

"It's a hobby," he said. "Plus I drove the chuck wagon at fourteen and worked in the mess house since I was eight."

"You worked so young?"

"I had chores when I was two, and my father would be after my hide if I didn't do them right and timely. He believed there was a moral benefit to work, that it built character."

"Do you think so?" Lydia asked with wonder. She had always thought it just built calluses. Work was something you did if your parents didn't have money.

The working man beside her, temporarily jobless, didn't answer. He was more interested in basting his rabbit, muttering off and on about how it was going to be tough, how he could make it tender if he only had the right implements and ingredients. With the pins on the dark ground, Lydia gave up on her hair. She sat leaning back on her arms, her knees up, and watched him. His hat lay beside him full of berries. With it off, his hair flopped down in his eyes when he bent over the fire. His dark hair—black as India ink in the night—had a bend to it, not curl so much as curve. The firelight made an arching shadow up his forehead from the way a piece hooked down over his brow into one eye. It flopped there, gleaming in the firelight, swinging as he moved.

She wanted to comb it back with her fingers, put him aright. An excuse to feel it. His hair had a texture so smooth that, even in disarray, it didn't look as if it would tangle—the sort of hair that, if one tied it into a knot, it would only slip right out.

Shadows flickered across his face. For a moment, the light—the angle and shadows of his hair and the bridge of his nose—hid his puffy eye, and she was brought up short again by how striking his face was. Or would be, if he hadn't argued with it this morning to five bandits. An attractive man. Moreover, his attractiveness went beyond his interesting looks. He had a way to him, a way of moving, smiling, responding. A rugged, bronzed man, cantankerous, but with a teasing smile and a . . . a what?

She wouldn't admit it immediately, but then, looking down into her skirts, she let herself acknowledge it: charm. He was somehow charming. For all his bluster and prickly disposition, she still wanted to talk to and look at Sam Cody. Indeed, she was fairly sure he'd turn the heads of most women with his hat-tipping and teasing and please-and-thank-you-ma'am-kindly. He might not be like the English gentlemen flirts of her association, but he was of the same species. A man who was confident, and successful, with the ladies.

Lydia realized she was holding her mouth tight, while scowling at a streak of dirt on her skirt so large and dark she could see it clearly by firelight.

As the rabbit's cooking progressed, she began to joke to Mr. Cody about knocking him down and stealing it from the fire. It smelled better and better, heavenly. He mock-defended it but wouldn't hurry, no matter how hungry she proclaimed herself to be. She was truly put out with him by the time he was mashing berries into the juices with "a soupçon of gin." (*Soupçon?* She couldn't put the word with his slow-talking drawl and homey phrases.) He also did something with the animal's liver at the end she decided not to ask about.

The end result though was a sauced, roasted feast, so surprisingly rich in flavor she ate till the bones were bare.

"Can you remember what you did?" she asked, wiping her fingers on the edge of her hem—the dress was never going to be the same. "I'd like you to write that down for—um, for the cook at Bleycott." *Our* cook, she almost said.

He laughed, sitting back. "I think the most important ingredient is a woman who hasn't eaten but one cucumber sandwich in a dozen hours."

The fire was down, low flames and red embers, enough to cast warm shadows across his smiling face. His mouth and tongue when he talked, she realized, were purplish from the berries. So must hers be. What messes. She laughed, too. Then became self-conscious again.

A ladies' man, she told herself again. A cowboy cook of a ladies' man.

Lydia liked looking at handsome men, but she certainly didn't take the handsome charmers of her own circle seriously. Among other reasons, she wasn't their counterpart. She was too earnest. Too thin. Not glamorous enough. Not meek enough of spirit—prone to contradicting them. So was it sour grapes or did she simply not prefer them? Might she rather that Boddington, who, bless him, liked her as she was, were strikingly handsome and a little more confident in manner?

Stupid question. Yes.

Was she attracted to Sam Cody, then?

Yes. All right, yes, she told herself. In a kind of trivial way. She couldn't decide if she liked him exactly, but he . . . he held her attention somehow. He was nothing like any man she knew.

"Thirsty?" he asked. She looked across the fire at him. He sat not quite halfway around from her, close though not within arm's reach.

She smiled ruefully. "Yes. I'd give quite a bit for a cup of tea right now."

He held up something, a bottle.

Oh, the gin. She shook her head. "Water would be nice."

"Well, there's a swamp back there not too far, if we could count on stumbling onto it, without stumbling into it. That's the only water I know of." He continued to hold the bottle in the air, an open offer. "It's all we have," he said.

She frowned. No, she thought.

"I'm going to drink it."

She thrust her jaw slightly forward, pondering. She'd only ever had a glass of port now and then, though to no ill effect. "Well, just a little maybe," she decided. "Do you think it's thirst-quenching?"

"Without a doubt." He took the neck of a bottle into one hand and twisted the cork out with the other, then, leaning onto his elbow, he stretched to offer the bottle of gin. "Ladies first."

She took it, stared at the light wavering through the clear liquor, sniffed it—not too bad, rather sweet smelling—then tilted the bottle back to her lips.

It burned the second it hit the back of her throat. She

drew in a breath to cool the sensation, but took air too quickly; the gin went down wrong. She ended up coughing and sputtering like a bad imitation of a character in one of Clive's absurd cowboy books, the greenhorn in the saloon.

"Just sips," he told her, leaning the full length of his body while stretching his long arm out. He patted her back.

She nodded. Once her eyes stopped watering, she tried another sip. It was merely warm going down the second time—she remembered not to breathe while she swallowed—and not too bad in small quantities.

As she handed the bottle back, she felt a little frisson, a ping, of wonder at herself: a sense of being free—inventive, good—yet frightened by the unpredictedness of the moment. How had this happened? Gin to quench her thirst. A dinner of rabbit eaten with her hands. An open fire for warmth. No roof. And a stranger who wore his hat day and night—he'd put it back on now that the berries were out of it—to pat her back when she coughed.

Looking over at him, she asked, "So what kind of work does a cowboy"—she corrected—"a cowboy's son do on this side of the ocean?" She tried to imagine why either should be sitting here on a moor in the middle of England.

"Nothin'." He took a drink of gin, then, leaning across on an elbow again, offered the bottle. "Like I said, the job in London for September was real clear about wanting a dependable married man. Jilting my fiancée pretty much cinches my ticket home."

"What were you going to be here, before your were fired?" She drank a bit more gin. It was pleasantly warm this time, not bad at all. Then handed it back.

As he took the bottle and sat back, he sent her a dubious look, one eyebrow raised, an expression that became one of his tormenting, crooked smiles. "A hired gun," he told her. His eyes brightened, devilish delight, when she looked alarmed. "Sort of," he added, then became more straightforward. "I was supposed to talk some sense into some folks here, scare 'em into bein' more reasonable."

"Ugh," she said.

He laughed. "Yep. It doesn't make me popular. But I'm good at it, what can I say? More?" He held up the bottle.

She shook her head. "In a minute. So will you miss it, this scaring people? Do you like doing it?"

"No," he said immediately. Then amended, "Though that's like asking if I liked pulling you out of that coach before it went down. I liked the result. But did I like doing it, no." He shook his head. "I'd rather have been in a hammock in the shade taking a little Mexican siesta with a tequila-and-lime in one hand—"

"What's tequila?"

"Like gin, only out of cactus juice." He continued, "And a dime novel open on my chest."

"So you can read," she teased him back, laughing. Then said, "My brother likes cheap novels, too."

A mistake. He twisted his mouth till he had to touch the corner—he'd made such a severe expression, it apparently hurt. With his mouth twisted to the side and his finger on it, he said, "By *cheap* you mean *proletarian* to your *highbrow* aesthetic?"

She was beginning to think it was impossible for them to be civil to each other. She had streaks of prejudice and pride that kept rearing their ugly heads, while he was a tetchy fool. Then the words, *proletarian, highbrow aesthetic*, registered. Where did an American ruffian get words like these?

She held out her hand, asking for the bottle. On receiving it, she took a larger drink before she asked, "So what's so blessed wrong with being a cowboy?"

"You think they're stupid and foolish."

She considered the possibility he was right. Then said, "I don't think *you're* either one."

He was momentarily disarmed. "I guess I just don't like bein' misjudged then, not for even a minute."

She nodded and grew silent. He took the bottle, and she wrapped her arms about her knees, setting her chin on them to stare into the fire. She didn't intend to say anything fur-

ther. Perhaps it was the silence or the night, maybe the gin.
A cozy intimacy for confidences. She murmured, "Everyone
is misjudged for a minute, sometimes longer. It's difficult to
take a person's measure, unless you know him well." She
shrugged, wistful. "I don't think a handful of people know
me. Not who I truly am. Maybe not even that."

When she slid a glance at him, he was staring at her, serious, contemplative.

He broke the protracted silence with, "You know, for a
snobby, complainin' woman, you sure have a streak of wis-
dom in you, Mrs. Brown."

Lydia had to couch her face to hide the pleasure the silly
backhanded comment caused her. Foolish. She put her
mouth and chin behind her knees with just her eyes watching the fire over her kneetops. Its flames lapped at the log.
The thickest piece, an old stump he'd found, glowed neatly
now. It was covered in little shrunken rectangles of ash, the
wood burning so that it glowed red from inside, from its
core.

She found herself giving voice to her most honest fear.
"Are we going to survive, do you think?"

He laughed. "Abso-dang-lutely."

"We were lucky to get the rabbit."

"Nah, I hit it accidentally. There's plenty out here. We
could live off the land till winter. Though we won't need
to—given the width of the moor, we could walk the whole
thing in a day or two."

As if to reinforce what he said, he lifted the gin bottle,
toasting her with it, then upended it. He drank till the bottle
glugged a burble of air.

She liked that he could be sanguine about their predica-
ment. He wasn't worried. Of course. They were going to be
perfectly all right. They'd go to sleep. They'd probably have
another rabbit in the morning for breakfast. Then they'd
walk south and get to the road. They'd stay on it till they either met someone or came to civilization. They weren't in
any real danger.

Though her arms were cold, and her back away from the

fire felt chilly. The wee hours promised uncomfortable temperatures. Unless of course two people were huddled together. She looked at him.

He wasn't saying anything. He knew it, too. He was waiting for her to come to the conclusion.

6

Within a short time Lydia was recognizably tipsy, but she didn't mind. She liked the feeling. The more gin she drank, the more she felt . . . happy, almost cocky, with their adventure: unhampered, spontaneous. She felt good. He was right. They were fine. And there was nothing very wrong with her. Truly. Except, she thought drunkenly, that her dinner menus didn't have rabbit and gin on them often enough.

Lydia kept up most of the conversation, telling the man across from her about Rose's wedding, for no particular reason other than he seemed quietly interested. "They had an accordion player for dancing, and everyone, even her grandmother, danced. Sometimes they sang with the music, too. . . ."

Sam listened with only half an ear, gratified to see Liddy so relaxed. He himself was exhausted, with a pretty strenuous day catching up with him. In the not too distant future, he figured, he'd be overwhelmed by sleep, but for now he fought it. For one, he was just cold enough to prefer drinking a little more gin to sleeping. And, for two, he couldn't seem to get enough of watching Lydia Brown laugh and gesture and talk, now that she had a little gin under her belt.

They were going to lie down together, he knew that, and it was another reason he avoided going officially to sleep for the night. He wasn't certain how well he'd tolerate putting himself up against Liddy Brown here, touching her to keep warm and not for anything else.

Her arms wide, Liddy demonstrated the width of some river at a town called Swansdown, then with a movement of hand and wrist the wiggly way the river narrowed then wound under a bridge. She was either showing him things like this or else hunched over, her arms folded into her knees and skirts, herself as near to their burning wood as she could be without being on top of it. She was cold; she was talkative. He remembered an old, apt expression of his pop's and smiled: She could speak ten words a second with gusts up to fifty. Ha, Pop would've liked her. With a little gin in her, Liddy put Sam in mind of Juliana, his pop's longtime Mexican mistress. Vivacious, friendly, open about her feelings, vague about the facts of her life—and seemingly without the first notion of unsavory motives in other human beings.

Liddy moved on to happily recapping their day, if he wasn't mistaken, though he couldn't think why she'd be so happy about it, when, sitting there, she reached absently up into her hair. She found the last several hairpins and drew them out, tossing them on the ground to keep company with the rest he'd dumped out earlier. He couldn't say he was sorry he'd disposed of them. Her hair was as crazy, as wild and copious as honeysuckle vines in June. She continued hunting through her hair, looking for any missing pins.

With the last one, she let her hair down completely, and the sight was even better than he'd expected. Her hair stood out in a curly cloud around her face. It spiraled down her back to her hips. It corkscrewed onto her shoulders. If he stuck his hand in it, he'd probably have had to disentangle himself with his free hand; he couldn't have combed his fingers through it. Her hair was that dense and curly.

When he finally horned in on the conversation, he found himself saying, "You're not married."

She threw him a discombobulated frown. She was going to insist, he thought, then surprised him by saying only, "You don't know that."

"You don't wear a ring."

"I lost it."

"There's no mark of a ring." He went on, "And there's something about you. You're—" He hesitated. "You know nothing of a man." He took a slow drink of gin before he said, "You're just a sweet girl, Liddy Brown. A sweet, unmarried young woman with a little bit of temper, a big, generous heart"—he laughed—"and a dangerous bent for adventure now that you've had a taste of it and survived it." He shook his head at her, smiling. "No more wild coach rides for you. It's making you into a regular thrill-seeker." He smiled at her, joking, but feeling admiration, too, and letting her see it.

Such a winning smile he had, Lydia thought, even if it came off crooked, using only half his face. His smile altered his words, bringing with them all the confusing, pleasant embarrassment of a pretty compliment. She felt a warm, flattered pleasure spread through her—though she couldn't think where exactly the compliment lay. A thrill-seeker? No, that wasn't her. She was too careful to value thrills for their own sake. Nonetheless, she felt emboldened: satisfied with herself for having survived the day and her own fear and worry, happy in the knowledge that she'd be less likely to be as frightened tomorrow.

She got up all at once, remembering something in her satchel.

"Gonna iron some clothes?" he called. He'd twisted around to watch her.

"What?"

"Nothing." He chuckled.

She bent over, dug into the bag, then stood up, shaking out petticoats and a shawl. "Blankets."

He laughed harder when she dropped one of her petticoats around his shoulders. "How sweet," he said. "And I'm sure it makes me look real debonaire." He nodded, though, smiling up at her; it no doubt improved the chill in the air. She sat again, wrapping herself up in the frillier petticoat, then her soft, fringy shawl. Swaddled and more comfortable, she picked up her brush again.

She used a silver brush—which made her, Sam noticed, the richest lady's maid he'd ever met, even if it was plate.

She grew quieter—tireder, he thought—as she tried to get a brush through her twining, winding hair. At one point, she stopped and stretched, yawning up out of her wrapping of frills and fringe. Just as she reached her slender arms up, a piece of moon came from between clouds with perfect timing to give small back light to her silhouette. It made her woolly mane into a nimbus of ringlets about her face and shoulders. A damn fine sight.

"Look!" she said suddenly and pointed over their fire toward the dark sky.

Distinct, black silhouettes crossed the glow overhead. It was a small flock of long-necked birds. They glided across the sliver of moon for a single stroke of wings, then were swallowed up again by the black sky.

"The Queen's swans," she said.

"Swans?"

"Yes. Queen Victoria owns all of the swans in England. The royal birds. Once a year, she counts them. Swan upping, it's called."

"Swan upping," he repeated. He looked at her. "Isn't there a fairy tale about a black swan?"

She thought a moment, huddling into her shawl and petticoat. She looked like a mound of clothes with a head on top. "Not that I know of."

He studied her, watching the way the firelight flickered over her face and hair. "You remind me of that somehow. I can't think which legend. But a dark swan." He laughed. "A dark horse."

"I'm not sure I'm flattered."

"I mean it flatteringly; I do. The black swan was enchanting." He frowned. "Or enchanted, I'm not sure which." He clarified, "Beautiful." Then wished he'd shut up.

She fixed a look on him, one that tried to measure intent. Then she pulled her legs up, wrapped her arms, shawl and all, around them, and set her chin on her knees, hugging herself tight. As she stared into the fire, she said, "The gin is getting to you."

He nodded, dropping his gaze. Something was sure getting to him. *Enchanting. Beautiful.* And, not to forget, *underpleasured.* Gin was as good a name for it as anything. Where was that bottle, anyway?

He asked, "You tired?"

She nodded.

"You ready to sleep then?"

She nodded again.

He voiced the big question. "You want me to bed down over here or you want me to come over there where we can keep each other warm?"

She rocked back, then bent her head and rocked forward, her mouth to her knees. She became just eyes and wild hair as she stared straight at the glowing ashes.

Right. He thought about telling her how she'd be safe, but then didn't. She liked to think the worst of him; let her. "Suit yourself," he said.

He pitched another rock or two from his spot, making it as unlumpy as possible, then slid his hat down over his eyes, folded his arms behind his head, and stretched out. He guessed they'd both just get cold then.

He was dozing when he felt something fall over him. A woman's lightweight shawl. It was soft—cashmere or camelhair, something really nice—and inundated with the smell of Liddy Brown, ginger, lemons, flowers, water lilies . . . the particular scent and oils from the skin of her arms, shoulders, hands, wherever the shawl had touched.

Her pale, delicately boned hand came across him, arranging the cover over his chest and shoulder. Then she turned over and slid under the shawl herself, up against his back.

It was a long night. Lydia began it curled on her side, her back against Sam's arm and hip. She lay rigid, not sure how to behave: unsettled, cold, and faintly tipsy. While Sam seemed to go right to sleep.

At some point, she must have dozed, because she awakened with a start to the strange realization that someone was shifting his position beside her. In the next instant, she felt his hand—the backs of his fingers as he rearranged their shawl covering—inadvertently brush her hip. Without intent or volition, she arched in response, her buttocks finding the side of his thigh. The movement was unplanned; it meant nothing, just a . . . an odd reaction.

After a second, though, he lifted the leg she pressed against—he lay on his back—planting that foot on the ground, his knee in the air. This left a kind of ghost sensation on her backside; she could have traced the place where his thigh had been. What a feeling.

She dropped back to sleep, turning the moment over in her mind. Glutting on it. The feel of his thigh. The strange warmth in her own belly. The shape of his round, hard leg; warm, muscular, strong. Her mind slid over these impressions into sleep, relived them, multiplied them, stretched them out. Her backside on his thigh seemed endlessly fascinating.

She slept fitfully, awakening several times more—she found no quick adjustment to sleeping next to another human being. Every time Sam moved, she came to consciousness. Sometimes she was aware that he was awake, too. Other times, she could hear his even breathing. She listened for it after a while, the sound of his deeply drawn breath while he slept. Sometimes he snored lightly. Interesting. She worried she made noise when she slept, some indelicate sound she had never listened to or thought to control.

The worst part of the night was just before dawn, when

the temperature dropped enough that Lydia kept breaking into shivers. She found herself both exhausted and alertly awake, too uncomfortably cold that sleep was even a possibility.

Her back was once more pressed along Mr. Cody's ribs and hip—she lay inevitably on her side. He was in and out of wakefulness, she could tell. His knee up, she could feel the side of his boot at her backside, the swaying movement in his hip as gravity pulled his leg into a drop each time he dozed. She fought shuddering as a chilly draft swept over them, funneled down the side of their rock protection. Wiggling, she got more of her back up against him, pressing till she could discern the feel of his individual ribs, his hipbone.

It occurred to her: This wasn't the warmest arrangement they could come up with.

She wished he might roll over and put the front of himself against her back, wrap his arms, himself around her; then she'd be snug. Or she could do the same, though he was so much larger. And would he mind? Could she simply curl herself around him? Oh, the idea of her cold skin finding his warmth sounded so good it made her head light.

She raised herself up on her forearm to look at him. Indeed, he was awake. He jerked when she moved, then his head turned as he seemed to focus on her.

"I'm cold," she said.

He tipped his hat up as if better to see her.

When he didn't say anything, she asked, "Aren't you?"

He nodded. "Yup."

She waited for the solution to occur to him. *Hold me.*

He didn't say or do anything for a long minute. Then he rolled himself away from her and up onto his feet. He left. Out of sight.

Lydia felt a plummet, deflated: rejected, abandoned.

Her unhappy feelings, though, were mitigated when he returned five minutes later and dropped an armload of wood beside their cold campfire. More matches, more stoking. He piled the old ashes with new twigs and branches, stooping on one knee. Their fire crackled to life again, sending out a faint, smoky smell while its welcome heat wafted out along the ground. He stayed with the fire for a few minutes, till the flames burned steadily, then he came back and settled once more lengthwise behind her.

Lydia returned to lying on her side, while he shifted around. Then again, without explanation, he moved away, once more gone. After a second, she twisted at the waist, laying her shoulders back onto the ground, looking for him.

She didn't have to look far. There he was above her, up on one elbow, rearranging himself. In the process, his shin came against her buttocks. He halted, looked down at her, their faces six inches away.

They lay motionless like that for a full minute, the top of his leg, his knee and thigh, against her.

There was just enough firelight to know his gaze dropped to her mouth. His face was at just enough angle to put most of his injuries in shadows. God above, minus the misfortunes of his morning, his face would be handsome. His jaw was squared, strong-boned there in the shadows, his firelit cheek ridged and channeled, angular. His brow jutted. From beneath it, his eyes watched her lips—she licked them once, unable to stop herself, because they felt dry, so dry, all at once.

There was a long, pregnant pause where neither of them moved, as if they dare not.

Then he let out a gust of air down his nose, turned, and rolled to lay his head onto his bent arm. He put his back against hers.

Pistons and packing rings, she thought. That's what all this was about.

Until today, she had never been alone with a man other than her father or brother for more than a few minutes (well, Boddington once, but that didn't count), and though all day she had ridden or traipsed along with Sam Cody, not until the night had their isolated, uninterrupted company seemed in any way worth noting. Now, though, it had become impossible to ignore.

Pistons and packing rings. Though whatever went on be-

tween a man and a woman wasn't just that. It was more personal; stronger, more engaging, encompassing: better. And it
began somehow with this feeling low in her belly and along
her skin. As if a wisp of smoke reached out, wrapped itself
around her, and drew her to him. A thin wisp. Hardly there.
But tenacious. She could resist it. She could choose to ignore it. But she couldn't make it let go of her.

Like the gin. She felt besotted, unbalanced for lying near
him. She kept thinking about him, the physical him. The
way he stretched out to sleep, the way he built fires, the way
he stooped or squatted on one toe with his arm over his knee.
God help her, she even liked the way he threw rocks. How
foolish was that? She liked his smile, or the half of it that
she'd gotten all day. She liked the rasp in his voice and the
deep, slow-drawling rhythm of his speech. . . .

"Sam," she murmured.

"Mm?"

"I'm cold."

"Go to sleep."

"Hold me."

He said nothing for long enough that she thought he was
going to ignore her again. Then he let out a snort. After
which—oh, the joy as she realized—she felt him turning,
rolling over. His hand and arm came over her, hooking
round her belly and hips. With the flat of his palm on her
stomach—Lord, how wonderful was *that* to feel!—he pulled
her back against him. Oh, yes, oh, yes. Behind her, he
curved his body to her as if it were the most natural thing in
the world. Heat. Contact. Goodness, why hadn't he done this
before? His arm was strong—he tucked her easily into him,
himself around her. Everywhere he felt hard, carved, so perfectly antithetical to her own softness. She let her hands
come to rest on his forearm, aware of a vigor in him that was
bone deep, an energy she hadn't understood exactly and
couldn't explain, yet she felt in his chest and arms and hips
and legs: a breathing, thriving virility. While his body temperature next to hers felt marvelously hot, warmer than she
could have—

Lydia was brought up short. She'd done that thing again, that push with her backside that she seemed to do without quite thinking it, as if her body pushed on its own. And the movement had yielded a discovery and a possible reason for his reluctance to hold her against him.

He'd been preserving his privacy and, in a way, hers.

For at her backside, through her dress, was an unmistakable—particularly vigorous—part of Mr. Cody's anatomy. A part that was rod-straight with a heft to it she hadn't suspected; weighty, substantial. More amazing still, she could feel him becoming thicker, heavier—while she had to fight an urge to squirm against him. She held herself rigidly still. While a long, steely presence settled into the cleave of her bum, the tip of him pushing solidly into the small of her back.

Well, sir, she thought. That's quite the piston you have there.

7

Sam awoke to a misty morning, a haze in the air that in the distance was so dense it blocked off visibility. There was no horizon, only the immediate vaporous vicinity: their dead fire, the filmy outline of their rock wall, the faint, milky silhouettes of a few bushes at the boundaries of perceivability. It was as if the dark of night had only lifted so far, then turned white. Overhead, cloud cover hung, thick and low, the sun perceptible only as a bleary bright spot where cotton-wool sky dissolved into mist.

It was like rising to the day in a little world of their own: His only perfectly clear view was of the woman lying next to him, the one who unwittingly had kept him up, so to speak, for most of the night. He couldn't remember a worse night's sleep. Beside him, Liddy lay tousled and unconscious, one arm thrown over her head, the other across her stomach. A damn fine sight, her chest rising and falling softly, her composure undefended. Her dress lay rumpled but dry around her. Remnants of mud dirtied her skirt, though the worst had dusted off—she'd loosened the laces of one muddy shoe, he noticed, her ankle noticeably swollen. Her face must've had a film of dirt on it, because in full daylight he could see two smudged tracks down her cheeks, evidence of her crying after their bout with the bog. He wanted to wipe the streaks away, then caught his hand back.

He wanted to do a lot of cussed fool things with this woman. Better he got himself going.

In the veiled light, he gathered and ate more purple berries as he checked the traps: He collected a rabbit, set a baby fox free, then sprang the rest of the snares and buried over the pit traps, one with a dead mouse in it, so that nothing further would stumble into harm when they weren't going to be around to enjoy the use of the kill.

When he got back to their camp, Liddy was sitting up, yawning and stretching. He handed her a hatful of berries, and they began: They argued over whether to eat the rabbit or get going. They argued over whether to head east across the moor or south and hope for the road. They argued over whether the mist would burn off or become heavier.

They ended up eating berries and making ready to head out as quickly as they could, since dim visibility was better than none—Sam convinced Liddy there was at least a possibility of rain, fog, or both. She held out longest in arguing for a breakfast of cooked rabbit. She really wanted more of what she'd had last night, which secretly made him happy, though he wouldn't say, since it would've weakened his side of the argument.

Argument. It was their byword. They seemed to take turns making each other mad. Still, it was one way to get to know someone, he guessed, through jostling and missteps.

As they gathered their things, he watched her hobbling and mulled over the best way to help. He would have made her a walking stick. Or just picked her up and carried her— she couldn't weigh much. Though he knew he'd have to negotiate what help he might be, especially the last, since she didn't like to be handled without permission, not even by accident, not even if it meant saving her from falling flat on her face. She'd rather fall. It was possible she'd even rather drown.

As he picked up the gin bottle—they'd finished off the short one—and driver's spare clothes, an idea too good not to mention came out his mouth. "You know, if we wrapped your ankle with these"—he picked up the socks and driver's shirt—"you could probably walk easier."

She surprised him. She blinked up at him, staring, then nodded.

"Great. Sit down here." Sam pointed and got right to it.

With his knife, he cut the sides of the socks, leaving the toe connected to make two long, knit strips. He ripped the shirt into lengths.

"Let's have your leg," he said. When he saw the black of stockings, though—sheer, expensive silk over a pale, slender leg—he said, "You'll, um, ah, have to take off your, um"— he paused—"this."

For the life of him, he couldn't say the word *stocking*. Pronouncing it took on such a prurient charge he was worried that forming it in his mouth would shoot stimulation from his tongue down through his body till his penis was standing there nodding at her again from his trousers.

Oblivious, she reached under her skirts to get the stocking started, rolling it along with a little black garter out into sight, a wad down her ankle then off her toe. She wiggled her toes, while Sam found himself staring at her bare foot, the high instep, the delicate ankle bone, the beginning of a firm-muscled calf. Her shin had a light covering of hair, little golden bits, sparse, as fine as down. He wanted to brush his hand along it, smooth it, pet her like a cat.

He held out his hands instead. "May I?" He threw her half an uncertain smile. "Since you like to be consulted on everything." He waited, partly tormenting her, partly uneasy about touching her for his own reasons.

With complete seriousness, she nodded. "Yes. Thank you." When she caught his eye, though, her expression grew uncertain. She knew he was making fun, but wasn't sure where or how: a woman who took her dignity very seriously.

He hooked his palm under her heel, tucking a strip of sock firmly against her ankle bone, then began to wrap her ankle, glancing up, wrapping, glancing up, wrapping. With each glimpse, he saw a thin woman with wild hair and mist hanging around her shoulders. Big eyes. Nothing special, though, he told himself.

Yet each time, he felt more uneasy: stranded in an eerie world—cloudlike today—alone with a woman he couldn't explain, his own impulses suggesting he might be losing touch with good sense.

He tried to analyze what he found so damn attractive here. Her voluptuous backside, yes. Her pretty breasts, yes. Her skinny body, no—though her leg here wasn't half bad, even though it was thin. Her face. Yes, something in her delicate face. The way she watched him. Her honey-brown eyes; warm, shining, sweet. They were giant, deep-lidded, with long, thick lashes—lashes so long, he realized, she must look at everything out from under their shadows.

These eyes were set low in a petite face under high eyebrows that made her seem always on the verge of a question. She had smooth skin, a short nose, a small round chin, and, God love her—she smiled and said, "Thank you for doing this"—deep dimples on either side of her wide mouth.

Jesus, he colored. He felt himself warm. He could barely get the words out. "You're welcome," he mumbled.

Then worse. Out the corner of his eye, he knew she stared at him. She lifted her brow and let her warm eyes widen on him in speculation.

When he looked up to face her fully, though, she looked away. A kind of cat-and-mouse of eye contact. Surprisingly, as she bent her head, he saw a slight smile spread onto her lips.

"Liddy—"

She gazed at him again, tilting her head, this time her eyes gliding over him before she looked away.

The hair of his arms lifted, sending ripples through him to his scrotum, tightening it until, with a rush of blood, he felt the beginning of an erection again. Jesus. All just from the way she tilted her head and looked at him, her manner as natural—and flirtatious—as a bird's flutter at mating.

He stared. Liddy had the instant sort of sweet, feminine attractiveness that made a man want to scoop her up, protect her with his life, hold her, soothe her. Penetrate her soft vulnerability.

Not a great impulse, since it didn't take a second to remember the little lady here was as vulnerable as a bee's pin. Physically delicate, tender-hearted, with a will of iron.

"There," he said.

She blinked, her long lashes brushing the tops of her cheekbones, and he felt a surge of such fierce, hot longing that he was dizzy with it for a moment. He wanted to plant a hand on either side at her hips, lean his weight out onto his arms, use it to press her back and down, and lie on top of her. Lord Almighty, he wanted to lay his body on her, writhe, feel her under him, push her legs apart until he was grinding himself against her—

He sat back onto heels.

"What's wrong?" she asked.

He shook his head. He prayed they found the road and a ride today, because if he had to lie down again beside her tonight, he would have to knock himself out to keep from spooning her into lovemaking. He wouldn't be able to stop himself.

Of course, she'd be able to stop him. *She'd* probably brain him, so maybe there was no worry. It wasn't as if Liddy Brown here couldn't take care of herself. Even though she, and apparently her whole family, liked to pretend she couldn't.

Sam stood. "Ready, then?"

Using the bright spot in the white sky as an easterly guide, Lydia and Mr. Cody headed south with the hope of intersecting the road. It shouldn't have been far, and by any measure the road was closer, quicker, than heading east—even though east in good weather should have been a more direct route off the moor. If the weather grew worse, though, knowing which direction to travel could become impossible. The roadway, meanwhile, if they could find it—even if they met no one, no traffic—might at least give them a sure path to follow.

Thus, they moved southward through the mist that hung about them, with her carrying what remained of the gin in one arm and Mr. Cody's hat full of whortleberries in the other, while Mr. Cody carried her satchel by its strap over his shoulder. Periodically, in swings of his far arm, she could glimpse a rabbit held by its ears, their next meal.

Something else she stole looks at: Sam Cody himself was different this morning without his hat. His beard had sprouted overnight, like black sand along his jaw, cheek, and lip. The swelling of his eye was down, though it had turned a colorful blue and purple at the socket. That and the rest— the bridge of his nose discolored and perhaps swollen, cuts at his cheekbone and mouth—made him look . . . reckless, which he probably was, come to think of it, to have gotten in such shape.

She loved his hat off, though. He was so much more open for perusal. His hair, which she'd known was dark, was truly very close to black. It curled at his neck. Thick, glossy commas of it lay over his white shirt collar in back— too long to be fashionable in London, but interesting. Appealing in an old, romantic way from days when men's hair was a show of their strength, masculinity, and good health. Samson hair.

None of this, however, was as interesting to Lydia as Mr. Cody's fair eyes—though by the light of day and without a hat to shade them, *fair* was hardly the word. His eyes were a deep, dusty blue—the color of the sky before rain, so blue they were almost purple. They stood out all the more remarkably this morning against the swarthiness of his unshaven face, so arresting against his dark hair she had to keep catching herself back from staring. Half a dozen times, as they'd gotten ready, as he'd wrapped her ankle, as he walked beside her now, he'd turned his head toward her, a quizzical look—a raise of black eyebrows—and she'd glanced away, shaking her own head. *Nothing.* Nothing except . . . he was appealing, beat up or not. How had she missed that at the beginning?

Ah, she realized, perhaps she *hadn't.* She recalled the feel of him around her—behind her—the strange sense of . . . not embarrassment or offense, but . . . pleasure.

She was still more or less occupied with this cataloging of the strange American's finer physical qualities—watching his trousered legs stride off long paces beside her—when she noticed the mist bundling into low, rolling ground fog. It wisped about her skirt. It kicked in slow-moving eddies at his legs, his boots, her own hems barely visible at a ghostly ground. It was eerie. It was beautiful.

It was also more difficult going. Unable to see the larger rocks or smaller bushes in their path till they were right on top of them, she and Mr. Cody had to slow their progress.

Five minutes later, they stopped simultaneously, frowning up into a low ceiling of clouds—low enough, it seemed, that if she had stood on his shoulders, she could have touched them. Lydia searched overhead for the bright spot above their horizontal line of vision that had just minutes ago guided them.

"Can you tell where the sun is?" she asked.

"Over there, I thought, but I—" He made a pull of his mouth. "But I'm not sure now." He sighed. "I think we've lost it."

The smell of the air had changed. A damp earthy odor, like loamy soil after rain, floated on the coolness. Meanwhile, the fog moved in solidly, visibly, like a billowing, slow-motion tide along the ground.

She should have been worried, even frightened, to see the fog roll in—closing off the world around them—yet it was so fascinating and purely lovely. Lydia opened her arms and rotated slowly, watching the white air gather as if the ground breathed cool winter breath. It roiled around her where it encompassed her skirts from her hips downward. She lifted her foot and knew she wiggled it at the ankle yet saw no sign of her own foot. She looked over her shoulder at Mr. Cody. "Isn't this an amazing place?"

He nodded, staring at her.

She said, "Look," thinking to show him. She held her arms out and spun, clearing a little space in the fog around her—it receded in response to her movement. Yet when she looked up, his regard—those startling eyes—was fixed on her with such contemplation, she had to look off. The strange, familiar elation rushed in. Along with a kind of embarrassment. A funny little war of emotions that brought a tension inside her.

She couldn't meet his regard, but the stir of emotion was somehow so nice. She just let it play over her as she stared off.

For as far as she could see the ground had become white and fluffy. It was like viewing a skyful of clouds from above. In the near distance the top of a little hill with its crumbling tor stood out like an island in a sea of vapor. She waded toward it, Mr. Cody behind her, as white, rolling air gathered, more and more abundant.

Within minutes, fog surrounded them, as dense as cotton wool. It blocked off all sense of direction, all sense of anything outside the two of them. It was as if they stood together inside a cloud.

So bizarre. Lydia knew fog from London, but never such a dramatically swift change, never so thick you couldn't see your hand in front of you. If she and Mr. Cody should take more than a step or two away from each other, they would disappear entirely from the other's sight.

She heard him drop the satchel and rabbit, one heavy, one light thud. Once deposited on the ground, the items were no longer part of the evident world. Then, as if diving down after them, the man beside her disappeared as well.

"Mr. Cody? Sam?" Lydia looked down through the fog

where a moment ago he had been. She was just able to make out a darkness that was presumably the top of his head.

"Here." His voice was bent close to the ground.

She followed it, kneeling down, then sitting back onto her heels—the fog traced the paths of air as she cut through it.

"This is unbelievable," she said. Unearthly. Through the haze, she saw Sam squatting. He was fiddling with something on the ground beside her, unbuckling—

"Hey!" She scrambled around in front of him, on the other side of her satchel. "Hey! Stay out of my things!" she said. She stood onto her knees, wrestling him for the satchel's handles, holding the bag together, its fastens loose, all but the last flap in the last buckle. "No!" she said emphatically.

He gave her a slant-mouth look as they faced each other. "I want to see what we have here."

They both held on, him pulling, her holding the closure together, an accelerating tug-of-war she could feel she would lose, if she didn't convince him to give in. "What *I* have," she told him. "The bag belongs to me."

"I carry it. Besides, I'd say, in dire straits, which I'd call these, what's in the only baggage we were able to save belongs to both of us."

"It's my bag. You can't appropriate it."

"All right, it's yours. But I want to look. I might think of a way to use what's inside that you haven't. It might help us." He made a snort of a laugh, a joke. "You don't by chance have a compass in here, do you?"

"No."

"Why can't I look? What do you have you're so damn afraid I'll see? What can it matter, under the circumstances?"

"No!" she said again as he pushed her hands out of the way and pulled the strap out of the last bar of its buckle. "No!" she repeated. She smacked his dark fingers as they took full possession of the handles. His hands were strong. When swatting at them didn't stop him, she hit his arm. He pulled the handles apart, the satchel open, with Lydia ending up batting at his arms and hands, his face, striking at anything in her fury. "Stop"—she couldn't halt him—"stop, stop! Stop it!"

For a few seconds, he attempted to look into the satchel under the barrage of her blows. Then, with an impatient grimace, he paused long enough to grab both her hands, crossing one over the other at the wrists, then wrapped his fingers around to hold her hands immobile with one of his as he pulled the edge of the satchel wide open with his other.

The strangest thing. She was furious and breathing hard—he had no right to snoop. If he'd have let go, she'd have hit him again. Yet at the same time the power in his grip of her wrists, the sensation of being held within his strength. Something changed. A feeling related to last night loosened her resistence. She felt herself give in, give herself over, oddly receptive to his hold of her.

He must have noticed it, because, though the satchel gaped, he looked up at her suddenly, and his frown became less angry and more puzzled—contemplative, even worried. He studied her.

She opened her mouth, the space it might take for a word to come out. What word? There was none. She wet her lips instead, a quick roll of them inward, a lick of her tongue. Lord, what a feeling. She felt her breathing grow shallow as her abdomen lit with a kind of glow that became warmer with each second, spreading from the low center of her into her limbs.

Attraction. It was the strangest sensation. Over nothing. She'd never felt anything quite like it, or rather had felt something like it, weak relatives to it. But this. This feeling was so . . . complicated, more fascinating by half than anything she'd known or imagined. Which left her baffled as to what to do.

She wanted more of it; she wanted to explore it. She was even coming to think she could predict the feeling—know how to elicit it, incite it.

All of which was so wildly inappropriate it left her breathless. How much could she allow herself out here, knowing full well the differences that separated them?

They stared at each other. She into a dark face, dark lashes at narrowed eyes with irises the color of bottle-blue glass. These eyes full of intelligence. And awareness. Beautiful eyes set into a handsomeness that was scruffy and bruised, but no less potent—more so, in fact: *Reckless,* she thought again. Raw. Uncivilized. Oh, the word *uncivilized* thrilled her to think it. His unshaven, cut face looked dangerous. The Wild, Wild West, she thought. She wanted to explore it.

Explore it, she did—she let her eyes travel over him, no pretense of doing anything else. Mr. Cody had a band of lighter skin at his hairline. His forehead showed where his face had been hidden from the sun by his hat brim. A sweet, tender detail.

Oh, she thought, if only he were a . . . a duke, for instance—higher in precedence than Boddington's father, a marquess. She wished they were in London. Or, no, Yorkshire. Yes, they could be on a moor in Yorkshire. And he was courting her with her family's approval. They might go on drives out onto the moor, just to be alone like this. He would speak properly, dress differently. And if he should kiss her? What would it feel like, his mouth? She wished he were a true candidate for the role her feelings wanted to lend him. Suitor. Swain. Then she could let herself go, smile and flirt, because what would it matter?

After a moment, he scowled deeper, then gave his head a quick shake. He pushed her hands away and looked down over the open rim of the satchel.

Lydia glanced into bag herself, saw an added embarrassment that she'd forgotten, and, as quickly, snatched up what lay on top of everything else. She tried to get it out of sight before he could recognize it.

He caught her arm by the elbow, brought her hand forward, and pried the book from her grip.

After which he smiled broadly, then laughed. He looked over at her. "I guess your brother and I aren't the only ones who like cheap novels." He faced the book around so she could see the silly paperback cover. *Buffalo Bill and the Stagecoach Bandits.* He turned the book over, reading the back. He grinned up, amused. "A double pleasure: Now you have to admit you're a hypocrite. Plus"—with glee—"I haven't read this one!" He set it down beside him, out of her reach. "I'll just take it, since you don't like these 'cheap, inelegant' books."

"It's not even mine. I can't—" Still on her knees, she reached over the satchel toward the book by his hip. As they jostled, she lost her balance, falling over—she caught herself by one hand in the dirt, one on his boot, all but facedown into his lap.

He helped her up by her shoulders, pushing her back. "Well, aren't we just getting cozy here."

They ended up face-to-face—hers frowning, his grinning—inches apart over the satchel.

He tilted his head at her, cajoling. "Come on," he said. "What do you want that would make you cooperative? My hat? You wanna wear my hat while I poke through this thing? We'll dump out the last berries. You have my hat. Or my boots?" He laughed. "You like those so much. You wanna wear my boots? I'll go in my socks; you can have 'em. But I'm looking in this bag, 'cause—"

"Don't be silly. Nothing like that—"

Sam reared his head back, his eyebrows rising. "But something. You want something from me." He blinked, laughed again. What he said surprised her, but the second she heard it she knew it was true: "I haven't named it yet," he told her, "but you want something from me." He laughed again, amused. "Go ahead. Tell me. I'm waiting."

Lydia wasn't sure. She sat back onto her heels, struggling to understand herself what she wanted.

He frowned, angled his head, a little wary. "Spit it out."

"I want to understand last night. I want you to show me—"

"Whoa." He held up his hands. "I'm not showin' you anything."

"No." She laughed, suddenly nervous, giddy. "Show me

how it feels—" She stammered. "Show me how it feels to kiss someone who—I—I want you to kiss me so I—"

The look on his face stopped her cold. His expression was as surprised as if she'd slapped his face. "No," he said with alarm.

"Oh." She stared, taken aback, then nodded, trying to look neutral, when she felt anything but.

An awful physical sensation dropped through her chest into her stomach. Disappointment, she thought. And shame. The shock on his face, the finality of his swift, single-word answer, made her feel like a trollop. And—oh, dear, hurt. Her feelings were hurt. Why? she wondered. Why didn't he want to kiss her? What was wrong with her? It had been a bold thing to say, but—

"I—I was only asking—" she began. "It was only a kiss," she tried to explain.

She'd kissed a handful of men and never found any of them less than enthusiastic for the privilege. The truth was, she'd done a bit more than kissing with Boddington, who was gentleman enough to pretend she hadn't, not only to others but even with her. It had been last summer. Right after he'd offered for her, she had let him run his hands over her and quite enjoyed it. Better still, she had parleyed this little sexual foray into some sort of advantage over him. Afterward, she neither accepted nor refused his offer, but rather left him dangling: He was sure by her actions that she would accept, then eventually unsure by her lack of confirmation, all the while seeming willing to stick around eternally if it meant he might one day fondle her again. Which so far she hadn't allowed, a fate he'd accepted.

With Mr. Cody, she felt confused after last night. She had virtually no experience with the physical evidence of a man's interest, or none but his. Nonetheless, she'd thought what she'd felt behind her last night had to do with his *wanting* to kiss her.

When she let herself look at him again, it was worse: He'd realized he'd hurt her feelings. Now he felt sorry for her. "Liddy," he said. She wished he'd stop saying this name he'd made up for her.

Then wished that was all he did. He came forward onto one knee, his arm dangling over the other for a second—till that hand reached across and touched her.

Sam couldn't help himself. He had to touch her somewhere, so, frowning with concern, he brushed back a piece of her hair—a wild, curling corkscrew that lay on her delicate shoulder. She shuddered when the backs of his fingers grazed her. He said again, "Liddy—"

"Stop saying that." She shot him a glance. "You make me feel awful."

"I don't mean to."

"Wicked, wrong"—she stammered unintelligibly for a few mutters—"sick, soft and hot inside, my stomach lifts—"

He laughed. "That doesn't sound very awful—"

"Stop laughing at me!"

"I'm not laughing at you. I'm laughing at, oh, fate or somethin'. Lid, I can't help it if I make you 'soft and hot' inside. You want me, that's all. And you feel guilty about it. You shouldn't. It's normal. Common even. Women are supposed to want men. And I want you, too, darlin'; so there." Under pressure, Sam got real down-home, no matter how he might like not to. He told her, "But we're not doin' anything about it, 'cause you're as innocent as a flop-eared pup for all your age and 'elegant' sophistication." Shaking his head, he repeated again what he'd said last night. "No more wild coach rides for you. They make you crazy." He added, "And they make me crazy, too—enough that, between the two of us, we could end up doing things that'd be bad for you." A breath. "I don't care who you say you you are. I can see you're a girl who shouldn't be giving herself to some passing—"

Some passing, two-bit cowpoke, he thought. Which wasn't him exactly, yet it was an image of himself that clung, especially when he felt unequal to what was being asked of him.

She said nothing, looking as forlorn as a woman could.

He forced a laugh, trying to lighten the mood, shaking his head in disbelief. "I gotta kiss you to make everything right? Come on, you don't want me to. Think about it."

More silence. She frowned down, no longer willing to voice a desire he realized he was playing too lightly with. She was serious. There were tender feelings here, things she worried about.

More earnestly, he told her, "Listen, Liddy. If I kiss you right, you aren't gonna be less hot and bothered, you're gonna be more. And I'm gonna get like I got last night—I know you noticed, 'cause it was impossible to miss. I don't relish the feelin' of wantin' you and bein' gentlemanly about it. Don't put me in that bind."

Her large eyes looked up at him. Very quietly, way too softly, way too appealing in tone, she said, "I want to know what it's like."

He let out a quick breath, exasperation, mild anxiety. "Well, I'm not the one who's gonna show you. I like feeling honorable. Which means I don't sleep with sweet little virgins, no matter how curious they are—as soon as we get ourselves out of our little fix here, you're going home: Remember that."

She looked up sharply, making a click with her tongue. "I wasn't suggesting we sleep together."

He laughed, then caught himself. He didn't want to sound too arrogant, but he'd felt the way she'd shivered when he'd moved her hair back. "Darlin'," he said gently, "I think we have ourselves here a pretty powerful attraction. Don't underestimate it. Or me." He didn't know if she'd accept the warning for what it was. "With all due respect," he said, "if I kiss you, I'll have you on your back in less than a hiccup."

Best to change the subject. He patted the satchel and asked, "So what's in here that's gonna cause such a stir?" He smiled what he hoped was a friendly smile. It was a friendly warning he'd given her, good-intentioned advice.

She only stared at him, then sat back and drew her knees

up, pulling her shawl up as she wrapped her arms around her legs.

After a few seconds, he dug down into her bag again. She just let him, though she was about as cheerful as a woman with a noose round her neck.

Inside the bag, he pushed her petticoats and some other lacy things aside. Beneath them, he found a long, flat leather case. Soft, expensive leather. He took it by its brass handles—its fittings were brass, too, all shine, spit, and polish. The whole thing gleamed as he lifted it out.

She gave both him and it an anxious glance, then looked away again. He set the case down on its side—the thing was longer than she was tall—then paused. He gave her a chance to explain. "You wanna say before I open it?"

"I, um—" She pressed her lips into that tight line she could make of them. "I—"

"What?"

"I—It's—" She said in a rush, "It's a bow." She bit her lip and looked down. "And if you dig at the side of the satchel, in with my handkerchiefs and, um, underthings are a leather finger-tip, an arm protector, and a quiver full of arrows."

"You're kidding."

"I'm not."

He sucked on a back tooth, staring at her. "You let me set traps and throw rocks all night when you had a bow with arrows in here?"

She frowned and talked quickly. "They're target arrows. They don't have barbs. If we hit an animal with one, it might fall out, the animal should almost certainly run off to die, and we should never have the chance to eat it."

"We could've chased it."

"In the dark?"

After a second, he nodded. "All right. That makes some sense."

She looked down again, literally hung her head, furrowing her brow, her whole face, till her expression became a wince. "I didn't want to tell you because I knew it would be hard to explain."

He shrugged without understanding. "You seem to have done it. That wasn't so hard."

She made another tight frown. "You'd better look at them first."

He lay the case out, flat on top of the satchel, flipped its latch, and opened the lid. The interior was a formed baize, shaped perfectly for what it held: a six-foot bow. An expensive one. Yew, he'd guess. One six-foot piece of perfect Italian or Spanish yew. In the States, the bow alone would have cost at least twenty dollars.

He glanced up at her over the lid. Fighting back a more sarcastic remark, he said, "Ladies' maids sure get paid a lot better on this side of the ocean than they do where I come from." Then, "Are you any good with it?"

"Awfully."

He snorted. "Does that mean you're awful or good?"

She didn't answer. She'd already squinched up her face again, shaking her head—little reluctant shakes as she said, "I'm not really a lady's maid."

"No kidding." He pulled a face, but the hurt on hers made him regret his sarcasm. More gently, he asked, "All right, what's the truth?"

"I'm—I—" She pressed her lips inward, then told the ground, "I'm a— Oh, you wouldn't know my family, but my father's a viscount. Do you know what that is?"

Sam let out a short abrupt laugh—"Yes"—then really let loose: He sat back onto his hind end, guffawing himself into deep belly laughter. When he could control it, he told her, "Oh, fine. Now you're near-royalty. Didn't your mama and daddy teach you it isn't nice to make up stories?"

"I am!"

"Right." His hand found the book at his hip. *Buffalo Bill and the Stagecoach Bandits.* He looked down at it. Oh, what a little liar she was. He ought to swat her, not laugh, but he could only shake his head. "You're hopeless," he told her.

She insisted, looking for all the world offended. "I really

am. I'm Lydia Bedford-Browne. My father's the Viscount Wendt."

Trying to keep a smirk off his face, he said, "And that coach at the bottom of the bog had a regal crest on it. Why, the queen is probably your aunt."

"Actually, she's my second cousin." He only laughed loudly for a few seconds because, when he did, her face fell—she looked crestfallen. "You don't believe me," she said.

"Look at yourself." She was getting better at story-telling, though, he had to admit. Her confusion seemed downright sincere. As she sat there in her plain dress. "You look like a schoolmarm from back home. A schoolmarm with a big imagination. Which we know you have."

She glanced down, her messy hair dangling onto her knees, onto her dirty skirt that covered her shins. She stared at herself for a minute, as if puzzled to find herself in a ready-made dress with no trim, if nice buttons. She glanced over at him, started to weave herself a new little explanation—"I wore something that— So people shouldn't—" Then made a pathetic frown and stopped, the wind gone from her sails. Though he had to give her this: She remained a contradiction. Her petticoats and shawl were expensive. Her bow and arrow setup was first-rate.

He rubbed his chin—it felt like coarse sandpaper—then his whole cheek. He grinned and tried to cheer her up. "I must look pretty terrible myself," he said. He picked up the book. "You want me to read first or you? I figure we can kill these bandits and a few buffalo, scalp an Indian or two, and save the Pony Express, all before this fog blows off."

Her face was hesitant, then a little ray of hope broke onto it, a shy smile. She nodded. "You read first," she said. After a few seconds, she offered a weak laugh. "If you come to any big words, just ask." Her smile grew bolder. "But I get to read the parts about the gunfights and any bad men who die like the dirty dogs they are. I love those, and I read them rather well. I've read most of those parts a dozen times at least."

Sam laughed, despite himself. She was a whang-doodle, this one. And, doggone, if he didn't like her for it. Oh, yeah, kiss her, he thought. Wouldn't he just like to, though? Starting with those two dimples, one over each butt cheek at the base of her spine.

8

Sam sat beside Liddy in a cocoon of fog, shoulder to shoulder, as they took turns reading a book he loved and she liked darn well, too, though she didn't like to admit it. The way they worked it, he read ten minutes, then she read.

He was on his third turn—doing trick shooting over his shoulder at a renegade band of Indians chasing him—when he realized out the corner of his eye she was smiling at the ground.

She sat, her knees up, her shawl pulled around her shoulders and legs, her chin on the tops of her knees, a swaddled bundle: while her mouth held a little smile—da Vinci would've liked the subtlety of it—that seemed out of keeping with the idea of shooting Indians. Sam read a page more, while her inscrutable smile persisted through wild riding, arrow dodging, and a lot of gore and blood.

"All right," he said finally. He dropped his arm over his

leg, his thumb holding the page. "What are you grinning at?"

She bowed her forehead into her knees immediately, as if by hiding she wouldn't have to answer.

"What?" he insisted, unable not to smile himself. He gave her a little nudge with his elbow.

She shook her head, then spoke into her muffling skirts. "Nothing." She let out a laugh, almost a giggle.

"Not nothing. What's making you smile like that?" So pretty.

She turned her head, leaning her cheek, and let her eyes slide to him. "All right. I was thinking it's flattering, what you said." When he didn't know what she meant, she explained, "About not kissing me because, well—" Her smile opened up as her eyes lowered, hesitantly pleased. "As if I'm some sort of femme fatale." Her smile went suddenly, shyly wide, spreading into her fine, generous mouth. "It's a relief." She laughed, so glad she was giddy. "You see, I thought you thought— Well, never mind. I'm so glad you don't think I'm a tart."

"But you are," he said stonily.

She blinked, her smile fading a little.

He let her off the hook. "The sweetest sort," he said and grinned. "A pie supper, remember?"

She repeated, "Pie supper." Her smile curled softly back again, just a line at her mouth, though big—it gleamed—at her eyes.

There he and she sat, grinning at each other for no particular reason. With Sam enjoying the hell out of the look of her: the way she met his gaze, the delicacy of her thin-limbed body folded up under her dark purple shawl (by daylight, the color of black plums, or, no, whortleberries, he thought), her wild hair lying over it in long, crazy gold and brown spirals that wound down her back, over her shoulders, down over her bosom. All of this adrift in white vapor. It was like sitting inside a cloud beside a disheveled, mischievous angel—

"Right." He returned his attention to the book, bringing it

back up in front of his eyes, and began to read. " 'Buffalo Bill, like knights errant of old, wanted justice and was willing to fight for it—' "

Quietly, she said over this, "And you couldn't do it."

"Do what?" He looked at her.

"You know." In case he didn't, smiling over her knees again, she told him: "You couldn't either have me on my back in the space of a—" She threw him a sly glance, then said, "A hiccup is rather quick."

Sam felt his mouth open, though no words came out. The hair at the back of his neck lifted. He said finally, after too long a silence, "I'm not responding to that." He turned back to the book. " 'The cavalry was ready—' "

"Anyway, you couldn't do it, and wrestling me there wouldn't count. I should have to go on my own."

He frowned over at her. "We're not having this conversation, Lid—"

"You couldn't."

"Don't tempt me."

"Couldn't."

"Could."

"Couldn't."

He laughed and turned toward her, dangling the book over his knee. "You know, if a woman asks for trouble, I usually give it to her." He put his tongue on a side tooth and considered. "All right, a hiccup was a figure of speech. I meant in a short time. How long do you think you could last?"

Her eyes widened, though her little smile didn't leave her face. He and she weren't serious here, he thought, just tormenting each other, out of boredom, because they had nothing better to do. "I don't know," she said. "Five minutes?"

"Five minutes!" He shook his head, chuckling. "Well I declare. I must be more attractive than I thought, if five minutes is all it'd take before your knees'd buckle."

She let out a squawk—"Ack!"—then protested, "It's longer than a hiccup."

"Yeah, but we already agreed that was too short. So how

long does it usually take? How long before I'd hold the record?"

"Ack!" was all she said again.

He winked his good eye at her. "Don't worry. We're not going to find out, so it doesn't matter."

She stared at him, looking disconcerted, then let out a release, a light laugh into her knees. "Right," she said, exactly as he usually said it, still game enough to pull his leg by mimicking him. She smiled down again at the ground, though a little less confidently—shyly, prettily.

He shook his head and lifted the book back up in front of his eyes. He and she were just having fun. Let her smile how she wanted.

Before he could start, she asked, "Do you read other kinds of books?"

He glanced at her. "You mean, besides catfish-dumb cowboy books?"

"I didn't say that." She supplied, "Austen?"

"Jane? No. Don't like her books. But Dickens and Collins. I've read all of theirs."

She nodded, smiled. "We both like books."

"We sure do." Sam was pleased she'd admit they had something in common, even if it wasn't every single author. He added, not wanting to make too much of it, "I wrote a book once."

She looked over at him. "Really?"

"Yeah, when I was young. When I was in school."

"About what?"

"About nothing. A bunch of sayings I liked." In fact, a reviewer of *A Texan in Massachusetts* had called it "a collection of witty aphorisms and surprising home truths." Sam wasn't so full of himself as to take such praise seriously. Still, as he sat there, he tried to figure out a way to work his little moment of glory into the conversation. Instead, though, the darnedest thing, what came out his mouth was: " 'Idiot country boy sayings,' my father called them. I gave him the book, and he threw it down the hole in the outhouse. 'Bunch of crap,' he said, pardon my French."

She looked honestly horrified. "What an awful father!"

"Oh, yeah." Sam raised his brow in appreciation. "My father was a humdinger. He went through five wives, survived two wars, was a bandit for a while, a sheriff for a while, worked the range for years, and could run a ranch, too. Lots of people respected him. But not many liked him. He was mean as blazes." He laughed. "Some days, I'm a whole lot more like him than I want to be."

He'd said too much again. Her eyes stared at him, wide with amazement and, possibly, appall. Then she asked, "You think people don't like you?"

"Some days." He studied her. "Though I think you do maybe."

She bowed her head, smiling almost with dismay. "I daresay."

He was fairly certain this meant yes. He added, "Even though I come from the darnedest background."

She nodded, another agreement. Why, they were full of accord this morning. She smiled that mysterious little smile of hers again and stared out over her knees.

They took turns, reading the whole Buffalo Bill book, which wasn't saying much since it was short. It was no more than noon when they finished. And still the fog didn't lift enough that they could see two feet in front of them.

Lydia, who'd read the last pages, quietly closed the book, then held it in her hands for several seconds and stared at it. She'd liked the stupid thing.

She'd read and liked all—oh, if she was honest, six: She'd purloined six Buffalo Bill novels from Clive, with at least twenty to go, judging from his stash in the bottom of his wardrobe. She'd liked them all. They were satisfying: Right won. Wrong was punished. The brave and truthful took the day. And she especially liked reading about all this with Sam Cody, while joking and sitting close enough that their shoulders brushed.

She let the book rest in her skirt and stretched, aware of Mr. Cody without looking at him. He stretched, too, unfolding his long legs, flexing a booted ankle as he leaned back onto one arm. He stretched one leg then the other, getting the blood flowing. They had both been so engrossed by the end of the book, they'd sat stock-still lest they miss a word.

He muttered something about that being a "darn good yarn."

"I *liked* it," she declared firmly. When he smiled over at her, she felt suddenly so good. She added, "And my brother has some photographs of some people in their knickers that I found under his books, and they purely fascinate me." Not to mention some drawings of a slightly obscene Greek play an American probably wouldn't know much about. "There is a whole world of things, I suspect, I'm not supposed to like that I love."

He raised his brow, mock horror, then laughed, teasing, "You go through your brother's drawers?"

"His wardrobe. I know I shouldn't." She joined him in rolling her eyes at herself. "Another horrible thing I ought not to like. But I do—I saw him hide something there after he'd been tormenting me about, oh, I think being late which I always am almost everywhere I go. This time, I was just angry enough to see what he'd hidden. And, *voilà,* a treasure trove of contraband. Our mother would kill him."

"How old is he?"

"Clive is twenty-two."

He smiled. "Old enough to take care of himself against his mother, then."

She rolled her eyes. "You don't know our mother."

"Your father can show him."

Lydia snorted at that. "If he were around enough." She leaned toward him, lowering her voice as if someone might hear. "I've never said this aloud," she began. "But I think my parents are waiting till Clive and I are married, then they will probably go their separate ways. They don't like each other."

"Ah," he said, his brow knitting with a look of empathy.

"I mean," she explained, "they might worry that a nice family shouldn't wish to marry into one with such a rift in it.

I think they might even consider divorce, which is so scandalous, isn't it?" She didn't wait for an answer, but glanced away. "Anyway, I think they're waiting it out. It's sad." She changed the subject. Brightly, she asked, "So are you related?"

He blinked. "Related?"

"To Buffalo Bill Cody. You have the same last name."

"To the mustachioed showman who runs the four-hundred-fifty-horse circus?" He snorted out a guffaw. "My pop used to say we were. Our cousin, William F." He said, "I don't think so, though. You've seen the show?"

"All four hundred and fifty horses, plus Sitting Bull and Annie Oakley." Another easy confession to Mr. Cody, who never looked down on anyone or anything, she realized. She liked him for that. Smiling, she asked, "You?"

He said, "Mm," which meant yes. "Complete with buffalo hunt. Twice."

She laughed. "Me, too. Clive sees it every time it comes to London. I think he's seen it four times. Where did you see it?"

"Chicago."

"Both times?"

"Yep."

Lydia let her mind drift. After a minute, she asked, "What's the farthest you've been from home?"

He said thoughtfully, "Here, pretty much. And it's too far. I want to go back."

"What's the best and worst thing you have seen away from home?" When he didn't seem to understand where the question came from, she explained, "It's a game my brother and I used to play to help us see the other side of things: What's the best and the worst thing about going away to boarding school, because he had to when he was six. What's the best and the worst thing about not going to university, because I wanted to but wasn't allowed."

Mr. Cody looked at her, a contemplative pause that tried to decide again whether to believe this upperclass reference

or not. After a moment, though, he let it go, as if no conclusion was truly necessary. He asked, "What's the best and
worst thing I've seen here?"

"All right, here."

He nodded, willing to play. "Don't laugh," he said. "I
half-like the moor. It reminds me of the Texas plains, except
for the mud, fog, and bogs." He chuckled, a kind of low
rumble in his chest. "Which I guess is a pretty big 'except.' "
He put one knee up, hanging his arm off it, and continued. "I
haven't camped out on the open range in I can't tell you how
long. I'm starting to like it." After a snort, he offered, "And
whortleberries." He glanced over at her, and their eyes
met—a frank, shared friendliness. "I really like whortleberries. They're the first English thing I can remember liking
wholeheartedly." His brow drew down, almost a perplexed
expression, as he stared directly at her and added, "Well, the
second thing, I guess."

The second thing? He meant her. He meant he liked
whortleberries best after her, which meant he liked her best
of all. Didn't it? Or was she misunderstanding?

Lydia couldn't bring herself to ask for clarification. Just
the possibility though made a warm, melting sensation at her
breastbone, liquid delight—a feeling that, despite herself,
seeped into her breasts and down her veins at the insides of
her arms.

"Here," she said. She handed the dime novel back to him,
into his lap, then lay back on the ground, turning away from
him, hiding her hot, wistful face. "Start again," she said.
"Let's read it again."

She lay there in her own kind of fog: contentment. How
lucky she was, she thought. He liked her. And here she'd
been an hour or two ago, sure she was going to have to beg,
plead, and promise to get him to keep her secret—not to tell
anyone whom he'd met out here—then he hadn't even believed her, even seeing what she'd thought of as undeniable
proof: her archery equipment. She thought of herself as an
archer, saw Miss Lydia Bedford-Browne in the bow some-

how. County champion, regional captain of the meet. But, of course, how silly. He didn't know that. He didn't know what to believe. Except what he saw.

Herself. Out here, she was just Liddy. Nothing more, nothing less. Which was perfect, really. She was glad not to be one of the Bedford-Brownes for now, someone other than the daughter to the Viscount Wendt.

Mr. Cody picked up the book from his lap and began to read once more.

Lydia tried his name out silently. *Sam* began to read. Sam, who liked and teased and kept Liddy warm. Liddy who didn't worry about her tonic—she realized that she hadn't missed it one bit, that out here, at least, she was fine without it. Liddy was different from how Lydia had always imagined herself: She was capable of saving herself from a bog, of eating roasted rabbit with her fingers, of laughing over the horrible-wonderful American Wild West Shows her mother made fun of, of eating whortleberries till her fingers and mouth were purple.

And of lying back and enjoying a foolishly marvelous story. For the *second* time, without guilt. As it was read in a voice that was both raspy and fluid, the deepest *basso profundo* she could imagine.

From the ground where she lay, she listened as she stared at Sam's dusty, broad-shouldered back. *Sam,* she said again to herself. She didn't even call Boddington by his first name (and for a worried second couldn't even remember it—oh, yes, *Wallace*). Above her, Sam was a fuzzier entity for her lying back staring up at him; his dark-suited hips—dark gray before dust and mud had altered the color—were distinct but his torso faded as it climbed upward into the mist. She could just make out his black head through the blanket of fog.

Sam's rough voice rolled through the heroic exploits of Buffalo Bill, Pony Express rider, killer of outlaws and wild Indians, saver of women and children. She'd begun to like the rhythms and tones of his speech. His American drawl had its own rhythm and predictable line length, not unlike poetry. She curled onto her side cozily, her hip against him, and just let the intonations pour over her as she lay in a doze.

He must have grown tired too—he couldn't have had a much better night's sleep than she—because somewhere along the way he gave up reading and ended up lying behind her. She knew he was there, had just become interested in the idea that his shoulder was against her back, that he was horizontal beside her, when she felt him move away. Nothing behind her, no contact, no sound.

She twisted at the waist to roll her shoulders back onto the ground, looking for him. It was the same maneuver as last night in the dark, their little dance, only now in the white: Their eyes met. He was on his side, up on an elbow, looking down, their faces close, nothing else but fog: Sam vivid, the rest of the world a haze.

"I thought you were asleep," he said down into her face.

"No." Black lashes, blue eyes. It was a purely gorgeous combination, no other word for it. And, yes, his nose had been swollen a little, because it had more definition today, along with the faint yellowing of bruise. She suspected it should be a thin nose, a blade, under better circumstances. There was a bump on the bridge. "Was your nose crooked before?" she asked in a murmur. No point in yelling into his face.

"No."

She frowned. "I think they broke it."

Gingerly, he touched the bony place where his nose went a degree off center. "It feels like it. Hurts like the dickens."

She winced. "I'm sorry." The black and blue under his eye made a neat outline of bone. The spot looked tender. She wanted to touch it at the top of his cheekbone, stroke the skin very, very lightly with the tip of her finger. Yet she held herself still.

Behind him, the fog was so perfectly blinding, so perfectly silent. Or almost silent—distantly now and then she could hear a faint trill. Frogs. Water somewhere, another bog. (Or even the same one, given how little progress they'd made.) Wherever, the sound was particularly of the moor; the strange, eerie place had a soul of its own.

It occurred to her: She wanted him to kiss her. *Kiss me.* Do something. *Touch me,* she wanted to say. *Oh, stupid man who is too noble to fool with virgins—I'm not* that *much of a virgin.*

She raised her eyes to his again, and their gazes held. He was going to, surely. Let him, she thought, oh, let him.

When he only frowned down at her, she tried to make a joke of it. "It wouldn't count now. I'm already on my back."

He blinked, startled, then burst forth with soft laughter so attractive it made her catch her breath. He dropped his head, shaking it. His hair brushed her chin, then neck. It was silky. She closed her eyes, waited. Nothing.

When she opened them again, he'd raised his head enough to contemplate her, a cautious frown on his face. Why she should feel so . . . intimately confident of him, she didn't know. Beard stubble shadowed his dark complexion to livid black, as if someone had smeared his lip, chin, cheeks, and neck in a neat pattern of dirt. His black hair hung over his forehead, the unkempt hook of hair she kept wanting to brush back. His remarkably blue eyes stared unwaveringly out of all this dark coloring, angel's eyes in a bandit's complexion.

One reason for her ease with him occurred to her: She had some sort of reciprocal power of him—and the realization made her spirit lift with the swiftness of a strong draft under spread wings.

He shook his head, in answer to nothing. His face, though, asked her to cooperate, to make doing nothing—no sexual contact—easy for him.

Lydia didn't want to. She wanted to be a siren. "Kiss me."

He laughed uneasily.

"I want you to," she said.

"No." Their faces were so close they all but talked into each other's mouths. "Roll over and go to sleep. We have to wait out the fog. We may as well get some rest."

Eye to eye, she argued silently by slowly shaking her

head. Then, harlot that she was, she wet her lips, opened her mouth slightly, and lifted her chin toward him.

He'd be doggone if he'd kiss her, Sam told himself. It could only lead to trouble. So what was he thinking? That he was going to bite her? Because the next thing he knew, his mouth was touching hers. No, he wouldn't kiss her. He'd just sort of feel if her lips were as warm and soft as they looked. See what that wide, pretty mouth was like against his.

Softer than petals. Though a lot better than petals. Warm and round and animate enough to move under the press of his lips. No, this wasn't kissing. This was brushing his lower lip against hers. Running the tip of his tongue along the edges between her lips. He'd only have a little more then stop. He'd have all the touching possible right up *to* a kiss. Small bites . . . of soft, sensitive lips . . . tasting. . . . All the while thinking, if he leaned into her just a little bit, he could have that sweet mouth, know it, take it, slather it, plumb it with his tongue, penetrate—

"Oh, God bless," he moaned and drew back.

She followed, lifting her head so her lips stayed with his. His retreat did no good.

He jerked back gracelessly, frowned, and let out a worried breath all but into her face, a held-back grunt of distress. "Liddy," he murmured, "we're out here alone. I could even convince myself right now that nothing matters since we may never see civilization again. My love life's a mess. I'm feeling lonesome and down about it. And you're pretty enough to put the sky to shame." He paused, then pleaded, "Don't—"

Which made no sense at all to Lydia. "Why 'don't'?"

He grabbed her hand and brought it down to the front of his trousers, till surprisingly under her palm was a round, thick ridge. "There," he said. "That's what you've asked about a couple times now—"

She jumped, hesitant, then was too curious. "Only once," she argued, then pressed her palm over him on her own. Oh, she thought. He was wonderful. Round. Not a ridge exactly, but long and perfectly cylindrical, hard, yet tender in some way. She let her fingers explore his shape.

This seemed to shock him. He let out breathy words— "My G-God, Liddy— What're you do-hoo-hooing— Ja-hee-ssus—"

While she explored the wonder of a male erection through his dusty trousers. His body wasn't anything like hers. Where she had nothing, an indentation, theoretically an entrance, he was substantial. She traced the shaft upward: with Sam gasping and cursing and praying, most of it unintelligible. What she did to him made her head light. She wanted to wrap her hand around him—

His fingers came down over the backs of hers and pushed hard, trapping her hand.

"Will you stop wiggling around there." Sam took a breath. "I know you felt me last night, but I want you to get a full understanding here of what's happening. My body, the blood in my veins, is working up a lot of steam here." He tried to give her some sort of example her virginal mind could grasp. "Think of an English army that comes up over the horizon, a thousand men, helmets, shields, spears, all shined and polished and pumped, ready to descend on . . . on just you."

She laughed. "A thousand men? All with their spears polished and pumped—"

"No, their spirits, their valor primed for the charge—"

"Primed and pumped?"

He floundered, laughed. "If you'd stop making fun of me long enough to listen—"

Lulled by their laughter, Sam loosened his hold of her hand: And she ran her two fingers boldly up the shaft of him to trace the ridge around the head of his penis.

"H-a-a!" he let out, then threw his leg over her, rolling up to lie half across her, chest to chest, as he took both her hands at the wrists. He pinned her out, straddling her hipbone, the top of his thigh wedged up between her legs. He let out a gust, exasperation, down into her face. "You're in over your head," he muttered, "and you just won't believe me."

She looked startled and, for the first time, as if she might grasp there was more trouble here than she wanted. Good. He didn't need to take his demonstration further.

So why didn't he let go?

He could feel their hearts knocking against each other where their chests met, the softness where his weight flattened the roundness of her breast. At her thin wrists, he could feel how much stronger he was than she. He found himself wanting to assert his strength, show her. He wanted her to feel his potency, God help him, in every sense.

Her eyes stayed wide on him, partly frightened, but so attentive: interested. She didn't back down. In fact, there, pinned half under him, something subtle changed in her face. Under his grip, he felt her let go, her whole body seeming to relax, breathe toward his. Capitulation.

"Jesus God," he murmured. He paused for a second longer, long enough to know he was right when, with a shake of his head, he said, "This is a such bad idea." Then he did it anyway.

He angled his head, opened his hurt mouth ever so gently, and pressed it down over her lips. Through those pretty lips, she made a little sound . . . the sough of a woman's pleasure. On a warm puff of breath, it mewed into his mouth, and Sam was undone.

He let go of her arms to take her face into his hand, a palm on her cheek, and penetrated her mouth with his tongue. For an instant, she squirmed. For the love of Pete, he thought, it was new to her. He cooed, "It'll be okay," and did it again. So much for his noble intentions, if ever he had any.

She let him. She gave her mouth up to him, letting him lead her into a full, deep kiss.

Pushing his tongue into her warm mouth was so pleasurable, it was unholy. The inside of her mouth was small. Foreign, female. He breathed in and, through their open mouths, her smell and heat and humidity entered his chest.

The feel of it made his heart thud so hard he could feel it down through his belly, all the way into his groin—his arousal there, already firm, rushed to full readiness. He was so hard and heavy so fast he was dizzy with it for several moments.

While Liddy followed and responded at every turn, as co-operative as a little bird being fed in the nest. She sighed when he slid his hand up into the back of her hair, digging upward till his fingers tangled in soft, snarly curls, his palm against her warm scalp. He glided his other hand down her side, past her hip and partly under her—suddenly in full-palmed possession of her unbelievably round backside. He pressed his thumb into one of the dimples where it met her spine. God Almighty—

He pulled her hips toward him with more force than he meant to, instinct driving. His muscles trembled from hold-ing back, from trying to go slow—he'd given up trying to stop. She startled when he first ground himself against her hipbone, but then she crooned. The sweet thing really took to lovemaking, even if she didn't know much about it, which was going to be a whopping good thing for some fellow, though it sure made her a rotten guardian of her own chastity at the moment.

He continued, kissing her, half on top of her, pressing against her, while images of full intercourse lit up his imag-ination. Lord oh Lord oh Lord. He kissed her hard enough that it was possible that the cut at the corner of his mouth opened again. He tasted the faint metallic tang of blood, though the cut didn't hurt. It mingled with the taste of her mouth; it became part of his awareness . . . the flavor of knowing the softness of her, the curves of her body against him, the promise of her open mouth, sultry with humidity and heat and pure responsiveness. He wanted her breasts bare. He wanted to touch her naked skin. Intimacy; he wanted it. He wanted her skirts up, his trousers open—

He pulled back and drew in a long, ragged breath. "Liddy," he murmured. She was breathing hard, too. Cussed woman. He couldn't decide if he wanted to give her directions—*lift your hip here so I can get at your skirt better*—or make one last attempt to warn her. He worried she didn't know what was happening.

Whichever, before he could get words out, he was already striking compromises with himself. Go 'head, kiss her deeply, draw her further into love play. Enjoy it. God knew it couldn't be more wonderful. You can stop when you need to.

While, in some darker place in his mind, a voice calculated: And if you don't stop, how could you keep her from getting pregnant? Could you pull out? You have nothing with you. Would you dare leave it to chance? God help him, he was as erect as a post, his blood flowing with the damnedest questions. While his cock was hot and fat with its own kind of answer; it felt blissful, it ached. He was sore after a whole night of fighting arousal. He couldn't endure any more. He didn't want to; he shouldn't have to. He wanted inside her. He wanted relief with a kind of narrowing focus that was making it difficult to think of much else.

Sam was wrestling metaphorically, then was all of a sudden up against a very concrete something that held him back: her hand. She'd seized his fingers as he'd started to pull up her skirt.

He halted dead still, a man instructed to do so.

After a moment, Lydia opened her eyes enough that from beneath her lashes she found Sam's face. So close. Oh, so nice. He stared down, doing nothing, motionless. She complained, "No, don't stop."

He looked confused. "You just stopped me."

"Well, from *that*."

He laughed—deep, devilish laughter. The sound fascinated her. She had heard of, though never actually heard, such a thing: a *dirty* laugh, full of sexuality. "Liddy," he said, "you're being seduced."

"No, I'm not," she said easily and smiled.

She closed her eyes again as she felt him shift his weight and run his fingers down the tendon of her neck till they rested at the indentation of her throat, at her collarbone. He flipped a button open. As easy as that, *flip*. She drifted in the sensation of his warm hand hovering near her breast.

A different world, all this—a warm, beautiful blur. It wasn't the real world, she wanted to tell him. They could dally a little, because they lay inside something else, a hiatus . . . a sweet limbo that didn't count. Where she could take perfect, poignant pleasure in a man's kiss and touch; never mind their differences. Here in the whiteness, the clouds, was a . . . a little miracle . . . of autonomy—no one to answer to but herself—of private pleasure and human connection.

Lying on damp ground in the cool blindness of fog, she raised her arms over her head again, stretching, lifting any barriers away with the hope that he'd understand he was free to continue. Within limits, of course.

He let out that laugh again, a little shudder of it that seemed to run up her arms. "Oh, yeah, this counts," he said.

"What?" she said dreamily.

"It counts. Less than a hiccup, too."

Oh, that. "No, it doesn't. I was already down."

"Do you want up?"

"No."

"Then it counts." More of his soft, low laughter as she shoved him in the chest. "I win," he announced.

What Sam won was another good look at Liddy's tongue, a quick, full extension, followed by a crinkled up face, a wrinkled nose at him.

He didn't even think about it—he just plain enjoyed her so much, right down to her amusing competitive streak, that, laughing, he leaned forward. He planted a full smacking buss on her twisted mouth that left her startled. She didn't have time to understand what was happening, to gauge her reaction. He was too quick.

Except that, when it was over, there they were again, an inch away: her face expectant, her wide, thick-lashed eyes looking up at him—he could've counted her eyelashes.

He asked. "Why don't you just dance naked in front of me?"

"Is that what you'd rather? Should that do it then?"

"Yeah," he said and laughed, though for the life of him Sam couldn't figure why everything now was striking him as funny. Along these lines, as if it were a joke she'd own up to finally, he murmured, "You're not really some muckety-muck's daughter, are you?"

"A viscount's. Yes."

She was lying. "Don't," he said. "Tell the truth."

"I am."

"All right, then lie to me." He laughed at himself for saying it, wanting it. "I could get playful with, well, a governess or a lady's maid—"

"*Well* nothing," Lydia told him, lifting her brow as she rested back on the ground. "How very un-American—undemocratic—of you to have different rules for different classes of women. Kiss me again."

She knew of course that he was right, that her family would be horrified had they known what she was doing. Yet they weren't here. And was this any of their business? And didn't they give her the most beastly advice sometimes?

She loved the feel of his mouth, the heat of it, the way he moved it over hers, the way it stirred her. She loved the press of his body against her, the breeze drifting over her skin where the throat of her dress was open. What else? What other pleasure might she like to explore in this glistening moment—which was temporary after all, she told herself. She and Sam would go their separate ways, and she didn't mind. She felt protected somehow, perhaps *because* they would.

He stared. She watched his smile grow tentative, uncertain.

"Oh, don't get distant again," she said.

His eyes narrowed. Such a serious look.

She risked telling him in a whisper, "You want to."

He broke eye contact and scowled into the fog.

When he looked back at her, she was surprised to find his impatience with her—his interesting, flattering exasperation she so enjoyed playing with—held a fleck of rage, indignity. His eyes, their blue, were dark, steely, a metallic sheen. Hard, bright. He said, "Yeah, I want to. I want to kiss you while I lie on top of you. I want to take your clothes off and touch you everywhere, while I pin you to the ground and kiss you hard—hard, wet kisses full on your mouth"—his dark, beard-stubbled face grew deadly earnest—"*in* your mouth. I want inside your mouth, inside your clothes, inside your body. I want to lie naked over you and slide myself inside you."

She blinked. "No," she said immediately. She felt herself flush. Then she knew a zing of anger herself. A kiss, she thought. A little more maybe. This was as playful as she dare be. "No," she said again.

He remained in full, sincere engagement with her watchfulness, eye to eye, and nodded. "It's a good decision, Liddy. I'm glad you've come to it. Now give me a little slack in the rope here, will ya? Roll over. Stop making life so difficult for me—and for you, too, if you think about it."

With that, he lifted his leg and rolled away, flat out on his back beside her. He crossed his foot to his knee, pushing his hand into his hair, and dug his fingers through it as if he might pull it out. He let out a long breath, blatantly adjusted the front of his trousers, then changed the subject.

"All right," he said, "your turn. What's the farthest you've been from home, and what's the best and worst thing *you've* seen?"

Lydia's mind went blank. Or almost blank. *Touch you everywhere?* "Um, I went to France once." *Hard, wet kisses full on your mouth.* "I saw a bare, I mean, a bear, no, a bull. I saw bulls, bullfighting." *In your mouth. Inside your clothes.* It was indecent. She shouldn't think of it.

Yet she could hardly think of anything else. *I want to lie naked over you and slide myself inside you.*

The fog thinned to reveal an evening sky, one area of the horizon slightly brighter than the rest—the setting sun, Sam hoped. West. Through a mist, the rocks and open spaces of the moor's terrain once more became visible. The world returned. Sam and Liddy found a near-toppling tor in the distance and fixed their direction on it, then congratulated themselves for sitting tight all day: Within a matter of yards, the ground sloped, grew spongy, then wet, then muddy.

For a time, the mud was broken up with drier patches of damp heath tufted with coarse-bladed grass gone to seed, lots of long stemmy spikes. Then muddier again, with both of them complaining, then they actually longed for it: Their southerly route, no matter how they tried to avoid it, became a horrible yellowish slime over which, to cross, they had to leap from one clump of grass to another.

The sky continued to clear, a moon appearing. Because they could see reasonably well, and because they had made such poor time all day, they pushed on, past their landmark tor, looking for the road. The going was slow though, their path turning from mess to mud to mess again. The land was lower than before. How could the road be this way? Lydia wondered. How could they be having such a hard time finding it?

As the sun set, the evening brought them some unwelcome eerie visitors—glowing eyes in the dark followed them for a time. They turned out to belong to half a dozen sheep, but Lydia knew a little of her old fear again. Then even Sam jumped when, as he and she treaded up a rocky rise, something clanked curiously under his foot, something metal. He picked it up, then they both wished he hadn't. It was rusted grappling irons, a reminder that the moor was home to a prison and the occasional escapee.

Lydia shivered and stayed so close to Sam after this that she occasionally bumped into his arm or side—though Sam couldn't imagine what he'd do if they were truly confronted with the convicts or hounds from hell she feared. He sympathized, though. Moving across the moor by moonlight was awe-inspiring. Not impossible, but fraught with enough unknowns, as well as perfectly explainable slipping or heels sinking suddenly and deeply into the wet ground, that even Sam was spooked.

The temperature dropped, and Liddy suggested they don their trusty petticoats for warmth, so they halted. She was reaching around to hand Sam his, when she suddenly stood, taking the wad of petticoat to her chest. Clutching it, she lifted her other moonlit arm and exclaimed, "Look! Oh, look!"

Sam turned to see what she meant. Through the dark in the far distance were lights.

"It's a cottage!" she said. "The lights of a house!"

Sure enough, at some distance off there seemed to be the tiny glows of windows. One extinguished as he watched, and another lit. People.

Without another thought—donning her ruffled wrap hurriedly as she walked—Liddy took off in the direction of the lights, and Sam followed.

It was funny, but he realized that his spirits fell a little more with each step they took. Civilization. He should be glad. They would probably sleep under a roof tonight. He'd be warm enough without wrapping up in a lot of women's ruffled underwear. Yet he wasn't glad. He almost wished he could stay out here. Wilderness Man. Liddy was right. He felt better about himself out here than he had in a long time. A lone wolf. He didn't screw up making a fire or killing a rabbit. Somehow neither of these was as complicated as getting to the church or attending endless engagement parties or simply getting his tail end across an ocean. No, out here was . . . simple. And he'd forgotten how good he was at *simple*, at pure, basic survival. It was the machinations of society that confounded him and made him hurt.

Come to think of it, he hadn't been a completely lone wolf out here. He glanced at Liddy. She was marching off paces, eager for warmth; he didn't blame her. But he admitted to himself at least: Civilization meant giving up his interesting, highly imaginative companion. And, surprising as it was to discover, he didn't relish parting company from Miss Brown, or whatever her name was.

For almost an hour they played hide and seek with the lights, heading toward them, losing them, catching them again. Liddy was racing for them with such vigor and single-mindedness that, at one point, Sam found himself holding her arm—she kept tripping over stones, not watching what she was doing, making her ankle give.

In the end, though, he and she stood with their toes sinking in mud, staring at what turned out to be no house at all. Only when they were right on top of the lights did they realize what they had beat a path for, going for all they were worth: methane rising off a bog, spontaneously igniting, burning, then going out.

Sam let out a long, loud laugh. "Oh, you gotta love the Dartmoor!" he said. "A bog. Another bog!"

"Well, I don't. Not at this minute." After a pause, she asked, "Have you any idea which direction we've walked? East? West?"

"Hm." He thought about it. "Maybe westerly. I'm not sure."

She sighed. "Bog candles, I think they're called." She laughed humorlessly, then added, "Pixie-led. That's what they say when someone is lost out on the moor for days. That pixies, for mischief, love to lead travelers round and round in circles."

"The pixies have had a good time with us."

"Indeed."

"Indeed," he repeated and laughed.

"I shouldn't find it funny, but I do." She laughed more genuinely. "We're lost. We are ridiculously and completely lost, while being probably no more than a dozen miles from where we started."

"I bet you're right."

"Should we feel dispirited, do you think?"

Oddest thing. Sam felt actually . . . relieved. "Nah. We'll just find more wood and get another fire going. We'll find our way off the moor tomorrow."

"Tomorrow." She laughed again. "Right."

Right. He was coming to love the way she used this word, her British pronunciation of it: his word. Their word. "Right," he said.

They were still lost. Well, wasn't that just . . . a fine ol' thing.

9

Finding wood was harder that night. Though visibility was better, there was less wood to find. By the light of a larger, brighter moon, Sam and Liddy took to the higher ground over the bog, but there found only clumps of heather. Eventually, Sam dug some of it up, roots, peat, and all, to augment their small supply of sticks.

This sort of fire pointed to its own kind of danger. The peat around the roots—the very ground of the hillocks over the bog—was porous and dry. It lit quickly, too quickly, suggesting that the ground itself could catch fire. Thus, Lydia and Sam put out their first fire, then cleared the area and covered the ground with rocks, before they lit what became a smoky fire—smoky but better than none.

Even with their difficulties, though, Lydia found herself having to fight the urge to hum a little tune as she threw twigs onto their small campfire. Rabbit again. And Sam. She loved that she had his sexual attention. She wasn't sure quite what to do with it, but she knew she adored having it. *Naked*. She wouldn't get naked for him, of course. But the idea fascinated her, and she wanted to think about it some more while staring across a fire at Sam's ever more sharpening features—the bumps and bruising continued to subside and reveal his face. It was angular, sharp-boned, even rather patrician.

Thank goodness for bog candles, she caught herself thinking.

She drew in a deep breath and felt . . . wonderful, somehow. Happy. In London, this past season, she'd known a growing and miserable feeling: discontent. Though, of course, at the end of the coming season, since she'd be twenty-five then, she intended to settle down. She would do as she ought: single her respectable number of suitors down to one mate. It was expected. She needed to do this. She needed to secure her future. Still, if anything, she felt hemmed in by all society "expected" of her lately.

Now, without anyone but herself to answer to—without witnesses, as it were—she felt a sense of . . . self-discovery. Freedom. Perhaps it was the notion that she could have drowned in a bog or starved to death or died of chill.

Well, goodness, she told herself. She could have died last week or the week before that. It was precisely what her parents worried about, that she would die, and one day she undoubtedly would, though not any time soon, she didn't think. For now, here she was, alive and thriving on a moor: in full knowledge that every day was a gift. It was as if, since she hadn't sunk or starved or shivered to death, she had regained something. As if her life belonged to her out here, that she could make decisions more clearly in her own best interests, do anything she wanted with her own particular days on this earth.

She felt as if she'd been reaching for this feeling for years, striving toward it. A sense of having shaken free of what others wanted for her. All that mattered was what she wanted for herself. What did it matter what she did, so long as it didn't hurt anyone else?

Or at least this was the fine speech she gave herself.

On their dry rise up from the bog, they settled in, cooking then eating rabbit with a side dish of frogs' legs, courtesy of Sam's efforts and tutoring. After making their fire, he took her down to the water again, where he taught her to chase frogs by the moonlight and the light of eerie, crackling, whiffing explosions of methane gas. After a while, though, what a lark. Her eyes adjusted. She became used to the idea—the gas indeed lit the bog as if by candlelight. Hundred-power candlelight. It was quite the perfect way to chase frogs.

Even if the frogs didn't cooperate as they should: Lydia laughed till her stomach hurt, splashing and grabbing till Sam's and her feet and sleeves were both good and wet. In the end, though, they triumphed once more in the art of survival.

"Frogs' legs *au lapin*," Sam said.

Which made her laugh, then made her blink. Sam's French was every bit as Texas-drawled as his English. But he still could understandably pronounce the word for *rabbit*.

When she asked him how, he said he'd spent three months in Paris last year.

"Ah, traveling with a Wild West Show, were you?" When he threw her a mock-angry look, she offered, "Or more gunfighting?"

"Exactement," he answered with satisfaction—his terrible accent sounded more like *eggs-act-a-moan*—then laughed. "The French should all be shot. I only took a couple of them down, though."

He wasn't serious, she knew. Or she didn't think so, at least. Difficult Sam wouldn't say more. He enjoyed talking her in circles, never answering her straight out.

After eating, they returned to a rivulet that emptied into the bog that they'd splattered into on their frog safari—literally splattered, for they hadn't seen it till they were ankle-deep. There, they washed, another welcome relief. She was able to rinse off two days' accumulation of grit from her face and arms. (While she and Sam argued over whether the rivulet offered a promising direction to walk tomorrow.

Surely, Lydia reasoned, it came from a larger body, and where there was large, flowing water there was almost always civilization. Sam thought they should simply locate south again and make another attempt at finding the elusive road. They tabled their disagreement, however, as a matter to consider by daylight, when their options should possibly be more obvious.)

Meanwhile, as they washed and argued, then sat more peacefully by their small fire, he and she kept up a constant stream of talk. They discussed nothing, anything. By the end of the evening, they sat with their heads bent together, their voices lowered as if someone might overhear them. Lost in a conversation of two.

"So you saw the bulls run in France?" Sam asked. He was stretched out on his side, leaning on one elbow. He had the gin bottle in one hand—he'd been hitting it fairly hard for the last half an hour.

"No. Bull*fights*. Would you have guessed they have bull-fights in France?"

"No."

"Well, they do. In the south near the Pyrenees. My uncle took me. I hated it. It was bloody and confusing. The men wave capes, while these massive, angry beasts attempt to kill them for doing it. It makes no sense. One man was gored in the thigh and stumbled. The bull gored him twice more be-fore someone could drag him to safety. I have no idea if he lived; he bled and bled. By the end, the bull's horns were red. I wanted them to shoot it."

"The bull?" Sam chuckled, not understanding, or else not sympathizing with, how much the scene had horrified her. He said, "The bull does nothing but defend himself. You don't like the bull?"

"He frightens me."

"They make him angry on purpose."

"Why does he let them? Why doesn't he just stop?"

"Sometimes he does stop, but they gouge him again." He snorted. "Liddy, they take him from his home, confine him, then bait him. Can you imagine? They drive you from the darkness into a bright, sunlit arena where everyone is cheering for your blood." He let out a low, macabre laugh, then said, "Me, I relate to the bull. It's the idiotic men I hate. They trap then taunt a dumb creature, who is helpless against its own nature. It's human, I guess, to rile him, but it's man at his ugliest. We are the ones who should stop; the bull has no choice."

She contemplated his face in the firelight. He'd closed his eyes and lay back. He was relaxed, just talking into the dark.

"So do they have bullfights in Paris?" she asked.

He laughed at that, a quiet sound, then answered, "No. Not that I know of."

"So have you been to a bullfight somewhere else?" He had surprising understanding of what she thought only she had seen.

"I know bulls."

Which wasn't an answer exactly.

He added, "The red cape. It treads somehow in his sacred place. Everyone has places like that." He made a soft sound, mumbled laughter, then said quite clearly, "Some of us are just loaded with them."

She shook her head. But he was drifting off. She could hear the faint change, the now familiar sound of his slightly heavier breathing when he fell asleep. In one night, she had discovered that, if he rolled to his back, he snored; she knew that a nudge made him turn, muttering apologies, then stop. What intimate information. And dear somehow. He was a very nice man, this American.

She took the gin bottle from his grasp, corked it, then rolled over and scooted backward against him, enjoying his simple, human heat. She hadn't realized, but, as the fire had died down, her back had grown chilly. He turned toward her, molding the warm front of him to the cold of her muscles, harboring her in the curve of his body.

Oh, yes. Oh, yes, she thought, please kiss me now.

He was relaxed, less defended than last night.

He was asleep, she realized. Oh, no. She turned slightly, thinking to jostle him. He was more than asleep. He'd drunk most of what remained of their bottle of gin—he was passed out.

Still, an hour or so later—of Lydia feeling puzzled and churning and somehow angry—he pulled her tightly against him, putting his face in the lee of her neck. He wrapped his arm round her waist, his knuckles lightly curled to her stomach.

The feel of him, his intimacy, made her squirm. It did something to her, something exciting, pleasing, sweet—

He muttered in his sleep.

"What?" she whispered. She didn't expect him to answer.

"Your hair"—the pause of a drowsy, deep inhalation, exhalation—"it smells so—" He fell into unconsciousness before he'd finished.

"So what?" She nudged him.

He jerked. "What?"

"My hair."

"Your hair?"

"What were you saying?"

"Oh." He laughed sleepily. "It smells good. Like ginger or something, lemons, flowers. You have the prettiest hair."

The prettiest hair. Talk about heat. That brought it. The idle compliment made her whole body hot. The pleasant excitement from a moment ago turned agitated. More yearning than interesting now: lacking.

Lydia wished Sam wasn't so full of exhaustion and gin, because suddenly she was wide awake. She wanted to talk more. And she wanted to start with the topic of why it felt so good for him simply to be smelling, and liking the smell of, her hair.

The fire burned low but remained warm, glowing, for a long time. Sam nodded back and forth beside it, half asleep. At first, he thought he was dreaming. He found himself watching a vision with heavy-lidded half-attention, then, his eyes still only slits, with full attention: Liddy by fireglow and the light of the moon, sitting up a foot away.

He watched his puzzling fixation: the woman who was

thin to the point of looking unhealthy at moments, at angles.
Yet with pretty features, striking in certain light, from certain perspectives—glimpses of beauty that were almost
poignant when paired with her frailness. Like her soft, idle
hands. A lady's hands. They were lovely—small, graceful,
softer than dew—yet their long-fingered slightness reminded him of cobwebs, little clear dust spiders. A fragility
he could blow away with a good puff of air.

It was a surprise, then, when she reached under her hair,
and, elbows up, lifted it on her arms, stretching. She
yawned, bathed in moonlight, her full breasts, their high,
round silhouettes, clearly delineated as she stretched in
three-quarter profile. What a unique combination she was.
Fragile of body, sturdy of spirit. Thin-limbed; full-bottomed;
small, bony hands with the ball of the thumb so plump he
would like to sink his teeth into it. She was voluptuous in
that arching moment, eyes closed, arms up, her hair lifted,
piled on them. Like a woman recovering from a spell: becoming herself.

He'd watched her in the past two days slowly change.
The story he hadn't been able to remember last night suddenly occurred to him—that of a swan slowly unfolding into
a woman. *Swan Lake*.

"Odette," he said. "The dark swan." The one who excited the prince and made him lose sight of the white swan-
princess. Was that what was happening? He certainly
didn't think much of Gwyn these days. Truth be told, he
hadn't felt as satisfied with life as he did right now in a
long time, and he'd never felt this content with Gwynevere
Pieters.

Liddy jumped at the sound of his voice, but settled back
after a moment and looked at him. "What are you talking
about?"

"That was the story I couldn't think of last night: *Swan
Lake*."

She was trying to escape something, he decided. What?
Or maybe it wasn't important, because it was done: She'd

escaped it here, a woman released from her swan state by the light of the moon, the light of the moor.

Her gaze lifted to him, a vague bafflement on her face. "You've been to the ballet?" She didn't wait for his response, though, continuing nervously—aware, maybe, that her tone had showed her surprise. "How very nice," she said brightly, conversationally, "that you've seen the ballet."

He twisted his mouth. "Yeah, sometimes, if I git tarred o' practicin' cattle calls, I go see them purdy girls dance."

She glanced at him, wide-eyed, then cast her eyes down.

"Sorry," he said. "I'm being ornery."

More humbly, she asked, "Do you like it?"

"Ballet?"

She nodded.

"A bunch of women dancin' on near-bare legs right there in front of me? Are you kiddin'? Of course I *like* it." He left a pause, sighed at himself. His father had thought the ballet was sissy. To this day, he could get defensive about his enjoyment of it. He gave a more serious answer. "Yes. I like the way ballerinas are aware of their bodies, their grace. I like the music." He waited. "And you?"

She grew wary.

He laughed at her. "Come on, Miss Viscount's Daughter." He still couldn't decide if he believed her or not, though the incongruous possibility worried him. He made fun. "You and the queen ever take the evening off so the two of you can go to the ballet?"

She had the good grace to hang her head—an acknowledgment of all the lies she'd told—then answered, "Sometimes."

Well, Sam thought. That was unexpected. No explanations or defense, she went straight for the truth.

Look at the two of them. He said, "I've never seen two bigger liars than us."

She looked up, her pretty eyes widening. "You've never been to the ballet then?"

He snorted. "Yeah, that's it. I read about the ballet someplace."

She looked disappointed. Let her be. She wasn't married. She wasn't in service. She didn't seem rich, but she didn't need money. And none of this mattered, because no matter who or what she was, she thought she was better than he was by a mile (though she liked him anyway and to a degree that embarrassed her). He was a dime novel to her.

Hell, if he didn't know better—the daughters of the English upperclass didn't travel alone—he'd have guessed she really *was* some sort of minor nobility.

As to himself, he felt no need to enlighten her, since she lied like a rug herself.

Normally, when Sam met a woman he wanted, he did a certain amount of scrambling. He hated it, but he did it. He'd make an effort to impress her: to cast himself in a powerful light. To his surprise and delight and sometimes consternation, none of this mattered with Liddy. She assumed the worst: then liked him anyway.

Who would have thought that a woman could be so wonderfully unambitious with regard to a man's money or power? Not that he was so all-fired impressive on either count, but still, most of the women he knew added that sort of thing into the measure of a man. He was delighted to be found attractive for nothing more than himself.

Delighted and not inclined to elaborate.

As Lydia watched Sam nod back to sleep, it occured to her: my heart's desire. It's him. I want him. All of it. What he'd said about kissing her and lying naked on top of her, being inside her clothes, inside—well, all of it, she thought. All of it. She wanted the long, lean man from Texas, builder of fires, hunter of rabbits, mess cook, campfire friend, and fine dramatic reader of cowboy books.

For a long time, she watched Sam lying there sleeping, till the fire was embers and there was so little light all she could see was his moonlit silhouette. Eventually, she let go of the feeling, the yearning for him. Freedom. I have this freedom in me. Strength and freedom.

She went to sleep with a sense of exhaustion, an ache in her muscles from use, and dreamed of walking the moor: traveling under the overcast sky, the cool air blowing across her, the earth passing under the feet.

10

What a silly thing love is! It is not half as useful as logic, for it does not prove anything and it is always telling one things that are not going to happen, and making one believe things that are not true.

OSCAR WILDE

The Nightingale and the Rose, 1888

Lydia and Sam awoke at almost the precise same time that morning, the two of them raising their heads all but simultaneously to the most beautiful sight: heather. The horizon was purple with it. A whole field of the short evergreen lay beyond in full, pale pinkish-purple bloom. Though the moonlight, the night before, had disclosed sparse, nearby clumps, it had hidden completely that, down in the shadow of their rise and just a little further out, the heather became dense, the only plant for miles. It turned the moor into waves, a fuchsia ocean of it.

Lydia was up in an instant, running toward the heather, out into little winding paths through it, raising up a wake of buzzing bees behind her.

"Be careful," Sam called. "Don't get stung."

It was gorgeous. Sturdy bushes, purple-stemmed, growing thigh-high, as high as the bush ever grew. And in per-

fect summer bloom. The field was covered in feathery
spikes of tiny bell-shaped flowers. She pulled off a green
shoot, its dense ranks of tiny, hairlike leaves growing in
whorls. The handsomest of plants in the most desolate of
landscapes.

She stuck a flowering piece into her hair, then danced out
into a small open space. There, she held out her hands and
spun till her skirt flared, till air brushed up under her skirts
against the silk of her knickers—it felt so nice. "Oh, the
moor. I love it, don't you? It makes me want to run, skip, do
somersaults and cartwheels like a child."

Sam watched her, his hands in his pockets, his head
faintly aching. She was a crazy woman, Liddy. "Yep, it's a
mysterious place."

It was, he thought. Stark. Beautiful. Impossible to predict. Yet so much the same sometimes it was hard to recognize where you were. A paradox.

And all the while he thought this, he was looking at
someone who was as hard to decipher, as fine to behold.

Liddy closed her eyes and leaned her head back, her face
toward the sun. "A high-scoring day," she said.

"High-scoring?"

She peeked at him from under her eyelashes, a kind of
squint. "An archer's idea of a fine day: sunny, with little or
no wind. Every arrow you shoot goes directly where you
send it. No excuses. But no trouble, either."

Then she spun again, a slender little top. He could see her
shoes with a glimpse now and then of an inch of shins, an
inch of calves, the finger of distance between her ankle
boots and the edge of her drawers. He could see where her
one ankle boot was laced wide over his wrapping. It felt
good to think her ankle was better because of it—and it had
to be, because she was all but doing a jig on it.

When she and her skirts settled, he discovered her face
beaming at him.

"The heather is lovely, isn't it?"

"Mm," he said, meaning yes.

"The Picts brewed mead from the flowers."

"The honeybees like it."

"Hill shepherds and deer stalkers laid it on the ground, flowers up, and made it into springy beds."

"No kidding."

"No kidding," she repeated his Americanism. She looked about them. "Such flowering abundance right around the corner from yesterday's mud and slime." She giggled. "Why, it's as pretty as a pie supper."

He laughed, too. "*Purdy*. If you wanna say it right, you gotta get the accent." He made fun of himself. "Purdy as a pah supper."

"Purdy as a pah supper," she said and laughed again. He enjoyed hearing her British voice try it out. "A good expression," she said. "How like you it is."

"*You* brought it up."

"Yes. All right. How like us."

Us. How like us.

They ate breakfast, buried their fire, but were slow getting going. Liddy was distracted by the beauty of the place; he was distracted by the beauty of Liddy. It seemed to take forever to simply pick up their things, pack the satchel, find their near-empty bottle of gin. Sam had done a fine job of swilling most of it last night; he could only pray they got off the moor today, because there wasn't enough left in the bottle to render him unconscious again. The sun was getting high in the sky, yet he and Liddy hadn't started for the day—they stood at the edge of the heather, arguing over whether to head south or go back and follow the small stream that ran into the bog, looking for a river and perhaps people in that direction, since their efforts so far at finding the road had proved pretty worthless.

That's when they heard the sound.

Liddy jumped, grabbed his arm, and squeezed, alarmed, a woman suddenly frightened. "Listen," she said.

She needn't have. It came again: a long, blasting whistle.

Sam grew stock-still, alert, trying to decide if his ears were playing tricks.

Very faintly in the far distance, it repeated: the distinct tones of what sure as the dickens sounded like a train toot-tooting along.

He dropped the bottle and satchel, emptying his arms, preparing for flight. He listened again, locating the direction of the sound, then took off at a dead run.

He tore down the slight rise, through one edge of the heather, half-slid his way through some muck, then raced up another ascent that became rock, a slope that was higher still. From the top, he could see it—though he didn't slow down: He ran faster, as fast as his legs could take him. Toward a train that was pretty far off, but, sure as shooting, there was a shiny engine, flashing with sunlight, leading a long, distantly rackety procession of cars. The whole thing, as he pounded his way toward it, looked almost magical, no tracks visible. It ran at the far edge of heather, ever so faintly clattering in rhythm.

It whistled again, the sound brighter. Oh, to make it before it disappeared. Sam pushed himself. *Run faster, harder. Catch it.* He matched his breath to the pounding of his feet, pumped his arms, stretched his stride, used everything he knew to beat a path that would intercept the chuffing line of cars.

Lydia followed Sam, though she was unable to keep up. She knew, though, with a sinking heart it was true: They hadn't found civilization, but it had found them.

Such confusion she felt as, skirts raised, she ran after Sam. Feelings . . . so many unsavory feelings rushed . . . she tried to push them away. No, she wasn't supposed to feel this sense of horror. Not the quick, plummeting anger, the deprivation. She should feel . . . relief. They would flag the train down. She would climb aboard. She might even know someone on it—almost surely she would. And Sam . . . Sam would—

What? Where would Sam go?

One thing was for certain. She wouldn't kiss his mouth again. She wouldn't get to lie beside him again or have rabbit cooked on an open fire.

She trailed after him, on his path yet farther and farther behind, with her shoes patting the stony earth, her wrapped ankle throbbing, hurting, her chest aching, her heart beating into her throat till she thought she'd be sick, all the while fighting an awful prescience: that in back of her, their cold, buried fire, their field of heather, the bog and fog and rivulet and stones and mud . . . all *that* was real, and she was leaving it behind—as she climbed the final rise and viewed the train: her old world. It looked like some sort of child's miniature. A Christmas toy set. The stupid train was dwarfed by all the purple, its smoke stack spewing pitiful little clouds against a wide blue sky.

She couldn't help thinking, *that*, the stupid train, was the mirage, the fantasy. The moor was real. It was alive. She was alive on it.

She stopped, catching her breath on the rocky summit. Looking down at Sam chasing the train, Lydia felt as if she were witnessing the end of the world. Loss. Below, he ran for all he was worth—and he was worth so much. Could that man ever run! He cut across the field at an angle, coming out of the heather at just the right point. The train was no more than halfway past. He waved. He jumped. He did everything but throw himself at the moving train. She could see him calling. She watched him run alongside the rattling cars, all but keeping up with them for a full minute, and her windpipe tightened, choking in her chest.

She only began to cry when she witnessed their small, almost pathetic, respite. Below, Sam's long legs covered great strides of land beside the steaming train, his fists, his bent arms swinging. Yet he lost ground. And the train, whoever controlled it, didn't so much as pause. No one saw him. The last cars transported goods, no windows, no one.

It was passing them by.

She went more slowly down into the far side of the heather,

wiping at her face as she made her way purposefully, without rush. When she caught up, Sam couldn't talk and breathe both. He was bent over by the empty tracks, his palms on his knees as he huffed and gasped. In trying to catch his breath, his body had to get past spasms to find enough oxygen. She had to wait till he could say anything.

When he did, all he could pant out was the obvious. "I— haa—I—haa—miss'd—haa—th'm."

"Trains run on schedules," she told him. "It will be back. Or even another one may come along today."

He nodded, his chest heaving, his lungs sucking air noisily. "We—we should—haah"—he panted—"should— haah—put something out"—more puffing—"a signal to get—*whoo*"—inhaled air—"their attention."

It was true. No one was likely to expect to see two people trying to flag down a train as it clacked across a vacant moor.

Then another discovery. Agreeing with him in a nod, Lydia turned, and there to the side, paralleling the tracks that stretched back, was a narrow river that wound beyond the heather.

"Are you all right?" she asked.

Sam nodded.

That was enough. Because she *wasn't* all right. But she thought she might be able to make herself so.

Without looking again at him, Lydia started for the river, at first walking briskly, then at a trot. Her running after him and the train had set off a mild attack of asthma, but now, as her feet jogged gently toward the sparkling water, she felt the tightness in her chest loosen on its own.

In the distance, the surface of the running river caught the sun, its light sparkling and shifting with the current. It drew her, while she felt her sense of absolute authority over herself return, larger, better—stronger, louder for having been drowned out by a stupid train whistle. No, she thought. No, she was never giving up this feeling again. Her old world could shriek all it wished; she wouldn't answer.

She ran. Now or never, she thought. It was now or never.

Now. It was now. *I want him.* There was no one here but

her and Sam. So why should she listen to the disapproval of people who weren't even here? They were just voices in her head. Quiet! This was private. Here. Now. It was just between them. Her and Sam.

Sam. *My heart's desire.*

The river wasn't wide or impressive in size, though—as Lydia rounded the heathered rise of land that hid it—its beauty and isolation made it a far more affecting sight than she was prepared for. The flowing water, limpid and flashing, unraveled into view like a burbling ribbon. At a far bend, where the land rose, it became a cascade of water—the river coming down the land in a series of short waterfalls, the current rushing, dropping a foot, running a short distance, dropping two feet, running another short ways, then plunging down over a granite wall into a spray that hit a wide spread of rocks.

She didn't see until she was right on top of it that, from there, the river flowed downward in sheets over terraces of the rocks, dropping over the last level smoothly to flow out into a small, peaceful, granite-banked pool before it became a river again.

Amazed, she bent, squatting into her skirts at the pool's edge. As she watched, a sleek brown animal dove beneath the water. She could see the creature in perfect detail as it swam away, its little eyes and snout and whiskers, its glossy coat, its paws tucked back: an otter. The water was that clear. It was deep and, like the river, sparkling. At the pool's far end, its rocky sides narrowed. There, the water flowed into the ribbon of river that had drawn her. At the near end, though, the sun shown through the spray of the falls, droplets glittering in the sunlight like tiny, airborne diamonds bouncing off the rocks.

Perfect. Lydia knew precisely what her business was here and got about it: She stood, slipping off her short jacket, then began at the buttons of her blouse. *Naked.* She couldn't quite do it in the end. She only stripped down as far as her white, cap-sleeve chemise and knickers, ribboned at the knees, standing in her bare feet. She had meant to take off her undergarments, too, but the water looked . . . too cold. . . . Or, no, her own shyness intruded, but never mind: She was brave enough. Without hesitation, she leaped out into the air over the pool and plunged in.

The water that swallowed her was icy, so cool it was barely tolerable at first. From beneath it, she let out a squeal of bubbles from the temperature. They rushed to the surface ahead of her as her face, along with another bubbling shriek, bobbed up, bursting into air again. She screamed a third time, of pleasure, enjoying the echo in the slight cavern of the low rocky pool. The sound, the crystal beauty, even the sharp coolness that was such a contrast to the warm sun on her face, felt rich to experience.

She turned in the water, treading as she looked up along the rim, her horizon, watching the thin line of ground she could see over the granite edge of the pool wall. She looked for Sam. He would come. He would follow. Her certainty of it made her heart beat like a bass drum in her chest. She could hear the glad rhythm in her ears as she rolled in the water, swimming one moment, floating to her back the next, checking the perimeters. He would appear. Yes, he would. There was nowhere else for him to go but here.

And when he arrived, she would seduce him. *You are being seduced.*

The idea made her feel positively godlike. Such a feeling. Realizing that she might, on her own, take for her own sake and pleasure a huge scoop of happiness was as surprising and uplifting as suddenly discovering that, with a leap into the air, she could fly.

Or dive down and swim. The cold water, as she glided down toward the bottom, was dark. It made her chest tight, but her asthma remained at bay. Another miracle of the moor. Why it wasn't more of a problem out here, she couldn't imagine. Years ago, when she'd been miraculously

free of it one summer, her brother had taught her to swim.
She still swam well enough despite a lack of practice. Physical. She liked the feeling of moving her body, of control-
ling it through the water. She might have been a tomboy
under different circumstances, she thought—with a health-
ier childhood, with a family who hadn't discouraged her
swimming and running and riding (though happily they approved of the archery). She felt sleek now, a little otter herself.

She swam, coming up periodically to draw in deep
breaths of sunny air. It entered her lungs and felt wondrous.
Like breathing liberty—license—shedding an old, outdated
restraint. I am an adult, she thought. This is what it's like to
feel adult, in charge of my own destiny. She came to the
rocks of the lowest waterfall, the last little rush over stony
surfaces, the river sheeting over them. Pushing on one rock,
she rolled—

That was when she saw him. Sam stood overhead on the
far bank, his knees slightly bent, tense, his body poised:
strong, sun-bright, energetic and handsome. She had just
enough time to notice his coat and vest were off—and,
oddly, his shirt hung open, his chest bare—before the tension in him found release. He sprang up, his body arching
out over the water. Arms extended he headed downward,
cutting into the water as cleanly as a knife. Lydia wanted to
applaud, he did it so beautifully.

Oh, yes. Pure excitement took hold as she watched his
head bob up: Closer, yards closer, he swam toward her. Yes,
oh, yes, oh, yes, oh, yes. Joy. What joy! What an amazing
feeling was happening to her out here on the moor, a kind of
celebration in living she hadn't known since she was a child.
As if she suddenly possessed her own life—fully in each
moment—her life consisting entirely of her own decisions,
inventions, and choices.

And there was an especially fine choice coming at her,
his stroke powerful and gliding, his wake as smooth as the
ripple of a swan.

I am allowed this, she assured herself. I get to have my own particular brand of happiness. Even though others might not understand my wanting a man who . . . a man who drove cows in America.

That was possibly even part of Sam's attraction. He existed comfortably at an elemental level, a man who could live outdoors for months at a time. He moved easily now through the water. Of course. She'd expected it, yet there was the gladdening sight: an athletic coordination, pure physical grace, as much as any human being might possess. She watched the slicing movement of his arms as they stroked strongly through the water. One reaching pull—he did an even stroke, his eyes never leaving hers—propelled him a dozen gliding feet closer, while his effort beneath the water didn't so much as disturb the surface.

She smiled as he swam toward her in his clothes, then began to laugh, both of them smiling broader, because they realized together: He'd dived in, clothes and all, because he'd thought she was in trouble. Unable to say why she was in the water, perhaps having heard her shrill outbursts when she'd first jumped in, Sam, the relentlessly heroic, had come in after her: out to save her again.

In the next moment, though, their laughter quieted. Yet he continued to swim toward her: neither of them mistaking that what was on his mind had anything to do with saving her. Unless it was to save her from climbing aboard the next train a virgin.

Lydia wedged herself into a nook formed by the last stony tier of falls, where two flat rocks came together behind her. There, she lifted herself up on her elbows, enough that her breasts broke the surface; water flowed round her elbows. She closed her eyes and leaned till the back of her head touched stone behind her, water pouring into her hair, making it flow like liquid onto the stones, over her shoulders. In front, she could feel the wet lawn of her chemise sticking to her breasts, feel the sunny air on them, on her cold, contracted nipples just above the water line. She arched as through half-closed eyes she watched Sam approach. An indiscreet, delicious game.

He drew nearer, and she could see the water beaded on his cheeks. The sky, reflected, made the water a bright, saturated bluebird azure, but the color was nothing compared to his eyes. They held hers like a mesmerist's. She couldn't look away from their dark, preternatural blue, so deep in hue, vivid against the line of his black lashes—he drew close enough that she could see water beaded in them, too. Such beautiful eyes. The most beautiful eyes she had ever seen on a man. Beautiful even against a puffy cheekbone, a nose a centimeter crooked, yellow at the bridge, black and blue at the socket.

Sam stopped in front of her, treading water simply to stare, taking her in where she balanced on her arms, chest out, in her small cove of rocks. Then he reached around her, taking hold of the rock at either side of her, and lifted himself up to rest his forearms outside hers, so that they both held their weight up on the same wet rocks. The stones were warm, then cool for a second in a thin wash of water. It flowed around her elbows and into the strait between their arms. She could feel the current gently pushing her toward him, sense his resistence to it as he held himself steady.

She was sure of what was going to happen. It was in his eyes, on his face—on her own, too, she didn't doubt as she looked up at him.

Before his mouth touched hers, the heat of his long, heavy body came over her like a shadow. His open shirt flapped loosely against her rib cage like sea grass. All these small anticipations, then the full presence of him as he pressed forward, trapping her against the rocks behind her with the muscular sturdiness of him, so solid, so contoured. Like the rocks themselves.

Oh, the sensation of Sam was lush. His bare chest was cold, though within moments his skin felt warm against her goose-fleshed breasts; hard muscles against her yielding breasts, flattening, rounding them upward on her rib cage.

He tilted his head, brushed his lips across hers, then he lifted himself higher on his arms—water running off him noisily—to bear forward and down on her from above her. He leaned his head to her, bringing the contrast of his cold lips against hers as he invaded this time with the furnacelike heat of the inside of his mouth, his tongue.

She heard him groan, felt him slide his body down hers, hard, rubbing as he pushed his tongue deeply into her mouth and pressed her back against the rock till the best way to breathe was to take the oxygen from his breath, inhale through his open mouth.

His kiss rolled down into her, from their mouths into her breasts, sinking down, low, low, into her body beneath the water, till she felt like a melting oven inside her own cold skin. She let him spread her legs with his knees. Then, by simply allowing her feet to float up, she had them around his hips. Where this instinct came from was a mystery. Lydia only knew she wanted him tightly between her legs with all the strength of her will. She dug her heels into the flexed muscles of his backside. Hard-muscled, his buttocks. She hugged him tightly like this, arms and legs and mouth and tongue.

Oh, the heat of him. Better, so much better than she had anticipated. And, best, as Sam kissed her—his weighty kiss that sank through her—the sensation pushed its way down till it lived between her legs, alive, hot, shivery, trembling.

Her body stirred against him, a yearning that roiled in her belly, the feeling between her legs becoming animate in a riveting, hypnotic way that left her in thrall to what she suddenly knew of him: to the robust feel of a growing *erection*. *Erection*. She thought the word, and it made her turn her head so she could push her open mouth harder down over his tongue; she wanted to swallow him.

Penis. His penis was hard and thick and unapologetic where it pressed along her sex—she felt herself open, unfolded somehow, her warmest place cooled by the water, heated by the friction of him as he rode against her. Cold water or not, his penis felt feverish. So did she. Inside, she felt molten. *Inside.* He rubbed himself up then slowly down through their clothes beneath the water. A little pocket of heat between them, their contact shockingly hot. It made her head dizzy, it made her limbs weak.

After perhaps two minutes of this blissful torment, kissing and kissing and rubbing against each other, he suddenly pulled back, pushing himself the full distance away of his arms.

He looked down into her face, panting, frowning, Serious Sam. His expression, as it could, carried the weight of the world. "Ah, Jesus," he muttered. His breathing was raspy, his voice hoarse. So delicious, the deep, masculine sound of him. So Sam. He closed his eyes and said in a husky whisper, "Liddy, if you are really English nobility, this will ruin you."

She laughed. "No, it won't. I'm not going to tell anyone."

He rolled his eyes, not joking, put out with her—now of all times. He actually moved away.

She couldn't believe it. "Sam!" She reached for him, letting herself fall into the water.

"You don't understand," he said. "You can't." He took a breath, as if to dive.

Lydia grabbed at him, catching him by the hair. They were both suddenly free-floating, treading water, clinging, wrestling in conversation. "I know what I'm doing," she protested. "I want you. I deserve this!"

"Ha," he said. He shook her off then faced her, his wet-haired head above the water. "The world doesn't owe you anything, Liddy Brown, and you better understand that." He took a breath, then groaned. "God, I want to make love to you like you can't believe." Another breath. "But there could be hell to pay, Miss Viscount's Daughter—"

She cut him off with an impatient breath. "Stop," she said. "I'm not a child." She inhaled gustily, then told him, "My suitors want my money and position, so let them have my money and—"

"No," he said. "The man who marries you will want this, too, I promise you."

"Well, I'm not asking *you* to marry me, Mr. Cody, if that's what you're worried about."

"Good thing," he said quickly. Then he blinked, frowned, glanced to the horizon. There was a funny moment before he met her eyes again and said, "Right."

Why was it a good thing? Sam wondered. Because somewhere these words—*I'm not asking you to marry me*—made him feel awful. When he should have felt excused, spared: Marrying her or anyone was the farthest thing from his mind at the moment. So why be wounded that she'd let him off?

He turned in the water, letting her paddle around him as he treaded—not unhappy to frustrate her: doing it on purpose.

Or maybe just watching. Her hair floated about her shoulders; it spread everywhere, like a living creature near the surface. Liddy, waterborne, was beautiful, eerie. Her breasts floated, her wet chemise clinging to them. High and round, they periodically broke the surface in little mounds, two perfect, gently bobbing, alabaster islands above the neckline of her chemise. In contrast, through thin, wavering fabric just beneath the water, he could see her dusky brown nipples. They wobbled in loose movement with her breasts—a brunette's nipples, a dark, ruby umber.

Have her. She wants you to. He puzzled them both, though, by swimming backward away from what he wanted, while the complexion of her face—in consternation—reddened. He was assailed by all the variations, the delicate colors of her skin, the textures. Her wet lashes flapped, so long and thick they brushed the tops of her cheekbones. Like butterfly wings, he thought, wet ones that spiked, clinging for a moment to her pinked cheeks. Everything about her . . . breasts, eyelashes, shoulders, hair . . . her hips, the heat of her sex he'd felt against him as he kissed her . . . everything about her arrested him. Liddy was so attractive to him from so many directions, he hardly knew himself near her. He could understand neither the strength of his attraction to her, nor the strength of his reservations.

The woman, in her innocence, continued, "My body is mine"—though it seemed his for perusal at the very least—"and I want to give it to you: to me, actually. I want to spend it as I like. On a lark if I so choose—"

Sam laughed, because it suddenly struck him. "That's it?" he asked. "I'm a—" He laughed again, because it seemed so preposterous. "A fling?" My God, he was a—that's right, the cowboy, a yokel to her who didn't count. Whom her ladyship here wanted to sleep with on the sly: for the sake of his body and the sake, possibly, of his two-bit cowtown Southern mouth. He'd never dreamed. Women always saw his money and position as part and parcel of him, or so he imagined. He didn't know whether to be insulted or flattered.

Both. Flattered she wanted him so obviously, so simply and without restraint. Insulted that she thought she could toss him over afterward, that he wasn't worth more.

Her desire confounded him, elated him, addled him. Have at it, he told himself. It wasn't every day a man got a chance at a woman as fine as Liddy Brown, with no strings attached. Perfect.

Yet it wasn't. An unaccountable anger rose up in him that was so fierce he didn't want to face it.

"You aren't being noble, Sam Cody," she told him.

He was. Yes, he was! He was thinking of her, too, damn it.

"You are being difficult," she said.

"I'm not." Except he knew he was difficult, because everyone told him so. It was just that he hated it, hated himself for it, wanted to be otherwise—

Sam dropped under the water. Liddy grabbed at him again, though he avoided her easily. Enough, he thought. He let the cold pool swallow him up, sinking down, down. The water was clear though relatively lightless just a few feet under.

"Sam!" he could hear far above in a muffle. "Sam!"

He ignored her, adjusting himself through his trousers in the liquid dark. His testicles were shrunk against his body from the frigid water, though they were active as the blazes and his gosh-darn peter was as hard as the granite walls around them. God love him, even this irritated him. He didn't want to feel arousal.

He launched his body forward, stretching out in the fluid dark. He gave a kick and glided toward the pool's edge. He swam, a single breath, then finally rose toward the light, toward the sparkle of the surface.

Lydia couldn't see Sam at all for a full minute, then saw his shiny head pop up, sending out ripples that ringed outward from his shoulders. He shook his head, slinging water, and headed toward the shoreline, where tall shrubs overhung the river.

Who could imagine that Sam could take his wayward, contrary self to such extremes? To kiss her like that, then leave her? No. Oh, no, she thought, as her eyes met the sight of his rising up out of the river, water streaming off him as he pulled himself up onto the rocks, his trousers and shirt stuck to his body. Oh, no, Lydia told herself again. Now was no time to become *ornery*, as he called it: difficult, she thought again. No, she thought. No!

She swam after him. He had just turned around, just raised his head from wiping his face with his hands, as she climbed up onto the rocks, then walked out of the river herself. In nothing but her soaking wet underclothes—thin cotton and lace and narrow little ribbons. She knew what she looked like. *Naked*, she thought again and felt triumphant. She was fully naked to him. Better than naked: almost naked. He stared. He gawked.

"Ha-a, God," he muttered. "Jesus. Liddy." He took a step back. "Lid—" he said again and broke off. She walked toward him. His face grew grave, his eyes narrowing, his expression openly angry. "I won't stop this time," he said. "I won't."

"Good. Don't. Show me." She danced her bare feet a few steps, letting her hips roll from side to side as she moved. She danced toward him, saying, "I'm dancing naked. I'm making it as hard as I can on you."

"Oh, you're making everything plenty hard." He let out a breathy laugh. "Jesus God, Liddy—"

Power. Oh, the power she had. It made her giddy. It made her sad: because it was her discovery, her triumph, but it was also the problem. Sam was afraid of her power over him. She was half-afraid of it herself, so she didn't blame him.

He stepped back. She pleaded her case. "Don't make me marry for society, for other people, *and* make love for other people, too. Let me make love one time for myself: for my heart's desire, remember?"

His face. The unblinking way his narrow eyes squinted at her, not trusting, yet waiting somewhere, watching, alert. He said, "I—I'm not for you. You've made it clear, Liddy. I— I'm not g—" He choked the word back a moment then let it out: "good enough."

She said with all the conviction she felt, so strong, as she came within arm's length of him, "You are right now. At this moment. You are everything I dream of in a man." A shiver ran through her—for the coolness of being wet, for trepidation of her own daring, and for the sheer vigor, the incredibly gorgeous vigor she felt throbbing in herself: the female potency to make tall, handsome Sam wet his lips, blink, eye her unavoidably up then down—and, angry or not, rise solidly to the occasion, so to speak. His wet trousers tented boldly.

She could see the outline of him—it took her aback a moment. His penis was long and thick. It stood out from his abdomen, an aggressively elegant part of him, straight as a rod and rounded like the end of a torpedo, but with the outline of a ridge, a head. She stared. He stepped spraddle-legged, shameless, to face her directly. Oh, yes. She wanted to touch him, see him, feel the heat of him again. Such intimacy. She wanted it. Though the logistics baffled her. She couldn't think how anything that size could fit inside her, yet she wanted just that. *Inside you.*

Mad, she thought. She must be mad to express these thoughts, even to herself. Yet she felt brave, willing to admit at least in silent conversation exactly what she wanted, what would be her chosen blessing if she were allowed to exert her will.

He murmured, sounding more bewildered than appreciative, "Jesus God, you are so beautiful."

In that moment, his saying so made her so; it made her
laugh. She couldn't help it. She felt such delight for the un-
equivocal earnestness in his voice, his eyes, no matter how
confused he was by his own response: His admiration as a
man, her chosen lover, was full and present, rich. A gift beyond measure.

The rest came quickly. Sam, muttering a stream of the
most colorful curses she'd ever heard, stepped suddenly to
her and pulled her up against him so strongly he yanked her
off her feet. He dropped them both to the ground—it took
her breath, as stomach-lifting and wonderful as a Ferris
wheel box plummeting with gravity. He landed on one knee
himself and broke her fall by catching her hips, then let them
both tumble. From here, in a kind of fit of purposefulness, he
moved them up a yard into a bed of ground cover, tiny soft
leaves with little white flowers, lightly fragrant, sunny-warm
and damp. There, he pushed her onto her back and brought
his weight onto her.

He let loose in a way that spoke oceans for his former restraint. He cupped her breast, rubbing his thumb across the
nipple, then bending his head, licking through the wet cotton, taking the tip of her breast into his mouth. Oh! She
arched. Oh! Her breath rushed out. A kind of cooperative
struggle ensued.

He pushed himself between her legs and pressed his hips
into hers, a rhythm, with Lydia not quite able to keep up with
her own arousal. Her stomach seemed to drop again. Blood
pounded. It was delicious; it was new and strong and unsettling. Sam kissed her full-mouthed, deep, slathering the insides of her cheeks, her teeth, her tongue, with his. His kiss
grew hard, passionate with want. Through the wet fabric of
drawers and trousers, they all but copulated. She felt light-
headed from it. It was as if she'd dropped into another pool,
a dark, hot one. Bottomless, powerful, and, she knew, if she
followed his lead, he could take her further down into it.

She simply let herself go, let him take them where he

would. She felt him push his knees against the insides of her thighs, opening her legs till she couldn't stretch them wider, at their limit. Then he brought his hand between them and touched her there through her wet drawers.

She leaped. "H-hea-vens." She jerked. Before she could catch her breath, he'd tugged at the wet drawstring. When it resisted—it had become knotted—he broke it, loosening the waist till there was nothing to stop his hand. He pulled her drawers down, sliding his hands with them down her bare belly, his cool fingers suddenly digging into the curls of hair. His fingertips registered all but icy against the heat of her . . . places. She knew the words, but they were suddenly inadequate. *Vulva. Vagina. Labia.* None of them were heady enough, shocking enough, delighted, panicky—

"A-ah h-ha-a hha!" So unexpectedly private and so perfect. She let him. . . . And couldn't catch her breath. "Ha-ah." Who could have been prepared for this? She tried to form words, though God only knew what she would have said to him, had she been able to speak. Stop? Thank you? This feels so wicked . . . oh, God, please, more, yes?

His fingers knew her better than she knew herself. His chilly fingertip found a small place that positively made her wild when he touched it. He teased her there, then slid his finger, so cool, down along where she was so warm, hot. She began to push against him, while he contained her.

He did the trick again, instructing her this time. "I want your legs wide, your body open to me. I want to look at you, touch you. Look," he told her.

She bent her head just in time to see him, to feel him, push his finger inside her.

Inside your body. What a feeling. To be penetrated, oh—

"Watch," he told her, and she did. She watched him withdraw his finger, spread her apart with his fingers and thumb, wide open, vulnerable to him, then push two fingers in all the way up to his knuckles.

"Ah—oh-hh-h—" Incoherent. Blind. Blaring white pleasure till her eyes ceased to see.

She could feel him move his fingers out, then in, out, then in. He bent his mouth to her ear, bringing his weight down onto her, and murmured in his deep, raspy voice, "I whaa—" He, too, was at the edge of control. He began again. "I wha-a-anted this from the first hour I stole looks at you across that coach. My f-finger—f-fingers-s—" He withdrew, then repenetrated, widening, as if filling her more . . . more fingers. . . . "My tongue, my penis inside you here"— He penetrated her deeply, and she arched against his hand, against him.

"Yes-s-s," she murmured. "Now." Whatever was building was starting to become unbearable. "Na-ha-how," she said.

He let out a faint snort and answered simply, soft and low, "No-o-o."

It was an argument he was destined to win. Because everything he did sent her higher, crazier, enraptured her more.

He lifted his weight enough to work at the buttons of her chemise. He must have been fairly dexterous, because the tiny buttons seemed to pop under his fingers, little flicks of fabric opening. He pealed her chemise off her breasts, off her shoulders, till it bound her arms lightly against her body. His bare chest brushed against her breasts, his wet shirt dragging lightly at her ribs. He bent his mouth to her cold nipple as he pushed his fingers into her again.

"Oh-my-dear-lord," a prayer, an invocation she muttered into his hair.

Lydia became unable to form any but the most inarticulate sounds, groaning, crooning as she turned her head from one side to the other. Oh, her breasts . . . open to him . . . to the heat of his mouth, to his sight and touch. He suckled one nipple as he seized the other with his fingers, squeezing. His fingertips were cold, his palm warm, his mouth as hot as Hades. His tongue and mouth pressed wetly over one breast then the other; he made the tips ache and constrict as if they could tighten like tiny fists. While he continued with his very wicked fingers lower.

He found that spot again between her legs, the place he'd touched, teased and abandoned. This time, though, when he touched her, she reached between her own legs and held his hand where she wanted it. She felt his hand move with knowing, their hands together in this intimate crook of her body. He began a rhythmic caress of the tiny place, this small part of her she wasn't very familiar with, yet he seemed to know all about. She responded strongly, her whole body quivering. He began to slide down her abdomen.

"Wha-what?" She lifted her head, unsure. No, this couldn't be right. "N-no—"

"Oh, yes," Sam murmured. He pushed away her reaching hands, her reservations.

When his hot mouth suddenly took her so intimately, she saw stars. He pressed his tongue, soft, then made it hard, the tip licking at her, and a second later, her body contracted with such strength, her muscles jerked. The pleasure of it was strong, strange, and unpredicted. Pleasure so powerful it was stronger than Lydia herself. All she could do was let it drive through her, let it have her, let it make her shudder.

A moment later, Sam was up on one arm, raising his hips. Lydia knew what was coming next. Through narrowed eyes she watched between their bodies, her mouth dry, her mind full of him. The sight, her vision was curtained by his shirt—he had no underwear, she realized. None. The front of his body was bare, from the top of his open shirt to the partly open fly his trousers—he unbuttoned it with one hand. Down the length of him was oh so handsome. Dark hair covered his broad chest, hair that narrowed to a line between his muscles, disappearing entirely to a flat, neat abdomen. No underwear. How wild, her American. The thought fled her mind in the next moment, though, when the last button of his fly gave and his naked penis swung into view—long, thick, weighty, a perfect instrument for penetration.

Lydia stared, riveted by a sight that made the backs of her eyes hot. He was gorgeous, his flesh, straight and solid, with

a raised, blue vein along the length. His penis was both delicate and powerful to look at, with a purplish head smooth as
sculpture. It was like the drawings she knew, yet not. More
colorful, more tender somehow. And larger, more steely
looking by half than what she'd understood. She couldn't
imagine how—

"Oh-h." She arched as he shifted and his erection fell onto
her belly, a firm stab at her umbilicus. Then, with a change of
angle at his hips, he dropped into the cleft of her sex, contact
that was shockingly hot—again, the surprising heat of him—
and smooth. He slid the full shaft up and down her, letting
her feel the length of him. He felt a yard long and as thick as
a log. Oh, she thought again, this could not possibly work—

She closed her eyes when she saw him reach to guide
himself with his hand. She felt the head itself slide up then
down once, along her waiting, open body. Hard. He was so
hard, yet the skin there delicate. An impossible perfection.
With it, he found her entrance, the tip of him homing. He
lowered his mouth to hers, gently bit her lip once, then covered her mouth with his and pushed his hips forward.

It was as if an impossibly small place, a tiny slit, sucked
in something the size of a plum.

"A-h-h—" he let out into her mouth.

Just the head was buried in her. So strange, the feeling. It
burned slightly. He put pressure, opening her only a bit further, then eased back a little. She didn't know why or what
he was doing, only that it burned more, yet felt somehow
right. She longed for him to do it again, do it more. "Yes,"
she murmured.

He did this small penetration several times again, each
time taking it a centimeter further, till she felt a slide, a
smooth movement. She felt him brace the second before,
then with a strong, neat thrust, he planted enough of himself
inside that she felt give, a sharper burning. She let out a startled breath, a surprised sound into his mouth: her maidenhead ruptured. Gone.

Surprise. That was her first reaction. It felt odd for a second. Filled. The burning ebbed, became faint. Filled. The satisfaction of it was so primal it was hard to absorb.

He let out soft sounds, gasps. He murmured, "There's more."

She waited for instruction, thinking that was what he meant. But his words were literal. He pushed further into her. He filled her more. Then more. He would slide out one inch, rock, then push in two.

"I ca-han't—" she fretted. He seemed huge to her. Were all men like this? Were all untried females so small?

"You're—fah-h-hine," he whispered, then murmured in a rush, "We'll go slow this first time," then on an exhalation, "You're so tah-hight—"

He began to move, balanced on one arm, reaching under her with the other to pull her hips with him, to show her the rhythm. The burning grew less; his presence inside her grew more, as he gently coaxed her body to accept him. It took patience on his part, while Lydia simply reeled. Sam inside her. Filled. The pleasure was unearthly.

She focused on the sublime sensation of Sam's moving in and out of her body. Tight, yet smooth. Who could have guessed? Oh, there was nothing like it anywhere, this feeling.

And Sam liked it too, because he was nothing short of delirious, which was perhaps most wonderful of all. As they moved together, his low-pitched voice became a mumble of syllables, endearments, sweet nonsense, while the satisfaction of having him inside her spread into a yearning to unite then reunite again and again. Something was building. She began to follow his movement, the sharp, full-throated hum of bliss—

Before she could find where they were going exactly, though, he suddenly groaned, jerked sharply, and called out, "Ah—Liddy, ah—Liddy, ai-i!"

And he was madly scrambling up and away from her, panicked in a new way she didn't understand. He pushed up onto his knees, withdrawing himself, as his body jerked and trembled. His face grimaced, and a shudder took him over.

Before it was finished, he was muttering profanity as she'd never heard from his mouth.

After several seconds of his flinching, he let out a long breath, then dropped to the ground away from her, at her side, flat out onto his back. He threw his arm over his eyes, a man distraught.

Lydia was left bewildered, half-fulfilled, up in the air. She asked tentatively, "Did I do something wrong?"

He lifted his arm, turning his head to look at her, and gasped out a laugh. "God, no." He let out another single, dry syllable, more irony than humor. He pushed his hand back into his hair, holding chunks between his fingers, and said, "It's just that—well, that has to be the worst possible way to keep a woman from getting pregnant."

"Oh." She nodded, trying to understand; she didn't precisely. She looked at herself. There was a wet smear of blood on her thigh. And something more. Full realization dawned. "Oh," she said again, more knowingly. "You withdrew before—um—" She nodded. "Right."

He laughed and answered, "Right." Then added, "In-doggone-deed."

She smiled and rolled to her side, curling against him.

They created their own language. While she created herself. It was lovely to have a friend like Sam. He knew her. What a simple sentence, yet how affecting. In three days, he knew aspects of her that people who'd known her all her life didn't seem to notice or else understand. And she knew him, was comfortable with him, trusted him completely.

As she lay there, quite naturally his arm came around her and she thought, *Aah.* Her muscles felt relaxed. Her limbs, her body, her neck and face and scalp . . . everywhere, she felt warm, cozy. And sleepy. There was something more here, but they would find it. For now, wet and messy and deflowered to a fare-thee-well, Lydia could not remember feeling so content.

* * *

In-doggone-deed. Sam was surprised to hear himself say this. He was surprised to be lying there holding Liddy, surprised by how nice she felt against him. *In-doggone-deed.* They shared more than words. He wished he could steal pieces of her and make them part of himself—her acceptance, her humor, her self-respect. Her respect of him.

He was "difficult," and she didn't mind. Well, she maybe minded, but she wouldn't stop coming at him for it. He wished he could fix his orneriness, be more polite. Or maybe he just wanted to be more direct, less protective of his shortcomings.

Sam watched Liddy close her eyes, her long eyelashes flapping to lie lacily—curling, copious—against the tops of her cheekbones. He kissed her eyelids gently, one then the other. He kissed her lips, a brush of mouths. Then he lay his head on her breast and let his own eyes close. A whangdoodle, this one, he told himself again as he drifted off. Liddy Brown took his breath away.

Later, as they attempted to gather their clothes up to get dressed again, Lydia told Sam, "Two lost souls." They were. They could barely dress for wanting to touch.

Lost indeed, she thought. In a fog of each other. On a stretch of land where it was difficult to know landmarks. Without a map. Rather like her life itself. Perhaps his, too, given his willingness to run the other direction from what his job and family expected of him. They were both in the process of trying to redraw the plans the world had handed them.

But redraw them how? Where? And could their plans include each other?

Did she want hers to include him?

She laughed at herself. Oh, if her parents were upset by her friendship with Rose, they should be fit to be tied by her desire to mold herself up against an American cow herder. But her desire was as clear as the tolling of a bell—and *she* was the bell. Something inside her kept striking, reverberating through her, hitting again and again, a ceaseless, ringing pulse. *Press your body to his. Feel his warmth, his solidness, the contours of him against you, kiss his mouth. . . .*

And she did. By the pool, they dressed, undressed, made love, dozed, attempted to dress again, and made love once more, all before twilight. Sam did his withdrawal each time. He became quite suave with it, in fact, though in his proficiency he groaned after the third time, saying, "I hate that part. I would give anything to let go inside you. Anything."

Sam seemed happy enough though, she thought. In the dimness of the setting sun, he took her hand and ran her down to the train tracks again. He showed her the reason he was missing his coat and vest, the reason he'd raced after her screaming with his shirt open on his bare chest, no combination. Apparently for underwear he wore something called a union suit—and it was red!

What he'd done was take off his red underclothes to use as a signal, the only thing he knew that was bright enough to stand out. He'd tied them to the end of her bow—while she was running and swimming and waiting for him, he'd been burying her bow (to her horror) in a pile of stones he'd built up around it. His underwear now flew from the top: a flag for the train tomorrow. So it couldn't pass them by again.

Sam would rescue them. He was determined.

Lydia laughed and laughed at his invention, so delighted by the effort—though she was secretly a little unsettled by it too. Yes, they had to be sure the train didn't pass them by again. Yes, they had to get off this blasted, beautiful moor. Yes, she had to get back to her own, her family. She and Sam—

She and Sam, what? His flying red underwear looked so alien to her. She knew only of her brother's or father's undergarments, and of those only vaguely from seeing the laundress trot them up the stairs in a stack to put them away: They were white. She couldn't imagine a man of her acquaintance wearing anything under his clothes that was . . . red.

She stared at the banner waving from the tip of her bow,

wondering what she was seeing incorrectly, what she wasn't grasping. Sam was the most interesting, attractive man she knew. What he'd done was smart. The train would be traveling fast and wouldn't be expecting to see them. It would see *that* at a distance.

So why did she want to hide every time she caught a glimpse of the red, flapping union suit wedged into her bowstring at the tip of her bow?

11

There are three groups of folks in the city of Houston
who have no legal rights, where someone else has to
sign for them like children: born idiots, the insane of
the asylums, and the entire female population.

SAMUEL JEREMIAH CODY
A Texan in Massachusetts

The evening was better than the afternoon, which was saying a great deal, since the afternoon was so splendid that Lydia never wanted it to end. Sam held her hand. He petted her.
He led; she followed. She led; he chased. Like children let
out to play, they dallied till it was pitch dark.

Once the sun set, their conversation turned to "the sensible thing to do."

Sam suggested, "We could walk along the train track,
even tonight if we wanted to." His voice, his breath, tickled
her ear.

She was scooted back against him, his bare chest against
her bare back as she sat between his legs, his arms around
her. They were half dressed, clothes on but open—oh, so delicious—his shirttail out, his trouser braces down, her dress
away from her neck so he could periodically brush his
mouth against the crook or her collarbone or the tendon up
the back of her nape. She could feel him, hear him, periodi-

cally pushing his nose, smelling, into her hair. Heaven. A little cozy warmth on a cool, moon-bright night, skin against skin.

"We don't really have to wait for the train tomorrow," he continued, being oh so sensible.

"We have a sure direction now," she agreed.

"Even in fog, even in dark, we could follow the train tracks."

"We'd get somewhere."

He sighed. Then he added, "Though I'm tired. How 'bout you?"

"Oh, yes." Lydia laughed. "What a strenuous day," she said. "Running down a train, swimming, a few friendly skirmishes, then having to make love all afternoon. Why, it was exhausting." She laughed again. "I think we should wait till morning. Then we'll set off straightaway."

She felt him nod, his cheek against the side of her hair. He whispered, "Or we could not set off at all. We could wait right here. I mean, the best we could do in the morning would be to get ourselves an hour or two closer. Plus I have the signal up. They won't miss us again."

What a good idea. She nodded. "All right. If that's what you want." How accommodating she felt. "We can stay here and wait for the next train." Whenever that might be.

"It'll come tomorrow, but till then we could have ourselves a—"

"A holiday," she supplied. She turned in his arms to look at him behind her.

The setting sun shadowed the features of his face. Smiling shadows. "Right," he said. "We'll take the day—"

"A day off—"

"Where we don't worry, where we don't do anything—"

"Except for ourselves."

Less a holiday than a honeymoon, she thought, but Lydia was so much in favor of the notion she twisted more to wedge herself into the crook of his shoulder and take his face tenderly into her hands. She pulled him down to kiss him again.

Sam. Hers, all night and all the next morning. At the very least. She would do her duty when she got back to London. She would dress and be courted and marry for the right reasons. But for now, oh, for now . . . why, trains probably didn't even run on the moor every day. There was no telling how often they ran. Why, perhaps not even once a week.

Sam and she built another smoky fire, again on the far side of the rise. Without discussing it, they knew they wanted the privacy of not being immediately visible from the tracks— which also explained how very ingenious Sam's flying red underwear was: On the off chance a train should come at a moment when they weren't in a precisely . . . ready condition, the red signal would stand in for them till they could get their clothes into place and present themselves.

They spent a lovely, comfy night secluded from view at the edge of the heather. In the heather, in fact—they cut pieces, like shepherds of old, and made a bed of it, a springy bower. Sleep, of course, was not the primary goal. When they weren't making love, they were whispering like two children in the night, like fond friends who explored their new bonds of attachment and regard.

Confidants. Lydia felt she could tell Sam anything. Things she couldn't even say to Rose or Meredith or Clive. No matter what she told or asked Sam, she had this sense of trust— he would listen and understand. And he confided back. Their secrets overlapped with physical pleasures, sexual longings. *Touch me here. I want to put myself there. Like this? Yes. What would you think if I wanted to do this? Oh. My. All right.* Till their physical intimacy seemed to give voice, enactment, to what was happening to them emotionally.

An aphorism Sam never put in his book: If women ever realized how good it felt to have small, soft fingers brush across the head of a man's penis, they would rule the world. Partly, he would never write the insight down because he thought of it as a secret that must be kept at all costs. Though, in fact, deep down, he suspected women *did* know, they *did* rule the world, and that was *their* secret—that somehow the power left to men was nothing, with women either too polite or too conniving to mention it.

He and Liddy ate a dinner of fish from the river, then made love off and on the rest of the evening and into the night—in ways that, for even Sam, who was relatively experienced, went beyond what was . . . he hated to use the word *normal*, but it was certainly beyond, and much, much better, than was normal for him.

Yes, Liddy had amazingly soft fingers. But never mind her fingers, Liddy thought to put her mouth on him, and the decision, her execution of it, leveled him. Literally. He ended up flat on his back from shock and pure slavelike rapture.

"Holy Moses, Lid," he said once he'd caught his breath from the whole ordeal, "what on this sweet earth made you do that?"

She looked surprised. "You did it to me, and I liked it." She frowned, squinting up into his face, as if looking for hints of a more complicated answer to his question. "Why?"

"I thought, when I did it, it scared you."

"It did." She smiled. "I liked that part too." She shrugged. "I rather like it when you scare me, in that way at least." She laughed at herself.

"Yes." He laughed, too. "And I like plenty the whole idea of you scaring me, I guess." He laughed harder. "Great plenty. A whole wagonload."

Ah, the joys of a woman's ignorance. Liddy had no idea that some people found such contact—mouths and private places—crude. Did he? Absolutely, he thought, smiling to himself. And that was part of the pleasure, he was sure. For pure contrariness, cantankerousness. The secret forbidden.

It seemed so un-English that Liddy would admit to liking his mouth on her. Though, come to think of it, it was very Liddy, both the directness and the sensuality of it. Liddy was apparently a whole lot more than just English.

Cripes, he thought. What if other English people were like that? What if they were all different, despite their seeming outer—and pretty snooty—similarities?

* * *

They made love. They played. At one point, as the fire was dying down, Liddy reached into Sam's inside coat pocket, a coat he had on at the moment. He'd just buttoned his shirt and vest, putting most of his clothes in order again. She rousted his coat pockets, then vest, feeling for contents, checking flaps inside and out. It was an unholy game she seemed to invent on the spur of the moment. Titillating. Inquisitive. Prying. Flattering.

"Don't go through my pockets," he complained, though he let her. He liked her hands on him. He liked that she was curious about him.

"Turnabout is fair play: You went through my bag."

He blinked, unable to think of any defense as Liddy lifted his arms. She frisked him thoroughly.

She located his flask from his inside left pocket, opened it, sniffed it, then whistled down into its emptiness.

"Do you drink a lot?" she asked.

"No. Though you'd never guess from the last couple days." He rolled his eyes. "You'll just have to trust me."

She brought forth his money clip with eight dollars and ten pounds sterling in it, a broken pocket watch—the bandits had stopped it cold at nine twenty-four in the morning three days ago—and his papers, including his passport.

She opened the passport with glee. " 'Samuel Jeremiah Cody,' " she quoted. " 'Six-foot-three. Two hundred twenty pounds. Fourteen-ten State Street, Chicago—' "

He took the passport, hoping she didn't notice how much he suddenly wanted it out of her sight. It was not the usual American passport, though she didn't seem to notice. It was a diplomatic passport. Their hands both held it for a moment. He opened his mouth, about to account for himself—though explanations were going to be a little dicey at such a late date and wouldn't likely mean much, considering they had to do with a job he'd lost that was only a temporary post anyway. Still, he realized, all the seals and embossing on the damn thing might give him a certain standing, which could come in handy, since he wanted to call on her—

Then he went from being embarrassed to being outright alarmed.

Liddy leaned forward, abandoning his watch, flask, and papers—too boring—to dip her hands into his trouser pockets, while she sat on her knees between his bent legs, her face against his chest.

He was confounded by their newfound intimacy—not that he minded, he was just flummoxed by the way she took hold of it. She liked to flex her prerogatives over him, test their limits, and darned if he knew what to do about any of it.

Then what she found in his right pocket slowed her down.

"What's this?" she asked as she pulled forth her hand, then sat against his knee. With her finger, she centered her find on her palm. She angled her hand a little, using the fire to illuminate the two little items he'd forgotten about: two wedding rings, a large and a small. Seeing them there, caught in firelight in Liddy's hand, made Sam sad and quiet.

"She threw mine at me," he explained. He wasn't certain why he'd picked it up. It had sailed at him from an upstairs window, hitting him behind the ear. For no reason, he'd stooped and retrieved it, putting it in his pocket. As if he could hide the whole business in the dark.

When he'd left his hotel on that fateful morning, three days ago now, his pocket had carried only one ring, hers, because Joseph, Gwyn's brother and his best man, didn't trust himself to remember it. Sam had carefully made sure he had it, then headed for the church.

Liddy looked surprised. "You were going to wear a ring?"

"Yeah, why?"

"It's just curious," she said. "A very un-English custom."

"Well, I'm not English, so no surprise."

"Was your bride?"

"English? No. From Chicago."

She held up the larger ring, looking through it into the fire. "It's ungentlemanly for an Englishman to wear one."

There was no criticism in her voice, only speculation. As if marveling over differing customs.

"It doesn't sound very gentlemanly to deny he's married."

"The idea is he doesn't need to be reminded: He knows."

After a minute, she asked quietly, "Do you love her?"

"Who?" he asked. Then said quickly, "Oh, Gwyn." He let out a snort, more bewildered than anything else. "I must. I keep trying to marry her." He shook his head.

It was a question that hadn't come up in awhile for him. The question that kept coming up, in fact, was: Did he love Liddy? He worried he did, which made no sense, because he sure knew Gwyn better and longer.

"What's she like?"

"Who?" he asked again, then felt himself redden. "Oh, Gwyn." He leaned back, thinking. "She's beautiful. A lot of men like her." A more distinctive feature occurred to him: "She has sad eyes. They look sad even when she laughs." It was true. It was as if Gwyn had some secret hardship to bear. "Every day brings a new woe," he said, laughing fondly, "a new crisis. She has very tender feelings. Though, of course," he said quickly—he should be defending her better—"she has happy times, too." When she got a new dress, for instance. Or received an extravagant gift.

Gwyn had a vulnerable ego that responded best to quick, strong intervention. Not that she was a bad person. She was generous with others. Usually she was . . . nice. Gwyn was possibly the nicest person he'd ever known—maybe nice to everyone *because* her own feelings were hurt so easily. She fretted endlessly over making anyone unhappy. To her credit, it had taken a lot for her to finally get angry with him—*two* botched weddings, for Pete's sake. 'Course, once she was started, she could have a real tantrum.

"What did she say?" Liddy asked. "About missing the wedding, I mean. When she threw the ring at you?"

He shrugged. "Oh . . . you know. A lot of mean things."

"Such as?"

He sighed, resisted a moment, then told her. "That I was afraid of marrying, a coward, a cad, twisted inside, that I'd never love anyone, couldn't, that I'm as crazy as my old man was." He sighed again. "All of which I worry are true."

Look at the evidence, he thought. To miss one wedding was an accident. To miss a second might be a coincidence—strange, but these things happen. But to miss the rescheduled nuptials? Hell, three times was a pattern. A dismal pattern, there was no doubt about it.

He sat there feeling real poorly about himself, staring at his knee, then happened to catch a glimpse of Liddy, the movement of her head.

She was shaking it, little, small shakes, smiling at him—it was that faint line she was so good at, a smile so subtle he had to study it in the firelight to know it was there. It was, and it contained little judgment and much acceptance. He smiled back.

And, like that, the bad feeling evaporated.

Liddy knew he had these bends and twists to him: He was as chambered and convoluted as a nautilus. And she liked him anyway. It was as if their connection—as if he could touch it somehow—had the power to make the worst of him acceptable to himself. So what if he was like his old man?

He wished he could like *himself* that way, the way she liked him.

He looked down, not sure where that sort of self-love came from: only that she had it herself.

In a lot of ways, she wasn't all that different from him. She was just as argumentative; she was contrary at times, hard to figure out. They were a pair. The big difference was, for the most part she liked Liddy Brown or whatever her real name was; she liked the person who was herself. And, to Sam, for all his thirty-six years of experience with the world, for all the people he knew, he thought the way she liked herself—the way she marched right into who she was, hardly any hesitation, at any given moment—was nothing short of a miracle.

She was something, Liddy. Us. *They* were something. Us-ness. Belonging. Close and real, known and accepted.

When he made love to her right after that, pushing himself inside her, watching her, touching her, feeling her wrap around him, squeeze him . . . he felt a kind of release between them, a relief that was so much more than sexual. Afterward, holding her as she drifted off, barely awake himself, he was aware of a calm settling over him, a peace he couldn't remember knowing since he was sixteen: when he'd first left home. When he'd been full of hope for his finding a place in the world. For fitting into it.

Birds somewhere knew the sun was rising before Lydia did. They chirped fiercely, awakening her from a groggy state. A dream. She'd been dreaming. She lay under Sam's heavy arm, remembering it—it was something pleasant.

Puddings. She laughed. Sam stirred. Noticing his eyes opening, she said, "I was dreaming of puddings! Can you imagine?"

She reached over her head, stretching, and felt his hand smooth down the inside of her arm, his palm from her wrist down to under her arm, along her ribs, into the curve of her waist, out over her hip. He slid his hand around her to cup her buttock, while he pressed his face, his warm breath, to her bosom. Oh, yes. She closed her eyes.

Smiling wistfully, she related, "I dreamed of puddings in a whole parade of fare, all carried on silver trays. A turbot of lobster with Dutch sauce. Cucumber. Meringues à la crème." A feast. "And rabbit," she added in tribute to Sam, though it hadn't been in her dream. She recalled suddenly a lost piece of slumbering creation. "And Clive!" she said with surprise. "My brother was in it." She laughed outright. "He was making fun of cook's raspberry-claret molds. He picked one up, dumping it off its dish into his hand, then, quivering it on his palm, said, 'Look. A living heart.' He did that once and made me roar with disgust and delight."

Sam murmured into her neck, "You miss your life."

Did she? She arched as his mouth made a wet path down her throat, downward into the open neckline of her dress. Yes, she supposed she did, but—*aah*—wasn't his mouth on her breast an admirable consolation, though?

They began the day the way they'd spent most of the night, making love. In fact, they'd hardly slept, as if each sleeping minute was a wasted one. Throughout the night, they'd made love till they dozed; they dozed only long enough to recuperate so they could make love again. They went at it till they were sore, then this morning ever so delicately went at it some more. Honeymoon mad: two people gone crazy for want of touching each other.

When they finally arose and got about the business of washing and finding breakfast, it was to a morning that was exactly as beautiful as the one before it, giving credence to the notion that their blissful state could last. The sun shone brightly over the heather in full summer bloom. It encouraged a generally irrational tenor that posed such questions as, Why say good-bye to this? Why not have it forever?

Foolishness, Lydia thought. The inquiries drifted through her mind, but she refused to ask them seriously.

It was easy enough to distract herself: easy enough to crowd out any thoughts but of her lover's physical presence. Sam was an extraordinary physical specimen—and faintly amusing about it. For all his humility and insecurity elsewhere, she realized, he knew he was handsome. Overall, he didn't seem to count it for much, but still he knew it and was willing to display it: Before breakfast, he and she washed off their busy night and morning in the river, and he just suddenly stripped down, without saying, just took his clothes off. Her mouth opened, dry; the sight of him left her speechless. And riveted.

It was nakedness so clearly for pure male show, for her benefit. It was this, not his immodesty (though he seemed indeed absolutely careless about his nudity) that made the impression. *Look at me.* She did. He swam naked for a while, and Lydia simply watched—with not a blink of maidenly reserve. Why be faint-hearted? When would she see such a wonder again?

Sam swam as sleekly as a fish: an angular, limber, long-limbed fish with wide, square shoulders and a strong, muscular back that narrowed in a neat V to tight, bunching buttocks—hard buttocks that showed pale white for an instant when he bent to dive beneath the water. When he broke the surface and walked out of the river, what a sight. Water poured off the breadth of his shoulders, sheeting down the sinewy brawn to his arms, so round, sculpted. . . . He had a powerful chest and abdomen. Everything about him was long—his arms, his fingers, his slender, graceful hands. He stepped onto dry land on tall legs. His thighs were chiseled, his calves cut with muscle; his legs flexed as he walked. High insteps in his bare feet, high arches, long toes. The muscular definition and proportion of Samuel J. Cody was so perfect that Michelangelo's *David* might have despaired, could he have seen.

And Lydia was slightly baffled to confront another fact: What swung between Sam's legs was considerably more than what *David* had, also. She wondered if sculptors, in an effort to be discreet, minimized the sexual apparatus of their stone men—she had never noticed anything the size of Sam and had been somewhat unprepared for it. Or was Sam simply . . . large? Impossible to say, other than he was longer and thicker, whether at rest or erect, than she had come reasonably to expect from textbook or art.

For breakfast, they ate a rabbit and two trout, then, after, returned to the riverbank, where they celebrated so much water by washing their hands of food. This time, Sam scrubbed his arms to his elbows, his shirtsleeves rolled back, while Lydia, folded down onto her knees, splashed her face in the clear, icy-cold river.

As she sat back onto her heels, wiping her face with her petticoat, she said, "It's a shame your superior will hold your personal life against you. What is it you were going to do? Seriously. What do you mean by gun fighting and talking sense into people?"

He laughed at himself. "I negotiate things. Or was going to. It was sort of a new job for me, something different. And I have a lot of bosses, not just one. It's political. An appointment I wanted."

An appointment? She raised her head, frowning, an inquiring look. "An 'appointment' to a post?" She smiled. Perhaps she'd heard wrong. "Or an appointment to *see* someone?"

"Sort of both, I guess—" He was about to say more, then stopped, shaking his head. "It doesn't matter. I didn't get either, I promise you." He sighed, reluctant to speak of his failure. Then he appeased her curiosity with something even more personal. He laughed and offered, "My pop never liked a thing I did. I didn't catch on quick enough or else I was too damn sharp for my own good. I was too young or too old or too sissy or too stubborn. I couldn't win.

"But he would love this: I can't get a job I want because I jilted one woman, I'm starting to think, I don't want. While I can't have the one I do because I've been too damn good at keeping her alive." He gave a sarcastic smile and said, "I don't figure, in your dream, you sat me down beside your brother?"

"No." She blinked. "You weren't in my dream, that I remember—"

He snorted. "If you'd been out here with the Prince of Wales, you know, you'd have died."

Lydia laughed a little uncomfortably. It was not far from true. Though the aging, portly prince was an avid sportsman, between the two of them, she and Bertie had roughly enough skills that, out here alone together, they both would likely have perished.

"Yet, if I happen to stay in London, just sort of hung around, I couldn't call on you, could I?"

She met his gaze, taken aback: He was serious. "You— you could—" she stammered.

No, he couldn't, she realized. Try as she might, as generous as she'd like to be with a man who fascinated her, who had helped her, saved her, she could not envision a future for herself and an American roughrider where his calling on her would be anything but painful.

He saw her answer in her confusion and let out a laugh, ending it suddenly when he bent over and plunged most of his head into the river. After a second, he lifted it again, slinging an arc of water off his hair as he wiped his face.

Then—as abruptly—changed the subject. He smiled wanly over at her. "I figure, tonight you'll have yourself a regular bath."

"A regular bath?" Tonight? Tonight, she'd imagined, she'd be lying in the warm circle of his arms again, up against his amazing bare chest. Why would she be taking a bath?

"Sure," he said. "In London. Or wherever the train takes us today."

Ah. The train. He expected it to keep a daily schedule, and it might. "What will you do?" she asked. "Where will you go?"

He shrugged as he slicked his hair back. His washed, un-shaven face looked lean and stark—he grew handsomer by the day as his features took on their normal proportion. "Back to Texas, I guess. September's hot as blazes, but Oc-tober starts to be nice. I haven't been there in a while." He pulled on one ear, fingering water from it, a quick, subtle movement.

"You'll herd cattle?"

He laughed as he rolled his shirtsleeves down over his thewy forearms—a smattering of fine black hair covered the backs of them, silky, she knew, to the touch. "Well, I'm too old for bronco-riding or bulldogging," he said, "so I guess it's plain old cowpunching, if I'm to be of any use." He paused to look at her. "Truth is, I sort of like it. I've found that piece of myself out here again. I liked riding the range, staying out all night when it suited me. I liked watching out for the animals under my care." He let out a self-critical breath, a man who found his own his tastes insufficiently no-ble. Or perhaps he thought she would and wanted the pre-emptive victory of deriding himself before she did. In either event, after a minute, he went with the notion anyway. Mat-ter-of-factly, he added, "Yep, that's where I guess I'm lick-ing my wounds, out on a Texas prairie somewhere."

She nodded. They understood each other, though she had to admit it was a melancholy understanding. At some point—today, tomorrow, certainly by the end of the week—

she'd be home too: returned to London society, where "cow-punching" or building fires, chasing horses, roasting rabbits, so much of the kindness Sam had shown her, would fall under the heading of "service" or "manual labor": worse than being in trade. Two worlds. Sam's competence in the wild, the physicality of his existence, drew her, excited her, even as she knew socially it put him beneath her. He was a working man, though for the life of her, there seemed something . . . uncommon about him. Still, his competence lay in the realm of her footmen and gardeners.

Though, it amused her to realize, her father would enjoy his hunting skills. A rabbit at fifty yards with a rock! Oh, yes. She smiled. Her father would have liked to meet Sam, which said a lot for why her father and mother did not get along: Her mother wouldn't have been able to build up enough interest in Sam for even a mild dislike; she simply wouldn't have noticed him. He was not beneath her contempt so much as beneath her awareness. In the Viscountess Wendt's world, there were the glittering, proper people and all the rest was furniture, some of which walked around on legs and could be asked to do things for her.

Lydia was lost in this morbid contemplation of the mother she loved, when she heard a sound—so removed from moors and trains—that her ears simply didn't put it in context. It registered only, oddly, as a kind of animal cry.

On the second call, it became human. "Miss Ly-y-y-di-ya-a-a!" A familiar voice, calling her name.

Lydia scrambled to her feet, straightening as she rotated three-hundred-sixty degrees, while the hair on her arms lifted. She scanned the horizon as if for a ghost.

Nothing. No one.

A second later, her name echoed again across the moor from a slightly different direction, fainter this time, more distant, but after the first call, recognizable. "Ly-y-y-di-ya-a-a!"

Oh, no, was her first coherent thought. Found. Though it was more a sense of being found *out*—caught—that hit her. It was like being shot. Guilt and fear, as solid as tiny bullets, struck suddenly and spread their pain. She wasn't ready—

Sam came up beside her and put his arm about her shoulder, as if he could protect her. With his other hand, he pointed. "Over there."

He directed her attention across the river toward a hill, to a rider coming up over it.

A woman on horseback at the summit struggled to control the animal. It refused the steep descent, turning away. With her back to them, as she strived to turn it around again, she called to someone else, a second party, "Here! Oh, here! I've found her! The smoke was her! She's over here!" Then she wheeled the horse around—it stomped, backed up, kicked a rock, then did as she encouraged. It carried her down the slope toward the river, her body thumping up and down wildly in the saddle as she yelled, exultant, "Miss Ly-di-ya-a-ah! Miss Ly-di-ya-a-ah! I've found you!"

It was Rose, valiantly staying atop one of Lydia's uncle's mares.

12

When Lydia recognized Rose, she glanced at Sam, and the words just popped out—in an emphatic, almost embarrassing whisper. "Don't say anything."

"About what?" Beside her, he was barely paying attention. She watched him in profile. He'd put on his vest, though it hung open. He'd set his hat on the back of his head, the brim up as his gaze followed Rose's progress.

She shrugged out of his grasp. "About—you know—that I—that we—"

Behind her, he laughed. "Why would I say anything?"

"I don't know, just don't." Even to her own ears, she sounded curt.

"All right," he said, humoring her.

She made a stiff nod.

On horseback, Rose descended the hillock, she and the animal skidding down the last of the embankment so quickly they plunged into the river with a rooster tail of water whooshing, horse and rider screaming.

Lydia crossed her arms, hugging herself. There she stood, Sam just behind her, Rose careening toward her. With a sense of disaster growing in the pit of her own stomach. Chaos. Fear, worry. Emotions bubbling up so fast she could barely grasp one before another replaced it: resentment, loss, surprise; discovery, exposure. Laid open to judgment.

She couldn't remember ever having anything she wouldn't tell Rose—or if not Rose, Clive or Meredith. Yet at her back stood a secret, six feet three inches of secret, that she couldn't imagine sharing with anyone. Sam was a *good* secret, she told herself. Never had she felt so free and capable and purely happy as she had with him out here on the moor. Yet she could think of no acceptable explanation she might offer for what he and she had done out here, not to Rose or her brother or cousin. Her mind went blank when she tried. And she loathed the feeling of not wanting them to know something about her.

Little, round Rose was out of breath when she dropped from the saddle onto the ground. Being winded, though, didn't stop her from running toward Lydia, talking, and gasping for breath all at the same time.

"Oh, Miss Lydia," she said on the intake, then on the exhale, "I can't tell you how relieved, why, we thought that, well, just anything could have happened, and Meredith and her brother and your uncle and aunt, oh, we've all just worried our heads sick." She stopped in front of Lydia, her hand to her chest as she took another deep breath. "The young Mr. Linton and his Lordship are on the east road, while Miss Meredith is just over the next ridge, goodness, we've been searching for days and couldn't even find the coach, though the horses came back, it just disappeared into the thin air, we didn't know what to think, then a fog set it, you wouldn't believe, it was so thick we couldn't see the horses under us, but then today, we'd been riding since dawn, and we saw a wisp of smoke—"

"Oh, stop," Lydia said, letting out weak laughter—better than crying, though for the life of her, she wanted to do both.

Rose halted, took another deep breath, and broke out laughing—sincere laughter. Standing on tiptoe, she threw her arms around Lydia and hugged her mistress so tightly she cut off air. "Oh, I can't tell you how glad I am to see you, miss."

"Thank you," Lydia said, pushing her back. "I'm glad to see you too." It was what she ought to say, which now added hypocrisy to her list of dissatisfactions with herself.

"Miss Meredith saw me from the other hill. She should be here shortly." She turned, paused, then, frowning, said to Sam, "You're the man from the station."

"Mr. Cody," Lydia said quickly. To Sam, "This is Rose Simms, my lady's maid."

Rose bobbed once, frowned, then said with protective rudeness, "You were drunk."

"I'm not now. Glad to meet you," Sam said, though he didn't look at her. His attention fixed on Lydia, he asked, "Can we talk?"

Talk? How were they going to "talk"? Lydia made a small shrug, a show of open palms, toward him.

Sam frowned, a dissatisfied look, while casually with one hand he buttoned his vest.

Rose meanwhile had marched off after something. At home, she could make herself all but invisible, while people "talked," by simply tidying up—it was how she got the best gossip. Of course, so far from their campsite there was nothing to tidy—until Lydia realized her maid had picked up a whitish splotch, a forgotten wad of wet clothes. Rose shook out her discarded drawers from yesterday, held them up, then lowered them enough to stare over their gaping, elephantine waist.

Lydia said quickly, "The drawstring broke."

The girl looked at her over them. "Your underwear broke?"

"It was very rough out here." Lydia tried to think of why

else her underwear might suffer. "Look at me. I'm a mess." Indeed, she was so, especially compared to Rose, whose hair was tied back neatly, her dress relatively fresh.

Her maid stared at her, eyes wide, then to Sam. Sam with his coat off, his vest buttoned wrong, the ruined underwear staring them all in the face—with, God help them, *his* underwear down there flying from the top of her bow. Oh, yes, Lydia thought, she could hardly wait till Rose saw *that*, which she would because they had to go retrieve it before it stopped a train.

"Doing the 'necessaries,' " Lydia added. "You know. In the wild. It wasn't easy."

The girl pondered the explanation a moment longer, like a indecipherable conundrum. Then she dropped her head, smiled sheepishly, and offered, "Of course. Never mind me." She folded the drawers over her arm. "It's my new status as a wife. It makes my mind wander to the oddest places." Leaning toward her friend and mistress, she lowered her voice. "Oh, miss, it was perfect. So perfect. We went to the Angel Inn, their best room. Oh, Miss Lydia, I have so much to tell you. . . ."

Sweet Rose carried on the conversation alone. She asked questions without getting answers. (Where are the rest of your things? Did you have enough tonic?) Lydia could only look fixedly at Sam. It seemed impossible that she was losing him so soon, so quickly: right now.

Rose continued, "So, you see, I begged Miss Meredith not to tell anyone I wasn't with you—she rallied her family and wired your parents, agreeing not to say for your sake. I think it's better for you, too, if people don't know you were"—she eyed Sam curiously—"on your own." She bit her lip before she continued. "Now, though, I'm asking for my sake: If your parents find out I let you travel alone, they'll dismiss me, Miss Lydia. It's an awful thing to ask you to do, but can we say I was with you?"

Lydia was brought up short. "My family thinks we're together?"

"So far everyone does, except for Miss Meredith, her brother, mother, and father."

"Don't people know I went to your wedding?"

"No." Rose corrected, "Well, my family, but they aren't very likely to talk to anyone." She waited, chewing her lip again.

"Oh." Lydia tried to digest the favor Rose asked. "Yes." Of course. "We'll say we were lost together. You're right, it's best for both of us if we hold to a story that you were with me." She looked at Sam, and the idea materialized—as if conscious thought had been bypassed completely—directly from her mouth: "And that he wasn't."

They all looked at one another as, simultaneously, they realized that the best way to guard Lydia's reputation and Rose's job lay within erasing Sam from the story altogether. But how to go about it?

Lydia stammered out, "The—the original lie—" Lies. Oh, dear, now there were layers of them. "That I—um, didn't go to your wedding, but went to the township trials for the Devon archery championship—yes, um, that should do. From there, we'll say, at Swansdown, you and I took your brother's cart to a meet, got lost, then survived on the moor till Meredith found us."

"Yes!" Rose agreed cheerfully. "And as soon as Miss Meredith arrives, we'll go back to Bleycott, where we'll put Mr. Cody on the next train." She looked at him. "We can send him off before anyone is the wiser."

They both turned to Sam, who said nothing. He stood watching them, his hat on straighter, the brim shading his eyes, his arms crossed.

Hesitantly, Rose asked him, "Is that all right? Will you do it?"

"Sure." To Lydia, he said, "Can I talk to you a minute?"

Rose was off again. "We'll say he's a friend of the young Mr. Linton, that he helped look for us—"

"Liddy," he interrupted.

Both women turned their heads to him abruptly.

"Liddy?" the maid repeated.

Over her head, Sam said, "See me. Let me call on you. I have money. I can get another post. I'm not completely without references—"

Oh, dear, that again. Before Lydia could answer, however, her maid had stepped squarely between Sam and herself. Rose, who never said a mean word to anyone, told him with umbrage, "Sir, you find your place. Just because fate put you alone with one of England's daughters does not give you the right to—"

"I want to see her," he repeated. "*See* her." As if he meant it literally, he pushed her out of the way. "Excuse us." He took Lydia by the arm. "I want to talk to you in private."

She went with him, thinking, Oh, damn you. She was just getting her balance, and now here he was, sure to throw her off again. Within a few feet the direction they took—toward the rush of the river's falls—was obviously going to put any conversation in raised voices. Sam stopped and called to Rose. "Could you excuse us?" He walked them back further, motioning her off.

The girl frowned when she realized what he was asking.

"Please," he said stiffly.

She puckered her mouth.

"It's all right," Lydia said. "Go on."

Rose pivoted around and walked off.

When she was near the far bend in the river, Sam said in a hush, "I don't want you to disappear. I want to see you."

Lydia frowned. "You can't. We've already been through this. My family wouldn't let you in the door."

"Don't you have some say in the matter?"

"About whether I turn my back on my mother and father and brother and cousins and aunts and uncles?" She looked at him, staring now.

While Sam said to himself, No? She couldn't mean no.

She squinched up her face, a pained expression. "Sam, I have to marry where my family approves."

"Well, there you go. I wasn't asking you to marry me."

He shook his head, trying to decide where to begin. "Liddy, I'm just saying, I'd like to call on you in the good, old-fashioned way, drive up in a buggy, arrive with flowers—"

Her eyes widened, appalled. "No."

He blinked, trying to absorb the word. A man couldn't get a more definite answer; no was exactly what she meant. He took a breath. "All right."

He tried to stay reasonable. It was her right. Her perfect right. Nonetheless, his blood rushed. The backs of his ears burned. *No*. He couldn't resist saying, "I thought I was everything you've dreamed of in a man."

"You are," she said. "You just aren't everything I've dreamed of in a husband."

It was like bricks hitting him in the chest. Fury, hurt. "Oh. Well. You'll forgive me, Your Majesty, if I mis-con-strue." He said the word with elaborate drawl. "It must mean something different on this side of the ocean when a woman bangs a man all night like a shithouse door in a gale."

She opened her mouth, speechless. He'd made her speechless.

God help him, if he'd said anything like that to Gwyn, she'd have burst into tears. Hell, she'd have passed out.

Liddy, though, let out a wounded breath, frowned at him, then recovered. She said quietly, "Stop punishing me for what I can't help. Stop being so difficult."

Difficult. When he wouldn't have minded hearing how much she admired him—something, anything positive—he got a good sharp pointer on how to improve.

"I'm not difficult." He was. God knew, he could be a pain in the backside.

"You are: difficult, stubborn, crude—"

He winced.

Her face softened. She reversed herself in midsentence, a look of concern overtaking her face.

It was unfair of her to become soft-hearted—soft-headed, he reminded himself—now that she had him where she wanted him. He felt down one, at her mercy. He hated the feeling of being at a competitive disadvantage, even when he wasn't competing per se, just in case he might have to, in case things got ugly—

On a whisper, her voice blew over him—the antithesis of ugly. It was a little breeze, a zephyr of understanding that he wanted so badly, he was afraid to believe he had it. "I have been so happy with you. It hurts me to leave you, hurts me much more than I could have imagined." She pressed her lips, rolling them inward a second, then looked away. "But I can't abandon my family and friends, and I can't take you with me into them."

"I'm rich," he blurted. Then was embarrassed—it felt like bragging, like wanting to buy her. He amended, "Well, pretty rich. Not as rich as John D. Rockefeller or anything."

She gave him a sad glance, a man grasping at straws. "You could be rich as a king, Sam, and it wouldn't matter. It's not money. It's a question of land and holdings, of class distinction and power—my parents expect their grandsons to sit in the House of Lords."

"Is that what *you* want?"

Oddly enough, the question seemed to make her angry. She glared, before she looked away. To a rock on the river-bank, she said, "I don't get everything I want. Not when I have a duty to—" She frowned, glanced at him. "When people will be upset if—" She didn't like that either and said so with a frustrated face. "Oh, I can't explain it. I can't let my family down."

"Don't let yourself down. What does your family—"

She cut him off vehemently. "I love them. I've loved them for twenty-four years: I've known you three days."

He shut his mouth. Of course. Why was he arguing? A man didn't convince a woman to be interested in him. Either she was, or she wasn't.

He nodded, a single jerk of his head, which he then bent, rubbing his forehead. He took his hat off to dig his fingers, his whole hand, back into his hair.

When he was quiet—he was afraid to open his mouth for

what would come out—she murmured, all but teary-eyed, "What do you expect of me?"

Nothing.

"What do you *expect*?" she pleaded.

"Not a damn thing. You're English, so is your family." He threw her a narrow look. "Class distinction and power," he repeated. "I came here to deal with the English and their stinking taste for hierarchies and dominion"—she blinked at the words; good, let her wonder where he got them and how he came to use them—"always eager to master and assert superiority: It's a country of snobs, and you and your family are some of the biggest."

"I'm not," she said. Her voice faltered, wounded. "That's unkind."

"It's true."

"It's you, not us," she insisted. "You see offense in every nuance and tone—"

At which point, her maid called, distracting him. Liddy, too. They both turned their heads in her direction, toward the rise that hid the young woman. She called again, whatever the hell she wanted.

Sam knew what he wanted: to reach out. He wanted to draw Liddy to him. He wanted to say with gesture what he felt. Not these mean words, but tenderness, dearness. God. Liddy. Look at us. If circumstances were different, he'd have been allowed to, and the rest would have been easy. His body would have said it for him: I need you, I want you; don't leave me.

That was when they heard the whistle. It was faint at first, a distant two-note signal that piped over the run of the river.

"The train," she said, her eyes widening. "Oh, no." She put her hand over her mouth, looking toward the craggy hill that hid the train from them and them from anyone on it.

Again the whistle came—loud, growing louder, piercing, and continuous: someone with his hand on the whistle cord who didn't let go.

Liddy swiveled around to face him, her fine eyes full of woe. Sam wished he could have done something for her, eased her fright. She said one word. "Rose."

A second later, as if summoned, the maid came racing round the slope, pointing, panting. "There's a train down there!"

"Did they see you?"

"I don't know." She frowned in dismay. "There's a kind of flag down there as well."

The bow. With Liddy's initials on it. And his underwear. Its flying out there in plain sight had seemed so practical when he hadn't slept with her, but now that he had, it felt downright incriminating. A red flag that said he'd had his clothes off.

He looked at Liddy, knowing this was all they were going to get: some angry words amounting to half an argument.

The maid asked, "You were this close to a train and didn't get home?" She looked flummoxed.

"Only since yesterday morning."

"Since yesterday morning," she repeated.

Yeah, right, now it all made sense.

"What do we do? Where is Meredith? Why isn't she here? We have to leave before anyone finds us."

"I don't know. She was on the opposite hill ten minutes ago."

The train's whistle blared again, different from yesterday: louder, more insistent, as if its locomotive had stopped, its whistle a long blast, a call: It didn't move.

Steam. Long, loud rushes of steam could be heard from a train resting motionless on its tracks.

"Oh, God," Liddy said. "Where can we hide?"

Sam laughed. "Nowhere. Not if they saw Rose. They'll come in this direction—the direction of a campsite, a horse, and the three of us, not to mention Meredith, if she suddenly shows up. I don't know where we'd hide all that."

"Oh, God," she groaned again. "*Now* what are we going to do? What are we going to tell people?"

"We could always try the truth," he suggested. Her gaze immediately jumped to his, though, the look in her eyes so woebegone at the mere thought that he instantly said, "Right. Never mind. I'm sure we can come up with something much better than that."

13

Now what are we going to do? It had been a rhetorical question. Lydia had never intended it to send Mr. Wilderness into rough-riding action. She would have thought of something herself within the minute, something much more satisfactory. If only Sam had given her a minute.

Instead, though, someone far off and below called out, "Hel-loo-oo-oo!" Clearly, people were coming from the train in their direction.

At which point, Sam said, "I wish we had time to discuss and vote on it, but we don't, so here's what we're doing."

He took Rose by both shoulders and walked her backward, half-carrying her by the arms to the edge of the riverbank. Only in the last several steps did she stumble and stammer out protests. Only at the last instant did she understand what was happening enough to scramble violently. Too late. He picked her up and pitched her, her small body sailing, frock flapping, arms and legs treading air, out into the river. Rose wailed the whole distance until she was swallowed up in a splash.

Sam turned toward Lydia, and she immediately backed away. "Just one moment," she said, holding up her hand.

There was no stopping him, though, or even slowing him. He feinted a leap in one direction, then went the other, catching her round the waist when she bolted.

"That wasn't fair!" she yelled as he carted her sideways under his arm against his ribs.

He only laughed at the edge of the river, then said, "I'm leaving. You have no man to explain. I'll find this Meredith if she is out there to find. All you have to do is figure out a way to account for my, um, our flag down there. Tell them they're yours. Tell them you sleep in a union suit. My mother used to, so there you go. Anyway, you'll find some way to make it believable." Half sarcastic, half appreciative, he laughed again. " 'Cause you've become one of the best liars I know, Lid. You're blue ribbon."

He turned her upright by the bottom and torso and said close to her ear, "Rose didn't look right for a woman who's been lost on the moor, and you, sweet thing, may as well match her. In you go. You can say you both went for a swim."

The river lay rushing before her one moment, while Lydia struggled against the man behind her—her elbow got in a good knock to his hat. Then the next, with a lift, she was in the air, the water beneath her. When she hit, it was shockingly cold, though not terribly deep. She went under, but quickly found the bottom with her feet.

She stood up waist-deep in the cold river, its current pulling at her skirts, Rose clambering beside her. Lydia pushed her wet hair from face, then held her posture like that, arms up, as her gaze found Sam.

On the riverbank, he'd moved quickly. He was over by the horse, his hands working at the buckle of a stirrup. He was changing the length.

Voices called, suddenly surprisingly clear. "Over here!" "No, I see smoke over there." "This way. I saw the girl this way." "Is it the two women, do you think?"

Sam was unfazed. He finished with the last stirrup, grabbed hold of the saddle, and swung up. Atop the horse, he raised his arm in a familiar gesture, reaching for his hat to straighten the brim: But it wasn't there. Lydia blinked, lowering her arms as she looked around, slowly swirling in the water. On land, Sam turned the horse full circle, scanning the area. They both saw his hat at the same time. Downriver from her, floating on its brim, his black Stetson with the silver beads drifted rapidly away, a loss.

Meanwhile, by the voices, she could hear there were a lot of people, a trainload, just down on the other side of the rise, swarming through the heather. Coming after her. While she stared after Sam. On horseback, he plashed across the river, then up the opposite slope.

At the top, he risked turning the horse. He lifted his hand, but only got it up partway before he lowered it as fast as he'd raised it. He stared down at her for a second. Then the cowboy reeled his horse around and kicked its sides. And, in a blink—a hiccup—Sam was gone, the place where he'd been the moment before oddly still: the sun shining down brightly, impassively, on the rocky knoll.

How could it? she wondered. When inside her a kind of shadow overtook her spirit. Lost. She had lost him in some huge way she hadn't expected: his good graces gone. She thought, He threw me in because he was angry with me. He didn't need to. He hates me for the choice I've made. He loathes me. He thinks I'm a liar, a snob. Names. My lover calls me names.

Irritation finally got her moving. What did he know of her real life? Who was he to judge? How dare he? Why, if he were standing here right now, she told herself, she might have a few things say. . . .

Lydia began to trudge and paddle her wet, bedraggled way to the riverbank, Rose slightly ahead. As it turned out, dragging a fully dressed body waist-deep in water to the shore was much more work than swimming there in her underclothes. It took enough time that a whole line of people had arrived to witness the last few feet of her struggle. Lydia barely saw them. Because all the while, in a kind of fury as she made for land, she argued mentally with Sam. She tried to convince her impression of him, indelibly bright in her mind, to forgive her for going home.

Oh, the things he told her in her mind. You tart. You snob. You child. The names he used. She explained about her family again. Such good reasoning. She dissected the idea of loyalty, then the idea of love. Didn't he understand the concepts? She argued every imaginable way for him to accept her decision. He should think kindly of her. He should stop saying mean things to her. He should leave her alone.

But the Sam in her mind wouldn't. He just wouldn't.

Men in bowler hats, in top hats, a fellow in a cap, women beneath parasols, a couple arm in arm, women holding small children by the hands. The train had all but emptied itself with curiosity. Half-sliding, half-walking, Lydia went down the steepest slope with this gathering group into the heather.

A young man, curious, shouldered his way beside her. "So you two young ladies have been lost on the moor for days?"

"No," she snapped, "we were out here for a stroll." She picked up her pace.

She was moving briskly, when she saw Sam's hat—one of its beads flashed sun at her like mirror. Chances were, she could have walked past it, and no one else would have noticed. The hat lay, caught on twigs at the bend in the river, in a shallow where the bank was low. Barely breaking stride, she detoured to snatch the hat up, then kept going.

She traipsed, gripping it, running her thumb along the smooth felt, over and over. Oh, Sam. To ride off without it. Then, as she saw him again in her mind's eye, another absence occurred to her—his shirtsleeves, his wrongly buttoned vest: Sam had not been wearing his coat at the river. It was still at their campsite.

The land leveled. Walking through the heather, the purple

wasn't as lovely as yesterday; it looked drier. Just beyond the heather, as they approached the train, Lydia could see stragglers, mostly women, waiting at various points along the line of cars. At the locomotive, the engine driver, a stoker, and two other uniformed railway people stood by.

So far, she had managed to avoid more than a handful of questions—people were reluctant to push for more answers than those that confirmed identities—confirming that "the poor, lost women" were "saved" by the train. This excitement had been enough to delay explanations. The trek down the slopes had worked to keep people quiet—the trek and perhaps awe for the way the two women looked. Though she could only imagine how she herself looked, Lydia could attest that Rose was a disaster. Her clothes stuck and clung, the hems wet, filthy. One sleeve had been torn. Her hair was matted. Her face had a smudge.

Oddly enough, it was with Rose that substantive questions began in earnest. Panting to catch up, she said, "Miss Lydia, slow down." She caught Lydia's arm, though Lydia jerked free. If the girl wanted to walk with her, she would have to keep up. Rose frowned. "Do you need your tonic? Do you have asthma? How can you walk so fast?"

Lydia led the way, in fact, everyone else behind, which *was* unlike her. She could never remember daring to do such a thing before, partly because she'd never been able. Partly perhaps because her mother felt it unseemly for a woman to lead anything.

Trotting to stay abreast, Rose whispered, slightly winded, under her breath, "The hat. What are you doing with his hat? Drop it."

Lydia brought it to her chest and clutched it.

"What's gotten into you? You're not helping."

The heather ended, and the train loomed up, large, waiting, silent all but for some faint hisses of steam and water puttering beneath. The driver held up his hands, quieting the people as they came up behind her. Then he turned to Lydia also. "We found this bow," he began.

"It's mine."

"And we were wondering what this"—Sam's red underwear—"was."

"A union suit, I think it's called."

Another man, in a top hat, couldn't resist stepping in to ask, "Whose is it? *What* is it?"

Someone laughed, followed by a round of tittering. Obviously, it was underwear. Strange underwear.

Lydia ran her fingers along the hat brim. A Stetson, a red union suit, and a dusty coat that might materialize at any moment. She opted for, "A man was traveling with us."

Rose coughed, then stammered out, "Y-yes, the f-first day, then he disappeared."

"Without his underwear?" came from another direction.

"It was an extra pair we thought to use as a signal."

"Why should he wander off?"

"He, um, drank a lot," Rose offered. "He was perfectly worthless, quite uncivilized."

Blank stares. As if to say, So that made him go off on his own in the middle of the moor, leaving two women?

Lydia thought to add, "One of those American cowboys." Faces turned toward her. She blinked and said, "He, um— he, um, drank a lot." What else? "We think he, ah, stumbled off to relieve himself then got—" Yes. "Um, lost. We don't know what became of him. That first night, he was on very good terms with the driver's gin, then in the morning—" She held out her hands. "We just couldn't find him."

"Even though we called and called," Rose added.

"What a fool," someone said.

"Oh, yes," Rose agreed quickly. "A drunken fool." She looked at Sam's hat and tsked. "Americans," she said.

One of the men laughed, then several more. A young woman offered, "Yes. An American from that Wild West Show last year went to a restaurant in London. When his steak came out a dash rare, he took out his gun and shot it." More laughter. It was the sort of story people loved to hear— and believe—about Americans who lived west of Boston.

One fellow, a foot shorter than Sam, held up the underwear. The legs dragged on the ground, the red underclothes of a giant. "Red," he said. That was the only word he needed to speak. Nearly everyone laughed, a great joke.

Questions began to come more regularly and from all quarters.

"How did you live?"

"What did you eat?"

"We ate—" Rose began.

"Rabbit," Lydia supplied. Goodness, it was getting easier. *You are blue ribbon.*

"Yes!" her maid agreed brightly. "Miss Lydia shot it with her bow."

And when the arrow fell out, Lydia told herself, we'd chase it down. And fish, she might have added, we netted fish in our skirts. Oh, the lies she could invent, so close to the truth.

And so it went. All in all, it could have been worse. Sam came off looking fairly foolish, though happily no one knew it was Sam. While Lydia and Rose, though they hadn't hidden the fact that a man was involved, had made the man of their story so witless as to render his manliness void. Two women and one fool under the stars together were not nearly so hard to dismiss as one woman and handsome, capable Sam.

And that was that. A first-class compartment had been vacated for them. As Lydia put her foot on the first step, several hands reached out to her.

"I have it," she said, shoving back anyone who dared help.

She only realized that she had alarmed people when behind her Rose said, "She's not herself." She took Lydia's arm—Lydia the invalid again, whose maid explained her behavior. "We're been out here so long . . . so worried . . . never thought to see civilization again—"

"I *have* it," Lydia said. She shrugged her away, grabbed her limp, damp skirts in one hand, gripped the handrail with the other, and heaved herself up. She climbed the four deep steps and enjoyed the exertion of it.

Someone handed them soft, dry blankets, then the door to

their compartment latched shut, making a neat end to her
first round of big, fat lies to, so far, a hundred or more people. Lydia let out a huge sigh as she plunked herself down
opposite Rose and let her head fall back.

"You shouldn't have kept his hat," her maid said across
the space.

"I wanted it." She lifted her head and set the hat on top of
it. The hat was too big, but her unkempt hair kept it from
sliding down over her eyes. So close to her nose, it smelled
exactly right. Sam. She lay her head back and did what
she'd seen him do: She tilted the hat forward until it covered her eyes. And, oh, the scent of him now. It filled her
lungs.

The train began to stoke up, steam whooshing, the first
chug and clank of iron wheels.

With the movement, Lydia felt her chest constrict, then
she caught back a sniff through her nose. Her eyes began to
ache, a feeling that said she might burst into tears. She
would not cry. *I will not cry. I won't.*

She managed not to. But it cost her a tightness in her
throat that made her muscles there feel as if they'd split. Her
chest became a knot down the center of her breastbone that
hurt all the way through her back into her shoulder blades.

Oh, Sam. The little refrain, without any other further re-
counting—oh, Sam, oh, Sam—kept running through her,
like a song she couldn't drive from her mind. *Oh, Sam.* As if
he were inside the hat, she saw him suddenly: Sam swimming toward her, her thinking, I deserve this. Him. My
pleasure. I deserve him. Oh, how she had longed for him.
She longed for him still.

But how wrong, her thinking. The world owed her nothing. She had to play by its rules or suffer its consequences. If
London society discovered what she'd done, her future as
she had always imagined it would evaporate. She would lose
her good name and the privileges and protections that went
with it: She would lose everything she had come to believe
already belonged to her.

I deserve this. What arrogance. What a mistake. No. More humbly, she prayed, *Oh, dear heaven, please protect me from what I deserve.*

Only when Sam heard the long whistle of a train did he pick up his pace to a canter. On a horse that was first-rate, though in a saddle that felt strange, he rode east. It was the direction that would bring him to civilization quickest on horseback— he'd already lain eyes on what had to be cousin Meredith, but only from the distance. Someone, a fancy fellow with another horse, was with her, her brother or father, he imagined. They looked to be taking care of something wrong with one of their mounts, a thrown shoe, a split hoof, hard to say, but she didn't need Sam, and Sam didn't want to introduce himself or explain where he didn't have to.

At his first opportunity, he'd wire this place called Bley-cott and arrange for the return of the animal under him. For now, though, his job was to get himself to London.

As to Liddy, he could manage without her. He'd enjoyed her gumption, her shrewdness, their rapport, certainly her body, and even her temper at times. The past three and a half days were already rare enough—a man couldn't expect so much good fortune to go on. No, they'd worn out the fantasy of it. They'd gotten down to reality. It was over; it had been grand.

Adiós, he thought. As he rode across the moor, it seemed alive with harsh beauty. Not that it mattered. He had to say good-bye to the Dartmoor, too. *Adiós. Adiós to the moor. Adiós, Miss Liddy Brown.* The valediction echoed through him, as if through a hollow place, an opening canyon of loneliness. Alone again. Isolated.

Mr. Wilderness. Mr. Lone Wolf. On the loose again. Roaming again.

An hour later, Lydia and Rose changed trains in Plymouth. The second train would take them all the way to London. Once more, a first-class compartment was reserved, which

they managed to lock behind them after only a minor skir-
mish with two persistent people, a reporter and photogra-
pher.

The train got going fairly quickly, then so did she and
Rose. Lydia told Rose about her adventure with Sam out on
the moor, or mostly she did. She recounted with enthusiasm
and in detail about crawling across a bog and roasting rabbits and reading stories while sitting in fog so white she had
to hold the book close to see the words. In fact, she told
Rose everything except for one little part—the part about the
kissing and swimming and, well . . . the lovemaking part.
And she was looking for an entry for that, feeling brave
enough to test the water, so to speak—

When Rose took over, giggling out her own story, the
story of her wedding night. It was sweet and dear.

"So afterward I say, 'I'm sorry I was so stupid about it,'
and Thomas says, 'I think it's beautiful, Rosie, that you were
stupid about it.' And he kisses me on the forehead. He just
beams at me, miss. I felt pure and glowing, I tell you." She
laughed. "An old married woman can give you some advice
now: It's worth it."

Lydia smiled, pleased for Rose. "What is?"

"Holding on to yourself, you know, for the blissful night.
One day, it'll be so wonderful for you, Miss Lydia."

"What if I didn't wait till the blissful night?" Surely, she
could tell Rose. She could tell Rose anything.

"What do you mean?"

"Hypothetically. What if you and Thomas weren't married? Would it be less wonderful?" She asked the question
fondly, teasing a little.

Her companion blinked. "Yes: It would be immoral."

Immoral? Lydia straightened in her seat. For a second,
sunlight blinked through the window, through a copse of
passing trees. Wheels clattered.

Rose said, "If you're not married, it's wrong. 'A great
moral failing,' Thomas calls it."

"And you think that too?"

The girl's eyes widened solemnly. "Yes, miss, I do." She

may as well have added, How can you question it? "It's a
dreadful serious thing between a man and a woman: It can
end in a child."

Unless you do something to prevent it, Lydia thought.
She felt worldly. And suddenly, oh, so alone.

She looked out the window, at jolly old England rattling
by. Stony fields, a bit of grass, some black-faced sheep. Ah,
Rose, she thought. There was no doubt that Thomas was
lucky to have her for his wife for a hundred reasons—
though Lydia did *not* think that Rose's having or not having
a maidenhead determined her overall worth as a partner.
Even though Sam had said the same thing. Still, she was
glad for Rose to have something that mattered so much to
her. Her husband's good opinion regarding her chastity was
hers.

So why this ache?

Oh. Lydia grew subdued.

By the size of her disappointment, she realized, in listen-
ing to Rose and all that went on in the best room at the Angel Inn, she'd grown hopeful that she herself could share
what went on by the river and lying in the heather all night.
She'd wanted to sort her thoughts out with her friend, talk
about her experiences on the moor that seemed so . . . so
amazing that not to share them with Rose and have her be
happy too was a kind of blow. But she couldn't. Because
Rose would not be happy.

She'd be appalled.

Immoral. The word left Lydia breathless. Yet she had no
response to it. She said nothing further, only staring out the
train window the rest of the way, watching her own reflec-
tion waver, like a ghost, over the passing countryside.

Goodness, what a day for judgments, and all at the hands
of people she liked who theoretically liked her. A liar. (She
was one and hated it.) A snob. (She hoped she wasn't.) Now
immoral. (From Rose's perspective, it was accurate: Her
employer was an immoral woman—a label Lydia did not
wear comfortably.)

She nursed hurt feelings and puzzlement with herself.

Who was she that people could say these things of her? Not the same person who had gotten lost on the moor four days ago.

Immoral? Did she feel immoral? No. She would do exactly as she'd done with Sam again. In a lifetime, she'd never know another man like him.

No, she felt solitary, separate: distanced from others because of secrets and judgments passed, some in anger, some in perfect sweetness without even knowing.

Seven hours later, Sam stepped off a different train down onto the platform at King's Cross Station. His mind was full of business: He intended to clean himself up, drop by the embassy to explain the debacle that was his existence (being vague about where he'd been exactly, so as not to be paired with and possibly compromise Liddy). He'd see if anyone there knew where to find his family—his grandmother, aunts, uncle, half-brother, and cousins—who were likely worried sick. He considered briefly tracking down Gwyn. He ought to. But in the end, it seemed already misery enough to have to have to face once more the wrath and disappointment of his own family—after which he intended to locate his bags in Dover, buy a ticket for the next crossing, and take himself home.

Full retreat. Nothing he could do. The world would always pull Liddy in the direction of old money and good English breeding; best he traveled as fast as he could in the other. *Adiós,* good-bye, *adieu.*

Good thing he didn't love her, because he sensed that the price of loving was something he didn't want to pay: a sense of deprivation in proportion to the strength of a man's feelings. Grief. How stupid would *that* be, to fall in love with a woman in four short days? Why, a man moron enough to do it might feel lost without her.

Nope, good thing. Sam's life fell right back into its old pattern—a man who was anything but lost. Though he arrived in a city that was new to him, London, the emotional territory was absolutely familiar—the exact same place he had been in seemingly forever. The same routine. The same petty triumphs. The same smug self-assurances. The same dissatisfactions, gripes, and grievances.

He arrived the same as he'd left: still himself, wishing he could get away from Sam Cody—proving a man could change professions, change women, change continents, yet still not change anything significant in his life.

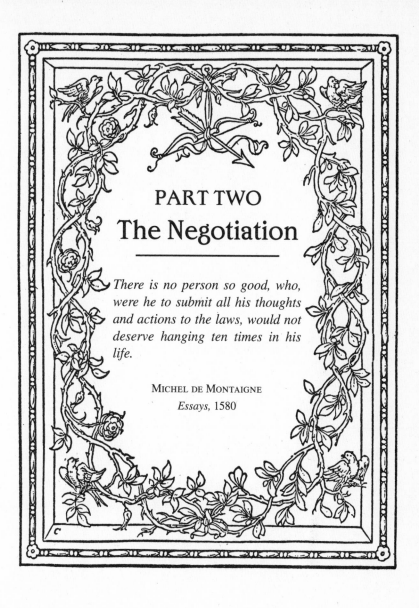

PART TWO
The Negotiation

There is no person so good, who, were he to submit all his thoughts and actions to the laws, would not deserve hanging ten times in his life.

MICHEL DE MONTAIGNE
Essays, 1580

14

*An ambassador is an honest man sent to lie abroad
for the good of his country.*

Sir Henry Wotton, first printed attribution
in *Ecclesiasticus* by Schroppe, 1611

" 'Sam Cody is a good fellow and the smartest man for the job.' I'm reading you this part, even though he didn't say to." Ian Patterson, the United States Ambassador to Britain, looked up over his glasses, his sallow face droll, then continued, " 'You tell him this. If he can make himself respectable enough to get his letter of credence to the Queen—if it looks like he can get accredited by the British government—then I'll stick my neck out for him. We have to have an interim ambassador. Under the circumstances, you understand, Ian. And Sam is there, with more understanding of this country's interests than any other person I can think of. Moreover, an interim post only requires the cooperation of a senatorial committee, which I can arrange, since Hobart names the committee. I'd be going out on a limb here, but Sam could do it, I know. I see no reason why he couldn't pack up his cowboy hat, smooth out his manners, put on a New York tuxedo, and beat the creamy-smooth Brits at their own game—even single and having jilted a senator's daughter. Twice, the idiot.' "

Ian folded the letter in half neatly and tapped its edge once on the surface of his desk, waiting. "It goes on," he said. "So what do you think?"

Sam squirmed in his chair as he frowned into the drawn face of a man making arrangements to vacate his post because his health was failing. Three months ago, Ian had weighed fifty pounds more. He looked like a different man from the one in Paris last winter, sitting here now behind a large mahogany desk that dwarfed him. Surprising and sad. Sam had always liked Ian. He hated to see him look so poorly.

Sam had come across the ocean thinking to work with Ian, not replace him. He'd been appointed by the president of the United States to the post of ambassador extraordinary to a canal treaty negotiation—giving him negotiating power over Ian in that one very particular area, that of reopening talks on an ocean-going link between the Pacific and the Atlantic oceans via a cut through Central America. It was an appointment that made great sense in light of Sam's role in the Spanish-American War and the treaty that ended it in Paris. Moreover, it was considered a great public advantage that a railroad man such as Sam would support the improvement that a canal would mean for shipping without a lot of fuss over what that improvement might do to shipping's competition with rail. Add to this Sam Cody's heroic reputation, built of tangential connection to Teddy Roosevelt's First Volunteer Cavalry, also known as the Rough Riders, and President McKinley had thought he had a viable candidate to launch talks on an old treaty that gave the British more rights over an unbuilt canal than they deserved. Sam should have been confirmed by the Senate in record time, his new career as a diplomat sealed.

It probably would have been if one senator, a Senator Pieters, hadn't cabled a long diatribe against Sam in an abrupt change of sides.

Sam had crossed the Atlantic early, his confirmation in the Senate all but assured, to marry the daughter of the senior senator from Illinois, the honorable John Pieters. The bride had taken to the romantic notion that, since she and her new husband were about to live in quaint, jolly old England, they should have a quaint, jolly old wedding there.

It was all one to Sam, just so long as he got married somewhere. One argument against his appointment had been that he'd be seen as too blunt and freewheeling—straight from Texas—for the good English queen. His supporters were afraid that on style alone, she might refuse him accreditation. His marriage—something he'd been planning anyway—was supposed to make him "respectable enough" for a queen known to tolerate more idiosyncrasy in a family man than in a slow-talking cowboy on the loose as a bachelor.

The rest was history. Sam had returned to London six days ago. His relatives turned out to be easy to find the second he opened his mouth. A hackney driver told him that the Americans "whot talk loike you does, guv, er et the Ritz." He stayed one night in the capital at the same hotel with them, then headed for Dover. There he'd claimed his bags from the Hotel Allegretto, returned to London, and booked the whole clan passage on the next steamer home.

When he went to board the ship at the end of the week, though, Ian and two more men from the State Department were waiting for him. They took his ticket and marched him off to the embassy, where he currently sat.

"I can't believe you didn't even come by," Ian said. "We were worried about you."

"I was going to. But then I read in the paper I hadn't been confirmed, and it seemed, you know, more discreet to just go, less painful for all concerned."

"For all but your friends."

"Yeah, well—" Sam never could understand this part: why people supported him as a friend, let alone a negotiator for his country. "Seems like I upset people more than help."

Ian laughed. "We like that you roust everyone from their

ruts. Sometimes that's just was people need: chased from
their safe positions like a flock of fussy birds up into the air
till feathers are flying."

"Yeah, well, I'm pretty good at that, I guess."

"Better than pretty good. You know how to leave the right
spots open so—if I may stretch the metaphor—when the
birds find new spots on the field our position is improved."

Sam laughed and scratched his ear. "I appreciate your
faith, Ian."

"So you'll do it?"

"Nah. Sorry. I'm sort of hankering after Texas these days.
You must have a next in command. Who is it? That Winslow
fellow? He'd be—"

"They'd run all over him. Heck, they've given me a hard
time. Sam, these cocky Brits need someone who isn't going
to play their game at all. You'd shake them up—then, before
they could wedge themselves in again, you'd have the terms
of a new treaty roughed out." As if it was a great draw, he
smiled his thin-lipped smile and said, "Gwynevere Pieters is
at the home of the man who'd be your British counterpart.
Parliament is out. Most MPs are in the country, hunting
grouse this time of year. Miss Pieters is among them,
trolling, so they say, for a new match, looking for a titled
Englishman this round. What do you say you go up and protect your interests there, too? See her, Sam. See if things
can't be patched up. Despite her father, Miss Pieters is a
lovely woman, truly beautiful and—"

"No thanks."

"You'd be feted royally. The Viscount Wendt puts on
quite the spread."

"I just can't see myself—who?" Sam frowned, squinting.
"Who did you say is the host?"

"Wendt. Jeremy Bedford-Browne, the Viscount Wendt.
Big outdoors fellow. He and a few of the more sporty members of Parliament stomp around his country property this
time of year, a lot of dogs, tweeds, rifles, and wellies. It's
Wendt at his most social—he avoids the season, doesn't like
parties, only sits in his seat at the House of Lords when

there's a vote coming up that he cares about. Mostly, he lob-
bies in the background. A very powerful fellow. He's given
us a hell of a time with this old treaty, holding us to the letter
while he's organized opposition to a new one like mortared
bricks in a wall. You could catch him now, though, in a relaxed atmosphere where he'd all but have to be civil."

"Wendt?" Sam repeated. "This is the Wendt whose
daughter was in the newspaper last week?"

"I'm not sure. Why?" Frowning, Ian twisted his dry-
looking, colorless mouth. "Now, Sam, the very thing we
don't want here—"

"Lydia," he said. "That would be her name."

The ambassador thought a moment. "Now that you mention it, yes. Wendt's daughter got herself lost out on the
Dartmoor for a few days, oh, maybe a week ago, though she
survived brilliantly." He guffawed. "If she's like her father,
she's a tough old goat. I'm not surprised she survived it.
What's that saying you have? About the snake?"

"Ah." Sam laughed. "So tough if a rattlesnake bit him—"

"Her, in this case."

Sam laughed harder. "Her. If a rattlesnake bit her, the
snake would die."

Ian smiled widely, a smile that somehow didn't meet his
rheumy eyes. "That's it." He tapped his gaunt fingers on the
desk with satisfaction. His nails were bluish. One of the
other men on the way in had murmured *cancer*, though Sam
didn't ask; he didn't want Ian to have to explain. Or maybe
he didn't want to know. It was about the saddest thing he
could think of, a man like Ian being cut down early. "You'll
do it?" the man across from him asked.

Sam told himself it was an act of charity, sympathy, of
gratefulness. A thanks to God: There but for Your grace go I.
"Sure. I'll give it a whack. Why not?"

Except, the minute the words were out his mouth, it was
Liddy he thought of, not his colleague; and the thoughts he
had of her were more of an earthly than heavenly turn of
mind.

Liddy. Liddy's smile, Liddy's skin, Liddy's body. He was

going to stand close to her again, see her again. It made him glad, he realized, to think he'd get a chance to apologize. A man ought not to spout off to a woman the way he had.

He laughed to himself. It looked like he was going to call on her and her family after all. And, knowing Liddy, he'd likely get himself a good smack across the shins for it. Why, he could hardly wait, now that he thought about it.

15

If thou does ought for nought,
always do it for thyself.
(If you do anything for nothing,
always do it for yourself.)

Yorkshire proverb

With shock on her face, Lydia's mother, the Viscountess Wendt, whispered to her daughter and the Marchioness of Motmarche, "I don't know where to put someone." It was a huge admission, since the viscountess prided herself on knowing where to put everyone.

Leaning near the marchioness, she continued, "The U.S. ambassador, Mr. Patterson, would normally go in before the high lord treasurer, but His Excellency is ill. He didn't come. Rather, he sent someone in his place. Where do I put him? At the front, where the ambassador might normally go in? Or at the foot of the table, where an American would go in otherwise?"

The marchioness, a slight but stately older woman, knew most of the rules of precedence, not for the same reason as her mother, Lydia suspected—because she cared so much where she herself stood—as because Lady Motmarche was as sharp as a tack and had attended every state event for the last forty years. The order of English precedence was as un-avoidable to her as who took which trick in a game of whist.

She asked, "Who is officially the ambassador from the United States at the moment?" Her voice was gentle.

In a voice as tight as the high string of a violin, the vis-countess told her, "That is the peculiar thing. I don't know. In his note, Mr. Patterson says he has stepped down from his post."

"Has the queen recognized the new man?"

"I don't know that either," the viscountess said with disgust.

"It would be highly unlikely for the queen to receive him on such short notice."

"It is highly unlikely that Mr. Patterson should simply wander off."

"Ah," the marchioness said. Her mild voice was some-how reassuring. "Graham"—her husband, the marquess—"said he was ill. I'm so sorry to hear he's leaving. He must be worse."

The viscountess frowned rather unsympathetically. "In-deed," she said. "But that still leaves us with the problem of what to do with this new fellow? Where do we put him?"

"Ask him," Lady Motmarche recommended. "Ask if he's been accredited by Her Majesty. We can hardly acknowl-edge him before she does."

"Oh, I hate that!" the viscountess said. The feathers in her hair bobbled as she jerked her head. "I hate to have to ask. It's so—"

Uncertain, Lydia thought. Her mother hated to speak to someone before she knew if she stood above them or not.

With a rush of taffeta and a clatter of crystal beads, her mother swooped off, leaving her daughter to think, Oh, I am being mean. Lydia tried to bring herself into line, but it was a difficult task.

The viscountess had been unbearable for the past two weeks. Tonight, she was in heaven; she was in hell. Nothing pleased her more than formal acknowledgment of her place in the British social order. Nothing ruffled her more than the possibility of getting something wrong, an embarrassment: of not getting her due.

Her due was connected tonight to the fact that the queen's grandson, the Prince of Wales's nephew, had three weeks ago serendipitously proposed to Lydia's cousin Meredith. The viscountess had pounced on the connection, making available her Yorkshire home for the engagement dinner. In fact, the Bedford-Brownes' historic country house—Castle Wiles—was a monument to spaciousness and old English style. Lydia's mother's sister-in-law, the bride's mother, had delighted in the invitation (one she didn't often receive, in fact).

Thus, Lydia stood in her childhood home, its urns and niches filled with enough flowers to put a funeral home to shame, in the drawing room that would open in fifteen minutes into a formal dining hall they almost never used, where would begin the most formal dinner she had ever attended: The Prince and Princess of Wales would enter the drawing room any moment.

Though the queen was missing, even she had sent her good wishes. The prince's royal yacht had cruised up the coast two days ago, his royal coach trundling him and his royal wife to their door this morning. He and the princess were upstairs readying themselves in the state bedchamber, where they would also sleep tonight. The viscountess was beside herself. It was the first time in more than two decades that royals had slept under her roof, and a fine pair of royals they were. The last time had only been the queen's German cousin. This time, it was her son, the future King of England.

Lydia squirmed. Her hands were sweating in her gloves as she waited. Dear Meredith and her groom-to-be had come downstairs five minutes ago. Presently, Lydia's mother was delicately making sure everyone knew their place in the formal procession into dinner, by order of title and patent. It was an "intimate" gathering, "family," as her mother kept saying: sixty or so of England's uppermost crust, gathered to celebrate a royal marriage—and to celebrate, so far as Constance

Bedford-Browne was concerned, the Bedford-Brownes' connection to it.

"Lydia." Her mother came up behind her daughter this time, taking a moment for one of her favorite complaints on her way across the room. She murmured, "You'd look so much better with your hair off your face." She shoved hair from her daughter's forehead with enough force to have removed axle grease from it. "Did you take your medicine?"

"I don't need it."

"Where's your father?"

"I don't know."

Her mother grimaced. "He'd best find his way down here. We're about to go in to dinner, and he's to escort the princess." She pulled a face. Under her breath she said, "You're paired with Baron DeBlah again." That's what she called him, *DeBlah*, when his name was DeBleu, very Norman. More brightly, she asked, "Where's Boddington?"

"I don't know."

Sharply, Lady Wendt met her daughter's eyes. "You don't know much, do you?"

"I know a great deal," Lydia said boldly, willing to cross her tonight for no good reason, other than they had been at odds ever since her return.

"Well," the viscountess said, dismissive, "you can help. The American I'm looking for is tall with very dark hair. The minister over there has seen him exactly once." She made an exasperated mew, then said, "Americans. He should have come straight to me. They never get any of this right, especially when they first arrive."

Small wonder, Lydia thought. Then sighed as she thought of the last American she'd spoken to at any length.

Sam. On the moor, she'd spread her wings, and he'd approved. She hadn't been aware then of how much she'd enjoyed his encouragement of her self-reliance—what her mother called impudence he had called pluck. She missed his encouragement now. From three people away, her mother caught her eye again. The viscountess raised her finger to her own forehead, motioning for her daughter to arrange her hair to suit her mother.

Lydia turned away instead, opening her fan with a flick of her wrist, *snap*. With small, short movements, she whipped the air about her face.

Oh, if her mother ever knew about Sam. Ha, if anyone did—

Lydia reminded herself not to think about him. Again. A good trick, reminding oneself *not* to think of someone. She did it anyway, for the hundredth time in the past two weeks. Why, if Emma Bovary or Tess of the D'Urbervilles or Anna Karenina, any of them, had simply done what she was doing—put her passionate attachment aside and kept her own counsel—her story should certainly have ended happier. A happy ending, that was what Lydia wanted. She was having none of this business, as in literature at least, where women who had an adventure—the exact sort that *men* were allowed to enjoy—had to be poisoned, hanged, or hit by a train. No, none of that.

Silence. Tell no one. That was the answer. That and forgetfulness. Intentional—calculated, premeditated—forgetfulness, if necessary. It was a variation on her father's British stiff upper lip. Bear up. Put it out of your mind. And soldier on.

Meanwhile, downstairs, a sure reminder entered her house with two other men, all of them stomping and shaking off rain. Sam handed his hat, longcoat, and umbrella to the servant who greeted them at the door. "I'm sorry we're late. Sheep," he explained. "A wagon slid into a flock of sheep. It was a regular free-for-all on the road from the station."

The servant looked at him blankly. Of course. The man behind Sam, John Winslow, stifled a silly laugh. Winslow, Patterson's right hand and heir apparent—so he had thought—was hoping for the interloper here to rip his britches or something, so Sam's explaining their delay to a servant made him real happy; he could barely contain himself. The third man, Michael Frazier, was more helpful, the three of them making up what Sam had thought would be the entire American contingent at Wendt's county home.

He was mistaken. They were led upstairs through an archway into a crowded drawing room, where Sam immediately saw the good Senator Pieters, his wife, his mother-in-law, his sister, and her husband. That is to say, the jilted bride's principles of the wedding party, including—no mercy—the bride herself: Gwyn, on the far side of the room, even wore white. She stood in a cloud of snowy lace with a huge pink rose at her waist. Why there should be so many Americans at a small, private English affair, he couldn't say, but there they were.

How cozy, he thought. He stayed at the edge of the room with the two embassy attachés, making small talk with a chatty grande dame august enough to attend alone, her husband being in Scotland "readying for the grouse."

Sam only half listened to her as, unavoidably, his eyes searched the room. He had to be careful, it turned out, or he'd make eye contact with Gwyn, who, he realized, was trying to get his attention. He couldn't tell if she wanted a chance to bash him in public or an opportunity to talk sense. Neither appealed to him.

He let people interpose and frustrate whatever she had in mind. With luck, he would sit nowhere near her at dinner. With great good fortune, he wouldn't talk to her all tonight—since everything he'd said, last time they'd talked, had been wrong, not a word available that didn't hurt her feelings. He had no faith that he could say hello right, not to Gwyn's way of thinking. Which brought Liddy clearly into his mind. No matter what he said to her, no matter how harebrained, she'd laugh or get angry or get playful. He liked how she could take care of herself.

He missed her.

He kept looking, knowing with utter certainty, as he scanned face after face, head after head, that he'd come here first and foremost with the hope of seeing her. Then, abruptly, his eyes stopped on a smallish, shining, brown head, curls contained in a silver net interwoven with silk flowers.

Instantly—before he'd fully formed the words inside his head, *It's Liddy*—his body understood her presence. As if an awareness of her could drop into his blood like a pebble into a pool: his surface breached, rings of reaction spreading through him. Nothing he could do. God, it was wonderful to see her. And, doggone, she was pretty: decked out like a queen. He smiled to himself. There was not a speck of dirt on her. The top of her dress looked iridescent or something. He couldn't see why clearly. Mother of pearl. Like her skin: creamy and polished. She turned, smiling to someone as she talked. Even across a room, her dark lashes defined her eyes. Her mouth was stained pink, neat, wide, perfect. The woman purely shone.

A second later—Sam had to lean his head—he saw a man bend toward her. The fellow was thick-waisted, but young and sturdy and, damn it, about as elegant a swell as England turned out. As the man angled his body near Liddy's, his posture was vaguely possessive, or wanted to be. Sam's pebble of awareness hatched: From his tiny consciousness of her came forth a dragon, a raging possessiveness—jealousy, fear, yearning. Sam felt competitive with the man, whoever he was, in a way that made him want to run over, pick the fellow up by his tailcoat, and sling him out the glass window onto the street two stories down.

She's mine, he wanted to say. Then had to look away. No, she wasn't. He was smart enough to stay put, say nothing, but his face felt hot.

And he couldn't keep his eyes away for long. He found himself staring at Liddy and the man beside her again. Surprisingly, from across the room, the man's gaze met his. Sam scowled, holding the fellow's attention. He couldn't help it. When the Englishman looked away, he was noticeably unsettled—he bent his head to Liddy and stepped back, completely out of the way. Oh, yes, an unobstructed view of her!

Oh, no: an unobstructed view of her turning sheet-white.

Sam tried to smile, tried to soften what had to be the

shock of seeing him here. Looking right at him, Liddy grabbed the shoulder of the man beside her as if she was going to fall. Beside her—now there was somewhere he'd like to be invited: beside Liddy. *Nod, Lid. Give me a little smile, one of your barely-there ones. Anything. Ask me over.*

She didn't. Instead, her face took on a kind of sick expression, as if she was ill. She looked away, turning her back.

Fine. He started over anyway, weaving his way through people. Some lady with a lot of feathers and glass beads tried to stop him; he ignored her. He just wanted to hear Liddy's voice, get close enough to see the smoothness of her skin, maybe catch a whiff . . . the way her skin always smelled so good. Then, too, he wouldn't mind finding out more about that fellow or getting rid of him.

All so mature. Sam, you better get a good hold of yourself. This is no moor. You are not alone. And you have promised to do a job that would be badly served by any sort of scene tonight.

Right, he told himself, as he twisted and turned his way past one person then the next. But just a word . . . a little moment . . . a passing scent . . .

"Excuse me?" said a voice behind him. Someone caught his arm.

"What?" He turned irritably.

The woman with the feathers wouldn't leave him alone. She had hold of him. "Would you be the man whom His Excellency Mr. Patterson sent?"

He frowned. "I guess. Why?"

"I'm Lady Wendt—"

He winced. "Oh, I'm sorry. I arrived late, and it's so crowded. My name is Samuel Cody. I'm taking Ian's place, that is, Mr. Patterson's."

"Indeed." She didn't care; she had something specific on her mind. "Have you seen the queen?" she asked.

He blinked. "The queen? Yes."

She frowned as if he'd misunderstood. "In London?" she asked.

"At Windsor. Her foreign minister arranged a meeting. Since there were extenuating circumstances."

"So you are the official ambassador?"

"Officially, I am the interim ambassador. Another man'll most likely be sent along by late autumn." He smiled. "But for the moment you are stuck with me."

She nodded, trying to grasp his meaning.

With a little bow, he clarified, "Samuel J. Cody, the new ambassador extraordinary and plenipotentiary from the United States, at your service, ma'am."

Her mouth opened. She was taken aback, possibly by his accent. *Madam.* It was *madam*, not *ma'am*, a nicety that never got high enough in his priorities to remember at the right moment.

"I'm sorry to be introducin' myself to you in this way," he said.

She only shook her head.

"But, you see," he continued, "Mr. Patterson had to return home to be with his family." He halted a moment, then went ahead and told her, "He's quite ill."

"Yes," she said. "I see." She frowned. "I'm sorry," she thought to say, though she seemed elsewhere. She was immediately looking round the room. "That puts everyone off one person."

He didn't know what she meant.

She looked upset. "I have to rematch every woman one man back. What a mess. I shall have to begin again."

He understood something was wrong, and it was his fault. "I'm sorry," he said with no idea what he apologized for.

She waved him off. "Nothing to do for it. It's fine. I'll fix it." She glanced at him. "You go in with the duchess. That woman over there." She indicated the talkative lady with the husband in Scotland, then threw him a smile so brief and insincere he almost didn't believe he'd seen it.

At which point, she walked away, allowing him to resume the pursuit of—

Criminy, her daughter. Lady Wendt. That was Liddy's mother. Jesus, no wonder Liddy was tough.

* * *

Lydia glanced over her shoulder because she was certain her
eyes deceived her. It had to be another tall man, someone
who looked like her cowboy from the moor.

But, no: It was he, trying to get around her mother—he
towered over her, taller, in fact, than anyone in the room. He
looked like an idealized version of himself, not like the Sam
she remembered, clean-shaven, his hair slicked back. He
was dressed in a high white collar, white bow tie, knife
pleats down his chest, a black coat, stephanotis at the black
satin buttonhole. Full evening dress. His face was lean, sun-
browned, taut and symmetrical: not so much as a bruise. His
posture, so familiar, was erect, purposeful. He looked determined, though her mother had him cornered—she would
throw him out. Lydia couldn't watch.

She jerked her head around, staring at Boddington's
chin—which was going up and down, on and on, about how
encouraging the queen's greetings were to her troops in
South Africa. Even with her back to Sam, though, Lydia
could feel him behind her. In an over-warm, crowded room,
with nothing in her since breakfast, his presence made for a
kind of nausea—a hot, acidic squabble in her stomach between anticipation and dread.

Why had he come? Why was he here?

Me. No, no, she dare not think it. Still, the look on his
face . . . *Me. He's come after me.* Oh, no, he mustn't. He'd
never make it past her mother, for one thing, guardian of society's rules, of circumspect, circumscribed life *comme il
faut.*

She glanced back again, only to see her mother smile at
him. As if her daughter's wild good time two weeks ago
were so large and sly it could even overcome the viscountess: as if Lydia's memories and dreams of Sam were allowed
to walk into her real life unannounced and turn it—and
her—upside down.

He moved toward her again, navigating his way through
people. Her heart raced. Her throat constricted. Once more,
she turned away. Boddington was watching him too, now.

A moment later, at her back, she heard, "Lid—ah—Miss Bedford-Browne?"

Slowly, she faced around and looked up.

Sam. *Impeccable* leaped to mind, though not in a million years would she have dreamed she'd associate the word with the beat-up, unshaven man she had known on the moor. Yet there he was: impeccable.

With entirely too much sincerity, he said, "I am so happy to see you."

His voice was the same; it seemed a miracle to hear it: deep, low, all but grating out his throat. It made her knees weak. She could feel her pulse leap at her wrists, her neck.

She couldn't think what to say. She and Sam stared at each other.

After a long, awkward minute, beside her Boddington asked, "Do you two know each other?"

"No," Lydia said at exactly the same moment that Sam said, "Yes."

He laughed. "Must you *always* say the opposite thing as I do, Miss Bedford-Browne? Must we always argue?"

She looked down, frowning, then felt positively giddy as, in the shadows on the floor, she recognized the toes of black cherry red cowboy boots. She swayed on her feet—it wasn't giddiness and shadows after all, but inkiness before her eyes. Don't be a ninny, she thought. Don't faint. But the room was so crowded and hot.

"Actually," Sam explained, "I tried to get to know her when she was in—"

"Plymouth," she said for fear he'd name the wrong town. "When I—I was, um—touring Devon's township archery trials." She took a breath, trying to steady herself.

"It was Bleycott," he said. "And she wouldn't have anything to do with me."

"Plymouth." She would insist with her dying breath, since the lie she and Rose had come up with didn't include her having gotten to Bleycott.

Alas, *dying breath* was looking to be entirely too accurate. The room wobbled before her eyes as if seen through

waves of rising heat. She felt a mist of perspiration at her lip,
her forehead—which she noticed only by contrast as her
face ran cold.

He said, "I was in Plymouth, but there were circumstances there that would've kept me from flirting with you. I
wouldn't've done it. Maybe it was that town near Bleycott,"
he suggested.

"Two Points."

"Right."

Right. She laughed, the noise of it, as it came from her
throat, sounding foolish and rattle-brained. She found herself grabbing rapid, short breaths.

Someone—oh, dear, her mother's voice—said, "Lydia?
Lydia? Where is your tonic?"

She had no idea. She didn't want any. It wouldn't help.
Nonetheless, before she could complain, an open bottle of
the bloody stuff appeared under her nose. The smell made
her gag. That was all it took.

The last thing she heard was, "Their Royal Majesties, the
Prince and Princess of Wales."

The last thing she felt was her damp, cold cheek collide
hard with Sam's smooth-pressed chest.

Lydia was out less than a minute. Just long enough for her to
collapse partway into Sam's arms and for her to realize that
he and Boddington were wrestling over who should have
possession of her inert body.

"I'm fine," she said, lifting herself awkwardly, gloved elbows up, trying to climb up out of both their arms.

"You're not fine," her mother said. "You haven't been
taking your tonic. You've been walking all over the place.
You're doing exactly as the doctors tell you not to. And now
look . . ." Her mother continued, but Lydia ignored her.

Her father, bless him, appeared. "I'd like to take my
daughter into dinner, Your Majesty, if you don't mind. . . ."
He was talking to the Prince of Wales, who stood with them
now, all belly from her slightly folded position. "I know,
highly irregular, but . . ."

Her father took over lovingly, the prince and princess more than willing, though briefly Lydia's mother argued.

The prince went in with Lady Wendt, the princess on the arm of—Lydia did *not* understand this at all—Sam Cody, she on her father's arm, though she should have been much farther down the table.

Before the soup course was finished, Lydia had overheard why an American cowboy was sitting at the end of the table with a blooded prince.

The United States ambassador? As it sank in, first she knew bewilderment, quickly followed by anger. She eyed him narrowly. A job? He was worried about a job? When he was the damned ambassador to her country? That wasn't a *job*! She wanted to kill him, poison his red mullet in Cardinal sauce, hang him by his white bow tie.

Her mind reeled as the same unanswerable question came up: What on God's earth was he doing here?

Other people didn't know quite what to make of him either, though, like she, they seemed to find his accent and cozy expressions interesting, amusing. Sam himself was guarded; he didn't speak much. At one point, in his earnest voice, he called the president a "straight shooter," which someone took literally.

"No," he said with slow, Texas charm. "I mean a fella who doesn't go in for a lot of tricks or fancy stuff. Just picks 'em off, one straight shot at a time. Direct. Effective."

As to the food she had so looked forward to at one point in the day, it was abominable. Lydia lost track of what was set before her. The wild game stank in her nostrils. After that, it all smelled the same—like old horse blankets, boiled. She stayed as long as she could, dizzily staring at Sam, nauseatingly pushing food about her plate, then realized she was just queasy enough that she might truly be sick.

"I'm so sorry," she said, standing. "You must excuse me."

Several gentlemen stood, including Sam.

Others were only halfway to their feet, before she said, "No, no. Everyone continue. I'll be fine. I just need to lie down."

At which point, with as much dignity as possible, Lydia

abandoned her family, friends, Sam, and the future King and Queen of England.

She intended to fly upstairs to her rooms, but at the last moment her feet took her down the staircase, through the long entry hall. She ran for the front double doors. Air.

It was a good decision. As soon as the cool night hit her face, she felt better.

She stood outside, breathing easier, fuming a little—how dare he? she kept thinking. How dare he show up at her house? She didn't care what his reasons. Seeing him was just so . . . complicated.

Then the door behind her softly opened and closed. She turned, and knew the silhouette.

"You," she said.

"Me." Sam laughed, and she felt so glad to hear his raspy laughter she wanted, oh, just to take a bath in it, run her hands over him, tickle him, make him laugh till tears ran down his face. His silhouette—not so unlike his shadow on a moonlit moor—said quietly, "I didn't mean to upset you."

She looked at him in the faint lights of her portico, servants at the doors, the drive filled with a line of carriages and waiting drivers.

And, impossibly, Sam standing there without a scratch on him. Not a smudge. His white shirtfront standing out in the dimness, so crisp she could have bounced a shilling off it. "You're certainly"—she paused, then said, "clean."

His low laughter again. "Yeah, you're clean, too." He added, blast him, "And you look real nice that way, Lid. Downright spectacular. I can't tell you how happy it makes me to see you again."

"I'm not happy to see you."

He dipped his head, shrugging in that way he had as he lifted one arm to rub the back of his neck. "Yeah, I know. I figured a woman who told me not to call wouldn't be over-joyed." In the dim light, she caught his smile—she realized it went into both sides of his face, a balanced, first-rate smile. "But, see, I got the job after all," he explained. "Or

sort of. It's a slightly different job. But it's a pretty good one.
I thought you might change your mind—"

"I haven't."

"Ah." He looked down.

"You have to leave."

"All right." He turned.

"No," she said.

He paused, glancing back over his shoulder.

"Not just now. Not the portico. The house. Here. You
have to leave my home."

He let out a breath, shook his head—whether in negation
or simple disbelief, she couldn't tell.

Then he turned and walked back into the house without
saying a word more. Through the door's sidelight, she
watched him climb the stairs again, returning, where in the
dining hall, she knew, he would be the tallest, handsomest,
straightest shooter in the room.

Sam returned to find that the ladies had left the large dining
room. The men were up from their chairs stretching their
legs, while Wendt himself traveled the room, pouring
brandy. A morbidly thin servant followed him with a silver
tray, offering cigars—like little corpses lined up side by side
in an open, polished rosewood casket.

"No, thank you," Sam said to the cigars.

On seeing him, Wendt set the brandy bottle onto the tray
and walked toward him, carrying two snifters, each with an
inch of amber liquor. "Cognac?" he asked.

"Thank you." Sam took what turned out to be very good
brandy.

Wendt offered it along with a raised brow. He asked,
"Pieters says you were originally coming over to open negotiations on the canal in Central America?"

"Yes."

Two other men joined them, the first English charge, Sam
realized. Either by design or practiced instinct, they more or
less circled him. With the good Senator Pieters right behind.

He walked toward the little gathering, at last free of the foot of the table so as to cause trouble, if he so chose.

"The Senate didn't confirm you," he said as he came up.

Sam held out one hand. "What can I say?"

"So how is it," Pieters asked stonily, "that, having failed to be approved as lead in a negotiation, you are now in charge of the entire embassy?"

"Interim Ambassador." Sam shrugged. "Patterson needed to go home. Meanwhile, we can't just close the embassy. I was here. I have a good idea of international U.S. concerns from having worked on the treaty in Paris in December." He smiled amiably. "Until the president can appoint someone whom the Senate will approve, I'm holding down the fort."

"Interim, hmm," said the shorter of the two unnamed Englishmen, who then exchanged glances with Wendt in a way that said they thought England didn't have to deal with him, that they could simply wait for the next fellow.

Sam told them, "The canal will be my main focus while I'm here. The president has asked me to bring home a draft of a new treaty."

"There is a Central American canal treaty already in place between our countries."

"A lot changes in fifty years." Sam laughed good-naturedly. "It's old."

"A lot changed in the past year," Wendt accused.

He was referring to the extraordinary U.S. victory over Spain in the recent and very short war between the two nations, a conflict that had bestowed the dubious honor of imperialism on Sam's country. The U.S. had gained Cuba, the Philippine Islands, as well as special authority over Puerto Rico and Guam.

The United States, a country of two oceans, now had concerns in both of them that made it, for the first time, a world power. And made a canal more necessary than ever.

"These days," Sam said, "a lot changes in fifty minutes. I have a direct telegraph line to the president, and he tells me daily he wants this new treaty. He's like a dog on a bone."

A point Sam didn't have to mention was that, last year,

loved being the crude ol' cowboy he was. In business—
even the business of diplomacy, the way he practiced it—it
could be a strength to be an aggressive, ornery-tempered
son-of-a-gun. It sure gave him the upper hand over those
trying to keep their dignity intact, hogtied by their own
ideas of civility.

Then he got gravy on top. As he was leaving the room, he
heard in a pretty loud voice full of a nice taste of outrage,
"This is intolerable." It was Pieters. "I don't know how he
got here, but if that man is staying, Wendt, I'm going. And
taking my entire family with me."

Oh, yes, please! Sam thought. And don't forget Gwyn.

16

If you want a red rose . . . you must build it out of music by moonlight, and stain it with your own heart's-blood.

OSCAR WILDE
The Nightingale and the Rose, 1888

Lydia retired early, but had a restless night. She didn't know what Sam intended. With a word, he could ruin her. Not that she expected him to, but his presence, the inadvertent possibility, left her feeling at risk. She hoped the morning should find him gone, a disturbing dream vanished back into wherever it came from.

Disturbing dream. She shouldn't have thought the words, because somewhere in the early hours of morning something brought on a terrifying one: She was in a vast place, a castle, a keep, though not exactly. It was dark and dank. There was a man far away, before an old stone wall—there was only one wall. She could barely see him from where she sat in a chair, her fingers clutching its wood arms. She was frightened. Somehow, she dare not move. The man at the crumbling wall was mixing something. It clinked in front of him. It was for her. Oh, no—

The next thing she knew, he was near, and the dimness of

the place had turned to black. She could feel his presence, yet couldn't see him. With panic, she realized, a dark sack had somehow gotten over her head, and her arms wouldn't lift to pull it off. The man took hold of her by her shoulders and drew her to him purposefully. He was going to do something, something unpleasant. She called out. "Your Excellency! I can't see! Help me!" Sam? Was she hoping the stranger was Sam?

He neither confirmed not refuted, only pulling her head against him while she struggled, blind. He was so much stronger. She could feel his power in the lock of his arms about her, in the hardness of the chest against her forehead and cheek. Behind, at her neck, he drew her hair up. She felt something cold there, a tingle. The feeling poured down into her spine, entering her, spreading, filling her as with liquid needles . . . or millions of tiny, cold-sparking stars—

Lydia jerked awake in her bed to a bright morning, her heart pounding, the dream vivid. Sam. Her strange nemesis in the dream had been his height. Tall, long-muscled, broad-chested. His chest. It *was* Sam. What had made her mind construct such a bizarre phantasm of him? What was she afraid of? The dream, its questions, made her shiver. The fear in it felt so real and horrid.

Yet there was something else . . . something horrifically fascinating within the dream as well. And *that* made her feel truly off-kilter: a stranger to herself.

"Good morning!" Rose said as she entered the room with Lydia's first-thing cup of tea.

It was their ritual: teacup in one hand, on her way to the bed, the maid grabbed a handful of dark green velvet at the window and carried the curtain with her. As she proceeded, behind her along the wide French window, sun opened up, pouring in across the floor to make neat patterns, lace shadows, that bent up and across the bed.

"Here you go." She handed over the tea as Lydia sat up, then walked back, pacing off the length of the other side of window, its velvet curtain in hand. The room brightened into full sun, a wavering contrast of sun-filled lace up a dresser, an armoire, a painted screen, a vanity and padded bench. One by one, Rose tied back the lace at the French windows. Through each, one could see a bit more, like a triptych that came together: a rolling expanse of green cut by a little stream to a distant pond and woods.

"Did you see who was here last night?" Lydia asked as she stirred tea.

"The prince and princess," the maid said cheerfully as she cranked open the first window. A light breeze entered, carrying the faint smell of roses from the side of the house. "Though they left early this morning."

"Oh, dear. Was I supposed to have been up to see them off? No one said." With a frown, Lydia recovered her former train of thought. "No, no, not them. Mr. Cody."

Rose looked over her shoulder, mouth pursed. "Oh, him. Yes. Though for an ambassador, I can't say much for him. He doesn't have a valet." She made a moue of disgust. "Which means I only know the gossip from the kitchen and upstairs staff."

"Upstairs gossip? Is he still here?"

"Yes, miss, he spent the night."

Lydia groaned. "Oh, do tell."

Her maid recited like a litany: "He went to bed late in the north guest room. He doesn't have but one bag, and that didn't arrive till this morning from the inn at Crawthorne. The other two men from the embassy left last night, as well as the American senator—there was some sort of rift. He's here alone as his Lordship's guest, though his Lordship doesn't like him. They got into a to-do last night also." She frowned, picked up a shawl that was over a chair, then disappeared into the dressing room. From there, her voice called, "The rest of the yesterday evening he was quiet and stayed to himself, except around midnight, when Miss Pinkerton and Miss Werther managed to involve him in a game of *vingt-et-un*, thinking they were teaching it to him."

She materialized from the interior room, carrying a dressing gown as she continued. "It turns out it's an American game, too. He beat them, and the ladies liked that he did, so boisterously that the servants were still talking about their shrieks and laughter this morning." She offered the gown out.

Lydia drained the last of her tea, set the cup on the bedside table, and stood, raising an arm into the gown.

Rose said, "You know, when we saw him last, he looked so different. I shouldn't have thought it was possible for him to look so—well, so genteel."

"His cheek and nose were swollen." Lydia puzzled a moment as her open gown dropped down onto her shoulders. "Or something. He's had a haircut. And of course neither he nor I was at our tidiest when we parted."

Her maid nodded, as if a haircut and clean face explained the difference.

Lydia risked looking at her and asking, "You think he's handsome?" She fought a smile. She wanted to say, He is so handsome, you can't imagine. His naked body is more beautiful than anything I've ever seen.

Rose looked bewildered by the question. "I suppose." Not smiling at all, she added, "Though handsome is as handsome does: There is a rumor he jilted someone, someone important, though I can't find out whom." She scowled as if it were an equal offense: "And a gentleman should have a valet. You would think an ambassador would maintain a certain appearance."

If only he would maintain a *dis*appearance, Lydia thought. But, alas, Samuel Cody did not evaporate like a dream. Nor, when she saw him, did he look the part of the mad monster—a Dr Miracle from *Hoffman* with flasks clinking like castanets, as in an opera she'd seen recently, which seemed to have combined with the moor and Sam to give her that awful dream. As to his more polished good looks, they had something to do with his clothes as well. Aside from his boots, his clothes were new and English-made—as if someone was advising him on how to be less contrary, at least in appearance.

The impression of his belonging here was furthered when

she saw that Clive had returned from London—a day late, so typical—and sat at the far end of the downstairs dining-room table, entertaining people over breakfast, Sam laughing with him, along with Meredith, her fiancé, Frederick, and Julianne Werther.

Behind them on the sideboard stood half a dozen heated, silver-domed servers—very much Lydia's father's style, not her mother's. It was the way her father arranged things on mornings when he, his neighbors, and friends rode out to terrorize the foxes of the district. Not even the season's cubbing, however, would start for a good several weeks, thus the arrangement of breakfast merely pointed out the absence of Lady Wendt.

Had Lydia's mother spent the night, even breakfast should have included liveried servants, a formal flow of food from the kitchen, and exact seating. Apparently, though, with royalty gone, Lady Wendt found no reason to stay. (Which meant that, once again, Clive had timed his arrival to coincide with his mother's departure.)

There were perhaps twenty in all downstairs having breakfast at the moment, some in the dining room, another half dozen having roamed to the terrace—one wall of the downstairs dining room was nothing but doors. These were all open this morning onto the long side brick terrace that overlooked the rose garden, a breeze gently stirring the room's heavy curtains.

Lydia had no sooner spotted Sam than he looked up, and their gazes fixed on each other. He immediately stood up, scooting back his chair, then paused when she looked away and kept walking, scowling.

Don't do that, she thought. Don't come to me, don't look at me as if we were lovers.

Oh, the thoughts, the fears that traveled through her head. She went straight over to the line of servers and began loading a plate—eggs, tomatoes, fried toast, marmalade. All the while her skin felt warm, colored by knowledge. Could anyone tell by looking at her? Did they suspect? Would they guess? Did it show? She felt guarded, afraid to look at him for fear of giving away a part of herself she wished to keep secret.

Out the corner of her eye, she was aware he remained standing, his hand gone into his hair the way it did when he was perplexed or frustrated. Memory took over from there. The way he shrugged sometimes when he talked . . . the way he slouched or straightened . . . his voice, his smell, the way he moved against her.

Oh, stop, she told herself and scooped up a huge serving of pineapple, only to realize after it was done that she had weighed down half her plate with it. She frowned at the mound of food. It wasn't just the pineapple; it was everything. She'd served herself enough to feed a small village.

Well, fine. She was ravenous after last night, and everything smelled wonderful, thank goodness. She was better. She was perfectly all right without her bloody tonic. She'd take her large meal out onto the terrace and eat it, every last bite.

She was on her way toward the wide terrace doorway when someone grabbed her from behind by the waist. She leaped and spun, ready to upbraid Sam for all she was worth: and dumped food down the front of her brother.

"You shrew!" he said, laughing as he madly wiped himself. Clive was a foot taller than she and thin as a reed. "You did that on purpose. You always hated this vest."

"Oh, I'm so sorry." Leveling her plate in one hand, with the other she brushed her napkin down Clive's loudest vest—a yellow, orange, red, and blue thing she thought in fact quite ugly.

He was in unusual good spirits. "Not to worry. I never much liked the vest myself. I only wear it to be perverse. You have ruined the shirt, though, and it was nice."

"I shall buy you another." She threw him a smile. "I cleaned up at Scorton. I took the ladies' Silver Arrow!"

"You didn't!"

"I did! And a tidy purse was attached to the honor, I must tell you. I can easily buy you a new shirt."

"You shall do no such thing. We shall buy champagne to

celebrate the best archer in the family." He laughed. "And spill *that* on you."

Oh, my, she was suddenly so glad to see Clive that, food down the front of him or not, she flung herself toward him on tiptoe—at six foot six, his was a hefty height to scale. She attempted to hug him.

While he held her off. "Careful, careful, careful, or you'll spill it down my back next." He jockeyed to balance the plate in her hand. "A fine greeting. I don't see you for a month, and you throw food all over me."

Sam watched, fascinated by the open affection Lydia showed her brother, part happy for her, part jealous: what he would have given for that greeting. Then—oh!—to hear her unself-conscious laugh again, burbling, belly-deep. Hearing it, the very first notes of it, was like hearing the opening bars of a familiar, favorite symphony. It stopped him in his tracks.

He wasn't the only one: Conversations came to a halt. Across the room, people turned, smiling, to listen. Because Liddy, caught in laughter, was gorgeous. The sound was riveting, infectious; it made a man want to join in, to laugh with her. The sight was wondrous. Her thin nose wrinkled. Her shoulders shook. Her small breasts quivered, and her cheeks pinked. Her face lit.

He defied anyone to leave the room when Lydia Bedford-Browne was laughing. Standing there, he forgot himself; all he could do was marvel.

Beside him, a man's voice said, "She comes with a piece of England attached, one of the richest dowries."

Sam glanced down at the young Englishman from last night—Boddington, he thought was the fellow's name. He'd plonked himself into a chair one place down, with no breakfast, no food. He just sat there, offering information the significance of which was lost on Sam, who shrugged. "I don't need money," he said, "and I don't want a piece of England."

"I know. That's the point. You can't appreciate all she is."

"She's more than a rich dowry."

"Absolutely," the other man agreed.

Sam's attention was drawn back to the brother and sister near the far doorway as Clive Bedford-Browne's voice rose—he looked like Liddy, only much taller, squared off, more masculine. His hair was a little darker.

He tormented his sister. "It isn't as if you haven't been busy. Out wandering the Dartmoor, I understand."

She pushed him playfully.

Clive continued, "With Rose and a disgusting chap who drank like a fish and had you walking in circles . . ."

Sam frowned, pushing his tongue against his teeth. Disgusting chap? With no sense of direction? Why was there any mention of a man at all? What story had Liddy and her maid come up with?

Not that it mattered, he told himself. All that mattered, of course, was that it was a good enough story to keep Liddy safe from any hint of the misconduct they'd gotten up to. As her brother continued, though, Sam's brow drew down.

"So did he have a mustache and six-shooter? Someone said he was a cowboy from the Wild West Show—"

Beside him, a voice interfered with his eavesdropping. The fellow Boddington asked, "Do you fancy her?"

"A little," Sam lied. "You?"

"A lot."

In silence, they both watched Liddy link her arm into her brother's, the two of them strolling through the terrace doorway and out of sight.

Sam slowly sat himself down, agitated. He threw a scowl at the Englishman, wishing for no reason in particular that he could think of an excuse to bludgeon the fellow. "So are you in love with her?" he asked.

The Englishman moved his jaw once as if chewing on a difficult question, then folded his arms across his chest like a schoolboy who realized suddenly he knew the right answer. "Indeed," he said. "I do believe I am."

Lydia had a long, delicious tête-à-tête with Clive over a much more agreeable breakfast of tea and toast, which he fetched for her. It was lovely. He brought the tea sweetened just as she liked it and the toast with the perfect amount of marmalade.

At one point, as the two of them sat on a bench alone, she'd thought to whisper to Clive about Sam, the real story on the moor, or at least part of it. "There was a man—" she began.

He paused, his eyes fixing on her. Something in her tone must have said already too much, for his brow lifted, his expression suddenly far too avid.

She covered by saying, "On the train," and shrugged. "I didn't give him the time of day." She couldn't help adding, "But he was so interesting—different." She shook her head. "Too different."

Clive frowned at her, then patted her hand.

Nonetheless, her spirits improved for having spent breakfast with him. Then churned up again when, on her way upstairs again, her father, on the landing above, called down to her. "Lydia."

She stopped and looked up, her foot on the first step.

Jeremy Bedford-Browne continued down the stairs, a balding, well-dressed man—thickset, yet with an alert mien that defied both the slight stoutness and age of his body. He was sixty-six and shorter than average: an inch shorter than his wife, only an inch taller than his daughter.

"I'd like to speak to you," he said as he came to a halt on the step above her. He looked down from the added height, laying his hand on a polished wood newel that was round as a cannonball.

"Yes?"

He patted the wood once, frowned, then said, "Last night, I more or less asked Boddington what he's waiting for, why he hasn't come to me to ask my permission to marry you."

"Oh, Father, no—"

"Oh, Father, yes. I *am* your father, which gives me the right, no, the responsibility to worry for your future: meddle with it, if I think it's appropriate." He cleared his throat. "Wallace says he isn't sure of you, of your affection for him." He held up his hand when, again, she tried to protest. "Lydia Jane, a man needs encouragement sometimes. He can't stand out in the open forever with little or no help. It's a woman's job to give him some sure ground to walk on." He frowned at her. "Shown favor, I feel sure this young gentleman would offer for you. We could see you engaged by the end of the week." He paused. "Boddington's a nice chap. I think he'd make a good husband." Softer, his voice imbued with an unfair degree of affection, he said, "It would make me very happy, Lydia, to see you so well settled."

"I, ah—"

"What?" he asked impatiently.

Her distress made her brave. "I'm not sure I'm ready to marry."

He raised his shoulders—her father was much less fazed by her newfound directness than was her mother. "Who's ever sure?" He made a short, dry laugh in his throat. "For that matter, who's ever ready?"

"Weren't you and Mother ever sure?"

He frowned swiftly and deeply, then said, "I was sure she'd be a good mother to my children and an energetic supporter to myself, which she is."

"What's wrong between the two of you?"

He was taken aback by the question. "Nothing." Then resigned. "Nothing important." He lifted his finger, pointing at her. "Boddington: Go over and say something nice to him."

"I'd like to say something nice to him later."

What cheek. Lydia reveled in it; she frightened herself. To exert here the same will as she had discovered, and come to love, in herself out on the moor felt dangerous. Yet necessary. No one, she had come to realize, was going to hand her life over to her. So she'd claim it.

Her father's brow drew down again. It was a look more of concern than censure.

She added quickly, "The new bow. I've been trying to get out onto the shooting range to test it for days now. Giles has put out the targets. I'm late. If I don't hurry, I won't be able to shoot eight full rounds and still be back in time to dress for dinner."

He nodded, studying her with a troubled expression. "Later then," he agreed.

"Yes, later. I'll say something nice."

She intended to. No reason not to. Boddington was a decent sort. Being kind to him was nothing less than he deserved.

17

Negotiations, like a poker game, usually have a sucker, a donator—if you look around the table and aren't sure who it is, it's probably you.

SAMUEL JEREMIAH CODY
A Texan in Massachusetts

If a person asked Boddington about love, he listed the qualities he wanted in a woman, like common sense and good manners and a comely degree of beauty. As if love were a rational decision that could be determined by measured attributes. As if a person chose the one he or she loved like a new suit of clothes. *I'll take one with pin tucks in seersucker.*

Proof that Boddington had yet to be in love—yet to be thrilled by it, tortured by it, leveled by it. Or so Lydia imagined, since this was how she envisioned it: a cataclysmic event. Certainly, no such event had passed between herself and Boddington. She was quite certain he wasn't in love with her, and equally sure she was not in love with him. On the other hand, they accepted and appreciated each other, which seemed not the worst basis for a married partnership.

So if she waited too long to show "favor," and he went elsewhere, how would she feel?

Disappointed.

Was that all?

Yes. There were other suitors. And she knew who she was and why they came.

They were drawn, first and foremost, to her family's fortune and position. On both sides, she came from notably powerful people. Even with this sizable advantage, though, she was by no means a favorite. She tended to contradict men—an unpopular trait. (Generously, Boddington told her she did so because she was smart and didn't like to hide it— when she contradicted him, he nodded, appeared to listen, and sometimes even laughed over it.) The surprise was that, after six social seasons, she still was not considered a failure for having not made a match. Rather, she had gathered the reputation for being difficult to please—some might say, nigh onto impossible.

Her strength lay in an ease she had with the opposite sex, a healthy liking for men combined with a liking of herself. And in her . . . *wiles*, her brother called them. By which he meant: Rose was good with her hair; Lydia herself was good with her clothes; and, perhaps most important, she had an intuition for gazing and smiling along in a playful manner. As a result—smart, contradicting, or not—every season one or two of the new gallants succumbed to her charm. The fact that one of them, the Earl of Boddington, son and heir to the Marquess of Ernswick, had for two years now been competing for her attention gave her in fact a certain amount of cachet—though the day he lost interest her stock would drop.

Stock. That was how she, and every other member of her family so far as she knew, approached marriage: as business, a negotiation. She might have liked for it to have included her being in love, but love, she was wise enough to admit, wasn't something she could command. It would happen, or it would not. And life must go on, regardless.

Perhaps because there was so much Lydia couldn't control, the fact that she had almost uncanny control over one thing fascinated her. She could hit a straw target with an arrow from sixty yards with remarkable accuracy.

She shot a thirty-two-pound bow, a heavy pull for a

woman, a bow that was also long for her sex, five feet, eight inches; it was taller than she was. A week ago, a new bow had arrived from Wales, where it had been handmade for her. She had already tried it out briefly in London at Regent's Park and knew it to throw an arrow smoothly, barely any jar: a good cast. Today, though, was the first she would have a chance to shoot as long as she liked, all day if she wished, and get a feel for how her new equipment was going to work at competitions.

Thus, the moment her father let her go, she was up the stairs like an arrow herself. She quickly dressed, gathered her equipment, then headed down again toward a day to be spent out on the target field.

Coming outside, however, she got only as far as the side terrace before she stopped. She'd walked out into the middle of a dramatic story, apparently—one Sam was telling to the rapt audience of Clive, Julianne Werther, and Elizabeth Pinkerton.

He waved his arm and said, "The Indians came up over the hill. First only about sixty or so, but they kept coming and pretty soon"—he spread out the other arm—"they lined the whole horizon. And, doggone, you have never seen anything so fearsome as a thousand Comanches on horseback—"

Julianne tilted her heart-shaped face and asked, "So is that how you did this?" She reached toward him, her fingers outlining in the air the cut at his mouth, the faintest red mark of a fresh scar.

. Elizabeth answered for him. "Oh, you didn't hear?" she delighted in telling the group. "Mr. Cody was a hero in Devon. He stopped five thugs from robbing the greengrocer's wife in Plymouth. Before he leveled them all, he was hit in the face. Five of them, one of him, and he won, hands down." To Sam, she asked, "So did the Indians attack?"

His back to Lydia, he started to say something. "No—"

"They aren't really that fearsome, are they?" Julianne asked. "I mean, they're just savages."

"Heck, no," he corrected. "They're so slick, they can make your eyeballs pop out far enough to get a rope on 'em." The young ladies looked frightened for a moment, then tittered—they realized he was speaking metaphorically. He must have given them his down-home smile, because a second later they both blushed, then tittered more. "In battle," he told them, "the Comanches can ride at full gallop hanging off the side of their horses or even underneath. You can't even see them."

From the doorway, Lydia found herself scoffing. "That sounds like something fresh from one of those cowboy novels."

He turned around, surprised, then a huge, toothsome smile bloomed across his face—revealing truly fine teeth, one crooked incisor, the rest straight, all a gleaming white. He had a fine smile, broad and easy. It beamed at her as it covered her once from head to toe. "How would you know?" he teased.

"I wouldn't. It just sounds—" She hemmed, frowning. "Outrageous."

He tilted his head. "It's true." Then he undid her. He reached and lifted her new bow off her shoulder and down her arm; he took it off her, saying, "Ah, and this—"

"Wait!" she said. He'd ruined the last one.

He turned away, out of reach, leaving her to grab at his arm.

She realized there were more people. At the side of the terrace, just beyond Clive, Julianne, and Elizabeth, stood Meredith and Frederick, Lady Motmarche, her stepson Charles and his wife, all of them seemingly fascinated by Sam's wild story.

He held her bow in front of him as if he knew how to shoot it, then looked at her over his shoulder, asking, "You feelin' better?"

"Why?"

"You weren't feelin' well last night."

"Oh." She blinked. "Yes." *Thank you,* she should have said, but couldn't. If his looking at her in front of people at breakfast was embarrassing, having him tease her in front of them now was impossible. It made her tongue thick.

To the others, he used her bow to demonstrate. "They can also gallop on their horses bareback like this"—he pulled the bowstring back—"the horses' ribs in the grips of their legs. . . ."

Lydia frowned as she watched and listened. His deep, resonating voice, oh—the way he gestured his arms, the way he braced his legs, his balance . . . his rueful expression every time his eyes glanced at her . . . It all made her so self-conscious eventually that she didn't know where to look. She studied the yellow bricks at her feet.

The story wasn't long. It ended with some sort of parley, the upshot of which hadn't made him happy—he'd been negotiating for the Indians, oddly enough, and the best he'd been able to do he still considered unfair.

Fairness. Sam had an admirable sense of it. There was something noble in him that could not be passed down in letters of patent. She wondered how many people standing here might consider this quality worthy enough reason for one of their own to have lain down with it, embraced it in a very literal sense.

In the lull at the end of Sam's story, she held out her hand. "May I have that back?" Her leather arm brace dangled from her wrist, not yet properly in place.

He turned toward her, and his smile faltered. "Certainly." With a look of puzzlement, he handed over her bow.

"Thank you," she managed this time.

To get past, she had to march between him and his audience. She moved quickly, head up, trying to look more confident that she felt. Hypocrisy. She was coming to be on frighteningly familiar terms with it. Yet it seemed so necessary. The situation so unsettled her. Why?

Her heart was thudding by the time she took the terrace steps. Then she cut through the garden at a dead run.

Sam pardoned himself shortly after, then went in, through the house, and out a side entrance, all so he could go down the parlor steps into the same garden without being seen. He walked out into a crisp August coolness that always took him aback every time he stepped outside: clear and sunny and barely seventy degrees.

He tried to follow Liddy directly, then was flummoxed when the rose garden joined a series of hedged gardens that led in different directions. He wasn't sure which way she'd gone. He'd all but given up when he came through a copse of trees, and a whole vista opened up, a wide view of rolling English fields as far as the eye could see. And there she was: the Englishwoman who fascinated him a hundred yards off in profile, her arm cocked, an arrow in her bow. She let it go, and it flew. She watched it, lowering her bow into her skirts, vigilant. He didn't care where the arrow went, but she did. She focused on nothing else—allowing him, as he walked toward her, to focus on her to his heart's content.

Ooh, Liddy was a fancy thing. She stood out against the horizon, a slim, green piece of femininity, greener than the fields around her, deep, mossy, vibrant. As he got closer, the green of her was marked with bits of reddish-rust—velvet trim, he thought. Then, no, fox. Fox, for goodness' sakes—the dress itself was velvet, like no dress any woman would wear on a Texas summer day, but perfect for northern England. Reddish gloves—suede—folded into her jacket's band at the waist. Her style was more subtle than Gwyn's, not as pale and frilly, and infinitely more striking. From her simple dress on the moor, he would never have guessed Liddy could be such a showhorse: a thin, ordinary-looking girl who put herself together extraordinarily well, a real competitor, Lid.

She wore another little hat. He remembered the one out on the moor that became so sweetly crooked. This one was on straight, or at least on right—it sat forward at an angle on her head, more dark green with several short, almost hairlike feathers, white, that ruffled in the breeze.

She didn't see him as he came up, her concentration was that focused—she'd loaded another arrow. He watched her draw back her bowstring again to aim down the shaft at a round target on a stand in the distance. A round target painted with circles. She uncurled her fingers—they were covered by leather tabs—the smallest, smoothest of little

he corrected, "folks are so silly about underwear anyway, they laugh in public over them no matter what color they are." He looked at her. "Did the red make you laugh?"

"It made me uncomfortable."

"Why? And what's so crazy about my hat?" He missed it. He wished he had it.

"Well, red is so—" She frowned at him, stumped, then said, "So loud. And the hat is so—"

Oh, yeah. That again. He understood. "So not-English," he offered.

She sighed. "Yes." She bent her head. "You should leave. You don't belong here." She pulled a face.

He changed the subject. Squinting toward her target, he said, "You're good. Really good."

"Yes, I am. The regional champion. Just this past week."

"I'm not surprised. Congratulations."

When he looked at her again, she'd tilted her head, standing there holding her bow, staring at him. She took a quick breath, looked down, then up again, and, as if it pained her to say it, said nonetheless, "Look. I appreciate your trying to be civil, reassuring, as you call it. But in truth I'd just like you to leave."

"Leave?"

"You make me nervous."

"Nervous?"

"Yes. Leave. Leave Yorkshire."

"I can't. I have obligations—"

"Yes, you can. You just get on a ship and go."

More alarmed, he said, "Leave England? You want me to leave the damn country?" How crazy was this? "Liddy—"

"I'll shoot you for it," she said suddenly. "Right now. And my prize, if I win, is you go."

He drew his brow up and scratched his head. "I can't very well leave England—"

"Yorkshire then. If I win, you walk back to the house, go upstairs, pack, and call for a carriage. You go. We'll shoot for it."

He laughed. "I'd be crazy to shoot against you. You're better than I am."

"Oh, come now." She smiled that little line of a smile of hers. "Where's your sense of competition?"

"Nowhere." He snorted. "How much competition would it be, me shooting against the regional champion?"

"*Women's* champion," she amended. "The men's competition is much more rigorous, of course. More arrows, farther distances."

He laughed at her attempt. "I don't know anything about an English bow. I'd lose."

"But you're so good with a Comanche bow and arrow," she said, the syrupy curve of her smile challenging again his story this morning.

"They're not the same thing."

"Then a handicap."

He paused, looked at her. "How much of a handicap?"

"Whites. The outside circle. None of my arrows that land in it will count. It's a standard winner's handicap. I've played it before."

And still won, he'd bet. Though he found himself ruminating, staring at the target.

"Ten arrows," she said. "Two rounds of five arrows each at sixty yards. How's that?" When he didn't dispute this time, she tilted her head and made that little line of a smile he was so fond of. It was a wicked smile, he was coming to understand. Which was probably why he liked it so much. "We go by points." She named the painted rings of the target from the outside in: "One point for whites, three for blacks, five for blue, seven red, and nine points for a gold. Do you understand it?"

Sure, he thought. "And blacks, too," he added.

"What?"

"I want blacks, too, in the handicap. They don't count either."

She frowned, studying him, which made him sure it was the right move. "Well, I—"

"Come on," he encouraged. "You're the champion, and I've never done it before."

"Oh, all right," she said—Miss Cocky—and smiled more of that same smile. Or at least he thought she was being cocky. He hoped so. She sure did agree quickly.

Which was how he realized he had agreed too. The dare was on.

He nodded again as he looked at the target in the distance. How hard could it be? he asked himself. It wasn't even moving.

While, beside him, the woman broke into cackles, the witch: raucous caterwauls of pleasure.

Given her laughter, Sam was a little nervous as he tromped out to the targets—butts, she called them—to gather her arrows and set up their match. The State Department would not want to see him back in London. So why he'd taken the fool challenge was a mystery to him.

Till Liddy bent down to get an arrow that was buried in the ground at the foot of the target (proof she could miss), and her bottom went straight up in the air. Staring at her backside, he smiled. "More motion than an ocean," he murmured.

"Pardon?" She looked around, upside down at him, and the arrow released into her hand.

"Um, nothin'. A Texas saying."

She stood up, swinging around with a swish of skirts. "About what?"

"Um—the targets." Sam busied himself, pulling arrows from the "butt." "Hardly seems fair. No motion. They can't move."

"They're straw."

"Right. I'm just saying, um—rabbits are more my line."

"Good," she said and laughed again, cheerfully sadistic at his discomfort.

Once the targets were set to her satisfaction—at sixty yards, when she'd been shooting fifty—she was quick to get started.

"Ladies first," he said and, like that, *thwack,* she shot a bull's-eye immediately. Arrow in the grass or not, he began to wonder if she shot anything else.

"Nine points," she chimed out, turning toward him with a smile.

She invited conversation as she shot her round. "So how did a cowboy end up a diplomat?"

He shrugged. "It was something different to do."

She glanced at him, then aimed another arrow. "Cowboys can't afford to be in the company you're in." She let the arrow go. It flew across the field, straight for the target, which sucked it in. A red. Just outside the gold center. Thank goodness. "Sixteen," she said.

"This one can."

She reached back, pulling another arrow from the quiver as she glanced at him under her elbow—she threw him another peeved look that once more accused him of withholding information.

"Railroads," he said quickly. "Railroads and cattle. The combination's been good to me."

"And the diplomatic appointment?"

"I volunteered for the quick war we had with Spain a year and a half ago, then ended up translating at the first treaty talks."

"Translating?"

He laughed. "All my pop's mistresses were Mexican. You wouldn't believe what I can say in Spanish—nothing gets by me. Anyway, by the second round of talks, I was negotiating. The U.S. didn't have much experience with foreign wars and acquisitions. I was there. I could speak the language. And it turned out I was good at bringing everyone's interests together. I used the same approach I use in business. Ended up going to Havana, Manila, Madrid, then Paris. By then I was working for the State Department." He paused, then finished up. "McKinley thought I'd make a good person for the English negotiations on the canal through Central America, since it floats around the same ideas as the other treaties. And that, more or less, has brought me here."

Thw-w-wack. Another bull's-eye. Sam stared at the target. Jesus, he didn't stand a chance.

"Twenty-five," she said, then paused to look at him, puzzled. "So what about all the cowboy talk? As if you ride the range?"

"I have. I did. I want to again."

Though it wasn't the same anymore. As he watched her shoot a total of thirty-seven points in five arrows—two golds, two reds, and a blue (she didn't need the goshdamn whites or blacks!)—he flapped his jaw: about the bad winter in '85, the summer that followed that was so dry the grass smoked and rivers dried up to nothing but paths of wet rocks. Then the next winter, a blizzard with temperatures to forty-six below.

"It was worse than anything anyone knew."

Liddy had let her hand, her bow come to rest in her skirts. She'd fixed on him all the attention she'd up to now given the target, her head tilted, the feather on her hat fluttering in the light breeze. And Sam suddenly didn't want to stop talking. He wanted her to keep looking at him like that—he wanted to stand forever where he was: in the heart of her interest, speculation, and questions.

She encouraged him. "Go on."

"It cut the heart out of my father. I went to see him, to help. He had cattle suffocating in drifts of snow as they tried to find shelter in gulches—maddened, ice-encrusted, staggering into town, starving, desperate for warmth. When the snow finally melted, the coulees were deep with dead cows. My pop lost ninety percent of his herd.

"He died the year after and left me the ranch, where I did what he and I, one time, had argued over: I fenced all the land I dared, kept the herd small on purpose, and grew hay, alfalfa, and sorghum for feed. When I'd suggested this before, Pop had said I 'thought small.' Turned out, that was the way to think. I have a foreman who manages it now. The ranch makes good money." Sam grew quiet.

Liddy's regard remained fixed on him, full of . . . curiosity, sympathy, something. "I'm sorry," she said. "When was the last time you were there?"

He shrugged. "A couple years ago." He smiled at her, teasing. "So can I stay? I mean, that was a pretty sad story."

She laughed, and their gazes held, the two of them smiling. So like the moor for a minute. Then she said, "No. Here." She held the bow toward him. "Your turn." But she asked, "You didn't live with your father?"

"Till I was sixteen. We got on terrible. When my mother died—she'd left long before that—my grandmother came to visit, to bring me some of her things. When Gram went back to Chicago, I went with her."

"Where you made good money in railroads."

He smiled and nodded, mostly because he liked agreeing with her. "More or less."

He and she contemplated each other through the bow held in her fist between them. With her other hand, she pushed hair from her face, the white hat feather flitting for a second against her bare hand with its strap and strip of leather protecting her draw fingers.

Ordinary? Had he thought the word *ordinary* in the context of her looks? There was nothing ordinary about Liddy's thin face, starting with her gold-brown eyes, rimmed in long, thick lashes. Intelligent, circumspect eyes.

"Your round," she said.

He quirked an eyebrow as he took the bow. "Can I take a few practice arrows?"

"Be my guest. Would you like these?" She held up her fingertips covered in leather.

"Nah," he said. "That's for sissies."

His first three practice shots missed that target completely, with him swearing and Liddy laughing till she was bent over into her skirts.

"Why?" he asked. "Why are you so happy to make me leave?"

She halted, her smile fading a little. "That's right," she

said as if just realizing. "If you leave, I won't get to enjoy your terrible shooting."

"Oh, come on," he complained. "You're nail-spitting mad. Why?"

She was smiling, but he'd called it right. Her expression opened up with awareness. "I don't know," she said, then frowned down at the ground. "You. I hate the hypocrisy of doing one thing and pretending another. I can't stand it."

"Me?"

She shrugged, baffled by herself. "The moor," she began, then shook her head. "Oh, the pretending that—" She stopped, looked away, refused to go further.

He understood anyway. "Darlin'," he said, "I'm not the source of the—the hypocrisy, as you call it. I get the impression you were living fine with it before I arrived. It's the truth you don't like. I remind you that, for three and a half days, you were free and happy: yourself without so many restraints."

She looked at him, one uppity eyebrow raised, putting a sarcastic slant to her mouth. "It's not that simple."

"Isn't it? Seems to me you want to be yourself—have your fling on the moor—and have everyone approve. You want the impossible."

She laughed, though not with perfect ease. "I want to live in a way that allows me to be honest with the people I love."

"I'd worry more about living in a way that's honest with yourself."

She rolled her eyes. His answer was too straightforward for her English tastes. She said bluntly, "I just want you to go. You make me nervous."

Nervous? It could have been the wind. It had picked up a little. But it was a fact, now that he thought of it: He'd watched her shots go from golds and reds to reds and blues. It seemed possible he distracted her. *Nervous.* He filed the word away.

Thankfully, he himself improved the more he practiced. On the very first arrow that counted, he hit gold. His own accuracy so startled him, he just stared at it; he couldn't think of a single smart-mouthed thing to say, a true indication of how astounded he was. He glanced at Liddy, wanting her to acknowledge the amazing shot—he'd never do it twice.

So what'd she do? With that one eyebrow arched a little higher than the other, she contemplated him a minute longer than was polite, then let out her breathy laugh. "Oh, jolly good," she said.

He laughed, too, because her tone meant the opposite. So Liddy. "Not going to celebrate my good shots, huh?"

"No."

Sadly, he didn't have any more to celebrate this round. Though he wasn't all that unhappy with himself by the end: the one gold, two reds, a blue, and one stinking white—but it counted, he reminded her, and, in this way, refreshed her memory that hers wouldn't. He was at twenty-nine points, down eight. Not bad for a man who hadn't shot a bow and arrow in six years and had never shot an English one—or Welsh one, as she corrected him, those being apparently better in her mind. It was a good one, he had to admit. An easy pull, hardly any shimmy, straight and true. He expected to do better next time around.

And she needed to do worse.

He handed the bow back, both of them giving a little jump as their hands brushed. Nervous, he thought. Why, it would be unfair to make her nervous on purpose.

He watched her load and shoot her first arrow. It was pure music watching her deliberation, her concentration: her expertise. Then *swoof-ff. Thunk.* Magic. Sam stared at the target in the distance, then laughed in wonder. She'd struck so close to the three arrows already dead center in the gold that she'd chipped the feathers off one—a spark of blue drifted to the ground. He could barely credit her skill. "Chihuahua, you're good."

Out the corner of his eye, he saw her cast her eyes down. This time, she blushed, the tops of her cheekbones pinking up.

He looked at her directly and watched the color spread across her nose, all the way from hairline to hairline. He said, "You're a regular Annie Oakley." He smiled with genuine appreciation. "Though a lot prettier," he added. "Hell, they should write books about *you.*"

Her eyes jumped to his, wide, then away.

As she loaded again, he found his favorite tooth and pushed his tongue against it. She'd do it again. The woman was a machine. And, fair or not, he couldn't very well afford to lose. Meanwhile, something else occurred to him: He hadn't mentioned what he wanted for his prize—mostly because everything he wanted was obscene. He would settle for less, but, in any case, he didn't want her to clean up his preferences too much before he had her beat. Liddy, on the other hand, had neglected to discuss his prize because she hadn't thought of the possibility she could lose.

She should really start thinking about it. As a favor to her, he mentioned, "I don't want to catch you unaware here now." She glanced. He continued. "I've been thinkin' about what I want when I win."

She let out a little laugh as she raised the loaded bow. "Your prize is you get to stay."

"I already get to stay. Your father invited me."

"Well, don't worry about it. You aren't going to win anyway." She aimed down the shaft of the arrow.

"I think we should worry about it. I mean, just for form's sake."

She uncurled her fingers—

Just as she let the arrow go, he said, "If I win, you sleep with me."

"What?" she swiveled, laughing—it was nervous laughter, breathless disbelief. She shook her head, her lips parting in what wanted to be an open-mouthed smile: a woman who'd heard wrong about to make a joke of what he couldn't possibly have said.

Th-wh-h-ip. They turned together toward the sound. Her arrow had pierced the blue circle, missing both the red and gold of the target's center.

Smiling to himself, Sam said, "For a whole night." For a week, a month, a year. His love slave. She'd never do it, but, aah, what a fond thought. "Yep, seems fair to me. If I lose, I put a whole lot more distance between us. If you do, you put a whole lot less."

"No," she said, glaring.

An idea came to him, an inspiration of the moment. "All right. Your knickers, shoes, and stockings. Your underthings. Oh, and your hat, too, come to think of it. After all, you already have my hat and underwear. It's only right." He kept blathering. He didn't want her to shoot. Not till he had a moment to—to negotiate a little here. He chuckled. "Actually, I was pretty sure you'd balk at sleeping with me, so this is a good compromise."

She snorted once, ignored him, and raised the bow again. "I won't give you my knickers, either. So name something else."

"Oh, no. I'm happy with what I've asked for. I like the idea of you goin' back to the house bare-legged and drawer-less, mindful every barefoot step I beat you fair and square."

She looked a little more worried this time when she glanced over at him. Then she let out a little breath and said, "Oh, yes. Quite fair. You're trying to throw me off. It won't work."

He raised his hands, a show of palms. "Good enough. I'll be quiet."

She fussed this time, setting the arrow's nock in the bow-string twice, not happy the first time with her grip of it. She straightened her arm, white-knuckled, the bow in her fist, aiming down the arrow—

"Just so long as you agree, right?" he asked. "I don't mean to interrupt here. I apologize. But, see, I wouldn't want us to shoot without having agreed. I don't want you complainin' after it's over."

She looked across her own arm, cocking that eyebrow at him the way she could. "Don't worry. I won't. You're going to lose."

The arrow flew, singing through the air, then *thwapped*

into the target at—aha! Sam wanted to crow. A black! Her
worst shot.

"A shame," he said, containing himself as he tsked. Then
he remembered and couldn't hold it in. He laughed outright:
"A black, which doesn't even count for you. You may as well
have missed."

Slowly, she turned toward him, the bow down—if there
had been an arrow in it he wouldn't have trusted her not to
put it through him—fury all over her face. Ooh, she was a
fierce thing. "You're cheating," she said.

"No, I'm not. We've talked all the way through all these
shots. We're just having what you Brits call a chat."

"Well, shut up. I'm finished chatting."

"Right." He winked at her. Fourteen points and only two
arrows left. The best she could do was thirty-two. Why, he
could probably beat thirty-two. Thing was, she had that
damn thirty-seven to add to it, with his having a mere
twenty-nine.

She reached over her shoulder, pulling an arrow from the
quiver.

"You never said," he reminded her. "About my winning.
You agree, right?"

She only loaded the arrow.

"Your knickers. If you lose, you'll peel them off right
where you stand, hand them over, no hedging."

She paused, her concentration broken. She looked at the
ground, then she looked at him. "No," she said. "It isn't all
right. You can't have anything so intimate. Not that it matters. But, no, so stop tormenting me with it."

"You don't get to say."

"Of course I do."

"I didn't. You just told me, if you win, I leave. I don't like
that, either. It seems a little extreme."

"Are we doing this or not?" she asked.

"Sure we are. Just agree." When all she did was glower,
he said, "You're the one who's so cocky. If you're so sure
you'll win, just nod, allow me to have my fantasies here."

She blinked. He'd called her on it. She jerked her head once. A nod, he thought.

That's what he gave her credit for, at least. "Fine. Shoot," he said.

He'd let her be from here, he thought. Let silence and imagination work on her—imagination, whoa . . . Would she ever look good with no shoes, stockings, or knickers. And her hat off and hair down . . . yep, there was plenty for her imagination to grab hold of.

The truth was, his own had gotten way out of hand. He watched her carefully, though not for the pleasure of seeing her pluck off one amazing shot after another now. He couldn't have cared less if her every arrow sought ground; he prayed they would. While he drifted in the bliss of watching her body, its sway, the tilt of her head on her long neck, the way her back curved in at her narrow waist, the way the fabric of her dress pulled taut over the valley of spine. He speculated, fascinated to know, if she'd really take off her drawers out here for him. And her stockings and shoes and hat. He remembered her underthings being silky out on the moor, fancy, full of ribbons. Had there been lace? Would they be warm from her bottom?

Oh, her bottom. He loved her backside. There was probably something wrong with him for being so taken with it. Nonetheless, he remembered that part of her anatomy dearly: the way it swelled out so quick from her waist, how soft and firm it was under his hands . . . the way it tucked neatly, the moons narrowing, as it went under her to give way into her sex. . . .

She shot two whites in row, then stood there biting her lip, staring at her debacle: the target just close enough to see the blue feathers in all the wrong places.

Sam accepted the bow while he calculated. She'd shot a gold, a blue, a black, and two white. With her handicap, all he needed was twenty-three points to win.

Alas, however, it turned out now she distracted him as badly. Lordy, the idea of her taking her drawers off out here raised his temperature five degrees. He felt feverish from fantasy. Of his first three arrows, one missed the target completely, then he hit a red and black—with Lydia clicking her tongue, daring to gloat. He was quick to tell her that, for him, that was ten points. She was fast in saying that was a long way from enough. While he admitted to himself that his managing to hit the butt at all was the real miracle. *Butt.* Doggone, what a stupid name for a target. And didn't he know the butt he wanted to go after and exactly what arrow he wanted to bury where?

He had two more arrows. *Now, try here, Sam, to keep your attention out of knicker-stripping territory long enough to find thirteen points.* With his fourth arrow he made a stinking blue—and Liddy clapped her hands.

"Ah, the sissy's going to win," she said, wagging her leather fingertip at him.

He needed a red to tie.

He was shocked when he hit gold. So was she. The arrow hit, and they both gaped. Then Sam laughed from sheer relief. He hadn't been aware of how wound up he'd been till the tension let go and pure joy let loose in his chest, reverberating, deep and free. Oh, such laughter. Dirty laughter. Dirty elation. He looked at Liddy. "I get your knickers. Start shuckin'."

Her gaze snapped up to his. "You aren't going to take that win, are you?"

"Sure I am."

"I outshot you. Why, if *your* blacks and whites hadn't counted—"

"Yeah, but they did."

She scowled, looked around as if people were standing everywhere, then said, "They can see us from the house."

"Move toward the trees. I want your knickers."

She stood there, planted, putting her fists on her hips. "You have a childish interest in underwear."

"Actually, it's a pretty grown-up interest, when it comes to yours."

"Asking for them is immature of you."

"Is it?" He laughed. "Then I wish I was ashamed. I'm

not. I'll take my winnings now, thank you: your hat, shoes, stockings"—he wiggled his eyebrows, grinning—"and drawers." Ah, some days were real good fun. He moved aside, making way with a little bow, extending his arm, palm out, toward the trees. "After you, Your Majesty. Move on over to the shade. You can take 'em off there. And if you can do it slow, you'll only make me happier, so just reach on up there and take your time."

18

We are all pulled along by our pleasures—but we know the real one when we give up all the others for it.

SAMUEL JEREMIAH CODY
A Texan in Massachusetts

What had become of a man's needing encouragement, Lydia wondered, as her father had counseled?

Refusing to budge, she said, "You c-can't have my hat and shoes. People would see that i-if—if you came in with—"

For some reason, this made Sam hoot. When he calmed down enough, he said, "All right, I'm feeling generous. Just your knickers, then. I'll make do with those."

"No."

His laughter quieted, his smile developing a squint that made her take a step back. "Look," he said, "I risked having to explain my departure to the U.S. State Department, not to mention the President of the United States. And I came damn close to losing, so you can pay up. *I* would have."

She dared to raise her finger at him, a gentle reprimand. "You see, you're more honest than I am—"

"Wh-h-hoo," he said, letting out a gust. "I'm about to make an honest woman of you, Lid. You take 'em off, or I'll take 'em off for you."

"You wouldn't dare." She blinked, frowned. "It's bad enough that you get to stay." She complained again, still trying to absorb that she'd lost. "I out*shot* you."

"Right. And now I'm going to give *you* a handicap. You get five seconds' head start. Decide what direction you're running and go. When I catch you, I'm having your knickers."

"God, no!"

"One."

"You wouldn't!"

"Two."

"Jesus!" she breathed, a whisper.

"Three."

"Bloody hell!" She took off toward the house, the trees.

She never heard *four*; he didn't wait. "You cheated!" she started screaming as she ran. She flew, but he was right on her heels. "You cheated you cheated you cheated. . . ."

The second she made the shade of the trees something pulled at the back of her skirts. They grew taut, her legs caught back in them. At the same time, his arm came round her middle, then his body collided full force at the back of her. Her teeth snapped. And she tumbled, screaming again. "You cheater! You bloody cheater!"

She and Sam fell to the ground together, tussling. He wanted her on her back, himself on top, but she'd be damned if she'd let him get her there. In the end, he pinned her on her stomach, his full weight on her.

She let her forehead drop to the ground. "Ah, bloody hell," she muttered again and gave a pound of her fist to the grass. She could barely move, her quiver twisted around on her shoulder.

In the next seconds, they both grew still. Just the pant of their hard breathing from their run and scuffle.

In the loamy damp of earth, cool from shade, her nose

brushing the soft glume of grass, there was Sam: his cheek just over hers, warm, his mouth at her ear. "*Bloody* isn't nice, is it?" A deep-voiced murmur, his gravelly whisper.

The plane of his chest rested on her back, broad and heavy. Lower, she could feel his abdomen at the small of her spine, the weight of his hips on her buttocks. "Let me up," she murmured.

She lay there, the woodsy scent coming off his hair where it flopped on her temple, faint under the odor of soap that she recognized from her own house—her parents' soap on Sam Cody. It was so at odds with the other knowledge: that, through their bunched clothing, between her bum and his pelvis, there was a solid erection taking shape. He didn't try to hide it.

The sum seemed impossible. A collision of worlds.

He shifted his weight onto one forearm to untangle her quiver from her arm and draw it over her head. As he freed her, she felt him roll slightly and bring his leg in, between hers. He gently made his leg a place—there was no practical way to resist—his other leg had already landed between hers in their tumble. When he pushed his legs out, hers went with them, further apart: splayed on her stomach under him. "It isn't nice, is it?"

"W-what?" Nice? The feel of him was pleasurable beyond any memory of it. Unearthly. Her blood danced, alive in a way it hadn't been since the moor.

"The way the English use *bloody*," he said.

In the tent of his body, she muttered into the ground, "Not at all. I never use it." She had to correct, "Not aloud." Then groaned to realize, "Except with you." She wobbled her forehead in the prickly, soft grass, side to side. "I never used it, even to myself, *until* you, in fact."

She could feel his breath on her neck, the *ha* of voiceless laughter. He said in her ear, "You're becoming a regular bandito, Lid. And it wears good on you, I gotta say. More power to you."

"Let me up."

"Your knickers," he whispered. "You gonna hand them over?"

"You can't mean that."

"Oh, I do."

"You're heavy. Get off."

Instinctively, he raised up a little on his arms—just enough leeway that she could get a palm on the ground and push, lifting one shoulder as she twisted to look back at him. A mistake.

It was quite horrible of her. But there, under him, inside his arms, inside the harbor of his body, with her buttocks pressed tight against him, she twisted and oh— Never mind his handsome, sun-brown face, the breadth of his shoulders and chest. No, it was the warmth and smell of his skin that undid her—she breathed it in. How welcome and familiar! She wanted to rub her nose against his chest and neck and face till her skin smelled of him. She wanted to rub her cheek down his body. Against his flat belly, his strong thighs, along his penis, put her lips, her mouth down over it . . .

She wet her lips, her mouth dry, then bent her forehead back to the ground. Oh, Lord. She couldn't look: her wild good time come home to roost—roosting right on top of her, in fact.

She told the ground, "I want you to leave."

"That's nice, but you lost." He continued with more heat than she would have expected, "You poke fun. You make me feel bad—"

"That's not hard to do," she pointed out.

"Well, too bad for you, 'cause now I took you out here and beat your pants off." He laughed. "Literally. Now who of us is peeling them off you? You or me?"

She glanced over her shoulder again, pressed her lips together, then blew out through them an exasperated breath. None of this was right. He threw her off. She couldn't think how to handle it, what to do. "Diplomats don't behave as you do," she complained.

"One does."

"You'll be recalled."

As he spoke, he lifted her arm, rolling it to get at the inside where the band held her arm protector to it. He undid it, saying, "You're kiddin', right?" At this awkward angle, their eyes met—he smiled down at her. The shade made his eyes dark, a dusky slate-blue, bluer than the sky behind him, starkly fair against his thick, black eyelashes. "Or else you know nothin' of the long tradition of American diplomacy, starting with Ben Franklin. Why, we're a regular bunch of wild fellas away from home. So are the British, by the way." His smile broadened into rich, chuckling sarcasm. "And, as I remember, you behave a little differently away from home, too, don't you?"

The last two words were muddled: He'd taken her other arm, bending it at the elbow, her hand toward him. She jumped when he bit her fingers, but he was only pulling the leather finger tabs off with his teeth. Oh, his thumb pressed into the ball of hers . . . his teeth pulling . . . he made her shiver. There was the sudden give as the tabs released. He opened his mouth to drop them. They fell at her neck to lay on the ground against the top of her collarbone. Another shudder, goose bumps.

She turned back toward the ground and told the earth, "All right. You've won. Let me up. I'll do it."

"And a kiss," he said.

"What?" She glanced over her shoulder again, and her back arched. And there was no mistaking—at her bum, he was full and solid. God help her, every part of him was so perfectly masculine, especially that part, nothing halfway about it any longer. He had to be mad even to suggest—

"I'm sorry, but it's a penalty kiss," he said, almost sounding apologetic. "For having to chase you down." He laughed softly, deep-voiced.

They were both mad. Because, despite herself, she let out a little burst, laughing, too. It was so ridiculous. "No." While the feel of him at her backside made her eyes glaze. He shifted a degree, and suddenly—perfectly—long, hard Sam nestled into the indentation between her buttocks. God

bless—she closed her eyes and bent her head to the ground
again.

"Come on, Liddy." So gently, his voice descending to the
sweetest whisper, he said, "Kiss me," and brought his mouth
to her neck.

Shivers again, goose bumps, deep, melting quivers . . .
No, no, this couldn't be, she kept thinking. The wrong feelings in the wrong surroundings. He brushed his mouth up
her nape and into her hair, drew a deep breath, and let out a
muted sigh or moan, it was impossible to tell.

Then, so quickly she didn't realize what he was about until it had happened: He lifted onto his arm, pushed her shoulder, came down in the space beside her, up against her, then
rolled them both back. Like that, she was under him, looking
up into his face, his hair tickling her temple as he brought
his mouth down.

She was going to turn away, going to thrash in his arms
so he couldn't find her lips. But this happened in fantasy, for
when his mouth brushed hers, all the wonderful, uninhibited
pleasure of the moor was suddenly with her. As if he could
carry it inside him, breathe it alive again into her throat: re-
suscitate it.

He twisted his head and pressed a full, passionate kiss
into her mouth, tongue, teeth, lips, hot and wet, shifting his
weight as he brought his hips against her till he'd found just
the right fit. He pushed his hips against her and groaned
softly, a sound that echoed down into the hollow of her
throat. While his face blurred and the clouds and treetops
spun. She arched, glimpsing blue sky just before she closed
her eyes and dropped into the sensation of him, hot like sun
everywhere their bodies met.

For a moment, she was back on the moor, so willing.
More than willing: aggressive, wanting him. Oh, the freedom to have him, to feel him enter her. Her hips answered
his. What a kiss. She opened her mouth and kissed him back.
He tasted faintly sweet, like the orange marmalade from
breakfast. He smelled, oh . . . he smelled like Sam . . . sunny,
a leafy woods, with the faint tangy scent as off new leather.

She caressed the back of his head, smoothed his hair with one palm then the other, petting him. Oh, oh—

She didn't want the kiss to end. She followed it . . . the intimate penetration of his tongue . . . his long body stretched out on her . . . his pelvis pushing, the outline of his penis distinct, grinding through their clothes at her belly, her pubis—

She shocked herself. She wanted to lift her legs up around him.

But they weren't on the moor, and if someone happened to look from an upstairs window . . . *This can't be right,* she thought again, disoriented. The wrong feelings in the wrong place. Or the right feelings in the wrong place.

With him on her skirts, thankfully, he held her legs back. She couldn't raise them round his hips, but her shifting around trying to brought some semblance of good sense. She broke free of his mouth, turning her head, pushing at his chest. "This is—something is—" Something was wrong. Something sent her into a state of alarm.

"You like it, Lid," he whispered, insisting: "You like it."

She could only shake her head, struggling to bring herself back. "I—I don't—"

He waited till she looked at him—his expression was at once pained and tender. "You could come to my room," he began, then knew she wouldn't. "I could come to yours—" He stopped, scowled, looked at her chin. He tried to invent ways. Then met her eyes and told her, "We could slip out here, walk to the trees. Tonight. Under the stars if you like. I want to make love to you again—"

"You're insane."

"What was so sane about a moor?"

"It wasn't here." More bluntly, "I won't. Not in this place among these people."

"Why?"

Because there was the moor. And there was her life here at Castle Wiles and in London at Mayfair. The two were separate, not related, and had to stay that way—as different and discrete as Devon was from Yorkshire or the city capital.

When he spoke again, it was almost as if he'd read her
mind. "Liddy," he said, "you're trying to make yourself into
two different people. Just be the one you are."

She put the back of her hand over her mouth, arm up,
holding it there, then closed her eyes. Indeed. She felt torn in
half ever since Sam's arrival.

No, before that. By something going on inside her. And
angry for it, absolutely ripped apart. How had she become so
different from her family? From her friends? When had this
happened? She felt foolish, critical of herself. "How many
of my friends might relish gallivanting across a moor," she
muttered—or lying on her back looking up at sky, treetops,
and Louche American Sam—"for no better reason than it
was exciting and fun?"

"How many would have gone to Rose's wedding?"

Ah. Rose's wedding. He was right. Her departure from
orthodoxy predated him. At least she was consistent.

Somewhere at her heart she was more a democrat than
those around her. *A democrat.* When the queen called a person the name, it was as close as she got to a curse.

At which point, Sam shifted, laying his shoulder down
onto her, the full weight of his heavy chest. At the other side,
his weight lifted. She felt her skirt raising on that side.

"Ai!" she said. "Stop!"

He let out a snort at her laughable prohibition, while her
skirt kept coming up. "So what color are your knickers"—he
snorted—"my knickers now. And how do you hold up your
stockings these days? With those little hooks that attach to a
lady's corset or with little lace elastics? It was the prettiest
elastic out on the moor—"

"All right, all right! I will! I'll give them to you! Just let
me up!"

He paused, tilted his head, watching her as if to assess her
sincerity. He raised one eyebrow.

"I will indeed," she affirmed.

"Indeed?" He raised both eyebrows, suspicious of that
particular answer. His jaw set.

"Really," she told him, an Americanism; she never said it. Till now. "So you have to let me up. I can't very well get them off with your lying on top of me."

He squinted, distrustful. Then with a push, let air and sunlight between them. Lydia scrambled for it immediately. She was out from under him before he was even to his feet.

She stood up on wobbly legs, putting both her hands to her head. Oh, her hair—and her hat was missing. She looked around, dusting her skirts. She had grass all over her. "Have you seen my hat?" When he didn't answer, "And my bow? What became of my bow?" She picked up her quiver. The leather was off-square; she pushed at it, fixing it. The feathers of the three arrows still in it were bent; there was no fixing those.

Sam walked over, leaning his long arm down, and picked up her hat, then fetched her bow. As he brought them back, he said, "You're good. The best I've ever seen."

She blurted, "I'm going to the Grand National. I'm going to win." It was a relief to talk about something else. "Last year, I came in fifth, a contender. This year, I'm better." She knew she was. And she didn't just want to win: "This year, if the wind's right, I'll set records."

"A high-scoring day," he said and looked at her.

"Yes." She ventured a smile. Yes. She had the skill. Though some things could cancel it out.

She frowned suddenly at Sam, a perplexed moment. She remembered her first qualifying meet for the Grand National, the one before the Scorton. It had been this past July. Her menses had come four days early, making the meeting into an ordeal. Her flow was irregular, hard to predict, but when it came it was profuse. In July, she'd barely made the cut, scoring just what she needed to remain on the register, then getting Clive to cart her home.

That had been two weeks before Rose's wedding—she furrowed her brow deeply, pondered a moment—almost five weeks ago. A Saturday. She counted backward to the exact day. Four weeks and five days. Lydia stared hard at Sam—he

stood there holding her bow and hat—thinking. If her flow
came every twenty-eight days, which it didn't, she was five
days late.

She asked, "You know that thing you did? You know,
where you, um—pulled out? It always works, doesn't it?"

"When we made love on the moor?"

"Yes."

"Withdrawal?"

"Is that what it's called?"

"Or coitus interruptus. And, yes, it works. Usually.
Why?" He contemplated her narrowly, though he could simply have been looking into the sun.

She shook her head, turning. "Nothing."

"You're not late, are you?"

"No, I'm fine."

This won her another long look, puzzlement, then a nod.
Good.

She shook her head. No, she wasn't late. Well, she was,
but she was often untimely. Her menses would come. She'd
been upset. Too much excitement had thrown it off. "May I
have my hat, please?"

"May I have my knickers, please?"

She blinked and let out a little breathy laugh. "You, ah—
you aren't really going to make me, are you?"

"Yes."

Another breath escaped, *pffah*. She encouraged sanity.
"You're joking." She smiled, inviting him to smile, too, to let
it go.

His gaze held fast. "I'm not joking."

She thought perhaps if she just walked away—

She tried it, but he caught her arm.

Such a look, so quintessentially Sam. He looked down at
her from his tall, broad-shouldered height as if all his discontent with the world, with himself, her, and the many im-
perfections of existence, had condensed into this moment: a
brooding glare—it was his face's most natural expression. It
set people back; it made him seem fiercer than he was.

He told her, "Liddy, I really do want the token of my win."

"I'll give you—" Yes, a sacrifice. "All right, my hat."

He snorted. "I want what we agreed."

"I never agreed."

"You did. If not before, just now on the ground."

"Under coercion," she said and frowned. "Besides, my, um—" She licked her lips, lubrication. She couldn't even say *knickers* to his face. "They're too intimate."

He scowled blackly then drew in a huff, one of admission; he couldn't deny it.

She said quickly, "A stocking. I'll give you a stocking."

He frowned deeper, a glower as dark as a Dartmoor night.

When he didn't object outright, she quickly turned, drawing up, wadding, the hems of her skirts to her garter as she bent out of his line of vision. She rolled her stocking down, shaking off her slipper as she did, then yanked the stocking off her bare toe. As she shoved her foot bare back into her shoe, she swiveled around to him, holding the stocking.

"Here," she said, trying to smile graciously. "Your win."

"You're a lot like your fellow countrymen. I say what I want, what I'm entitled to. You say no. Finally, you grudgingly give me a tenth of what I ask for, then think you can get up and go."

She could see where Sam's moodiness might unnerve some people, because his expression at the moment provoked anxiety even in a woman who knew him to be a fairly nice human being.

Then he almost didn't even get his "tenth."

They both jumped to hear a voice call from within the copse of trees. "Lydia!"

She was jamming the stocking into the first available hiding place, the arrow quiver, when the stocking was summarily yanked out of her fingers. For one frightening moment, she wasn't sure who had it. Clive had trotted from between two rather near trees.

"Ah, there you are," he said. "I couldn't see you, though

Father told me you were out here. He wants you upstairs in his study, posthaste."

Sam's hand, she noticed, was in his pocket. Her stocking had to be in there too. She hoped. Clive looked innocent.

More crossly than she'd intended, she asked him, "Why? Father knows I'm busy out here shooting."

Her brother blinked as Sam's presence registered—who it was she stood beside. He looked from her to Sam to her again, as if to say, Busy? You don't look busy, not with shooting at least. "Hello, Mr. Cody," he said. "I didn't realize you were out here." To Lydia, "Father didn't say why he wanted you. A boatload of telegrams has arrived though—someone in London has kept the telegraph office busy in Crawthorne, I must say. Perhaps it has something to do with those."

There were a strained few seconds, neither Sam nor Lydia recovering themselves quick enough.

At first, Clive looked at them, frowning from one to the other. "Is something wrong?"

"I beat her," Sam muttered.

"What?" Her brother's long face transformed with a spreading smile. With wonder, he started to say, "You beat Lydia at—"

"He didn't," she said grimly. "I gave him a huge handicap. I outshot him."

Clive began to laugh. "I can't believe it! You let him beat you! What did he win?"

Even Sam looked taken aback by the question. Lydia, of course, was undone. "Nothing," she told him, too loudly. "Nothing at all." She grabbed her hat from Sam, took her bow, then had to step forward: She used her skirts to hide her finger tabs and arm protector where they lay on the ground. She stood over them.

"Oh, I'm sorry," Clive contradicted, very amused now. "I know you, Lydia. You've never taken me or any of my friends for less than twenty quid." To Sam, he asked, "Did she give you whites?"

"Whites and blacks."

"Whoo!" He whistled.

She led the way toward the trees at a march.

Her brother fell in beside her on one side, saying, "You must have been *very* confident, Lyd." Clive, a head taller than she, looked directly over her at Sam, who had fallen in step at her other side. "So what did you bet, Mr. Cody?"

Sam glanced at him, his own hands in his pockets as they walked three abreast into the small woods. "Nothing," he said. "Just as she said."

Clive looked sideways at them both, leafy shade playing over his amused expression. He shook his head, grinning. "Not bloody likely. My sister is a greedy thing. You bet a lot, something good, and Lydia matched it—and lost!" He twisted his mouth—he thought he was teasing with his hint of lewd speculation. "What, hmm?"

Lydia wanted to kill him; she'd strangle him in his sleep tonight. "Shut up," she said. As they trudged up out of the trees and into the back gardens, she threw him a murderous glare.

Which only made Clive's eyes dance, then he broke out into peals of laughter.

Had he realized how truly compromised she was, he would never have teased in this vein. But so long as he thought her upright and chaste—it was beyond his imagination that his sister should be anything but virginal—she was in for it. She wished she'd told him. She wished he knew. She wished he could be on her side—though she couldn't imagine how to say enough, without incriminating herself horribly, to get him there.

So she walked back to the house, her brother on one side of her, ribbing her and Sam mercilessly.

Sam on her other, as they came up out of the trees into the back gardens, actually had the nerve to murmur under his breath, "We're not finished, Lid."

She threw him a quick frown askance. His expression still wanted to argue. Oh, grand. Caught between the two, a clown and a madman.

She looked from one to the other, right, then left. Then

straight ahead as they walked into the rose garden toward the back parlor door, where she knew an odd, uncomfortable flutter in her chest. For a dozen, rapid heartbeats, she felt frantic.

19

There is one thing worse than an absolutely loveless marriage. A marriage in which there is love, but on one side only.

Oscar Wilde
An Ideal Husband, 1895

Liddy all but slammed the door on Sam as he came in behind her. He caught it—it impacted the heel of his hand with a loud smack—still thinking he could get her alone, follow her, speak to her, get some sort of satisfaction.

He touched her arm. She belted him, elbow to the solar plexis.

"Oof."

Half a dozen people witnessed the blow. Boddington, Miss Pinkerton, another young woman, and two other men, all sitting in the parlor—everyone but Clive, who was behind Sam and missed the action.

"Good Lord, did you see that?" Boddington proceeded to describe the action for Clive and anyone else who would listen.

Clive chimed in, "Ah, getting along well, I see." He laughed. "He beat her on the target range—"

Liddy, halfway to the door, whirled, facing them all in the middle of the room. "He didn't!" To Sam, she said for the third or fourth time now, "I outshot you."

"She gave me a handicap. I beat her, and she won't own up."

Though of course it wasn't the archery match he wanted her to acknowledge. It was the other, *after* the match in the shade: the fact that she gave him a "handicap" there, let him catch her, pin her to the ground: wanted him to, liked it.

Admit your attraction, give in to me. Love me, Lydia.

She doesn't want you. The thought came from nowhere and made him so low, it stopped him in his tracks. Lower than low, his spirits in the mud. Sam let himself drop into a chair beside Clive, spraddle-legged, rancor and unhappiness at the surface of him in a way he couldn't remember in a long time. Sad and angry and confused. He let Liddy go, watching her flounce out of the room.

She doesn't want you. You aren't good enough. Stop trying.

Clive was asking something about the Isthmus of Panama, something about the engineering feat of a possible canal there, but Sam couldn't even say exactly what his question was. "Mm," he answered.

He sat there, his hand in his pocket, fingering a black silk stocking exactly like the one that, when he'd first seen it on the moor, had made his head spin. He crushed it now in his fist out of view, knowing its soft, springy texture, its warmth, the faint dampness of it still from her skin. Clive talked. Sam pretended interest, attention. While the dispiriting, hateful refrain echoed through him: *She doesn't want you, she won't have you.*

Knocking on her father's study door, Lydia realized that, at the top of the house, facing north, if anyone could see out onto the target range, it should be he from here. Oh, splendid.

Alas, when she came in, he had his back to her: Jeremy Bedford-Browne was looking out the high, diamond-mullioned window behind his desk onto the estate's rear gardens and the very cluster of trees that had hidden, she hoped, herself and Sam.

"You sent for me?"

He turned, his hands behind his back. "I sent Clive after you when I realized Mr. Cody was, ah—negotiating something out there with you. What, Lydia?"

"Um, nothing." She had to fight an urge to spill everything. *Oh, let me tell you. I was alone out there for four days with this man who upsets me . . . he excites me. Sit down, I need advice from someone who cares. . . .* What a tirade was inside her. Yet she stood quietly.

Stoic, the same as ever, her father came forward, glancing down at his desk. On the desk's surface lay random squares of yellow paper, telegrams, a disorganized slew of them— among discarded cigar trimmings, a pair of eyeglasses, a crumpled wad of paper, and last month's page off a small calendar. So like her father. Though his dogs and horses were perfectly exercised and fed, well-bred, fairly everything else was left to an as-it-came, need-be basis. Her mother kept the desk, his study, the house organized. When the viscountess left, everything slowly went to pieces until her return, when she would resurrect it all again.

"What are those?" she asked, nodding at the telegrams.

He made a helpless gesture. "A dozen wires from London." He lifted his brow, relentless. "Tell me what you know of Samuel Cody."

Out of the blue came the memory, *He reads Buffalo Bill novels really well.* But she said, "Not much," then thought to add a single bit, a good part. "He's well off."

"My dear"—he indicated the telegrams—"he could pay off the national debt and buy the navy in the bargain. Do you know who Gwynevere Pieters is?"

"The American heiress?" Lydia had met her just yesterday afternoon before the engagement dinner. Very pretty, particularly feminine, very rich. Word had it that mutual friends, the Duke and Duchess of Garmary, intended to bring her out this season. Ho hum, Lydia had thought, another American girl out to marry an English lord.

"He jilted her a month ago. Did you know that?"

She shook her head, frowning, then nodded again, confused. "I, um, didn't know whom— But, yes, I knew he'd missed his wedding."

"Her father's a senator. He, she, her family were here last night. That must have been damn uncomfortable. I had no idea. But did it stop Mr. Cody? No. He even badgered the man after dinner. The fellow is so bold." He took a quick breath, then said, "Lydia, he went outside after you today. You know him. How?"

"Um—" A dozen stories passed through her mind; invention was there. Then she surprised—and frightened—herself. Out came the truth. "The man on the moor, it was Sam."

Her father's eyebrows rose up in surprise—no doubt as much for her accidental use of Sam's given name as for anything else—then drew down again quickly, a fierce, single line of disapproval. "You and Rose were out four days alone with this—this jilting lothario—this obnoxious, belligerent—"

"Rose wasn't with us." Sam was right. Her "proper" life was, had been, and would continue to be hypocritical unless she herself changed it. *Honest with the people I love.* She said, "I went to her wedding. She was on her honeymoon. I was on my way to Meredith's when the coach crashed. Mr. Cody was on it. He saved my life." *Brave and truthful.* Buffalo Bill would have been proud of her—though her knees shook.

Her father's mouth opened. It worked a moment with no words coming out as he stood there trying to absorb what she'd said. He glanced down at the telegrams, then picked one up. "He wrote a book," he said.

Lydia blinked, then asked, "Really?" She remembered Sam's telling her of the one his father had put down the latrine.

"Yes, when he was at Harvard."

"Harvard?"

"It's a fairly good American school—mostly rich society boys from the Northeast who pay their way in, but still good. I can't imagine his fitting in."

No, neither could she. "How did he get there?"

"I'm not sure. His mother's side is from Boston, it seems." Her father continued, "Mr. Cody is either the humblest man I know. Or"—*more likely,* her father's tone said—"the biggest, most devious pretender alive."

She offered, "He can hit a rabbit at fifty yards with a stone," adding, "in near-darkness."

"So could the devil." Her father's face remained stern. He shuffled through telegrams. "He's not a good risk, Lydia. He's left women standing at the altar of three weddings." He looked at another wire, then tossed it toward her. "His family is a disaster: His father was a known outlaw."

"And a sheriff and a rancher."

A good risk? Anything could happen. In the end even good old Boddington could leave her, divorce her, or simply treat her so badly she'd wish he would. Risk? Her father wanted her to marry safety? She no longer believed in it—not since bogs and cotton-wool fogs and drunken coach drivers. The memory made something in her, that strength from the moor rise up. A warm vein-dilating surge. It felt good. And dangerous. Full of peril in the real world where bravery, honesty, even strength were not always rewarded.

Her father scowled. "He wants to overturn a treaty my father helped write." Having said this, he muttered down to papers that he sorted blindly, "Worse than a Liberal."

It occurred to her: "Where did you get those telegrams? Who are they from?"

"One from a friend in Washington. The rest from your mother."

"Mother? How? Why?"

"Because we didn't know him, and a lot seems suddenly to be riding on him. And, too, last night she saw—more accurately than I realized, the perceptive woman—that, besides my own business with him, he is interested in you."

"You and mother?" Lydia repeated, bewildered. It was as
if her parents were ganging up on her.

He nodded. "She's on her way."

"On her way here? She just left."

"Yes. She made London by noon. The embassy knows
him there. She visited Whitehall, then his"—he looked
down—"his grandmother and aunt. Your mother found the
information we wanted, then wired it to me." When Lydia
could only stare, nonplussed, he angled his head, frowning
at her. "We are good business partners, your mother and I.
We have been, consistently, for twenty-eight years. Don't
underestimate the value of that."

"Do you love her?" she found herself asking.

Her father's eyes shifted to a point just beyond her shoulder. For a moment, he stared into space. Then he answered
the question backward. "She doesn't love me, Lydia."

By the end of the day, if Sam walked into a room where Lydia was already present, or vice versa, someone might say,
"Oo-ooh," and even bait them a little. They became, in a day,
famously at odds. He tormented her obliquely about owing
him something. She retaliated with stories of the cowpoke
from the moor, letting whoever was in their company do the
rest. Her friends and relations were keen to make fun, while
only she knew the "cowpoke" was sitting there. *It served
him right,* she thought. *Cowpoke, indeed.*

Gwynevere Pieters. The name sat sourly in Lydia's mind
whenever she happened to glance at her lover from the
moor. A rich debutante. That wasn't precisely the impression she'd gotten of the Gwyn whom Sam had described.
Served him right.

Lydia was ruthless. She brought up again the red union
suit and invented stories of a drunken fellow walking around
in it. She used the truth: *We walked in circles, while he drank
the better part of two bottles of gin.* No one understood the
point as she did, but everyone was game. Oh, the fun they all
had. With Sam and Lydia parrying back and forth like children smacking at each other.

"I have never seen two people develop such instant antipathy," Boddington observed, pointing out, laughing, how well he and Lydia got on. "They do nothing but fight."

Clive added, "We ought to send her in to negotiate with you, Cody. *She* unsettles you."

While Lydia justified her meanness to him by saying, Sam of all people should realize she was making the moor story up, exaggerating. The fool on the Dartmoor was fantasy, not at all how he had been. It shouldn't bother him. Or only a little. She was just giving him a pinch.

Yet, clearly, her teasing affected him beyond that. She watched him grow more and more upset, till he finally stood to his feet. It was a kind of sad triumph to realize he could barely contain himself. He was distraught.

Foolish Sam, undone by stories.

When he left, though, taking a parting shot—he called her a shrew who could drive any man to drink—Lydia grew quiet. She bit her lip, looked down, and blushed. "What are you so goshdamn afraid of?" he murmured as he passed her.

What *was* she afraid of? That desire should overtake her again? No, that was ridiculous—mostly because it already had. She had a squirming awareness of her attraction to Samuel J. Cody.

No, she was afraid of her own will, that force in her that had been so wonderful and strong on the moor: She was afraid she would find a way to act on her desire. And that, by doing so, in the context of her real life, she would accidentally destroy it. The fabric of her existence here in Yorkshire and London, her social standing, her future, seemed fragile by comparison to her existence on the moor—not held together with as much . . . vitality, vigor . . . desire.

Her heart's desire: She feared that she would reach for it.

She deserved Sam's animosity, she decided. Yes, a shrew. He kept her secrets. In fact, he ate a lot of crow to do it. While she used his chivalry to hurt him—she didn't understand how exactly, nor had she intended to hurt him to the degree she seemed to, but she knew she had done it—willfully—and was ashamed.

*   *   *

Indeed, the next morning her mother arrived. She brought more papers, she and Lydia's father calling Lydia once more into the upstairs study.

On her way up, Clive stopped her. "What *is* this? What's going on? There's some sort of intrigue, and I'm being left out. You have to tell me."

"I will later," she promised.

Upstairs, Constance Bedford-Browne sat to the side of the desk, behind which Lydia's father stood. Though position would have said he commanded the room, there was no doubt that the viscountess, off to the side, in the shadows, by dint of personality, was the room's mistress.

She began, "Your father tells me you were alone with Mr. Cody on the moor."

"Yes."

"Does anyone else know? Besides Mr. Cody, that is." She clicked her tongue, disapproval.

"Rose and Meredith. Meredith's mother and father, I think."

Her parents exchanged looks, betrayed. Meredith's father was Lydia's mother's brother. With disgust, the viscountess told her husband, "Lionel should have said. How ridiculous to keep such a secret from us."

Jeremy Bedford-Browne nodded sagely as he pulled his desk chair out and sat.

The viscountess tapped her beads together. She was rarely without yards and yards of them looped round her neck. She had a mannerism of taking two parallel strings, a knuckle between, and rocking them over her finger. It made a little *tick-tick* if a room was quiet. As this one was. *Tick-tick. Tick-tick.* From the shadows, the viscountess stood. She produced a stack of papers that had been on her lap, walking them to the desk. "I think you should see these," she said.

Lydia came forward, querying her mother, then her father with a glance.

"Here." Her mother offered the top page.

She took it.

"It's copies of agreements signed in Manila, Havana, and the formal Treaty of Paris, all courtesy of my uncle." Frowning, she said, "All mete out tough terms on Spain, but not only Spain. By omission, they are very rough on the people of Cuba and the Philippines, both of whom thought they would be self-governing. No one wins in these agreements but the United States. They get everything."

Why did that surprise her mother? Lydia looked from one parent to the other. "The U.S. won."

"The U.S. fought alongside the native people, made promises to them. These treaties were negotiated by men who came in and gave no concessions anywhere, very single-minded men."

"Ah, you are speaking of Mr. Cody. You're saying he's unrelenting."

"He's impossible. They spirited him out of Paris last December, because he became so belligerent the other side challenged him to a duel. He suggested"—she smiled— "spears on bareback ponies, quite sarcastic, this young man. The thing is, it seems he could have done it. According to his grandmother, he lived with the Comanches for two years. His father offered him in exchange, taking the chief's grandson, his idea of an education. The rest here—" She glanced down at the pile, tapping them once, then said, "The rest are: a brief account of Mr. Cody's background from Whitehall, courtesy of your uncle, my brother, and notes from a talk I had with Mr. Cody's grandmother in London."

The viscountess glanced at her husband, assuring Lydia they were a force united, then said to her daughter, "I want you to know that, if he is pressuring you in any way, because of the mere fluke of being alone with him in compromising circumstances, well, you have a family that will fight him—"

"No. I tried to tell Father. It's nothing like that—"

"Your father has noted his interest in you. And others notice that the two of you argue a great deal."

He father clarified, "What we're saying is, you don't have

to marry someone you don't like, no matter what happened, Lydia."

"I don't?"

"No."

Well. What a relief. They wanted her to like her choice. "About Boddington," she began. "I *like* him. I mean, he's very decent. But I'm not sure I want to marry him."

Her parents looked at each other with shared confusion and unhappiness. "All right," her father said.

"It's not all right!" her mother argued. "She has to marry where her parents say." She added, glaring, "I did."

Jeremy Bedford-Browne stiffened in the way a man will brace himself after a sharp blow has already come, a reflex after the fact. "And you're unhappy with their choice?"

"No," his wife said quickly, as if caught unaware. "I— I'm not." They stared at each other.

Her husband glanced at his daughter, then down. "Well, Lydia doesn't have to."

The room grew quiet, not even the sound of aquamarine beads.

After several long seconds, her mother said into the lull, "At least we have taken care of Mr. Cody. I think we should ask him to leave. His attention to Lydia is entirely inappropriate."

"No, I have other things about which I need to speak to him," her husband said. "I want him here. But I'll mention in passing that Lydia is more or less spoken for. By the way," to his daughter, "now would be an excellent time to spend some hours with Boddington." He smiled kindly. "To make up your mind."

"Yes!" her mother seconded.

Yes! Lydia thought. Since she didn't have to marry him— though she didn't think it would take hours—it was best she tell him she wasn't going to.

Wendt was the hunter of all hunters. His chief joys were fox and grouse, though he didn't mind the occasional hare or carted deer, and he raised pheasant by hand, or his gamekeeper did, so, whenever the viscount wished, he could release the birds to "shoot them over dogs." His stables were impressive. His kennels were monumental. He had beagles, foxhounds, harriers, setters, retrievers, and plain old mutts because occasionally the dogs got out and crossbred where they weren't supposed to, but he was so fond of them he never culled a pup. He just kept them, scratched them, and fed them. And hired more kennel huntsmen.

Coming back from a tour of Wendt's hunting haven, Sam and Wendt started up the steps of the rear terrace. They paused, however, when, halfway up, they could see that Boddington and Liddy were huddled on the far side alone, having a heart-to-heart. Sam and Wendt stood shoulder to shoulder on the step, watching for a second.

How attentive and kind Liddy was to the Englishman, the antithesis of how she treated *him*, Sam thought. She leaned toward ol' Boddie and touched his hand. He looked delighted for a blink, then utterly downcast. Yep, Liddy could do that to a fellow. From the heights to down a hole in a single second.

He and her father watched a moment, then Wendt took him by the shoulder and turned *him* around. "Best to leave them alone." He added as he led the way up through the garden, "We expect her to marry Boddington"—as they marched along the gravel, the viscount studied his crunching boots—"or someone very much like him."

Lower and lower. Sam wanted to spit. He wanted to rail. Stuck here when, between Liddy and her whole family, he was sure getting a lot of hints. Hands off. Leave her alone. Under any other circumstances, heck, he'd be gone by now.

Back on the terrace, however, he'd left a very different situation from what he thought, and Lydia wasn't too happy with it herself.

She'd taken Boddington's hand, looked him in the eye, and told him she would always be his friend and never his wife. At which point, he'd flatly denied he had still been considering the match.

"My mistake, then," she said. "I—ah—I just wanted to be clear. In case."

They sat there for perhaps a full, awkward minute. Then, in a murmur, more candidly, he admitted, "Actually, I *did* hope."

"Thank you. That's very kind of you to say. And I'm sorry."

"I'm surprised," he added.

Yes, wouldn't everyone be? "You will have no trouble. You will have your pick."

"Obviously not," he said, deadpan.

His eyes were a very dark brown, she realized. Something she'd never noticed.

While puzzlingly, in her mind, she could see the color of Sam's. Or colors. She knew the varying blues of his eyes according to light and mood. Why? she wondered. They were so often angry, these eyes: lately, with her. Edgy, melancholy. Why remember them?

Why think of him at all?

That evening at dusk, Sam wandered back to the terrace, then down to the target area, where he and Liddy had been shooting. Perhaps he was hoping to find her—he'd seen her walk down earlier, another day of practice. She wasn't here now. She wasn't anywhere. She'd disappeared, her parents, brother, friends, everyone seeming to run interference. He didn't know where she was.

He found an arrow, though, its feathers bent. Feathers. He picked it up. He remembered her hat, dyed beaver felt, so soft in his hand, its plumage as delicate as lace, ostrich. He held her arrow out, a finger at each end. It was light and well-balanced, smooth, perfect—even the broken feathers of her arrow were beautiful to him. Peacock, he realized. Peacock. Ostrich. Captive birds.

Ah, he remembered his dark swan of the moor.

At Castle Wiles, Liddy performed, she glided, she preened as she was supposed to. But privately, out on the moor . . . He still had this image of her, the plain dress, her hair wild and coming down in crazy corkscrews all over the place—it was so neat in the net she wore now.

Where was she as she had been on the moor? Anywhere? Did she wake in disarray in the morning? Did she ever escape captivity here, ever escape what everyone expected of her, to be simply herself?

Or did she only get to release arrows toward a straw target, angrily zinging them through their short span of freedom?

20

*Always play fair, but especially with cheaters: They
know what cards they dealt you.*

SAMUEL JEREMIAH CODY
A Texan in Massachusetts

Sam and her father seemed to have developed a great deal to
say to each other. Their heads were bent together over late
morning tea. They went hunting after that, a whole group
taking off after carted deer—using Boddington's father's
staghounds. It was a sport that never made much sense to
Lydia, involving the release of a stag from a cart, then chasing the fast, leaping thing for hours all over the countryside,
all so they could put him back in the cart again. Her father
had a great time with it, however, though the stag must
surely have been tired of it. This time, her father, with Sam's
help, was the one to corner the poor beast, ahead of all the
others. She hadn't seen her father so happy in months.

The next morning, he and Sam were both gone again, this
time just the two of them with her father's pack of harriers
and two servants to help manage the dogs: after hare. She
could have told them that, with Sam, all they needed was a

hatful of rocks—and be sure to have him cook any you bag.

They didn't return till late in the day—though a package arrived for her in the morning's post from a London address she didn't recognize. It included a note—"Enjoy. *Box Canyon Shoot Out* is the best," signed, "Sam." Books. Six Buffalo Bills and one Annie Oakley novel, not a one of which had she read nor did Clive own. Lydia was thrilled and spent the rest of the day upstairs reading: She had Rose bring dinner to her. It was hare, prepared beautifully with some sort of berries—not whortleberries, but almost as good.

That following day, at afternoon tea, she finally saw Sam for the first time for any duration since their archery match—he, her father, and several other men had been driving grouse since dawn. The season had opened. They all looked exhausted. Nonetheless, they made it to tea, and she made a point of sitting in the chair nearest Sam, of being nice, watching herself. She would not say a single word to give offense. She would be considerate, sensitive.

He, too, seemed cautious—and puzzled, even wary of her presence. All of which bred a kind of distance between them. They couldn't behave and be themselves, too; she wanted to laugh. She wanted to cry. Oh, Sam.

The tea biscuits began to taste dry; they didn't sit well. The tea smelled flat, stale.

"I received the books," she said as she stirred her tea.

"Books?"

"The American novels."

"Ah. I sent them before—" He stopped.

She looked at him. "Before what?"

"Before I realized."

"Realized what?"

He shrugged, stared at her a moment, sighed, then got up and left.

Lydia sat there, slowly sinking into misery.

She spent the rest of the day hoping against hope for a kind word from him, which never came. What a fool: The expectation left her wretched. Oh, what upheaval of emotion. She went upstairs and cried. Cried!

Why? So what if he'd called her a shrew the last time they'd spoken at any length? She *was* one then. Now she wasn't. Didn't he notice? What did he *want*? Her knickers, she thought. Well, that was too much. And everything else was too little.

Later that afternoon, a seemingly brilliant notion, she remembered she still had his hat. Yes, the perfect thing. Not too much, not too little. He loved his hat. She would return it, a gift.

She went upstairs and dug out his Stetson from the moor. How light and lovely it felt as she set it into her lap, onto her aqua satin skirt. She ran her fingers along the felt brim. She straightened the beads on the band, while the sunlit lace of her bedroom wavered its pattern over the black hat. She lifted it by the crown and put her face into it, closing her eyes when she discovered that the inside was filled with the smell of Sam's head, his hair. She almost didn't want to part with it. Though she would. To please him.

Then she stymied herself. She couldn't just send it. She should write a note. She took paper and pen, each from one of the many small arabesqued drawers of her writing desk (Sam's dark, uncomplicated hat looking as out of place atop the delicate secretaire as Sam himself would sitting on it), and drafted a dozen notes. None was right. She finally came up with the clever composition: *Here is your hat. Liddy.*

All wrong, of course. Again, too little. She riffled through crumpled ones; they all seemed to say nothing or gush: *Here is your beautiful hat. I hate to give it up. It so reminds me of you.* She felt caught between extremes. Which plunged her into doldrums again.

She felt a stranger to herself. Oh, how could she have known, she wondered, that her mind had these peculiar, dark places? Lightless moors, uncharted, terrifying for their lack of visible landmark or familiarity, any sign of boundary. She didn't understand herself. She wasn't like this.

Or, yes, she knew the feeling vaguely. It had nibbled at her once or twice in her lifetime, like a little misbehaving thing, a pup, who insisted on using an earlobe or toe to teethe. Only the pup had grown huge and undisciplined. And ravenous. It had turned out to be, not a flop-eared old dog after all, but a wolf, a wild-eyed hound that prowled the moor of her mind. Where it now ate her alive: She lay in the dark belly of her misery, confused, on edge.

What was wrong with her, that she felt like this? It wasn't Sam. It must be her menses. That was it. It was here.

It wasn't. And she actually looked for it this time. In her clothes, in her body. Nothing. Lydia went to her bed and lay down. There, she put her hand to her breast. It was tender, a sure sign her flow was coming. It was. Oh, goodness, was it late—nine days now.

Her breasts felt full. Fuller than usual.

She was different, it occurred to her. She slept a lot. Food didn't taste the same. She often felt queasy. No, don't be silly—

She refused to think of the word, nor even the possibility. Meanwhile, her mind paraded all the people before her who might enjoy her fall from grace, if—well, if. Even those who wouldn't, her friends, wouldn't be able to help. So she couldn't be. Besides, Sam had saved her from it. It wasn't possible. That thing he did, it prevented it absolutely. It always worked.

It usually worked.

Sam got the box that night. It was waiting for him on his bed. Puzzled, he opened it, then leaned it toward the light. His hat. The one Liddy had taken over. He tried to think of a good reason she'd send it back—and couldn't. Boy, was she saying good riddance to every last bit of him from her life. He lifted his dusty old Stetson from the box, and a note fell off its brim. *Here is your hat.* Yep, here it was. Have it back. Good-bye. Seeing the hat suddenly made him feel so bad he had to put it in the box again, hide it. She didn't want it.

She didn't want him.

*   *   *

The next morning, Lydia arose to a sunny day, a high-scoring day. Rose was in gay spirits. She brought a breakfast of toast and tea; it was good. Lydia ate it looking out into the breezeless, beautiful morning, and all seemed well. Yes, she was feeling much better. Bright as sunshine, she told herself.

She was on her way downstairs, dressed for shooting, when, with about two moments' notice, she suddenly rushed back upstairs—she made it as far as the hallway water closet, where she promptly heaved up her wonderful break-fast along with the remnants of last night's dinner.

Her mouth full of acrid taste, Lydia blotted her wet chin, stared into the porcelain toilet, and burst into tears again. With the door closed, she sat down on the little stool by the door in the W.C. There, bent over into her own lap, her face in her hands, she wept for half an hour.

It was the darkest, loneliest half hour of her twenty-four-year existence. Her moor-wolf of misery shook her by the heels and swallowed her whole.

Shortly after, Lydia was summoned to her mother's rooms. Her worst fear regarding her parents was coming to pass: that she should spend the rest of her life endlessly called on the carpet, all for having been wicked for really only a day. It didn't seem right. And they didn't even know the worst of it.

Her parents' apartments were on opposite ends of the house. Thus, on the south side of the house, in her mother's sitting room, she found the viscountess at her writing desk.

"Come in, dear."

Constance Bedford-Browne sat at a small black lacquer secretaire, tapping a stack of papers on which she set a book. Her hand on it, she turned. "Wallace told me. I'm sorry. I'd hoped the two of you would get on together." Her mother shook her head, frowned, then said, "Don't look so defensive, Lydia. I only wish to talk to you, mother to daughter. I'm worried for you."

"Don't worry, Mother." It would have been the perfect opportunity to say *I'm pregnant.* Yet that seemed a little she was right. And, two, she'd thought that pleasing others didn't matter, that she could act against the wishes of her family, the dictates of society, and simply live with the secret: And she was wrong.

She needed the people who loved her to know her. She couldn't hide what she was from them.

This was what she was thinking when Rose came into her room that evening. Rose with her shoulders bent forward and her eyes puffy. An unhappy posture, the face of a woman who'd been crying.

She brought Lydia's nightgown to her in her dressing room, then in the bedroom beyond opened the valve of the gas lights and closed the window curtains. The gas jets hissed softly. Lydia walked out into a bedroom that glowed. The light, however, did nothing for Rose's mood. It only further revealed her glumness.

"Is Thomas all right?" Lydia asked.

"Yes, miss."

"You?"

She glanced over. "I'm all right."

No, she wasn't. The girl's happy mein from this morning—from all the days since her marriage—was gone. She looked forlorn.

"What's wrong?"

Rose came to the foot of the bed, then, as she did when they both had time to talk, she and Lydia sat on the edge. She straightened the books on the night stand into a neat stack as if they needed her attention, then said, "I'm disappointed." She rolled her lips in, pressed them, then explained further. "My monthly came. It was late, but it came. I'm not pregnant." She caught back a little sniff.

Lydia shifted and moved up onto her knees to put her arm around the girl. Rose leaned into her. "You wanted to be?"

"Yes. Oh, yes."

"I'm sorry. How sad, then." Lydia sat there for a few seconds, holding her friend, patting her arm. "And how sad for me: I am."

Rose arched around enough to look up at her. "You can't

much. Lydia hadn't said the words aloud to herself yet. No, she looked for a better way. . . .

Despite reassurance, her mother's face looked worried anyway. She continued. "Your father told me you were down shooting rounds of arrows with Mr. Cody. You enter a room, and he doesn't see anyone else. Most of the time, he seems to be fuming angry. He reminds me of a man denied, who thinks he's entitled, somehow—"

Lydia shook her head. "He knows he's not."

Her mother seemed surprised by her quick, certain response, then made a nod, acceptance. She insisted still, "The two of you are connected somehow."

"We, ah—we grew to know each other out on the moor." It was a relief her parents knew at least this much, she realized. She shrugged, remaining vague. "We have things to say to each other, things to resolve." She hoped they did.

Her mother's expression remained thoughtful. She nodded again. "All right." From her papers, she separated out a small, thin volume bound in yellow cloth, offering it toward Lydia. *A Texan in Massachusetts* by Samuel Jeremiah Cody. "A book," she said, offering it. "His grandmother gave it to me. He wrote it when he was in school and the first months after when he worked in Boston as a banker. He saw it published when he was twenty-one."

"A banker? How odd." Lydia took the book. "I can't imagine Sam as a banker."

"Nor could anyone else. They fired him."

She laughed. Of course.

"He was fired from a total of—" Her mother looked down at another of her slips, before saying, "fourteen jobs over the first three years he was out of school."

Again, Lydia laughed, a small, more uncontrollable burst, which made her mother glare anxiously in her direction. Her mother wanted to be sure of Lydia's feelings for this intruder—or, more accurately, to be sure of her feelings against him.

The viscountess continued, "He reorganized his father's ranch in the meantime, which took several years to make money, but eventually did. With the profit, he bought part interest in a small railroad. That made money. It all seems to have snowballed from there. He was already rich when, two years ago, a geyser of crude oil erupted on one corner of his land in Texas. It did a lot of damage, but he seems even to have turned that around." She again consulted the small paper sticking out from the rest. "I should have thought so much petroleum was good for nothing but making a million bottles of elixir or hair tonic. But, no, he seems to have sold the rights to drill for it, for a sizable amount of money as well as for shares, to a company called"—another paper—"Standard Oil."

She frowned, blinked, then told Lydia as if not quite believing her own words, "According to this"—she lifted the last paper, giving it a shake—"his net worth is in the millions." Frowning deeper, she told her daughter, "He is a most puzzling person: both the largest failure and grandest success I have ever heard of."

Her mother was unsettled. She wanted to despise Sam, dismiss him, but somehow had backed herself into the inability to do so.

And none of it mattered to Lydia. It was all irrelevant. Without realizing, she had decided weeks ago on a moor whom the father of her children would be. Or child. Perhaps it would just be child. Sam was not the easiest person to get to march in step with anyone else. There was some doubt they should become lifelong mates, though that is what she wanted. A revelation.

"Do you love Father?" she asked suddenly.

"Of course."

"He believes you don't."

"I can't think why."

"Because you leave all the time. Mostly you live in London, and he lives here."

"We don't have much in common. I don't like to hunt. He doesn't like London society. That doesn't leave us much." She smiled. "We have you and Clive, of course. We're both greatly interested in the two of you and your welfare."

"Why did you marry Father?"

Her mother smiled politely, her usual smile. gaze left Lydia's and the smile grew almost sw "He was gentle," she said. "And he wrote the mos letters."

"Does he write to you?"

"Not anymore." She shrugged, wistful. "Th lovely. One summer, he wrote every single day. If I letter one day, I knew it was the post, not him. The the stray letter would catch up: I'd get two."

"Do you write to him?"

Her mother looked at her, startled. "No."

"Did you then?"

"Sometimes." She smiled all at once, broadly. ' him telegrams now." As if defending with a list: "Lyd everything he needs. I had two children by him wh continue to support together. I am faithful, loyal. Ho he doubt my love?" She looked at the papers in her then murmured almost to herself, "The telegrams w about Mr. Cody, of course. Nothing else." Softer still, haps I don't love him. I can't remember."

Lydia looked down, and there was the book her m had placed in her hands. Standing there, she opened it, ous for the man who had written it years ago.

She never got beyond the first page, however, for she read there made her throat tighten. She brought her to her mouth. "Oh, no," she murmured.

She offered the page out, as if her mother might re and understand.

The viscountess's gaze dropped, read, then raised a She gave her daughter a quizzical look over the open b She didn't understand at all, of course.

The opening page read: *This book is dedicated to my ther, Joseph Jeremiah "Heck" Cody, whom I love very m and admire more than any man I know.*

Two ideas from the moor haunted Lydia. One, she'd thou that she could not have Sam and please her family, too: A

be. You're not—" Her face grew horrified, her eyes wide. Her mouth made a little O of alarm. "You didn't!"

"I did. On the moor. Mr. Cody was so—" She started to smile.

With conviction, the girl said immediately, "Oh, that evil, evil man!"

"No, no, not at all. He didn't think we should. I did. It's entirely my own doing." Lydia did smile finally, the first she had over the whole business. "Well, my half of it is entirely my half-doing." She made a weak laugh. "My *un*doing." She wished to make it into a joke, to have Rose laugh, too.

Her maid, though, bit her lip, stared, then looked down. "Excuse me," she said. She stretched her legs toward the floor, straightening her back, and slipped off the bed. She walked from the room.

Nothing. She said nothing. Not censure, not consolation. Nothing at all.

Lydia waited for a few minutes, thinking Rose would come back, trying to remain cheerful. When it became obvious that the girl wasn't returning anytime soon, Lydia found herself staring at the lace counterpane, poking her finger into its holes, poking at shadows, sitting alone.

Over the next several days, she sometimes caught Rose frowning grimly in her direction. Sometimes it was as though the girl was simply disappointed, very disappointed. Sometimes it seemed she was angry.

Rose kept the confidence, thank God, but hers and Lydia's chattiness, the friendship itself, truncated. It was as if Lydia as a person had disappeared off the map of her world. As if her mistress had done what she herself had dared not do, no "decent" girl do, and consequently Lydia and their relationship would suffer so that her sacrifice to stay decent might mean something.

She chose an allegiance to an ideal over Lydia.

Rather like her mother would, when she found out, Lydia thought. Perhaps her father, too. He certainly enjoyed Boddington's father's staghounds. They might very possibly choose society's approval over her—certainly her mother loved it well. It was this reason, perhaps, this feared echo, that made Rose's abandonment so utterly heartbreaking.

That and its likelihood of being a predictor of what a long, lonely road lay ahead.

21

*Every man's passions make him different, and the
choice of them'll make him odd by somebody's
benchmark. We're all somebody's cross-threaded
oddball.*

SAMUEL JEREMIAH CODY
A Texan in Massachusetts

That week, Sam saw Liddy exactly four times. Once on the
terrace with Boddington. Another time midweek, through
an interior east-side window—he'd looked up from a
telegram he was composing to the secretary of state and
happened to see her crossing the terrace. She went down
into the rose garden, a pretty, slender young woman in dark
violet with another of her little matching hats, her bow
over her shoulder, her quiver, arm protectors dangling in
her fingers, swinging as she walked. She was on the move.
She practiced a lot, a woman in love with the flight of an
arrow.

He saw her again at tea—the day he received his hat—
where it was so unbearable to see her obliged to be nice to
him, he had to get up and leave. The fourth and last time
was the morning after that. He was coming into the house
through the mud room from shooting all day with her father.

The area Wendt shot was moorland. Amazingly, the countryside had burst out into bloom: heather—the north moors were apparently a little behind the southern ones. To Wendt, the healthy abundance of it meant red grouse, bagloads, which fed on the heath. The season had opened two days ago, the viscount and his many arriving friends avid, out every day at the crack of dawn. To Sam, seeing so much heather again—a little shorter, a little purpler—was painful; it was heaven.

The northern moor was hillier than the southern one, not as rocky, not as wild somehow. Or at least the portion of it over which Sam shot wasn't—they did what was called "driving": Beaters sent the grouse up out of the bushes toward the shooters who hid behind butts (more butts, the British were crazy for the word). You fired at oncoming birds. It was a duck shoot, so to speak—with short spans of time in between for retrievers to gather the dead birds. The Yorkshire moor was reminiscent enough of the Dartmoor that Sam was pensive through most of it, thinking of the daughter—Wendt had some of her mannerisms and used a lot of her expressions. It was eerie. Family. They were a piece.

"Plenty of bogs this time of year," the viscount said, speaking of Yorkshire as they came into the house. "They feed all the rivers on the moor like sponges, soaking up winter rains, then letting it go all summer into rivers and pools."

Sam looked up, and Liddy was standing there. She and he stared at each other. *Rivers and pools.* Their eyes held. She opened her mouth as if she had something to say, then closed it, glancing at her father, then him again, all the while looking so fidgety and forlorn—yep, still here, Liddy—that he wanted to turn right around and go back out. Her father clapped him on the back then—the worse Sam and the daughter got on, the better he and the father seemed to—and shepherded him inside.

And thus it went.

Though he saw little of Liddy it was as if there was a physical connection between them. He wanted it. He guarded it fiercely. His, this connection to her. It was a joy; it was a torture.

Nothing gave Sam more pleasure than his and Liddy's moments together—so tenuous, in his mind, threaded like beads of dew onto a spider's thread. *Us,* he wanted to whisper in the mud room. Nothing harrowed him so much as that he might not be delicate enough in his grasp of their connection, to weave it into something substantial, something to last a lifetime. He had to have her help to do it. A man and woman did it together. He himself was clumsy with emotion. He lacked insight, sensitivity. Would she help? He wasn't sure what she wanted of him. He felt exposed to speak of his feelings in honest terms, his feelings were so—

It was why they were called "tender" feelings, he guessed. He felt vulnerable. Speaking of love was easy enough, if a man didn't have it at the heart of him. If he did, though—well, it seemed to take more bravery than he had to whisper the word to Liddy. Love. He was in love with her, and she was mad at him.

She sent him his hat.

She doesn't want you. Why say anything? What was the point?

The mud room was Thursday. From Thursday afternoon to Saturday, Sam didn't see Liddy at all: and he'd learned to watch for her. The writing desk at the east-side window had become the place from which he wrote all his correspondence—his sentry post. But she didn't go down to the archery range, not on Friday nor Saturday, not once, and both were good days, high-scoring days. He couldn't think what she was doing with herself.

Then the viscountess's sister's uncle-in-law's boy—the British aristocracy were as intermarried as the tiniest, far-off town in Texas—a cellist, came from Derbyshire for what

Sam thought was a concert. Wendt himself was disgruntled, but his wife was in residence and kept "mucking up the shooting season something awful with these damn cream teas and concert cotillions."

When Sam walked into the upstairs music room that evening, though, all the furniture was pulled back: It was no concert. Typical. He'd misunderstood. He was forever singing off the wrong song sheet these days, so distracted he'd had to ask Wendt to repeat himself—twice—when the viscount had said he'd be willing to set up a meeting in London for September to put some of the ideas they'd talked about on paper—the beginning of formally drafting a new treaty—ideas they'd discussed between the booms of guns and the barks of dogs.

In the music room, chairs lined the walls, their single file broken with occasional small tables sporting little fringed lamps. A cello and piano stood waiting in the corner. Dancing. Not Sam's favorite pastime. Though he should probably stay: Among the people who drifted in were not just neighbors and houseguests but newcomers. At least four members of Parliament, if he wasn't mistaken, their families in tow, had arrived to partake of what Wendt modestly called "the best grouse moor south of Scotland"—men it would be helpful to woo to his terms.

About five minutes into talking to one of them, though, as the cellist and pianist tuned up, who should walk in? None other, God help him, than Gwynevere Pieters on the arm of Boddington, of all people. The two of them took over a table, ol' Boddie looking smug enough to strut sitting down. For one quick minute, Sam reconsidered going back to his room. Then he saw Liddy. And didn't want to. Couldn't have anyway. He was riveted.

She glided into the room just as the music started, a long-necked swan tonight: She wore a black plume in her hair. She was a sight for sore eyes. That wild hair of hers was tamed back into a smooth, shining coil, only hints of wayward ringlets where wisps escaped at her nape. Her dress fit low on her shoulders, blue-black taffeta, a kind of gun-metal blue, a metallic sheen to it. She sparkled—cut jet and dark blue sapphires, tiny ones set in malachite at her throat and ears and hands. Her skin was like cream against the dark, glittering colors. While her breasts—

Whoa, her breasts. Most of both of them was in view, and memory didn't do them justice. He remembered their being round, more generous than expected on such a slim girl: He didn't remember their being . . . plump, so full they could take over the neckline of a dress. He wet his lips, staring, recollecting way too well: Her nipples were dusky pink. Rosy. Little things, no more than a pinch of flesh in his fingers, set on small areolae, little geranium-pink circles no bigger than the bowl of a soupspoon on dove-white.

Oh, yeah, this was what he should be thinking of now. He looked down at his feet. His boots needed a shine. When he looked up, he blinked, stepped back: Liddy was headed in his direction, looking right at him. She was going to tell him to leave again. *And take your hat with you.*

Sam turned to the woman standing next to him, a sweet-faced thing who was a little on the heavy side. He didn't know her. "Excuse me." He smiled. "Would you like to dance?" She looked bewildered but delighted, and off they went.

As they turned across the floor with half a dozen other couples, Sam caught glimpses of Liddy. She stood at the side, watching him, stalled, a look of dismay on her face. When the dance ended, he was way too close to her, only three or four people between them. She raised her hand to get his attention. She got past one person, called, "Sam, I need to talk to you. I have something to say—"

Yeah, right. "Go home," he thought. He took hold of a lady between them, and out he went again, spinning into a waltz. He knew he was behaving badly. He should stop. Yet it was more than just not wanting to hear how she'd like him to leave again. There was pride in him somewhere that was wounded.

I'm defending myself. From attack, insisted a voice at

the back of his brain. Though attack from where was a little
blurry. You've gone wild. He could hear in his own mind
that he was defensive, self-justifying—and hated himself
for it.

She'd rejected him, that's all. It happened every day to
one man or another. Hell, there sat Boddington. She'd rejected him, too, word had it.

Besides, Liddy was too skinny anyway. Her hands were
bony. Her eyes, her hair were brown, the most common
color.

Yet still, whenever his eyes found her as he circled the
room, he could do nothing but stare. If only he didn't like so
well bony hands and plain brown eyes.

No, she wasn't pretty. Not from every angle. She wasn't
soft-spoken like a woman should be. In fact, she liked to
contradict him—she liked to contradict anyone, even men.
Especially men. She thought she was so smart, so special.
She wasn't kind-hearted; she was soft-headed. Why, she had
compassion for . . . for everyone, damn it. She wasn't very
selective or discriminating.

Hell, she'd had the poor taste to cozy up to him: to sleep
with him. How discerning was that? You'd think Miss Prissy
Brit could do better.

She ended up dancing with someone else, some kid
maybe twenty-four, twenty-five. Watching her spin backward in someone else's arms made Sam feel awful. Oh, he
recognized the feeling: jealous. And he knew his own usual
reaction—anger, rudeness. He kept trying to check it, stop it,
but it kept coming on.

And there was something else afoot. There were only
about thirty or so people in the room yet, but Boddington
was up, moving through them. People were looking at Sam
and at Liddy. He realized that Boddington, Clive, and others
were aware he was running from her, or waltzing from her,
that is, while she was trying to make him stop, get his attention: the two of them fussing, at it again, the joke of the

"Was. Yes."

"Miss Pieters is an heiress." Her tone put some sort of fault in the statement—his. "Why didn't you mention that?"

He was flustered for a minute, unsure of his reasons, then said simply, "I didn't think of it. I wasn't marrying her for her money."

Liddy's hands came onto her hips, her chin up. "No. That *you* have money. She wouldn't marry the poor country boy you pretend to be."

"I *am* a country boy."

"Who has a *lot* of money. Obviously. Who never said in almost four days of being alone together." She was accusing him of being deceptive and underhanded—a month ago.

"There was no place to spend it on the moor. It didn't seem important." He blinked, looked down, then said, "And I liked that you liked me without it. Besides, I did tell you—"

"Yes, as we were leaving, and then you even took it back. 'Not as rich as John D. Rockefeller,' you said."

"I'm not. More like Vanderbilt. Rockefeller is richer than both of us together. So now is it all right? Now that I'm rich, can we be friends?"

She sniffed.

"Can we dance at least? People are staring."

She blinked. They started again.

Her hand at his shoulder, she said, "I have something to tell you."

"What?" He glared down, bracing himself. Here it comes.

Her eyes went wide, looking up at him, almost frightened. Upset. She bit her lip, chewing the side of it, and a funny frown took over her face—the inside tips of her eyebrows rising even though the rest of them went down. A look of dismay. "Why are you so mean to me?"

"That's what you wanna tell me? I'm mean to you?" He stopped in the middle of the floor.

She stopped again, too. Stop and start.

"Why are you so mean to *me*?" he asked, pointing a finger at her.

"I'm not." She looked surprised, then humble. "Well, I'm not anymore. I'm good to you."

"You're not." As evidence, "You sent me my hat."

Her expression grew more bewildered by the minute. She answered, confusing him, "Because you like it." She furrowed her brow again. "Don't distract. You're vile to me. You have been. Ever since our archery competition, where I beat you."

He leaned toward her. "I. Beat. You," he said, separating the words, drawling them out with Southern emphasis. *Ah. Beet. Yoo-oo.*

She blinked, frowned, pressed her mouth again, then took him aback. "All right," she said. "You beat me. There? Are you happy?"

He wasn't. It must have showed.

Because she said, "No. You're never happy, are you?"

"Not often. But what does that have to do with anything?"

Her hands drew into fists, which she shook in front of her. "What does it take to make you give in?" she asked. "What would make you look at me kindly again?"

Kindly? He looked at her kindly all the time. He went from confused to confounded.

"All right," she said. "You beat me. I gave you a handicap because I thought I could shoot rings around you, but you shot better than I ever dreamed. Next to me," she said modestly, "you're the best archer here. There. Is that enough?" She spit the question out, fierce.

"I knew all that."

"What then?" Her agitation grew.

Oddly enough, he liked seeing it. It made him feel alive, affecting. At least he counted for something. "The other."

"What other?"

In the shade, Liddy: He might have said: *Admit you want me. Say you're sorry you sent my hat back, that you want me gone, all so you can look good to people you can't even be yourself with. Say I'm the one, you need me. Want me.* He couldn't bring himself to utter the words privately, though,

She wasn't. Not at all. She started to cry at the base of the stairs, where she hiked up her skirts. She took the staircase, the landing, and the next rise of stairs at a run. She was sobbing uncontrollably by the time she entered her rooms.

22

Those who see any difference between soul and body have neither.

Oscar Wilde
Chameleon, December 1894

Some time later—it seemed hours, though it was undoubt-edly less—Lydia found herself collapsed, quietly numb, on the floor of her dressing room, her dress only partly off, be-cause it had a lot of hooks at the back she couldn't reach, and she hadn't yet been able to bring herself to ring for Rose. Alone. Never had she felt so alone.

She thought of the moor and how marvelous it had been to believe she had in Sam one person—what a huge differ-ence just one made—who understood, who accepted and sometimes even approved of, her struggle to be, to find, who she was beyond what others expected. Unless, apparently, it was what *he* expected. He wanted her to be as she was on the moor all the time, the runaway lady's maid. Not the daughter of a viscount and all that implied—all that he found . . . pompous and . . . well, those other things. How much must he despise her to be willing to humiliate—repudiate, abase—her in front of everyone?

where to go, what to do. Bad? He wasn't bad; he was a failure at it. Half the time, he couldn't even take a hand that was
held out to him.

"I'll do right by you," he told her. "You know that, don't
you?"

"Right?" she repeated, then snorted. "No, thank you. I
don't want anyone taking care of me or doing things for me
or to me—I'm not sick, I'm just pregnant. I don't need pity
or help. You've done enough." She added with a kind of
teary snort of laughter, "No medicine," but that really confused him because he wasn't offering her any.

Sam was lost for a minute. How to bring the two of them
together after so much hurt and misstep? Union, friendship.
Love. How did a man make it all work, when he had failed at
it—at connection—pretty much all his life?

Love*making*. The idea popped into his mind. He *was* good
at that. And the next thing he knew, he felt a smile inside
himself he had to hold back. He said, "So you're pregnant."

She only rolled her watery eyes up at him, then pulled a
sarcastic face.

"Now wait a second here, Lid," he told her, "there's a
good side to it."

"Oh, certainly, from your viewpoint at least: *You're* not
pregnant."

"No, no, you can't *get* pregnant."

"I *am* already, you—you—"

He held up his hand before she strained herself finding
more names to call him. "Easy, there. What I mean is, now.
You can't get pregnant again. You already are."

Her large brown eyes fixed on him. "Pardon?" she said.
Ha, he had her attention.

He let his grin show in what he hoped was a disarming
way. "I mean, remember that penalty kiss? How I just sort of
wrestled you down and—" Whoa, just thinking about it
made his pecker shift around in his trousers. Oh, yeah, this
was a great plan, he thought.

"What penalty kiss?" She said it deadpan, straightening
her back like a ramrod was down it.

"The one at the edge of the trees." He raised his eyebrows, teasing, smiling, and said, "Where I sort of chased you down."

"Don't get cute with me, Sam Cody."

Cute. Oh, yeah, he was cute all right. He felt his grin broaden. "The penalty kiss," he repeated. "You can't have forgotten about that. It was so goshdarn wonderful—"

She said quickly, "I don't remember any—"

He laughed. He loved it when she lied. He couldn't help it; he just did. "Well, don't worry, darlin'. I'll remind you."

"Don't 'darlin' ' me. You said awful things to me downstairs—"

"I take them back." He rethought that. "Well, some at least."

She rose up slightly, her eyes widening. "Some?" She threw something hard, another item from the dressing room floor, a shoetree.

He jerked his leg to keep from being hit as he said, "Most of it was true." Then laughed: "Like now. You are a shrew, you know."

"Oh!" she said in frustration. "Well, I certainly don't want to hear about it in front of everyone, my family, my friends." She gave a snort of outrage. "Even your stupid Gwyn heard what you said, not to mention some others of my acquaintance who aren't that fond of me: ridiculed by His Excellency the U.S. ambassador. You humiliated me."

He stopped smiling and pushed back the brim of his hat. "And for that, I'm sorry. You have to forgive me."

"I don't either have to. And I don't."

He laughed. "All right. That'll make the penalty more fun, I guess."

"What are you talking about—"

"The penalty." He paused, thoughtful a moment, then said, "See, I thought I was coming up here to say I was sorry. But now that I've said it—and had it so ungenerously received—I think maybe I came up here after all to get those knickers you owe me."

"My what! How can any man have such gall?"

She drew back, as he took a step forward—just enough to reach behind him and take the doorknob. Her expression registered a startled flicker, dawning understanding, as he swung the door to, and its latch clicked closed.

She scooted backward, away from him. "Don't you dare—"

He interrupted. "Now, see, I know you're going to fight being playful about all this, but I can't see any other way around it." He let himself lean back on the door and look around. How to get close to her without getting kicked in the shins?

"I'm not over being angry with you, Sam Cody—"

"Right." Children. They were two children at times. But since they were, well, they might as well enjoy being hare-brained. Children knew how to play at least. "So be angry." He smiled, wiggling his eyebrows at her. "That ought to make it into a different kinda fun."

Lydia blinked, scowled, and got her feet under her. Oh, no, she thought. Not on her life. Not over her dead body. He'd hurt her feelings, really hurt her, and he hadn't made it right. Though she felt a little better somehow; stronger.

She remembered, "R-Rose will be up any moment." She pushed herself all the way up, standing, poised, at ready.

The smug American, still smiling, made a click of his tongue and a reluctant shake of his head. "Actually, she won't."

"Yes, she will. She comes in every night to help me undress. I was waiting for her."

"Not tonight." His pulled his hand from his pocket and produced a long, recognizable key. "You see, I found this in the door, so I locked it. I didn't want us to be disturbed after all the trouble I had getting in here. No one's coming in."

Lydia frowned at the key to her room, then at him. "Um, Sam—" She took a step back, a hanging dress making her jump when it came over her shoulder. She reiterated, "I'm, ah—I'm not very happy with you at the moment."

He laughed. "And who could blame you. I can be a horse's ass. What can I tell you?" When she liked this vein, cocking an eyebrow at him, he continued. "I make mistakes. Sometimes they're painful ones. I told you, I'm sorry."

She blinked at him. *I'm sorry?* These two words were supposed to fix her hurt? Perhaps she was being petty, but they didn't. They weren't large enough; they didn't feel commensurate to the offense.

He repeated again, softer, "I can't do anything more about it now, Lid. It's past; it's done." He touched his hat brim, a little salute, then said, "Thank you for my hat. My appreciation is pretty miserably delayed in coming, but thank you."

"You're welcome."

She scowled deeper. Her feelings were supposed to be all better now? She was being too demanding. Vindictive, she told herself. She should forgive him, let it go. But she couldn't get over her anger; the pain of his accusations downstairs clung to it, fresh again each time she thought of his mean words.

Oblivious, he said, "So I'm thinking—" He paused and set his jaw the way he could, as if putting his tongue on a back tooth. "I'm thinking that, to start with, I want you on your hands and knees, so I can take off those knickers personally."

"Oh, no"—she shook her head, backing up into the dress further—"absolutely not." Outrageous. This was outrageous! "You can't do this! I'm still furious with you—"

"You'll get over it." He grinned.

She didn't want to get over it. She pressed her lips together tight. Then had a bright idea. She told him, "All right, I should have given them to you already. I will." She bent over and reached under her dress. This would stop him.

What noisy skirts she had. They made a terrible din as she wiggled, her hands lost in a shushy churn of blue-black taffeta, black tulle, and black lace frothing in her arms from beneath. She stripped off black silk knickers. "Here." She tossed them at him.

"Thank you." There at the closed door, he caught them,

making a magnanimous nod, then brought her knickers to his face. With them at his nose and chin, he tilted his head back slightly, rubbing the silk between his fingers, and closed his eyes. Voiceless, he let out air through the sound— "*Aah*"—satisfaction. "Now about that penalty—"

"There's no penalty—"

"Yeah, there is. And it's huge this time, Lid." He cocked his head, looking at her again out from under the brim of his hat, the way his mouth pulled, his grin, rather reminiscent of the moor.

She shook her head. "No, no, I *gave* them to you. You can't complain now—"

"Oh, I can: It took more than a week, and, though here I stand, it was such a hardship getting up here to claim them. To get up here past your mother, father, and brother, who all, by the way, have told me to pack my bags and get on out of Dodge, I had to climb out my window, down a trellis to the library, then sneak up the hall." He glanced around her dressing room as if there might be someone else he'd have to sidestep.

What his eyes found, however, was the valve by the door to the gas jets. He reached and with a turn closed it, cutting the gas to the lights. After a few seconds, along the walls the fixtures *whiffed*. They went out in a little concatenation of popping air, *puff, puff, puff, puff*. . . all the way down one wall, behind Lydia—the room growing dimmer—across and up the other.

She only knew Sam had stepped forward into the dressing room by a sense of movement somehow: in utter darkness. Her dressing room had no windows. There was a grill high over the door for circulation. If she stared, she could see twenty feet overhead a scrollwork of gray, muted moonlight coming from her bedroom. More a delicate reminder of light's absence than anything else. In front of her somewhere, Sam laughed his low, dirty laughter, the one that didn't always mean something was funny, but she couldn't see him. And she looked, turning in the dark.

She could only follow the path of his sound—his rough sigh at he brushed his hand across the back of her skirts, her buttocks, then moved away, then the knock of a hanger as he came round her shoulder. Blind.

"S-Sam?" Lydia called.

He said nothing, though she had a sense of his circling her.

She stammered, "I—I'm afraid of the dark."

"I know." His deep voice, a whisper, was right beside her.

She jumped when he took her face, but let him turn it, raise it toward him. She could smell his breath, the tang of after-dinner cognac, faintly stale, deeply stirring. She realized, there in the dark, she was frightened, fascinated: excited. Oh, Sam. His mouth brushed her bottom lip, stopping to catch it in his teeth, pulling a second, then letting go to brush his mouth, warm and soft, against hers again. When he laughed again in the dark, that evil laugh of his that could sound so truly wicked, she could feel his warm breath on her neck.

"Liddy," he murmured near her ear. Oh. His sweet name for her. How good to hear it; thank God he said it. Because it eased something just enough that she didn't scream, when he kissed her shoulder, just the touch of his mouth in the crook, then his low voice murmured, "Get down onto your knees and forearms."

The hair on her arms stood on end. On the moor, they had given each other directions. They were regular magpies when they made love. Do this. Try that. I want you here, like so.

Her knees and forearms? In a dark little cupboard of a room? It felt different. "W-what?" she asked. Except she knew she'd heard correctly. "No." She laughed, a jittery laugh. Nerves.

She knew him to be right beside her, but she kept misjudging exactly where he was. She reached toward where she thought she'd find his arm, and nothing. Then she'd startle and run into his chest at her back.

When his hands took hold again, she leaped, half-glad to their solidness, half-alarmed by the way they turned her, then his arm came around her, pulling her into the front of him, as he put the flat of his warm palm on her abdomen and pressed, sliding his hand down.

She let out another giddy laugh. What ambivalence. She found all this thrilling, blast it. She wanted it somehow; she wanted him. Yet it all felt so doomed; as lovers, partners, they were both too hardheaded.

"Come on," he encouraged. "Down on your hands and knees." As he smoothed his palm down to her pubis, rubbing the heel of his hand against her. He ran it up her belly to her ribs, over a breast, cupping it, then over her collarbone to her neck. She didn't stop him. She dare not, she told herself, as if he wouldn't allow it. He turned her face toward him, to face him over her own shoulder, and kissed her, open-mouthed. A lascivious kiss, deep, wet, full-mouthed. Oh, heaven . . .

He kissed her as he pinned her arms down and behind her, so she could neither fight nor embrace him. It was oddly frightening, thrilling, in tenor with that crazy dream several weeks ago. He turned her by her arms, kissing his way around till his mouth was at her neck, his breath going hotly down the vertebra of her spine. She closed her eyes, floating down into dark delirium.

He used his braced weight to push them both down onto the floor. He pushed her down into exactly the position he'd said, though now she was half in love with sensation. He put something—a bunched dress or petticoat—at her face and neck. "Hold on to this."

Delicately, he undid hooks. She had no idea how he could do it in the dark, but he released her clothes, as efficient as Rose. He didn't take them off though. Once they were loose, he simply put his hands inside, feeling under her to her breasts, freeing her completely, then downward—where she was bare because she'd given him her underwear.

Bare. He moved her skirts up. What a mess of her he

made. He drew back. She was aware he was undoing his
trousers—and shamefully happy to recognize the movement. He pushed her legs wider, touched her between them,
and she leaped and called out.

"*H-h-oh.*" She caught her breath as his fingers entered
her.

He bent and kissed her then, at the base of her spine, off-
center, first on one side, then the other. He muttered fond
words, "beautiful" . . . "soft" . . . "the sweetest." His hands
worked her buttocks, smoothing over them, kneading. Then
he took hold of her at the bend of her thigh and thrust himself inside her.

"*H-aa!*"

It was a feverish coupling. Pleasure pitched. It was odd; it
was strong. She knew, too, that he intended to stay inside her
to the end, and she anticipated it with a kind of relief. Oh,
good, I won't lose you, not then, not at that perfect moment.

When it arrived, it wasn't as she expected. He grew excited in a way that made him groan and clench his jaw, his
teeth snapping together. His body seemed to touch something, a place inside her, and a new sensation . . . more than
before somehow . . . inside pleasure, spasms. . . . She felt
her body grip him as surely as if her fingers had reached out
and squeezed. He called out softly, trying to muffle his
noise. Sharp, sweet contractions of pleasure began at the
core of her, then carried deeper, joined him, the two of them
jerking and panting into fulfillment that lasted and lasted
and lasted, then echoed in a way that left them still and
waiting.

What a position to discover oneself in. Her bum in the air.
There was no dignity in sexuality, she decided. Nor did she
wish there to be.

Lydia collapsed on her side into the pile of satiny fabric.
Sam's body, his arms, came around hers, his knees tucking
up into the backs of hers. She could feel him at her bare
backside, his open trousers, his naked member, still thick,
but spent, his vulnerable genitals tucked under her bum, so

warm and sweetly fitting up against her. She must have dozed. For when she came aware again it was with his jostling her shoulder.

The dressing room door was open. There was light, a lamp, coming from the bedroom. He murmured, "Liddy, I have to sneak out of here before I get us into more trouble. Before I leave, though, I'll go face your father. I'm going to offer for you. He'll tell me no, but tomorrow you tell him why. Or do you want me to?"

"God, no—" What did she want? From the floor of her dressing room, she looked up at Sam's silhouette sitting beside her.

He said, "You shouldn't have to worry about any of this. I'll take care of it." He'd save her.

She grabbed his arm—not because she was glad he would. But because it occurred to her: He wouldn't do it to her liking. She didn't want him to rush around fixing anything. "Let me tell them," she said. "I'll tell them everything. Where will you be staying?"

"The inn at Crawthorne, I guess."

She nodded. Yes. She wished he'd say he loved her. She wished they were on better terms. They had managed their usual cooperation—the physical sort. No two people knew how to make love better than they did. Yet she felt more worried than anything else.

On the moor, she'd learned what her life could be like if she herself directed it as best she could. Independence. Now she felt the threat of being overrun again. She feared the idea of Sam, the rich ambassador, in league with her parents, the viscount and viscountess. Plans. They would all have plans for her. While she wasn't sure what she wanted. She felt shoved along by them, by fate, and her lack of understanding of herself, her own indecision—if she couldn't make a choice of her own, she would be forced to swallow theirs.

The dream. She remembered the crazy dream she'd had when Sam had first arrived. The dream of the madman making medicine for her. No medicine, she thought. And a little whiff of the strength and freedom she'd felt out on the Dartmoor was with her again, just a little breath of it.

No medicine, she thought again. Why should I need it? I don't want it. I'm not ill.

I'm just me.

23

It's a bad idea to give advice. If you have to, though, just remember, no bending things to suit your own ends, 'cause, see, people never use advice the way you aim it. If it isn't plumb as an oak, in their hands it can curve and hit anything anywhere, including you.

SAMUEL JEREMIAH CODY
A Texan in Massachusetts

Her father's estate agent had an office in a manor house near the property's front gate, the first building of the estate after passing under the gatehouse. That was where they all met the next afternoon: Her father and his solicitor sat at the long table, her father's main estate agent and amanuensis, plus two bookkeepers. Her mother stood by the window, her back to the room, quietly livid, Lydia thought. It had helped Lydia that the viscountess had insisted on being present, because the bride also insisted. "The strong women of my house," her father had grumbled. And Sam. He pulled out a chair and sat at the table as soon as Lydia had settled into a stuffed chair near the window off to the side. Sam didn't wear his hat, but rather a pressed and tailored English suit of clothes, vest, high collar, a necktie, dressed respectfully for the occasion of the groom's shearing.

Then, no, one of the "bookkeepers" turned out to be *his* solicitor. Likewise, the amanuensis was not her father's but rather worked for His Excellency the U.S. ambassador extraordinaire and plenipotentiary to Britain. It made Lydia frown every time she realized this was Sam.

And thus they began: her parents, with their representative army, meant to convey how difficult it would be if Sam didn't cooperate; Sam and his representatives, their presence and attitude saying that, if the English intended to drive the American into unfavorable terms by using their position and power here, at the very least he would not go lying down. A marriage contract—forced due to pregnancy—was not the cheerful negotiation it might otherwise have been.

Her father began, "We are all here to assure that Lydia is well taken care of in this marriage settlement. I hope we are agreed. It is her welfare that comes first."

Ah, yes, her welfare. The family drum—let us take care of the weak and defenseless girl. Here's your tonic. Don't go out in the cold. You can't go off to school, because—why?—we love you and you don't need it. With Sam added now, there to save her, who, according to the cowboys she was reading now furiously, really needed a white hat.

Control. She had so little. She should simply accept that. Yet Lydia bristled. She crossed her legs one way, then the conversation at the table—dry lawyer conversation—stopped when she kicked up a leg to cross them the other way, the churn of her skirts being loud enough to draw attention.

The weak girl, she kept thinking. What was annoying was that she *was* weak. Politically. Economically. Her parents were right to worry. A husband could do great harm if the woman and her property weren't protected from an unscrupulous man. The implication, of course, was horrid as her parents went over everything, point by point. They didn't know Sam, their concerns said. They couldn't trust him: He wasn't of their own.

And she was weak, gestationally speaking. Even her powerful parents found her being six weeks pregnant a huge negotiating disadvantage. Though—for the benefit of the solicitors and other strangers involved—no one was mentioning her state. So English. So much unspoken. Like code.

Yes, yes, she thought, *carry on. I don't want to raise a child alone. I don't want to be an outcast. Yes, I'll marry him. In fact, I love him. I'm in an awkward position (rather like last night,* she thought, *amused by the irony).*

So she listened at first, as her father, mother, and Sam discussed the marriage arrangements. Money, property, who received what, what she had coming, what they would give. Business. Sam accounted for his money. Billions. She thought she'd heard wrong and asked for the number of zeros. Nine. Which, at first, made everyone else in the room look at each other. In Britain, a billion had twelve. Only a small cultural misunderstanding, however. In America a billion did have nine zeros, and Sam was nigh onto the tenth. And, given his assets and their growth, why, in time it might well become a British billion. Meanwhile, he had property in Texas, Massachusetts, Illinois, and Virginia. Rich as Rockefeller, in fact, for which—oh, Sam of the insane modesty—even apologized.

"I know I told you, Lid, I wasn't as rich as John D. I was surprised myself when these wires came in this morning. It's that doggone oil on my land and the partnership I got into a year or two ago." He shook head.

So did her parents. They're information had been old. As Sam liked to say, things sure could change quickly in that growing, thriving country on the other side of the Atlantic.

When her father couldn't complain, when in fact he'd been left speechless for the third or fourth time after being handed telegraph wires, bank statements, evidence of stock certificates, bonds, partnerships, corporations, the viscount grew gruff and slightly impossible. "And you have to live here," he asserted.

Sam frowned. "I can't. I mean, I can live here a lot—we can—but I can't be chained here. I like what I do with the State Department."

Her father brought his bottom lip up, tight against his upper. "And her property? What do you intend to do with her property? You can't carry England with you as you travel the world. She comes with a house in London, an estate near York. How will you manage those?"

"I—ah—I don't know. I haven't even seen them. I'll get to them as I can."

The viscount wasn't happy.

"You certainly have a modest life-style for so much money," her mother said over her shoulder from where she stood by the window.

"Do I?" Sam smiled, then dared a glance in Lydia's direction. "I think she's going to be expensive. I'm glad I have it."

Insane. Indeed, Lydia thought, Sam had a crazy streak in him. A streak she understood by extrapolation: She certainly knew lately what it was like to be angry with herself, but he was hard on himself most of the time; he couldn't stop. His style was different. He didn't fret or cry. Sam became angry; and, when in emotional pain, he sometimes distracted himself by running someone over the rails.

While a voice inside him was always running Sam over them. She could have sympathy for him, but—she had to own up—she couldn't do anything about it.

Control, she thought again. *Oh, how very little I have.*

Her parents segued into wedding arrangements.

"I'll marry her anywhere," Sam said.

"If you show up," her mother threw from across the room. Oh, she was seething—forced into a monied match, so lucrative in the filthiest sense: Goodness, some of his *riche* was so *nouveau* he hadn't even counted it yet.

"I'll do what's right," he told her parents, his face sober at the criticism of his past.

What's right. The words again struck Lydia. "Right," she said from her chair. "We must all do what's right. Why, if this got out, it would be an international incident: U.S. ambassador gets House of Lord's daughter pregnant."

They all looked at her, her parents and Sam chagrined to hear their worst fears put into words. While the solicitors' eyes widened as they leaned forward—juicy things were going on here, things that could feed a battalion of lawyers. For years.

"Well, don't worry about me," she said. "*I* won't tell anyone." To Sam, "And you needn't feel you have to marry me." What was she saying? Everyone blinked. *Do right.* She didn't want him to marry her because it was "right"—she didn't want him to have to swallow anything unpalatable either. She wanted him to live with her, stay with her, because he loved her.

"Why not?" he asked.

"You're unhappy about it. Businesswise, it's turning into a rousting."

"Well, I have to admit, it would make me happier if you'd own up—" He stopped, rephrased, "You're not humble here, Liddy—"

"That's what you want? Humility?" Then she caught what he'd censored and asked, "Own up to what?"

His brow drew down, Sam's quintessential dark look. "It would be, ah—it would be nice to hear you admit you—you're in love with me."

She wasn't going to at first. She balked—he'd admitted nothing, an emotional mute. She caught herself, though. She said quietly, meaning it, "I'm in love with you." There. It was out.

His mouth opened. He looked down, up, then across the room at the bookshelf, all the while his smile growing. It was lovely to see it. He looked at her parents. "She's in love me," he repeated, as if just to hear the words again.

Quiet reigned in the room for five or six ticks of the mantel clock. Then her father asked curtly, "Well?"

"Well what?" Sam asked.

"Do you love her?"

Sam blinked. "I'm marrying her."

Her father, wiser than Lydia had ever given him credit for, grew unceremonious on her behalf. "Listen, you, you—" He clamped his lower lip over his upper till it was white, bit down a minute, then continued. "Who cares that you intend to marry her. Do you love her?"

Sam blinked as if Jeremy Bedford-Browne were mad to ask the question. "Well, yes," he said like an obvious fact.

Lydia leaned to sit, her elbows on her knees, at the front of her chair.

Sam stammered, "I—I've wanted her, I think, from, from the moment I first sobered up across from her." He laughed nervously. It seemed a declaration was forthcoming. Then it wasn't. He looked down at the papers and said, "I can't promise that amount on the Yorkshire property until I see it. It's too much. I could buy and sell half the places in England for that."

Her father immediately took exception—you couldn't buy what Lydia's property was. Heritage, tradition, England . . . And they were all at it again, her father adding, "One of the reasons we don't like an outsider's marrying our daughter is you will take her away from us." An outsider. Don't take her away. It was the burden and pleasure of being well loved. Then he came back to, "And you aren't marrying her if we can't work out the terms, and part of the terms are that you love her."

Testy, Sam snapped, "Which is actually none of your business."

Her father stood, his chair scraping back. "Whether you will care for my daughter is most certainly my business. If you aren't smart enough to love her, you can't have her. Not even in her present condition, which *you*"—he leaned across the table—"couldn't have been thinking too clearly about when you put her into it."

Sam's eyes narrowed. Then he said in as rapid-fire drawl as she had ever heard from him, "Well, for God's sake, of course I love her. I love her. I'm delirious. I'm wild for her. Why else would I marry her?"

"She's pregnant."

"Fine. I love that she's pregnant. I love her. I'm in love. I'm very in love. I'm head over heels. Is that enough?"

From her chair, Lydia blew out a long, flummoxed sigh and stood up. Enough.

She herself had butted heads with everyone here, trying to maintain her independence, just as Sam was doing. Yet the heart of such struggle was wrong. They were both calling contrariness independence, when these weren't the same thing. She didn't have to fight for control of her life. She only needed to take it, have it, live it.

"Excuse me," she said. "These negotiations and this marriage are off. I don't want them." She took a deep breath. "Sam, you find it easy enough to humiliate me in front of people, then you dicker over terms, while you can't even say you love me in a civilized fashion.

"I want someone who can proclaim he loves me to the world, without shame, despite the fact that I'm far from perfect. I need your loving gestures to be as large as your means ones.

"Which I am beginning to believe is a lot like coupling between a man and woman: to have the most fun, one can't cling to a lot of ceremony." To her astounded parents, she said, "I trust Sam. That's not the issue. I just don't think we'll make good mates. I know this is going to be hard for you to accept, but I think I'm going to have the baby on my own. It will probably be hard on all of us, but I don't want to marry Sam this way. That would be worse."

She walked around the chair's arm and proceeded toward the door; she had things to do.

"What way? I thought this was your way," Sam asked behind her.

"Lydia?" her father called.

"Lydia!" her mother demanded.

"What?" Sam asked. "What!" He sounded desperate. Good. Maybe a little desperation would help him stop being so protective. Commit, Sam. Commit to me. Trust me. And for God's sake do what I'm going to do: Trust yourself.

As she got to the door, almost in unison—it was laughable—her parents said, "Where are you going, Lydia Jane?"

With the knob in her hand, she turned and told all of them, "To the Grand National. I've missed a lot practice. I'd best get back to it."

Amazed at herself, she opened the door and walked out: She felt fine. She felt good.

* * *

The day was beautiful, she realized, as she walked the mile home up the drive. It was still early enough to get in some practice.

Then, upstairs in her room, as she gathered her equipment, it occurred to her: Why did a baby have to be bad? A baby. She was going to have a baby. Babies were lovely. One of her own would be delightful. Her mother might collapse of shame, of course, but even that, when she thought about it, wasn't all that terrible. Let her. Her father would be sad, but only for her. If *she* wasn't sad about it, why—

She wasn't. Why did a baby have to be terrible? She'd already decided she wasn't marrying Lord Fancy Choice, a great relief. Now she would either marry Sam because he could prove a loving mate, or not marry him because he couldn't—it was entirely out of her hands.

Perhaps they'd be lovers, she thought. Difficult lovers. He would visit periodically, chase her around the house, bounce the baby on his knee, then leave—because they couldn't work out their differences beyond this.

In any event, she'd already determined she'd go her own way. Goodness, did this ever put the seal to it. But never mind. She had money and property of her own—the discussion this afternoon, if nothing else, had pointed that out. Of course, a lot of people would shun her as her belly grew. But her family would still love her. Her friends would stand by her, surely. And wouldn't a pregnancy, sans husband, determine once and for all who her friends were?

It frightened her a little to test these notions. She didn't expect the testing to be easy or smooth. But neither did it have to be so onerous as she and everyone else were making it. No one could make her ashamed without her permission. She wasn't going to hide anymore, not the fact that she'd slept with the man she loved, nor the fact that she was carrying his child, not her faults nor her strengths. She was just going to be who she was and let others think as they would. Enough.

She came down through the house, out the terrace and

through the garden, heading toward her targets: and knew suddenly that sense of power, control over her life, she'd known on the moor. There it was, blowing through her like a wind. It was back. It was hers. She came out onto the archery range for the first time in almost a week, feeling better than she had in ages—free and capable. She was capable of finding happiness, if not in every moment, then in spans of it, an unending pursuit and succession of it.

Like arrows. From quiver to target, *thwh-h-whip*. Then again, *thwh-h-whip*. And again . . . out into the air. Like flying. Repeating, repeating the short flight, always aiming toward gold. Sometimes hitting it.

24

Wickedness is a myth invented by good people to account for the curious attractiveness of others.

OSCAR WILDE
Chameleon, December 1894

At dusk, as Lydia entered the house, she stumbled onto an unusual sight. Clive had his arm at a doorway, where he had Rose trapped behind the servants' stairwell.

"What are you doing?" Lydia asked.

He jumped, then let out a sigh of relief. "Oh, you." He quirked an eyebrow. "Something is up, and no one is telling me anything, so I'm pestering Rose."

"I didn't tell him." Rose stood on tiptoe to call over his arm. It was the longest sentence she'd uttered in days—while the way she phrased her brand of loyalty implicated there was something to tell.

"Thank you," Lydia told her. "Let her go, Clive."

He did, and Rose skittered away, spooked by the whole business.

As Lydia watched her go, she thought, I've told the wrong person. Rose might very well never get over my transgression.

She looked at her brother there by the stairwell. "Clive," she said, "I'm pregnant, and Sam is the father."

He didn't blink. He shrugged, in fact. "I'd supposed as much, what with all the flurry. Congratulations."

"I'm not marrying him."

"Ah. Well. That will be sticky, but you'll get by." As if a brilliant solution, he offered, "You can live at Castle Wiles forever, even after I inherit it. And I'll give you a jolly good allowance, whatever you think is right. There you go." He smiled.

She laughed, then hugged him. "I have the house in London. I'd probably live there. I like London." In fact, it was a great anomaly for all of them, mother, father, brother, and sister, to have been out in the country together for so long. "But thank you."

"I'll visit then. A lot. I'll walk the baby."

"You're—" She met his eyes fondly. "You're a cracker-jack, Clive," she said. "A humdinger."

"A what?"

She shook her head—never mind—smiling. Oh, but he was, he truly was.

He held her for a few minutes, patting her back. She felt so happy suddenly. Amazing. She felt good for no better reason than someone knew who she was—and loved her, accepted her, someone she herself loved so much.

Then Clive pushed her back, lifting a long finger, asked, "So what have they said? Tell."

"They?"

"Mother and Father."

"They're shocked. I feel badly for them. I'm not what they bargained for."

He rolled his eyes. "Oh, it's Mother. I mean, Father is all right with things, but the old girl—it's just so awful to disappoint her. I hate to disappoint her myself." He paused, frowned, then held out his hands. "But sometimes there's no help for it. You see, the person I'm in love with will drive her dotty also."

"Oh, Clive!" Lydia was so surprised. "You're in love! Who?"

He grinned shyly. "In London. A big secret." He looked delighted, full of joy, as he pronounced the name: "Barnaby Winthrope."

"Barnaby? Barnaby's a man."

"Yes." He looked down, smiling sheepishly. "I am well acquainted with the fact."

Lydia put her hand over her mouth, then laughed. They both did. They laughed for five minutes, while hanging all over each other there in the corridor.

They were lucky, she thought.

She was lucky. She was strong and healthy with a baby inside her. She had the resources to take care of it and herself, come what may. She had a family who might take exception to her behavior, but they would never abandon her—or trade her to the Indians or put anything important to her down a latrine hole.

"We're lucky," she said again, this time aloud to Clive as they were parting.

"I know," he said and kissed her head.

The day before the Grand National, as Lydia was coming downstairs, her father was going up, having gathered the morning's post.

As he came by her, he was taking a thick letter—pages—from its envelope. He was so intent on it he didn't even see her as they passed. Then, just above her in the middle of the staircase, he suddenly stopped, turned the page, and just stood reading, a look of concern coming onto his face.

"What is it?" Lydia asked.

He startled, glancing down at her. "I—I'm not sure." He frowned again at the sheets, peering, shaking his head, as if unable to decipher the handwriting. Or perhaps what the handwriting had to say. When he looked up from the pages again, his expression had changed from concern to bewilderment. He told her, "Your mother has written me a letter."

25

Stout arm, strong bow and steady, Union, Trueheart and Courtesy.

Official motto
British Grand National Archery Society

The Grand National Archery Meet was an annual all-comers event that determined the best archer in Britain, male and female—a competitive ideal as old as Robin Hood or William Tell. Archers could be independent, though most were part of archery societies—in the program Lydia Bedford-Browne was listed as a member of the Royal Thornewood Foresters. The champion would be determined by points, though not exactly the way Sam and Liddy had counted them. The calculation was a little confusing as Sam heard it from people around him where he sat in the grandstand. The upshot, though, seemed to be that the committee wanted to reward evenhanded skill—an archer, for instance, who shot a lot of golds while also sometimes missing the target entirely was less likely to be named champion than someone who hit reds over and over. Thus, the highest gross score did not necessarily take the big "cup," though there was also an award for this as well as for highest number of hits and most central gold.

Thus, four levels of winning: the big one—the championship—and the three areas of excellence—high score, high hits, best gold. That was it. The York *Herald* put a price of two hundred pounds on the prizes, mostly in money, "cups" of various amounts. This didn't count private purses—the queen herself offered twenty-five pounds to the high score from her own Royal British Bowman. Nor did it include betting, which Sam found, at least in his corner of the grandstand, to be fast and furious all morning, even in rain. There was also a rule—explained to him as an archer out on the field miraculously collected—that anyone who made three golds at one "end" received a shilling from all participating archers of the same sex. Thus, it was possible for an archer to leave the meet with less money in his or her pocket, not more.

This year the committee had commandeered the Wyesmire Racecourse for the event, where on a large plot of grassy ground, directly in front of a grandstand, thirty targets, fifteen at each end of sixty yards, were currently pitched. On the other side of this narrow stretch, at a distance opposite the grandstand, was a spacious marquee tent, a covered bandstand to one side, another smaller tent to the other. The tents were for the organizers and participants of the event. The bandstand sported a soggy brass band at the moment. They were just filing in after being rained out. As to the grounds themselves, 195 archers had gathered to shoot, 108 of them women, and with the rain clearing up, they were attracting a pretty good crowd.

It was overcast but sunny presently. All morning, the men's hundred yards had been a struggle, with rain eventually emptying out the grandstand and sending archers under the tents. Till noon, they had battled heavy showers and high winds that would come up at right angles to the paths of the arrows, blowing them off course—even occasionally into wrong targets.

By the time luncheon was over, however, the sky had

cleared. The wind had dropped to a stiff breeze, and the carriages began to return—the fashionable set out on what stood a chance of becoming a nice summer day. There was a murmur when the afternoon arrivals included the Viscount and Viscountess Wendt and their son, the Baron Lorschester, that is to say, Clive, all of whom climbed into the grandstand in a group that also comprised the Earl of Boddington and the Marquess and Marchioness of Motmarche—both the viscount and the marquess, Sam was told, had daughters competing, which relieved him, because so far he hadn't seen Liddy. Among the people in the stand, "nob spotting," as the man beside Sam called it, turned out to be a minor side sport. Happily, the nobs didn't spot Sam. He preferred to bypass sociability today, not that they were feeling too social toward him. They'd kicked him out of their house. He was living in Crawthorne.

Then he spotted someone he thought he should talk to: Gwynevere Pieters arrived with her parents. As they came up into the grandstand, Sam excused himself between people and followed the Pieterses up till they took their seats. There, he found just room enough to plunk himself down beside the woman he'd courted two years, then jilted, twice.

She startled when she realized who it was who'd sat down next to her, then she made one of her little moue-presses of her mouth, about to object.

"Before you have me thrown down the grandstand here," Sam began, "let me say something, okay?" He went on quickly. "I'm sorry I wasn't there for you like I promised. There were reasons, but still you were right. I wasn't the groom—and I wouldn't have been the husband—you needed."

She closed her mouth. A pretty mouth. Her whole face was really pretty, in fact. Oval, symmetrical, nice eyes. Gwyn was a beautiful woman.

"But I think it was for the best, you know?" he continued. "You're going to find someone just right for you." He believed it, his sincerity in his voice.

She contemplated him still with vestiges of that frown in

her eyes, on her lips, then gave a quick nod and looked away, out onto the field.

"You all right?" he asked.

"Yes," she said, "I'm doing fine." Her voice was musical. He remembered all the things he'd found attractive about her (not the least of which was that every man in the grandstand kept glancing her way—Gwyn was so pretty some days she could hurt your eyes). The thing was, though he saw and heard all he'd liked and still found them attractive, he didn't want her. Sort of like seeing a pretty, delicate little music box, enjoying its sound and fanciness, but sort of liking it better at the store than needing it for his own.

"I'm glad," he said and nodded. He smiled in her direction, though she didn't see it. "That's real good." He felt real good himself, in fact. Happy with himself, which was a rare enough occurrence for Samuel J. Cody.

Then he got distracted because, finally, at the side of the field, he spotted his favorite nob of all: Liddy. The second his eyes found her, automatically he raised his hand, as if to wave, and forgot everything else around him. Of course she didn't know to look. She was huddled with the rest at the edge of a tent, her shooting glove off, her hand out, measuring the wind. Oh, come on, he thought. Die down, wind. Drop off completely.

At long last, with spectators shoulder to shoulder and chomping at the bit to see something happen, the committee handed out the target tickets for the women's competition. The field was wet—galoshes were the order of the day—but the band took its positions on the opposite side of the archery range. The bugles sounded, commanding the first set of lady archers to go to their respective targets—each would shoot at two, standing beside one as she shot at its far counterpart. Then the flagmaster waved his signal, and the women's Grand National Archery Meeting was under way.

Fifteen ladies at a time all shot an "end" together, three arrows—Sam kept asking the English people around him questions. At first they were taken aback, but after a while every Englishman near him was explaining. After an "end," the ladies crossed over the green, where their scores were marked; then the archers turned and shot in the other direction. They repeated this little procession till they shot a "national": forty-eight arrows at sixty yards, twenty-four at fifty. After which, a woman's champion would be declared.

It was a pretty sight, the ladies—though Liddy wasn't among the first batch—in their crisp, colorful dresses, moving in a group up or down the green, then arrows flitting, glancing white to and fro against a bank of dark grass and green tents in the distance. When the shooting paused for the next fifteen women, though, with Liddy coming out of the smaller side tent with them, Sam couldn't stand it. He was too far away to see exactly what was happening, too far from the action. Down there. That was where he needed to be. He stood and made his way down the grandstand.

It took a little Texas finagling to turn his grandstand ticket into a marquee pass—Sam told the man who questioned him he was Liddy's coach. The damn fellow actually went out to ask her. She looked up from the sideline—she hadn't taken the field yet—and over at him as she said something to the man, then she turned away, strapping on her arm brace. She must have said yes, because the fellow let him in.

The tents had chairs and tables set up under them, with water, cider-cup, tea, coffee, the like: rest and refreshments for archers and others connected with the sporting event. It turned out, though, that the tent wasn't close enough. Sam left it to watch Liddy from an area in danger enough of catching an arrow that the judges kept making him step back. He stood as close as they'd let him to the range.

He laughed out loud when her first three shots, her first end, were all gold. Every woman had to give her a shilling, which she took very sweetly. She had two little pouches affixed to a belt at her waist, weighed down now with roughly fifty shillings each. The pouches matched her hat, which had a feather pinned at the side into where the brim was bent to the crown. Ah, Liddy.

Her second end brought a white, a red, and a "pin-hole"— which turned out to be good, very good: a dead-center gold,

a contender for best shot of the women's meet. It was
marked on her target. Sam's heart thrilled for her. She was
going to win. She'd just begun, of course, but he felt it in his
bones. She was the best out there. The calmest, the most
skilled, the prettiest, the smartest—

He looked down at his boots, daydreaming. She'd win.
She'd be so happy that when he showed her what he'd
brought her, she'd want it. He'd say he loved her—he figured that's what he'd messed up before. They'd celebrate.
When he looked up again, she'd shot two more ends, neither
of them quite as good as her opening, but still competing
well.

And so it went, Sam watching, afraid to breathe one
minute, wool-gathering the next, fueled up on elation and
expectation mixed with a generous amount of anxiety. Sure
enough, the sixty-yard shoot finished with Liddy as high
score, though another lady, by one, had most hits. In terms
of round points, they were tied.

As the targets were set to fifty yards, she came in but was
all business. She said to him as she walked under the tent to
get water, "I need more arrows. They're over there." She
pointed, then smiled faintly and added, "Coach."

He brought her a handful, turning her around and putting
them into her quiver himself.

"Thank you," she said.

"My pleasure."

"And can you take my galoshes? The field is dryer now."

"Absolutely."

She chucked them off, *clonk, clonk*, then said, "Oh, and
here." She emptied more than a hundred shillings into one of
the galoshes, leaving her waist pouches empty again.

Sam stuck her overshoes in a corner, then turned around:
She was gone.

He spotted her salmon-pink dress, its shimmer as she
strolled out into the sun again, her bow at her shoulder. Gone.
He worried he'd made a mess of a good opportunity. No
more messes, he thought. That was why, when she glanced

back at him, out of desperation he mouthed the words, "I love you."

She stared a minute, stopping, then mouthed back, "I love you, too," and moved off. She went onto the field like a woman who had no new information. Nothing had changed.

He blinked. Doggone. *I love you* wasn't it. Or else he'd said it wrong. He hadn't made it very fancy or anything. All right, Sam, admit it, he told himself. You didn't even say it out loud. He stood there frowning and scratching his head. Darn her anyway, why did she have to make it so difficult?

Liddy shot her first three arrows at fifty yards—and collected another shilling from every woman—then started across the green toward the target. As she passed the bandstand, the band trumpeting some awful brass piece as the ladies marched, she let her eyes slide toward him. Their gazes caught.

"What?" he mouthed and held out his hands. "What you do want from me?" He made a face.

She looked away, smiling, as if he hadn't been meant to see her watching him, then she glanced back. It was that funny cat-and-mouse game of glances she could do that he liked so much. In the end, her gaze lit on him and held. Holding his attention, she pivoted, her sheening dress, golden-pink, swishing as she turned around. She walked backward toward the targets. Dang woman. Then she did something he hadn't seen since the moor: She stuck her tongue out at him. It caught him so off guard, his jaw opened and stayed there.

Then he laughed. He couldn't tell if she was angry or not; he didn't know what she wanted. Worse, he wasn't sure what he felt. Where, the second before, he'd been working his way toward *annoyed*, he was suddenly charmed. Darn her anyway.

"Aah, at it again, I see."

Sam jumped. Clive, right beside him, folded his arms over his chest. Sam asked, "How did you get down here?"

"Same way you did. I said, 'I'm with him,' and the fellow said, 'She has two coaches?' I answered, 'Yes,' " He glanced sideways, smiling. "So are you two getting married yet?"

"I hope so."

At midpoint, halfway through the twenty-four arrows, when she came in for a drink, he corralled her, Clive watching protectively but giving them a discreet distance. Sam started by saying, "I don't want to argue—"

She agreed immediately. "We shouldn't hurt each other's feelings."

"No, we shouldn't. If it happens, though, we should see it and try to fix it."

"Right," she said.

They agreed. So where was the problem? He was flummoxed. Why hadn't they been to the altar already? Why didn't the program say, "Mrs. Samuel J. Cody?" Or "Lydia Cody?"

" 'Course that'd leave you saddled with a two-bit cowboy—" he began.

"What does 'two-bit' mean?" she asked as she set down her glass, untouched. They stood inside the tent, a little private moment in the swarm of people.

"A quarter. It's American money: not much."

She scowled at him. "You?"

"Yeah, me."

"You know that's absurd, don't you?" She squinted, looking almost angry, as if he couldn't mean it. "You can climb out the window of a coach while it's careening. You can kill a rabbit at fifty yards with a stone—"

"A fluke, and you know it—"

"—then cook it. You know about bulls, then you turn around and talk about *Swan Lake*—you're much more sophisticated than you want to let on. You're a regular Indian with a bow and arrow. You swim like a fish. You read stories to a woman you've pulled from a bog, whom you actually make feel good about her part in it. And you—" She took in a breath then said softly, with so much passion—prickly, whispered passion, but passion nonetheless—that it caught him aback, "You make love like—like an angel."

He stopped. This was sounding pretty good.

Till she added, "Yes, you're tetchy and hardheaded and march conspicuously to your own drummer, because, so far as I can tell, you're afraid to march in step with anyone else—"

What did he want from her? Not this. Not a list of his faults.

"But, fiddlesticks, who cares?"

Again, she threw him off.

She told him, "I don't care about your faults."

He pulled his mouth sideways. "You sure are quick to list them."

She blinked. "Because I'm not blind. I know who you are. And I love you anyway."

"Well, thank you *awfully*, Your Majesty." He imitated her. "But you will pardon me if I'm not thrilled: My many short-comings are not what I want to be loved for."

"You want to be perfect?"

"I want to be good enough."

"You are."

He was? He frowned. So did this mean everything was all right? Did this mean he could drag her back out onto the moor and live with her there forever? Or at least marry her here?

No, it meant her next end at the targets had come up. They called her name in a list of several through a loudspeaker.

"Ooh," she said, taking off at a trot, holding her hat. "I have to shoot. Wish me luck."

"Knock 'em dead, Lid. You can do it, sweet thing." You're amazing, he said under his breath.

And she did. By the end of the fifty-yard shoot, Lydia Bedford-Browne was not only the high score, the high hits, best gold, *and* the champion: She'd broken the women's British record. Only one of her arrows the entire day missed the targets, the one that had set her back to a theoretical tie at sixty yards.

While the band played, her family and their friends—half the archers were her friends—came from the field, from the grandstand, the bandstand, and tents, from all over. Sam had to fight to get near her.

And when he did, all he could think to do was call to her, "Congratulations."

"Thank you." Many people jostled her and wanted her attention, but she watched him. It made him feel good, though he didn't know what to say from here.

Boddington, though, the big mouth, suddenly had a lot to say. "Straw targets," he was expounding as he came up with Gwyn Pieters on his arm. "A true marksman shoots at moving targets. Straw targets are nothing. I mean, they just stand there, waiting to be hit. Why, you should have seen us on the grousemoor. . . ."

At first, Sam ignored him. The man belittled Liddy's win, but let him. He was an ass.

It was too much, though, when the ass said, "It's a woman's sport. For skirts. Lydia's a nice woman, don't mistake me, but she sets too much store by all this. It's only straw." He mocked her. "Certainly, she's good when shooting straw, but she's never shot at anything live, nothing moving as I have or most of the men here. She isn't capable of real shooting. It's a silly woman's sport, archery—"

Sam couldn't resist. "So what do you want? Shall I grab a target and run up and down the field like a crazy grouse with one of your dogs after it?" Madder than he realized, he said, "Hell, she could shoot the eye of a mosquito at a hundred yards. She's a regular Annie Oakley."

"Annie Oakley?" Boddington asked.

"Yeah, the American markswoman who—"

"I know who she is," Boddie said. "And, no, you don't have run with a target. You could just stand there with the cigarette in your mouth—isn't that how Oakley does it? She shoots cigarettes and coins from men's mouths and fingers." He shuddered. "Ugh."

"She could do it," Sam said.

Lydia's eyes widened. "Sam—"

"She could."

"Fine," Boddington said. "Let's see it. I have fifty pounds that says she'll go wide. Or put an arrow through your cheek."

"Peanuts," Sam told him. "I'll bet a hundred—no, two hundred—no, five hundred"—he was sort of enjoying watching ol' Boddie's eyebrows go up—"that she pins the cigarette to the target without touching a hair on my head— five hundred pounds and my cheek against"—he looked around for something he might want, then spotted Boddington's new carriage—"against that." He pointed.

"Ha," Boddington said, though for a few seconds his eyes lingered nervously on his new vehicle. "The way the two of you fight," he said, "you'll be lucky, Cody, if she doesn't skewer your privates."

"I'm not worried—"

"Sam—" Liddy complained, louder.

Their eyes met. It suddenly occurred to him what he was doing: "No, you do it, Liddy: I'll trust you and cooperate."

Her eyes grew wide. She wet her lips and stared at him. Whoa. He could tell by her face he'd said the right thing. Finally. Accidentally. Because he meant it.

Hoping for a lucky streak, he continued, "And I'd like you to trust me and cooperate so I can take a shot at you. With this." He retrieved a small velvet box from his coat pocket, then tossed it. "Catch."

In a hand against her bosom, she did, then put her bow under her arm to examine the box in both hands.

Watching her open its small, hinged lid, Sam was suddenly on edge. "Oh, dang," he said, "don't embarrass me in public, okay? Even though I'd deserve it. If you don't want it, just sort of close it and—"

Her mouth, her face, her expression, opened in surprise at what she found inside. She stared down into a box smaller than the palm of her hand—looking, he knew, at a perfect diamond as large as the tip of her finger.

More nervous still, he apologized. "Look, I know it's a

little crass for it to be so big, but, see, I figured it had to be bigger and better than Gwyn's, since she'd tell you if it wasn't, and you're kind of competitive." Beneath the diamond, attached—he hoped she'd find it—was a platinum engagement ring.

She looked up at him, her amazed, open mouth drawing into a smile that gaped a little. Delicately, with three fingers out, she plucked the ring from its box, and put it on, wiggling her hand to stare at it.

She smiled up, one eyebrow raised at him, then bit the side of her lip. She teased, "Do you think it'll throw my shot off? It's awfully heavy."

"No. I think you'll do everything better wearing it. Does it fit?"

"Yes." She frowned and smiled, both, studying her finger. "Perfectly."

He admitted, "Your brother helped me." Then added, digging into his coat pocket again, "Oh, and something else." She waited as he reached around in an empty pocket. There was a moment of panic until he remembered he'd put it into his inside pocket. "Here," he said, finally and oh so nervously.

He handed over a piece of paper rolled tightly with the matching partner to the diamond ring, a wedding ring, holding the paper in its scroll. She took it, puzzled, sliding the ring off and unrolling his official offering.

"It's a special license." The fanciest—and quickest—way to get marriage in England. He wished he weren't such an expert on how to set up marriages, but there he was; at least he knew. "I had to move heaven and earth to get it by today."

"Our names are on it!" she said with surprise, then looked up at him. Earnestly, she asked, "Sam, do you think this is a good idea? I mean, we fight an awful lot."

"Yeah, I think it's a good idea. I really want this, Liddy. I want to marry you, live with you forever. I never wanted anything so much in my life." He laughed a little sheepishly. "And, yeah, I think it's okay if we fight. We do a lot things pretty intensely. You're right, it's no good, purposeless bickering. Still, if you're upset with me, you have to say. And I have to say if you rile me."

When that didn't seem enough, with every face turned to him, and—oh, own up, Cody, you're rambling: He couldn't shut up. "See, so long as we say what we need and leave off criticizing what the other one wants, we'll be okay, I think. Arguments are chances to meet each other halfway. And we will; we always will: as soon as we figure out where halfway is."

Liddy beamed at him. What a smile she had.

Someone sighed.

Another person, a lady's voice, said, "Oh, that's so sweet."

"How lovely," said someone behind him.

"They're in love."

"They'll do beautifully together."

Boddington interrupted with, "Yes, if she doesn't kill him. Are you going to do it?" he asked, real sarcastic. "Or are we going to stand here forever and watch the two of you make eyes at each other?" His own eyes kept going to the huge diamond ring. "Either hand over my five hundred pounds, Cody, or walk out there and let her shoot."

"Sure," Sam said and shrugged, Mr. Nonchalance. "Who has a cigarette?"

A dozen people did.

"Sam—" Liddy frowned at him.

"Do it," he told her.

"You want me to?"

"Yes. I'm going to trust you. You'll do fine." He added more playfully, "Plus you always wanted a carriage with a crest on it. Now we can have one. Win us his carriage."

He took one of the offered cigarettes. Boddington himself lit it, and Sam turned on his heels. He strolled casually out to the first target, one hand in his trouser pocket, the other holding out the burning tobacco, letting it swing with his arm.

He was not as relaxed as he looked, or hoped he looked. It occurred to him that now Liddy was excited.

Distracted.

A fine sweat was on his forehead by the time he reached the straw target and turned sideways. He bent down on one knee, planted the other foot in the ground, and rested his arm on his thigh, putting the cigarette at the gold. This was easy, he told himself.

It was hard. Out the corner of his eye, he knew when she loaded the arrow, then aimed. All over him, like goose bumps, he felt when the breeze picked up. She waited, everyone silent, Sam as tense as if steel ran down his spine. The wind blew his shirt against his chest. Maybe he should turn around. The way the wind was, it would drift the arrow from its path toward the cigarette right into his ear. That'd be dandy, he thought, an arrow through his head, in one ear, out the other.

After a full minute of his heart racing and the crowd so quiet he could hear a bird's chirping on the tent top, the breeze gently flapping everything in sight—Liddy eased the string back, lowered the bow into her skirts, and toed the ground. Boddington jeered. Sam couldn't hear what he said, but could see his mean mouth moving. Yep, he was going to have to flatten the fellow's nose; it was going to come to that. Then, no, Liddy looked back at the jackass, said something, then turned toward Sam again.

He had enough time to really, truly wish—repent—he hadn't made her nervous on purpose out on her practice range. Oh, the regret. And, please, oh, please, don't be nervous now, Lid.

Then the wind died down, she loaded, pulled, and, like that, shot.

Sam was still, utterly rigid, except for the wince as the feathers of the arrow literally kissed his mouth on their way past, the end of the cigarette exploding into shreds of tobacco. Bits of it flew at his face. He was left with a half inch of frayed cigarette clamped in his teeth for dear life—he'd intended to let go to the arrow, but its flight had been too quick. He took the wet piece out, then, smiling, filliped it up into an arc, showing Liddy what remained. People were already cheering as he ran toward her.

He had to climb through them to get to her. She grabbed his hand two people away and pulled him in.

When he got to her, he turned her around, grabbed her small waist, and lifted, saying, "Pull your skirt up, darlin', or you'll turn me into blind man's bluff."

She caught on right away. She was in the air over his head, pulling up skirts, laughing, getting her legs out, as he, bending, hoisted her up onto his shoulders. There, she grabbed his head, then kissed the top of it.

"I love you," she murmured.

He was supposed to say it back. He muttered, pretending the crowd was too noisy. As if he'd said it, only she'd just missed it; she just didn't hear him.

He couldn't declare himself. Even though the words were right there in his throat. They sang inside his brain, the perfect name of a blissful feeling. They were so true: *I love you, Liddy.* He could think them. They tortured him. *I love you; don't make me say it.*

Public declarations. There was a piece of him that always panicked here, he guessed. Partly, he was conditioned from experience: He'd messed up so many elaborate public vows. Partly, though, he'd messed them up because dedications, he thought— No, he meant *declarations.* Declarations worried him. Especially when they came with a lot of mixed emotions as they had with Gwyn and Zoe.

There were no mixed emotions here. His feelings were as pure as a man's got. He loved Liddy. He wanted her forever. He opened his mouth to tell her. And got stuck; his mind went blank.

From above him, he heard it again. "I love you," she said as, his hands on her ankles, he walked them toward the tent.

He answered, "You're going to marry me, right? You never said. You're going to, aren't you?"

"Quick as hiccup," she told him and laughed, then called down to him again, "I love you," this time with such gentleness. She added, "Give me the words, Sam. I swear, I won't throw them down the hole in the outhouse. I want them. I want you. I need you."

They came like sudden rain, a surprise as they left his mouth. "I love you, Liddy," he called up to her there on his shoulders. It was like a black sky's cracking open on parched land. He pried her hand from where it clutched his chin and kissed her palm. "I love you." It wasn't hard at all! "I love you, I love you. I want you for my wife. I trust you with my life. Marry me. Have children with me. Live with me. Sleep with me—"

"That's enough," she said and put her hand back, this time over his mouth.

Several people walking beside them, Clive now among them, laughed. Her parents, too. Sam realized he didn't know how long they'd been part of the group, though probably from the beginning. He thought he remembered seeing them come down from the stands to hug her after her win— criminy, he was hardly aware of what was around for the woman on top of his shoulders. Though then he grinned. Her father was smiling. Her mother was present, walking with them, which was saying something. Which he figured meant his relationship to Liddy, his and her affection for each other, had played out much more acceptably in the odd little drama that had just taken place.

Near the tent, because he and she were too tall to get in under the flap, he swung her down onto the ground again. He was proud when under the tent the organizers and judges gave her another round of applause. The record. The women's record goes to our new champion. The best archer in England. William Tell.

Annie Oakley, he thought.

He whispered in her ear at one point, "You know, you're going to have to shoot with a terrible handicap after this." He leered. Boy, oh, boy, was he eager suddenly to get her alone.

She raised her eyebrows toward him, then rolled her eyes and said, "Ooh, a handicap." She did that provocative little glance thing, looking away then back, with her barely-there little smile on her face.

He couldn't resist then. In front of everyone, he grabbed her, pulled her to him, and kissed her so soundly he knocked her hat off.

It blew in the light breeze, rolling across people's heads and fingertips, its flirtatious feather tickling the hands that tried to grab it.

While Sam had what he wanted. He petted Liddy's bare head, pulling out one corkscrew curl from the pins that kept it contained.

Ah, Liddy. She liked to compete, and didn't he enjoy it, though he couldn't imagine that it would have been her every suitors' favorite trait. He liked how smart she was, and how she didn't hide it, which probably didn't go down too well with some fellows either. It sure sat well with him, though. (Him and Boddington, whom he secretly half forgave for being such a pain in the backside, since not winning Liddy could make any sane man as crazy as a calf in the chute.) She was unusual in a lot of ways: smart, warm-hearted, and sassy as a jay. He liked the way she struggled toward independence, an emotional self-sufficiency, even though not many would appreciate the quality in a young women, especially of the upper class, who was supposed to think and do what she was told.

Best, seeing all this in her made Sam feel good about himself: clear-sighted. Having the good sense to fall in love with her was the best thing he'd ever done. It made him feel like a smart man.

While Lydia's mind, as Sam kissed her, swirled round and round the word he'd said. *Handicap.* Ooh.

She thought of the handicap he'd given that day on her own archery field: not much of one! Honest to God, counting to three when he'd offered to five. Oh, he cheated. How he cheated! It made her warm to remember the two of them out under the shade of the trees. Silly. Two grown people wrestling on the ground—oh, it made her uncomfortable to think of it; it made her laugh into his mouth. She was happy she'd gotten away with her knickers till . . . well, till she hadn't. But she had them again, which made her grin. She wanted to thumb her nose at him.

She wanted to play. Sam was so much fun.

Fun. Had she truly thought the word? Had all her angst and fighting with Sam been entertaining?

No. Some of it hadn't been. But, egad, some of it had! Or partly, provided it didn't go off-tilt. When they, neither one, took it too seriously, that's what it was: Fighting with Sam was fun. More than she could remember having since . . . well, Sam and the moor.

She searched for her anger and hurt feelings, but they were gone. She couldn't find them. Evaporated like cotton-wool fog.

The moor. She had consorted there with a different man altogether from whom she'd thought. A more respectable man. Well, not respectable exactly. Money didn't make one respectable. And certainly one couldn't call it gentlemanly to take a handicap, beat her with it on a women's archery practice field, and then ask for her drawers.

Which suddenly made Lydia think: Sam was *perfect,* actually. He was *almost* respectable: respectable enough. And more fun than she could explain to anyone who thought *respectable* was the main measure of a man. Or a woman either, for that matter. He was dependable, capable, and vastly entertaining—three qualities that beat respectable any day.

A funny happening that Sam, Liddy, their children would still be talking about on their sixty-seventh anniversary: Liddy put the wedding ring on her finger with the engagement ring, just seeing what they'd look like together, and the idea of getting married right then struck. She wanted to. Right there, on the archery range. There were two reverends, one deacon, and a magistrate, any of whom could do it. The special license didn't specify a location, so they were off.

What a day. Clive was especially thrilled with the idea. He ran around gathering the proper people, preventing the work crew from taking the tent down, and organizing the official paperwork. Lydia's mother's carriage had pulled out by then, but he even borrowed a horse so he could chase it down.

"What sacrifice," he called to Lydia and Sam as he galloped off.

Epilogue

We belong to a young nation, already of giant strength, yet whose political strength is but a forecast of power that is to come.

THEODORE ROOSEVELT
vice presidential address, 1898

Standing at the back of the tent with her father, awaiting the moment to walk toward Sam and the deacon, Lydia heard her mother's voice.

"Darling!"

She looked in the direction from which it came, and there was the viscountess working her way through Lydia's friends and family from the edge of the tent toward the front, all the while waving to get her attention. Lydia smiled, watching.

"Excuse me. Viscountess Wendt here," her mother said brusquely, shoving people out of the way. "Mother of the bride. Excuse me." Constance Bedford-Browne halted briefly when her and her daughter's gazes met. Over and between heads, she smiled—so sweetly, Lydia thought—then the viscountess lifted her own hand to her own forehead. "Fix your hair," she mouthed, pointing with her finger to demonstrate.

Lydia laughed. She felt her own smile rise up as if from the center of her chest, till happiness shone out her face, such affection. She reached up and pushed her hair back.

Her mother nodded, beaming as she shouldered herself a prime place in front. Then leaning to see between heads, she mouthed the words, "You look lovely, dear."

The music—her cousin's cello—began with mother and daughter smiling broadly at each other. Then, as Lydia took her father's arm, still staring at her mother, the viscountess's mouth mimed the words, "We love you."

Lydia's eyes grew so full—her heart so full—she could barely see. She looked away: And there was Sam standing at the end of the tent, shifting from foot to foot, staring at her. She began toward him, between the rows of chairs, through the crowd of gathered friends, a few strangers, to the sound to Chopin's waltz in C sharp, tears streaming down her cheeks, her face beaming.

Happiness. It was only the beginning. The odd wedding was followed by the best honeymoon with a better mate than Lydia had ever imagined for herself—literally, since Sam was nothing like the man she had grown up thinking she would marry. They returned from the honeymoon—a sojourn of various inns on the Dartmoor—to London and a very lovely season, after which came the beginning of a new family: On May 10 in the first year of the new millennium, Savannah Jane Cody was born, the namesake of her American grandmother, long gone but remembered fondly.

That summer, before they left for Japan—without a word of Japanese, Sam had been named to a diplomatic position there—they went to a picnic at the house Sam's grandmother had rented nearby in Harrogate. The occasion was the visit of Sam's aunt, uncle, two cousins, and half-brother, come to England to meet the bride and see the new baby.

They'd eaten something called "barbecued ribs" that Sam had cooked on a grill over an open fire. He liked them—he'd eaten them till he couldn't move. He sat in the grass now, on the other side of the picnic table under the shade of a huge

maple. He looked half asleep. He looked himself: wearing
blue denim trousers so faded and soft they looked at least as
old as he was—at the knee they had a small hole, showing
his underwear, a faded red. Lydia smiled and took him in:
his boots, their reddish leather, polished with black polish
till the red barely showed, his black Stetson, the silver beads
gleaming, his soft flannel shirt, plaid. He had Savannah
wrapped in his tan corduroy jacket—she was nestled in his
arms, also half asleep. Very un-English, very Sam. Very
hers.

"I'm through," he'd said a week ago. "They're taking the
draft of the treaty over to D.C., where the secretary of state
and the British ambassador'll hammer out the last." He'd
grinned. "Me and whoever's in my company, though, have
to stay in London to hold down the fort till they send the
next fellow over. Meanwhile, though, I'm dressing like I
want. I hope you don't mind."

Not at all. He dressed like his family. Or some of them.
His aunt wore elegant dresses. One uncle, though, was quite
western in his sartorial preferences. His cousins, from
Boston, were dapper. His Gramma Sadie looked surprisingly English in attire—when the others of his family
months ago had left on the ocean liner that Sam had been
taken off, she'd taken herself off with him. "If Sam and John
stay, I stay." His half-brother, John, lived in Europe. He'd
been on the continent for eight years, studying for most of it
under the tutelage of some fellow in Austria; he hadn't settled down yet, but was considering a medical practice in
England.

Gramma Sadie was tall, almost as tall as Sam. "You think
she's high up the mountain, you should've seen Gramps. He
was six-seven and big, a regular Paul Bunyan."

John, the doctor, was quiet, soft-spoken, though not with
the ladies. When they'd taken him to town, he'd surprised
her by flirting mercilessly. He came out with the ladies,
tending to be rather—oh, sweetly arrogant. He knew how
handsome he was, what a catch he would be, and played it
like a game of tag—at twenty-eight he hadn't slowed down

yet for any girl to catch him. He was handsome in a different way from Sam, more a Bostonian, though all American, and very dedicated to his profession. Lydia doubted, at least for the moment, that any woman would compete very well against it.

"You have a lovely family," she told Sam over the checkered tablecloth. Then, "How are you doing?" She had to stand up to look.

On the other side of the table, he'd slid down into the grass, laid out, Savannah a little bundle asleep on his chest, his hand relaxed over the lump of her thick-nappied bottom, his hat over his face.

From under it, he said, "I'm homesteading cloud nine, Lid. If I get any happier, I'll have to hire someone to help me enjoy it."

Author's Note

The events and characters here are made up, though the reader will no doubt realize there was eventually a treaty between the United States and Britain that agreed to the construction and regulation of a canal across the Isthmus of Panama. The details were indeed hammered out in London, then finally drafted in Washington, D.C., in 1901 by U.S. Secretary of State John Hay and Lord Julian Pauncefote, British ambassador to the United States. It was not ratified by the U.S. Senate until later revisions. Known as the Hay-Pauncefote Treaty, it superceded the older Clayton-Bulwer Treaty between Britain and the United States.

Also, the Grand National Archery Meeting is an actual event, to this day still held annually as it has been since 1844, while its variously named and organized antecedents were held for centuries before that. Archery is a rich English tradition; I hope I have most of its details right. I mention here that, though I based my archery meeting on historical facts, the one you find in these pages is an amalgam of a number of such meets; Lydia's Grand National as it is here never took place. I have also taken the liberty of inventing many place names in both Devon and Yorkshire—Wyesmire, Crawthorne, and Swansdown, to name but three.